D1367278

BABY

A Novel by Robert Lieberman

Crown Publishers, Inc.
New York

For my sons, Zorba and Boris, who always wanted
a book dedicated to them

Thanks to
Jim Salk, attorney
David Berman, musician
Two FBI agents, who wish to remain unnamed
One other lawyer, who will also remain anonymous
Don Smith, for help in Los Angeles, Ithaca, and Caracas
And, of course, Gunilla, who sparked this idea

Inquiries should be addressed to Crown Publishers, Inc., One Park Avenue, New York, New York 10016

Printed in the United States of America

Published simultaneously in Canada by General Publishing Company Limited

Library of Congress Cataloging in Publication Data

Lieberman, Robert.
Baby.

I. Title.
PS3562.I44B3 1981   813'.54   81-1491
ISBN: 0-517-544881

10 9 8 7 6 5 4 3 2 1
First Edition

Music to me is a power that justifies things.

—IGOR STRAVINSKY

ONE

There was something distinctly remarkable about the child. It was not just the extraordinary fact that she was born to a woman nearly sixty years of age. Nor that her mother was to vehemently insist that there was never a father. Nor the fact that, in this age of modern medicine, she was born in a field outside Ithaca, New York, without the benefit of obstetrician or blessing of a birth certificate. Nor that the child would never carry a name other than "Baby." All this was definitely strange. These oddities would be whispered about, openly discussed, ultimately examined in minute detail in the nation's media. But all this was peripheral. At the center of the maelstrom was Baby herself, born to Doris Rumsey, a child allegedly endowed with an incredible talent, a little girl who many said was nothing less than a miracle, a sacred gift to the world. Others, less generously inclined, called her and her performance a fraud, a carefully orchestrated hoax.

1

B y any measure, Doris Rumsey was an odd woman. She was a spinster in the classical sense, an anachronism, a woman with a prominently curved spine and a sense of dress that was fashionable in the early years of World War II. She could often be seen lunchtimes, when free of her duties at the Boynton Junior High Library, walking up Cayuga Street toward the Ithaca Commons. Hunched over as she had been since her teenage years, Doris would, if the weather were mild, be clad in a vintage crepe dress with padded shoulders, her hair perched on top of her head in a stiff roll. When it was bitingly cold, as it was now, those dresses would be hidden by an old wool coat, her hairdo covered by a matching hat decorated with a feather or a little bundle of berries.

Invariably during the school year, Doris Rumsey followed the same lunchtime route. It took her south along Cayuga Street, across Court, Buffalo, and then Seneca streets, and finally she would end up at the Home Dairy, a cafeteria where she would get on line with the other older folks, pick up the plat du jour and a cup of tea, and sit with her tray at the same corner table she had occupied for nearly thirty years.

Despite her contorted spine and her out-of-style fashions that set her apart from the rest of humanity, Doris Rumsey was a pleasant woman who tried in small ways to be sociable. Reticent and shy, she would nevertheless always make a point of stopping and exchanging greetings with the people she knew in town, offering a smile and some small talk about the weather or the flowers if they were in bloom, or the colors of the leaves if they were flaming and then, with her head thrust forward like a turtle, she would trudge the length of Cayuga Street back to school.

Originally, Doris Rumsey had worked as the sole librarian in the St. John's Elementary School on Buffalo Street, a few blocks from her home on Willow Avenue. It was a formidable brick structure with wire mesh protecting the windows and a high, cyclone fence encircling the yard. Doris had liked working in the elementary school, especially with the younger children. Once a week each class would line up and march down in a double line to Doris's domain on the first floor for their "library hour." An old classroom fitted with shelves and racks, Doris's library in the west wing was bursting with books and periodicals and encyclopedias. It was so crammed that with a class of twenty-five or thirty children, there was barely enough room for them to turn around. The little ones always arrived boisterous and fidgety, poking one another and laughing at silly jokes, but Miss Rumsey knew just how to handle them. Without waiting for the shoving and giggling to subside, she would reach for one of the storybooks on the shelf above her desk and in a slow, steady voice start to read. Without fail, within a few lines the children—especially the first- and second-graders—quickly fell into a mesmerized silence. For half an hour she would read them stories of adventure, of explorations in the wilderness, of children who played detectives, of heroic dogs, and of pioneering families. For the remaining minutes, while she had their attention, Doris Rumsey would tell them of the library, how this small, musty room packed with books was a "warehouse of knowledge" where they could find anything in the world they wanted to know, how it was all arranged in a simple order, and how there was no such thing as an "old" book. All books, she would earnestly tell them, are new books if we haven't read them.

Though Doris Rumsey was never married, would never have

a child of her own, it was apparent to the students that she loved them—apparent in the even, gentle-voiced manner in which she dealt with them, in the comforting way she might put her arm about a distressed child, apparent in her soft eyes. Miss Rumsey's barrenness was a source of sore disappointment that she had come to accept ever since her fifteenth year, when her spine began to inexplicably sag and bend under the weight of her upper body. Despite the use of all types of braces, consultations with specialists in Rochester and New York, her back continued to curve, becoming more deformed each year until, at the age of eighteen, she was for all purposes considered a hunchback. No man would ever look at her she knew, nor, as the doctors told her mother, would she ever have a child. Her older sister married, left town, and was killed in a tragic accident on her honeymoon. Her parents died within a year of each other. Alone in the world, Doris Rumsey stayed on in her modest family home on Willow Avenue, took a job with the school system, and tried to come to terms with her life. She adopted two stray cats that ultimately became four, sponsored a half-dozen children through the Christian Children's Fund, which gobbled up a large chunk of her monthly paycheck, began sporadically attending the Methodist church of her parents, and told herself there were surely worse afflictions in life than a **U**-shaped spine. Childless she was not, she would remind herself in moments of weakness. She had more than two hundred children of her own, not to mention those poor little ones overseas. Doris Rumsey was not one to complain. Not even when life dealt her one more cruel blow.

"Maybe it's time for a change," she had said with a fatalistic shrug when told that she was to be transferred to the new junior high.

"We're going to miss you, Doris," said Olive Eldridge, the principal, who was a friend as much as a colleague. Olive was a large, big-boned black woman with a world-wise smile and deep circles under her worried eyes. When she broke the news she couldn't look at Doris.

"You make it sound as though I'm moving to the end of the world," Doris had said with a smile.

That had been back in 1969. Her words later struck her as prophetic. The junior high school was a sprawling, noisy complex in a state perpetually bordering on anarchy.   There, a li-

7

brary was no longer a library; it was now called a resource center, and the children who came to her classes were not to be pacified with a fairy tale or a book of adventure. They were big, clumsy ruffians, silly as teenagers can be, and often as rude. Unlike the cramped but cozy little library at the elementary school, the junior high library was situated in the middle of the first floor, wall-less like the rest of the classrooms in this "open" school. There was a central hall, encircling the library from above, through which the students passed on their way between classes. From this balcony the students were afforded a tantalizing bird's-eye view of the resource center and their aging, hunchbacked librarian. The temptation seemed too much to withstand, and without fail there rained down from above paper planes, butter patties from the lunchroom, pieces of chalk, books grabbed from an innocent student, eggs. Once a coke bottle crashed by her desk and Miss Rumsey finally broke her silence. Her desk was moved to a more protected area, and two teachers were posted on either side of the balcony during class changes to prevent further incidents. Nonetheless, they continued and so, too, did the thefts and the needless destruction of books.

Doris Rumsey tried to make sense out of what was happening around her. She tried to come to grips with the ways of these students just as she had learned to live with her deformity, the childlessness of her life, and the long, empty weekends.

"I suppose I'm just getting on in years," she confided to Olive Eldridge when she ran into her one lunch at the Home Dairy. It was an unusual confession for Doris who was becoming progressively more indrawn—and more tired. She just didn't seem to have the spunk that she used to have.

"Things aren't like they used to be," said Olive with a nod, but she didn't bother elaborating. She, too, was getting on in years and felt equally baffled and overwhelmed by all that was going on in the world.

"Another—how many years is it?" Doris asked herself as though trying to measure out her energies and beginning to wonder if, maybe, she was feeling so low because she was coming down with some bug. "Six."

"And then?" Olive questioned with a full mouth, polishing off her eggplant parmigiana.

"Then I'll retire. I've always wanted to travel. That's it." Doris brightened. "I'll go on a trip!"

That meeting had occurred in early January. Making her way down the slush-filled streets just a week after that lunch, a biting north wind howling down Cayuga Lake and chilling her to the bone, Doris finally realized that there was indeed something strange going on in her body. Not only was she perpetually tired, but she couldn't seem to tolerate the cold any more. The winter, supposedly the mildest in years, seemed unbearable. Every time she went out, the cold ate right through her, causing her body to tremble and her teeth to chatter. To add to that, the very act of walking was becoming a chore. Her steps felt leaden and waterlogged. Just lifting a leg required an inordinate effort so that what ordinarily might have been a casual stroll, even in this weather, was making her huff and pant. Now that she thought about it, whatever it was that was happening had been going on for weeks already, maybe a month. Her wrists and knuckles were now swollen, she recognized, flexing them under her gloves. Her breasts ached, and her gut felt inexplicably bloated. As she headed into the icy wind that viciously cut through her old fur-collared coat, it suddenly occurred to Doris that she might be seriously ill, that she might not even make it to retirement, that her dream of travel would be nothing more than that, a dream.

The Oltzs were the first to sense something amiss with Miss Rumsey. A retired couple who lived in the large stucco house on the corner of Willow Avenue, they were the self-appointed guardians of the neighborhood. In the warm weather they would pull out chairs and post themselves on their porch, scrutinizing each passerby. They scolded dog owners who let their pets pee on their bushes, ordered children who dropped gum wrappers on the sidewalk to pick up their litter, reminded their neighbors when it was time to cut the grass or rake the leaves that were in imminent danger of blowing over onto their own immaculate lawn.

Aside from spending their days tending to their grounds, clipping their grass in a blade-by-blade fashion, stooping down to pick up individual leaves, shoveling their walk at the first hint of flurries, Charlie and Edna Oltz made it their first order of business to watch the comings and goings of their neighbors. They knew, for instance, when Muzzy, the alcoholic realtor who lived around the corner on Yates, was picked up by the ambulance after one of his severe bouts with the bottle; knew when that no-good daughter of the Hickeys had another fight with her parents; knew each and every time that black woman, Olive Eldridge, came over from her neighborhood across the creek to say hello to Doris Rumsey. It was therefore not unexpected for them to spot the change in Doris.

"Whatsa matter, Doris?" Charlie Oltz asked, leaning on the handle of his ice chopper and adjusting the red-checked hat on his head. His cheeks were flushed from the cold, and his walk was the only one on Willow Avenue that was perfectly ice free.

"Matter?" echoed Doris as he moved aside for her to pass on the walk. "Must be the winter," she smiled, forcing herself to pass briskly along.

"Can't complain about this one. Not yet, anyway," Oltz said and, taking off his wool cap, scratched his bald head as he watched Doris move down the street. Just as she had done an infinite number of times during the school year after lunch, she climbed the steps to her porch, picked up her mail, quickly checked her cats, and then hurried back to school. Oltz was still studying her as she walked in her hunched-over gait up the far end of the block and disappeared around the corner.

"Told you so, didn't I?" said Edna, slipping up unexpectedly next to her husband. She had been watching Doris from the window and, as soon as Doris was out of sight, she had rushed out to confer with Charlie.

Charlie Oltz took a long breath and exhaled a stream of white vapor. His eyes remained fixed on the vacant corner and then shifted down into the frozen creek bed that ran the length of the street. "Yeah"—he nodded thoughtfully—"she does look a mess. All sickly and pale and—"

"If you ask me, it's cancer. Or maybe something worse."

"Like what?" asked Oltz, turning to his wife and getting distinctly uncomfortable.

"God knows."

"Hope to hell it's not contagious."

10

2

Irwin Shockley lived on the Hill, as they say, meaning of course East Hill. He lived there with his wife, Ruth, and their four children in a rather sumptuous old stone house in Cayuga Heights that the family had painstakingly restored. His home sat on a little promontory, affording him vistas of the lake, West Hill, and the Fall Creek environs occupied by Doris Rumsey and her neighbors.

Professor Shockley was a tall, wiry man with dark, hungry eyes and a goatee lined with early threads of gray. He was a composer of music, a musician, though he now earned his livelihood teaching at the university. He taught a series of large lecture courses in music appreciation, gave instruction in theory and composition as well as occasional lessons in violin and cello. His teaching had been a compromise made several years ago when it seemed the only way he could earn a living and still be free to compose.

"Sometimes," he confessed to Ruth one afternoon when they were alone in the kitchen, "I feel that life is like a hunk of salami."

"Oh?" said Ruth puzzled. She was a bubbly, quick-witted woman who taught math at the college on South Hill. Large-boned, with dark, curly hair and an ever-present white smile, Ruth was the sort of person who rarely if ever was plagued by dark thoughts.

"A hunk of salami. And every day a slice is shaved off. If you try to object they say, 'What are you bellyaching about? It's only a thin slice.' But one day, I'm afraid, you wake up and find that the whole salami is gone."

"Sounds more like baloney to me," quipped Ruth, trying to buoy him.

Shockley smiled weakly, but his eyes, which were focused off into the distance, betrayed him. In his mind's eye, spread out before him like so many slices, he saw his history—saw himself again as a young man, barely twenty, envisioning a career as a full-time composer, a creator of music. A top grad of

11

the Eastman School, Shockley had been invited to become a protégé of the famous Gunther Schuller. Studying composition at Tanglewood under the venerable composer's tutelage, Shockley had written a number of progressively more promising pieces. Then 1965. At the age of twenty-four Shockley completed work on a tone poem, *The Last Star*. It was a deceptively simple piece born without terrible pain or labor, but it was a brilliant work, carrying all the earmarks of genius, and it burst upon the musical scene like a comet. It yanked him from the anonymity of struggling student to the heady heights of feted composer. He was wined, dined, and treated like visiting royalty. Every notable group in the country scrambled to perform the new work. *The Last Star* was played by the Baltimore Symphony, the Houston and San Francisco symphonies—to mention but a few. It was a powerful orchestral work that a notoriously vitriolic critic for the *New York Times* hailed as a singular modern masterpiece. Shockley could still quote the review: "Chromatically tonal with unique orchestration, Shockley's *Last Star* is a superb example of music that is harmonically rich and imaginative with a melody line that goes in unimagined directions."

Showered with lucrative invitations to conduct his own work, give lectures, just show his face, Shockley finally got the ultimate in recognition. Until the day he died he would never forget the thrill of receiving that telegram announcing his Pulitzer Prize.

Praise came in torrents. He was showered with offers of grants. The Koussevitsky Foundation. The Fromm Foundation. You name it—they were there trying to push money on him. With that kind of support and fired with optimism, Shockley went back to work. Employing the same basic and simple approach he had used to create *The Last Star*, he began to turn out new works.

But something was wrong. Looking at a new piece, he could see something was amiss but just couldn't put his finger on it. He would begin to rework it, making nervous changes, throwing out whole sections only to pick them up again and then discard them in a fit of rage. What had been a straightforward labor of love became convoluted agony.

The more he fiddled and rearranged, the more muddied the

12

waters. People in the business began to talk. His scores that once had been so eagerly snapped up by major orchestras could now find only second-rate groups. Slowly the grants dried up.

Finally, in the midseventies, near broke, Shockley accepted a position at the university and came to Ithaca. He knew then, as he knew today, that he was cashing in on his Pulitzer Prize. It was going to be a thick slice, but what else could he do? He had a family to feed, at that point three growing children who ate like young horses. Teaching music appreciation to freshmen didn't have to be the end of the line, did it? He would still compose—compose no matter where he was or what he was. He was born a composer and he would die one.

At the university he did, in fact, continue to compose. Determinedly he worked weekends, early mornings before class, sometimes nights. He whipped himself into generating prolific streams of composition, but the old joy and excitement of creating seemed to have evaporated, leaving in their place a dull and tasteless residue. Lofty sentiments aside, Irwin Shockley began secretly to fear that he had nothing more to say.

"You missed the punch line," said Ruth, poking him lovingly in the ribs and trying to rouse his spirits.

"Huh?" said Shockley, shaken from his reverie and looking up absently.

"Oh, Irwin, you're hopeless," she said and kissed him. Instinctively he wrapped his arms around her, held onto her tightly as though he could get a grip on the world through her.

"I understand," she said quietly a moment later when he moved away from her. He wondered if she really and truly did—if deep down inside, she, whose life had been so ordered and easy and linear, could really grasp his anguish.

"Sometimes I wake up at night—" he said, walking over to his favorite window that overlooked the valley, his sentence trailing off. His eyes traced Cascadilla Creek as it sliced across town, the ice-choked stream moving from the mouth of the gorge and out into the foot of the lake. For an instant his eyes settled on the point where Willow Avenue ran parallel to the creek bed, then moved on, and he picked up his thoughts. "Wake up in a cold sweat and think that I'm finished. That I'll never write another note. That this is just the tail end. The death throes."

"There are worse things," said Ruth worriedly.

"Oh. Of course." Shockley snapped out of his gloom. He was thinking of her and his children, and shuddered at unspeakable thoughts. "Then, other times—," he trailed off.

"Yes," Ruth prompted.

"I have this odd feeling that—"

He turned to look at her and, as he had guessed, she was wearing a nervous smile, her teeth big and gleaming.

"Go on."

"Oh, it's nothing." He laughed at himself.

"Tell me," she insisted.

"Well, that I'm at the turning point of my life. That this is just a phase. A hiatus. That I will do something, discover something, create something, that will forever transform me and those around me. Just like before. That *The Last Star* will turn out to have been the first star."

"That sounds optimistic to me," said Ruth.

"Yes. It is—I think."

3

Doris tried to ignore her growing list of complaints. She tried to forget the insidious nausea that came in the early morning and usually slackened by school time. Her fainting spells were few and far between, and things like that, she consoled herself, did happen as women got older. No matter how much she slept, Doris awoke in the morning feeling exhausted, and that, too, she tried to dismiss. What troubled her, however, were the nagging pains in her back. No matter what position she slept in or sat in, no matter how she held her frame, her back was killing her. Too, she was gaining weight despite the controls she tried to exert on her ravenous hunger. It was her growing weight, she reasoned, that was exerting more pressure on her spine and precipitating the pain. Buried deep in the back of her mind was the fear that her spine was softening again, that her hunch would worsen until she was bent over like a pretzel and reduced to a helpless cripple. If there was one thing Doris Rumsey didn't want to be, it was dependent on others. She would, she once told Olive, rather be dead than helpless.

Doris rarely saw a doctor. What she feared most about a visit with a physician was that she might have to undress and expose her disfigured body. She had all but ruled out going to a doctor when, coming home one gloomy February afternoon, the choice was made for her.

It happened on one of those typically leaden Ithaca days with the sky hanging dark and heavy, a low, sluggish veil dragged across the university that stood on the hill towering over her Fall Creek house. On that February afternoon, a Thursday to be exact, Doris had been shopping in the P&C Supermarket on Hancock Street. Her arms loaded with two unwieldy bags of groceries, she was trudging up Willow Avenue, sidestepping the treacherous patches of ice in front of the Poyers', who were off wintering in Florida, when suddenly and inexplicably her heart started to pound and she burst out into a rush of sweat that drenched her in a matter of seconds. Frightened, she picked up her pace and made a mad rush for her house. As she pushed forward on legs of jelly, Doris tried to still her terror by concentrating on her house. If she could just make it to the front door, she told herself, she'd be safe. Nearing her walk, she was concentrating on the peeling porch trim when suddenly the entire house began to lurch. The sidewalk heaved under her, the trees on the street rolled over to one side, and then everything went black. When she opened her eyes a few seconds later, Charlie Oltz was already there, dressed in shirt-sleeves and bending over her.

"Oh, I must have slipped," Doris said, struggling to find her feet that were somewhere under her. She was lying amidst a clutter of broken glass, cracked eggs, and cat-food tins. A head of lettuce had rolled away and come to a stop at the porch steps.

"You didn't slip. You conked out!"

"Call an ambulance, Charlie!" ordered Edna, who was standing there breathlessly.

"No. It was ice," objected Doris, still on her back.

"Ice, my foot!" argued Edna stridently. "We were standing in the window and saw you. You conked out. Are you going to call an ambulance, Charlie, or do I have to?"

"No. Please," said Doris, as she pulled herself up, hanging on to Oltz's arm.

"You shouldn't let her move," Edna reprimanded her husband. "I'm calling the ambulance myself," said Edna, beginning to storm away. Edna believed in positive action.

"Mrs. Oltz. Please," Doris called out weakly. She tried to go after her, but her knees began to cave in, and forlornly she settled down on the front stoop with the help of Mr. Oltz. Edna stopped and turned around.

"Look at you," Edna said. "You can't even stand on your feet."

"I'm just a little shook up."

"I think you'd better see a doctor." Edna softened her stance now that the color was coming back into Doris's face.

"OK," Doris conceded.

"Charlie 'll get the car; you just sit there."

"Now?" Doris asked distressed.

Edna had called ahead to Dr. Melcher's office, and when Charlie drove up, the doctor whisked Doris past all the other patients in his waiting room, taking her directly into his examination room. Making her lie down on his table despite her objections, Dr. Melcher felt her pulse, listened to her heart, and took her blood pressure. He looked under her eyelids, peered into her throat and ears, and asked her about her general health. Reluctantly Doris told him about her back pains.

"Did you have them just before you fainted?"

"I don't remember," she answered.

"Look," said Melcher, absently twisting the tubes of his stethoscope, "I don't see anything immediately wrong, and I can't give you a full physical right now. I'd like you to go up to the hospital and take some tests."

"What kind of tests?"

"Oh, all kinds," he answered evasively.

"When?"

"We could send you up right now. How are you feeling?"

16

"Perfect," said Doris with a shrug and a purposeful smile.

"Do you think you can go home and come tomorrow for the tests?"

"Sure," said Doris, who was actually feeling well, as well as usual—which made her feel foolish taking up the doctor's time.

"Tomorrow, then," Dr. Melcher said and watched as she walked out of his office.

"What'd the Doc say?" asked Oltz, jumping to his feet when she emerged into the waiting room. He followed her out the building on Buffalo Street and led her to his parked car.

"Nothing. He says I'm fine. Perfectly healthy."

"When's he going to see you again?" asked Oltz, who needed some worthwhile tidbit to report to Edna.

"He isn't," answered Doris and, lifting up the end of her long wool coat, she carefully lowered herself into the car.

Doris's condition began to steadily deteriorate in March. Her back pains became progressively more severe, with the moments of relief few and far between. Continuing to gain weight at a frightening pace, her thighs and midsection and breasts were now swollen to proportions that seemed to her almost double what they had once been. The dresses that had served her so well through the years no longer fit, and Doris was forced to go out and replace them. Even her trusty gray wool winter coat that had once been so floppingly comfortable could hardly be buttoned around her. To add to her distress, she was plagued by unmentionable afflictions—her bowels were forever churning and producing vile gas, she suffered from extreme constipation and, as a result, developed painful hemorrhoids. To top it all off, Doris's teeth were rapidly deteriorating—old fillings began falling out, new cavities were developing, her gums were bleeding, and she was plagued by a sour breath that even she could smell and that no amount of mouthwash could disguise.

Doris's condition distressed her and made concentrating on her work nearly impossible. She dropped books. She lost vital loan records. On a number of embarrassing occasions, she tripped over her own feet in front of a library class. Sensing her decline, some of the crueler students at the junior high took the opportunity to goad Doris from the balcony with taunts of "Clumsy Rumsey!" She tried to ignore it, but the fun caught on and inevitably the slogan appeared as graffiti on the walls, scribbled under caricatures depicting one grossly bloated and hunchbacked school librarian.

Though Doris was able to ignore her morning nausea, learned to anticipate her fainting spells, managed to somehow muddle through the day, the aches in her teeth became unbearable, and she finally went to see Dr. Markowitz, the kind, old dentist who had his office on the third floor of the Bank Building.

Markowitz peered into her mouth, poked around with a tool for a few moments and then, pushing his glasses up over his forehead said, "Mrs. Rumsey, your teeth are in terrible shape. And your gums too. Are you eating right?"

"The usual," answered Doris, trying to hide her anguish.

"Maybe you should try to leave off the starchy foods and eat more healthy things," he gently suggested, purposely avoiding looking at her recently developed double chin. "Milk. Skim milk, preferably. Eggs. Cheese."

"I do."

"You need more calcium. Also vitamin C."

"I understand."

"You know they have to go."

"Who?"

"Your teeth. I can't save them."

"Oh," she said, fighting her tears.

"Not all. We can try to save the bottom row. But the top—There's nothing left there to be filled," he said sympathetically. "I can fit you with a plate and it'll look even better than before. No one will know."

4

Though he considered himself above superstition, Irwin Shockley believed that fate always dealt its cards in clusters. That is, bad news—or good—had a way of being bunched up and delivered to the recipient in rapid-fire order.

Stepping out of his house on a windy January morning, only the vaguest hint of a thaw in the air, the sky overcast as it had been most of the winter, Shockley sensed from the outset that this was going to be a dismal Monday.

On the way to work, whether by self-fulfilling prophecy or just plain bad luck, Shockley's car skidded on a solitary patch of ice, and he ended up slamming his wheels into the curb and knocking the front end out of alignment.

Then, at school, Shockley ran into his colleague, Ernst Rosenzweig, who was standing at the foot of the stairs leading up to his office.

"Did you hear?" said Rosenzweig, making small talk.

"About Tuesday's meeting?" asked Shockley, reading Rosenzweig's mind. The hallway was crowded with students moving off to their first morning classes, and the two men were momentarily jostled together against the banister.

"Doesn't look good," said Rosenzweig, tugging at the long strands of white hair at the nape of his neck. "Doesn't look good at all. There's going to be some big changes. Austerity, they say."

"No sense anticipating. The best thing is—" Shockley had begun when, suddenly, he caught his name mentioned above the general din. He strained to listen. A familiar voice at the top of the staircase was talking.

"Shockley?" The voice from above laughed. "Are you kidding? Shockley's a fucking has-been!"

Feeling his pulse race, Shockley tried to speak but his voice deserted him. Anxiously he looked at Rosenzweig, who was busily pretending not to hear.

"It was good. I'll grant you that," continued the voice belonging to Martin Gross, a grad student who was taking a

19

composition course with Shockley. "But it was a fluke. A stroke of luck. Call it what you want. But one piece doesn't make a career."

Shockley stood rooted to the ground, looking at Rosenzweig, who kept staring at his shoes.

"Look, Irwin," said Rosenzweig, gathering his wits, "I've got to run off to class." And before Shockley could say anything, he quickly disappeared into the milling crowd.

Shockley stood abandoned at the bottom of the staircase. From above he could still hear Gross dissecting his career.

"Tell me, what's he done that's worthwhile in the last—?"

Taking hold of the railing, Shockley turned and slowly marched up the stairs to his office. Step by step he climbed toward the second floor.

"Like I said, one piece doesn't make—"

When Shockley got to the landing, sure enough, there was Gross talking to a new grad student, a young woman. When he saw Shockley, Gross's jaw fell open. The girl blanched and almost dropped her books. Without breaking stride, Shockley walked past them, his eyes meeting Gross's for an instant. Holding himself erect, he walked down the wooden planking of the hallway, his footsteps echoing loudly in his own ears. He reached his office, unlocked it, stepped in, and closed the door sharply. Gross, he thought to himself tossing his briefcase on his desk, who was he but an arrogant, two-faced little twerp! He had yet to write a single original piece himself. What did he know about music, much less life. And with that, Shockley dismissed the man from his mind.

But the words returned to him all through the morning as he labored to prepare his classes. *A fucking has-been!* Shockley struggled to shrug it off, but Gross's words had already burrowed themselves deep into his mind and sat there like a parasite, draining his energies. He knew he should give it no credence. That, even if it were true and he was washed up, Gross—who had a tin ear—was in no position to hand out death warrants. But—But—The words stung.

Maybe, Shockley mulled as he sat alone over a cup of coffee in the Temple of Zeus in Goldwin-Smith Hall, maybe Gross was right. Shockley looked up from his tepid coffee and noticed the heavy plaster replicas of Greek statues lining one side of the basement coffeehouse. They seemed to be staring down at him, admonishing him. Perhaps, as he had said to Ruth, this was just a bleak period. When you most need the muse to strike, it deserts you. A work of art must gestate like a fetus. Patience, he reminded himself, patience.

When Shockley got back to his office, there was a note stuck in the door. It was from Krieger, his department chairman, asking him to drop by his office.

"Times are getting harder," said Krieger, deciding not to mince words. Krieger was a diminutive fat man, who seemed lost in the immensity of his overstuffed chair. He was a reputed expert in fourteenth-century lute notation and really didn't give a damn about Shockley's music.

"Which means?" Shockley asked, though he sensed what was coming.

"Which means we have to cut back. A decision's been reached. The university's curtailing our funds." Krieger reached over and lifted a piece of paper as though it lent more authority to what he was saying. "I'm letting three of our faculty go. We're all going to have to pitch in and take up the slack. That means no more released time for composition."

"But—"

"It's not just you," Krieger interrupted him, and then Shockley knew that he was being singled out. "You're going to have to take some more of the freshman courses this term."

"The big ones."

"Yes. And they're going to be even larger." Krieger nodded, showing no emotion.

"Look, Irwin," Krieger said after a moment's silence. "It's not the end of the world. You'll still find time to compose."

"I will," answered Shockley, and he said it as much for his own benefit as Krieger's.

Oblivious of his surroundings, Shockley walked the short stretch of corridor back to his office. His mind was in a turmoil. First there was Gross pronouncing the death sentence on his career, he thought bitterly. Now Krieger had come along and precipitously stolen his last remnants of free time. If bad news really came in clusters of three, he thought, slumping down at his desk, what would the third thing be? What else could they possibly do to him?

The phone on his desk rang.

He reached for it.

On the other end was Burt Marra, director of the university orchestra. When Marra started to hint what was on his mind, Shockley almost burst out laughing.

"You're kidding!" Shockley exclaimed.

"No. I wish I were. I know what it means to you, Irwin. But we're making some changes. The students need a more balanced repertoire. They're complaining that they want to play some of the standards."

Shockley listened but remained silent.

"And your works are expensive." Marra fidgeted uncomfortably. "I have to bring in extra harpists. You need eight horns, I have only four. Try to understand. We have to pay these people. And now with the new belt-tightening, well, something had to give."

Silence.

"It was a consensus agreement," Marra said, trying to squirm off the hook. "But it's just for the summer concert and next fall," said Marra, meaning that they would not be performing Shockley's new works. "By the winter season things will probably improve." He tried to dangle out a little hope. "Look, if we get some additional funding, your works will be the first to—"

"If," repeated Shockley, breaking his silence.

"Irwin, it's not the end of the world," said Marra, oddly enough invoking the same words that Krieger had used but an hour earlier.

That day Shockley went through the motions of teaching. He gave his lectures, met with his grad students, and managed to muddle through his private lessons. When the day was over, he bundled up and went to his car. Driving numbly through the darkened streets, he tried not to dwell on the misfortunes of the day. There was nothing to be gained pursuing them. Tomorrow, he thought, slowing down as he neared his home, tomorrow he would salvage what he could, rethink his life. He was damned if he was going to give up composing just because things weren't exactly going his way. Shockley pulled into the garage, grabbed his briefcase, and headed for his warm house.

"We've got a problem with Randy," said Ruth before he was hardly in the door. She was referring to their thirteen-year-old,

22

whose primary interests, as of late, were girls, coins, electronic games, and expensive clothes—in that order.

"Again?" he asked.

"He was thrown out of violin class. Mr. Hoover just called with the good news. If Randy's not going to practice, he doesn't want anything more to do with him."

"The world of music will never be the same," said Shockley, a little distantly.

"Is that all you have to say?" asked Ruth.

Shockley shrugged. He had come to the point where he had all but abandoned the hope of seeing any of his children turning into musicians. Randy, his only son, was a lost case. Annette at fifteen was a different matter. Though she practiced her violin unstintingly and was technically sound, she lacked that indefinable little something separating accomplishment from art. Just at that moment, as though for his benefit, he heard the discordant sound of a cello groaning in the den. Stepping into the room, he took a peek at Julie, his ten-year-old daughter, who sat half hidden behind her instrument. The raspy sounds ceased, and she looked up.

"Hi, Daddy." She smiled tentatively, her smile reminiscent of Ruth's.

"Don't try to con me." He tried to look menacing but then broke into a grin.

"Oh, I wasn't," Julie said in her usual open way, her eyes searching his. "I meant to start earlier, but—"

"So start," he urged and stood listening for a minute, feigning interest as she laboriously weeded her way through an exercise.

"That's my little girl." He stood over Julie, urging her on gently, watching her little fingers bridge the strings. "Don't rush. You're not trying to catch a train. Keep the notes clean. Yes, yes, that's it. And put a little feeling into it," he said, trying to sound a note of encouragement. But at that moment he still felt removed from his home and feared that his tone undercut his words. He headed to the kitchen, where he could hear Ruth preparing dinner.

"What are we going to do about Randy?" asked Ruth, hunting in the cupboard for a pot.

"Huh?" Shockley asked. He was staring out the doorway at

Cindy, his youngest. She was stooped over a miniature table she had set up in the far end of the living room. Seated around the table was a slew of dolls, a family Shockley surmised, doing a quick count. Mother, father, three daughters, and one son. Knees to her chest, with her pink undies peeking out, Cindy was carrying on an animated discussion with her family, and Shockley longed to eavesdrop. For a moment he stood watching her play, drinking her in. With big, brown eyes and long, silky tresses, she was still slightly chubby, still a baby. Seeing her, Shockley never failed to be overcome with the urge to protect her. Of all his children, she seemed to be the most sensitive, the most vulnerable. He was scrupulous to avoid favorites, but he knew that there was one. In her, right or wrong, he saw himself as a child.

"I was asking you about Randy, but you seem off in some other world."

Shockley drew a long breath.

"What can you do? Obviously he wants out. We could break his arm, but it's only going to make it tougher for him to practice."

"He's going to regret it," Ruth said, sounding an ominous note.

"Tell him, not me."

"I have."

"I give up," he said, sounding   resigned than bitter. "From now on it's every man and woman for themselves. If Randy or the girls don't want to learn an instrument, that's fine with me," said Shockley, who came from a long line of musicians. Four generations to be exact. Four generations of performers and composers and conductors. Try as he might, he knew that the tradition was now at an end and there was really little he could do about it.

"You can't take that attitude. If you do, Julie will give up before she's even started. And Cindy. She's flighty like Randy. If you don't give her encouragement—"

"I suppose you're right," Shockley agreed halfheartedly.

"What's the matter with you these days? You agree with everything I say. Which means you don't care."

"And I agree with that too." Shockley grinned, pouring himself a drink, and for the first time, Ruth noticed that his hand was shaking.

24

5

B y the time late April rolled around and all the daffodils and crocuses around the Rumsey house were out in full bloom, Doris's request to the school system for a leave of absence was all but a formality. She had already repeatedly lost days on end to illness, and on those days that she did drag herself to work, she could barely function at her job.

Mr. Lisk, the acting principal, finally called her on the phone during one of her stretches of absence and suggested that she take the leave.

"I was thinking of that," admitted Doris.

"If you could get us a doctor's note, you could have a medical leave."

"Yes," Doris agreed, but she knew that she would no more seek out a physician for a note than she would return to Dr. Melcher for those tests or go back to Markowitz, to be fitted with the false teeth that would replace the upper row he had already removed. For Doris had ceased being distressed about the future. Standing naked in front of the miror one evening— an act she had scrupulously avoided all her life—she saw the grotesque swelling in her midsection, observed the way her insides all but seemed to explode, extending her belly and pressing out her navel, saw that and knew that the malignancy that had grown to the size of a football was taking over her body. Looking down at the enormousness of the hard, protruding mass, she realized that there could be little time left and, furthermore, she didn't seem to want much more. Nothing could have been further from her mind than to subject herself to operation after operation. To chemotherapy. Or radiation. Or heaven knows what. She had witnessed what they had done to her good friend, Theresa Thames, and, thank you, wanted no part of it. When she left this earth she wanted to leave it in one whole unmutilated piece.

Resigned that she had reached her last days, Doris took to walking. Though her feet ached, her back pained, she felt compelled to wander. Each morning she would get up, eat breakfast when the nausea was tolerable and, pulling on her old winter coat, would begin one of her long, agonizing treks. Some days she would walk south along the floor of the valley, beginning in Ithaca and heading toward mountainous Newfield. Despite her cumbersome weight, she would waddle up the steep hills leading out of the city, climbing until she reached a height where, looking back, she could see Ithaca spread before her like a child's play village.

Drawn to the outdoors, Doris became something of a movable fixture in the county. An odd sight, Doris Rumsey could be seen walking sometimes across the university quads, shuffling along in her now-crumpled shoes, her feather-bedecked hat perched awkwardly on her head, her top teeth missing, her stockings loose and wrinkled and worn with holes. As she passed through the university, students who had not seen her before would stare and she, unfazed, might acknowledge their looks with a nod or even a gentle smile before moving on.

At peace with herself and her fate, Doris Rumsey walked and walked and walked. Along the dangerous trails that wound along the lips of the deep gorges. Beside the highways that skirted the east and west shores of the lake. Through the residential neighborhoods of the downtown and once right past the front door of the Shockley home in the Heights.

Though Doris would not be likely to confess why she walked, in her soul she knew the reason: She was going to die, and in her last days she wanted to experience everything that there was to see, to hear, to taste, and to feel—all that might have escaped her in life. And the only way to see it was on foot. Out in the open air she could smell the fecund soil stirring with spring, touch the soft, new buds on the trees bulging and ready to burst, witness the geese as they flew overhead in formation back home to the north, laugh and pity the inevitable straggler honking its way back into line. An aging vagabond, guiltless and cut loose from the world of responsibilities and job, Doris would plant herself on a hilltop and sit there listening, entranced by the mellifluous sound of wind whistling through the bare branches of a tree. By a slow running stream she would pause and listen for the familiar notes caused by the silky, cold water caressing the rocks. The birds sang to her a new song. The trees creaked in harmony. The leaves rustled in a gust that miraculously melted her last vestiges of anguish.

On the days that she felt poorly and couldn't face a long hike into the countryside, Doris would usually manage to walk the five short blocks leading to the Commons. It was a small but pleasant pedestrian mall that had been formed by cutting off a section of State Street and installing trees where there had once been parking meters. On the Commons Doris would find herself a warm, sunny spot and, like many of the students from the college or university, would buy herself a bagel and sit in her sheltered nook contentedly chewing, pressing the tough meat of the bread against her now-healed upper gums, chewing and chewing like a teething infant until the bread was soft enough to finally swallow. And there she would pass her time reminiscing about the old days when she was a young girl in this town, the days before her spine had weakened. She would remember going to the State Theater when it still was a music hall. Joining her father fishing on the banks of the lake. A winter sleigh ride in the countryside.

In her mind's eye, as she sat dozing in the sun, Doris saw her life pass before her, and she told herself that it had, after all, not been so bad. Admittedly she had not had a man to love her. (She could still remember the envious way she used to watch couples strolling arm in arm, stopping to steal a kiss. And even now, she could not help but watch a pair of lovers through the corner of her eye.) Nor had she been able to experience having a child of her own. But all things considered, she had had almost sixty years of health. What more could anyone ask for? Nothing, perhaps, except to pass quietly and painlessly from this earth. And for that she prayed. Prayed fervently.

Surrounded by long tortuous hills, the roads around Ithaca were something of a cyclist's nightmare. A notable exception was the stretch from Shockley's house in the Heights to the university, which was a near-level run broken only by a few mild grades. In May, when the rains stopped and it turned dry and hot and the grass was growing dense, Shockley dusted off his bike and began cycling to and from work. The trips were an invigorating pleasure for him that kept him in shape, saved gas, and made him feel mildly virtuous. Perhaps most importantly, they gave him a chance to clear his head and make the transition between work and home.

Riding home early one evening, the sun low, yet agreeably warm, Shockley let his mind run while absently making his way along University Avenue. As he pedaled over the steel-mesh bridge spanning Six Mile Gorge, water gushing through the yawning chasm hundreds of feet below, Shockley was thinking back to the dreary January day when he had been assaulted by that barrage of bad news. Though that bleak day stood in stark contrast to this glorious spring evening, its effects, he mulled, pedaling on, continued to ripple through his life. The extra courses overflowing with bodies, the endless papers that had to be graded, the small hassles that ordinarily were manageable, all had conspired to take a chunk out of his life. The remnants of time that he still managed to carve out for himself were unproductive. Though he had resolutely promised himself that he would continue to compose in the face of all adversity, when he did sit down to work, his mind was scattered in a hundred directions and, try as he might to focus on a new piece, there was always some little item popping up in the corner of his mind to distract him. Though he rarely complained, Shockley wondered how much longer he could go on.

Coming off the end of the bridge onto the macadam, Shockley gave a quick backward glance to the cascading waterfall at Beebe Dam and then turned onto Wait Avenue. He was moving along at a steady clip, still lost in his thoughts and the rhythms of his stride, when suddenly, looking up, he saw smack in his path the rounded back of an old woman moving directly ahead of him in the road. With but inches to spare, Shockley frantically jammed on his brakes and, yanking his wheel to the left, managed to just brush past her before finally coming to a jerking halt and nearly tumbling off his bike.

Collecting himself and beginning a profuse apology, Shockley watched in bafflement as the woman, apparently oblivious of the near collision, continued unfazed along the side of the road, mumbling to herself as she moved along. His heart still pounding, Shockley got back on his bike and, tramping on the pedals, began to move on. A few hundred yards farther down the road he found himself slowing down and turning around to catch a glimpse of this strange woman. Everything about her struck him as odd. Though it was a balmy evening and Shockley was comfortable in only shirt-sleeves, the old lady, he noticed, was dressed in a clumsy winter coat with matching feathered hat. Her gait also seemed strange. It was a slow, shuffling walk in which, hunched over, under her coat, she propelled herself forward by dragging her feet ahead and stepping down on the backs of her crushed shoes. There was a sidewalk that followed Wait Avenue, but here was this queer lady walking in the street alongside the gutter. Well, he thought to himself with a perplexed shrug as he turned onto Cayuga Heights Road, Ithaca sure has some peculiar people. And then, before he could give her much more thought, he was turning into his familiar driveway, pedaling up the slow incline toward his garage, and a familiar child's voice was calling out to him.

"Daddy!" cried Cindy, spotting him from the back yard. Deserting her toys in the grass, she rushed forward to greet him and, as he stood straddling his bike, she leaped up into his arms nearly bowling him over.

"Whoa there!" He laughed, catching his balance as she wrapped her arms around him and hugged him tight. "Take it easy on the old man." He grinned, tickled by her effusiveness.

"Take me for a ride," she said, turning her face up to him. "One of those speedy rides."

"What about dinner?"

"It can wait. Please," she pleaded.

"OK, hop on." And putting her on the crossbar, he turned back down the drive. "Now hold on tight and keep your feet away from the spokes," he said as they careened down the inclined drive.

"Faster. Come on. Lots faster," she urged him, laughing excitedly as he shifted gears and began to force the pedals harder and harder, the bike picking up speed until they were whizzing down the street of stately homes, Cindy's mouth open to catch the wind as she hung on for dear life.

"More, more," she coaxed, and Shockley continued to pour on power, putting his might into his feet until his muscles began to ache and he could barely catch his breath. Then he coasted, slowed down, and, wheeling in a wide circle, headed back to the house.

"Wow," uttered Cindy, catching her own breath.

With sweat dripping into his eyes and a momentary sense of well-being invading his tired body, Shockley shifted down to his lowest gear and turned into his drive. As he closed the last few feet to the top of the knoll, he suddenly realized he was

29

thinking about that crazy old lady. He had seen her somewhere before in Ithaca, he thought, coming to a stop and letting Cindy slide off, but just couldn't place her.

6

By the time Doris finally figured out just what it was that was happening to her, it was too late to do anything about it. There was no single symptom that finally made it dawn on her that rainy Tuesday in mid-June. Rather, the revelation was brought about by a mounting backlog of evidence—edema, sore and grossly swollen breasts, morning sickness, protruding belly, lethargy, and those strange, internal movements—singular events coalescing in her mind like fine particles of mist merging spontaneously to form a single, perfect droplet. As she wandered through the streets of town, the dribbling trees soaking the feathers on her hat, the truth finally assailed her. Those sharp spasms she had first attributed to gas could be only one thing—the undeniable kicks of a growing fetus.

She was pregnant. Gravid. With child. As absurd and ludicrous and shameful as it was, there was no denying it. Parthenogenesis. She remembered once reading about it, and that day Doris pulled herself over to the library and looked it up again. High in the stacks of the county library, she read of how, instead of the normal situation in which the male gamete enters and activates an egg in the female of a given species, it was possible for an egg to develop spontaneously because it had inexplicably acquired the full diploid number of chromosomes and become self-activated. Parthenogenesis. It was common among plant lice and aphids, bees, crustaceans, and lizards. Thumbing through the cumulative sets of *Index Medicus*, Doris discovered how parthenogenesis had been experimentally induced, how unfertilized frog eggs pricked with a needle amazingly developed into living young, how rabbit ova subjected to temperature change or saline solution had ultimately produced living rabbits, how local anesthetic and tranquilizers had induced parthenogenic activation of mouse oocytes. When it came to humans, mythology was filled with stories of virgin births. But so, too, Doris found, was history, alleged cases occurring around the globe—none ever satisfactorily confirmed, but then, none ever scientifically disproved. Among Doris's research, one sentence discovered in an encyclopedia lodged in her mind, and long after she had left the library that day, it kept repeating in her thoughts: "In origin, parthenogenesis is not primitive but has arisen by mutation in many species." In this infinite universe all things were apparently possible. Though the odds were one in ten billion, it had nonetheless actually happened. And it was to her, she realized. Miss Rumsey. Doris Rumsey. A singularity. An aberration. A mutation. A freak!

But why? Why me? She shuddered. Better to have died a slow, agonizing death, consumed by a malignancy, than to be a freak, she railed against the stormy heavens. Why, of all the human beings on this planet, why had she been singled out for this curse?

Later that night, when the rains lifted and the skies cleared, Doris looked up at the stars that glowed beyond the halo of light surrounding the city and wondered if this thing, this infant that was surely in her, weren't a punishment brought on by her secret longing for a child, brought on, perhaps, by unvoiced envy?

A few days later, Olive Eldridge came by to see her.

"It's been ages, Doris," she said, trying not to be too obtrusive as she glanced around the house. It was not by chance that she dropped in. Olive had heard all the rumors around school about Doris's disintegration and she had come by to take a look for herself—and to see what she could do for her old friend.

Once in the house, Olive couldn't help but notice how Doris's ordinarily tidy house seemed neglected. The furniture was covered with dust. There were piles of forgotten refuse spilling over the garbage bags in the kitchen. Dirty dishes lay piled in the sink. The kitty-litter box looked as if it had gone unattended for weeks, and the stench of rotted food caused Olive to gag.

"Is there something I can do for you?" asked Olive, trying to disguise her disgust. "Are you ill? Are you—"

"I'm fine," said Doris, shamefully averting her eyes.

"Let me give you a hand cleaning up. You can't live like *this*."

"I was going to straighten everything up tomorrow. I just haven't gotten around to it."

"Doris, let me help you. Let me take you to a doctor."

"No!" objected Doris adamantly. She knew that if the truth ever got out, whatever peace she had left in her life would be taken from her. It was her shame, her punishment, and what she needed most was privacy.

"Just let me—"

"Please. I just want to be left alone," said Doris, shaking her head. "I think you'd better go now," she uttered, and, shuffling through the dark hallway, showed Olive the door.

After Olive left, Doris sank down on the couch and wept bitterly, crying until she fell into a deep, dreamless sleep. The next morning she got up and, without so much as breakfast, pulled on her coat and headed out the door. That day she walked and wandered until dark, praying to God for forgiveness and understanding. Once she even considered stepping into a church, but she didn't want to be seen like this, seen in her sin.

The days passed. The weather turned hot and sticky for a spell, then rained, cooled off under a north wind, then started the cycle all over again. As Ithaca finds itself caught on the break point between the sultry heat of the southern states and the crisp arctic air of Canada, a mere wind determining a violent shift in temperature, so too was Doris's life balanced on a fine line. One minute she might find within herself the steely determination to meet whatever future awaited her, the next she might be staring down from the lip of a gorge into a rocky abyss contemplating the ultimate sin.

Doris wept, prayed, debated, despaired, gained courage, lost it again. But through it all, the days marched on, and the thing within her womb continued to develop and expand and slowly descend. It kicked her, poked her, jabbed her with sharp bones from within, and turned around in her stomach as though it were doing somersaults. Mercilessly it grew and expanded until the skin that stretched over Doris's belly felt paper thin and ready to burst. Then in the early morning hours of June 21, the day on which the sun reached its zenith, the inevitable and unmistakable sharp warning pangs roused her from her sleep. Pulling herself from bed, Doris Rumsey dressed, washed herself, combed her hair for the first time in weeks, and, putting on her coat, headed out into the countryside to meet her long-dreaded appointment.

Hurrying along the road that led north out of the city, Doris began to sense within a few miles the telltale drip that ran down her legs. Anxiously she pushed on, halting only when her contractions came in cruel clusters, forcing her to double over at the side of the road. In even shorter stretches between pains she determinedly plodded on and on, panting and puffing and murmuring, driving herself to the very limit of her endurance until, just outside of Lansing, her waters broke with a sudden gush, and looking worriedly down at the inert puddle that lay on the macadam, she knew she could go no farther. She turned off the road into a field planted with young oats and, stepping as cautiously as she could over the tender plants, trekked across the seeming vastness of the clearing. Finding a secluded spot in a hedgerow at the far end of that field, Doris Rumsey accepted the commandments of her pain and, sinking to her knees, she slowly lowered herself to the earth.

The pains came and went, returning each time with greater frequency and more violence. They lasted all that morning, through the afternoon, and into dusk. As the sun exploded on the horizon, burning a fiery red in the streams of high clouds above her, Doris cried out, beat her fists into the ground, bit down on her sleeves until they tasted of blood. The racking pain came without abatement, twisting, tearing, contracting her aged body until it was a single knot of torment, and Doris was now certain that this was what hell must be like. And then, in her instance of greatest anguish, she let out a piercing howl that echoed across the still countryside.

"Oh, Lord!" she wailed. "What have I ever done to deserve this?"

And in that moment, Baby was born.

Even before she returned home the next day with Baby swaddled in her old, gray coat, Doris knew that there was something distinctly unusual about her newborn infant.

After a long, arduous delivery, mother and child had slept out that first night in the hedgerow, the two of them falling into a deep, exhausted sleep. When Doris awoke the next morning at dawn, she opened her eyes with a start. Around her, birds sang, insects buzzed, a bee alighted noisily from a wild flower just behind her head. A breeze blew across the field, ruffling up her hair. She had been sleeping outside in the country she realized and then, feeling the dull residue of pain inside her, recalled what had happened. Looking down she saw the baby that lay against her body. The infant's eyes were already miraculously open, and she was looking up at her mother as though patiently waiting for her to rise.

Lifting herself on an elbow, Doris took a closer look. In the early morning light that reached just over the hill, she saw for the first time what a beautiful child she had gotten. Born with golden wisps of hair, fine, even features, and a cherubic countenance, the child looked to Doris like nothing short of an angel. As she continued to examine her, marveling at her perfectly formed little hands and feet, Doris realized that the baby was actually watching her, staring back up at her with a knowing, expectant look in her powder-blue eyes.

Clutching her baby tightly, Doris slowly got up and sat on a large shale rock that jutted out of the ground. She squinted out at the sun rising behind the trees in the distance. Overhead and in the fields on either side, the birds were busily beginning their day, their calls and chirps filling the air and getting louder as the sun rose. It was their activity that finally made Doris aware, by contrast, how oddly silent her baby was. Since birth, her baby had not issued so much as a single sound. Frightened that the infant had been born mute, she began to shake her baby, hoping to elicit a cry. She shook her repeatedly, jolting the child almost violently, yet the baby gave not a whimper or cry, but just continued to look up at her mother, a puzzled expression coming into her eyes that made Doris stop.

Instinctively Doris opened her blouse and offered the child her milk-heavy breast. Finding Doris's nipple between her lips, the baby began to fumble unsurely with it and then, with a little coaxing, she finally began to drink, sucking away hungrily. In a few minutes the child emptied both breasts, and Doris found that she had barely enough milk to satisfy her. When the child was finished and pulled away, Doris waited hopefully for some sound, but other than a small burp there was nothing. Finally she gathered the baby up in her coat and began the trek home.

In her attic Doris found an old wicker basket. She put a pillow in it, covered it with a fresh sheet, and put the child in the makeshift crib. Still, as the day wore on, the child neither cried, nor called, nor complained. Later, holding her tight to her breast, she fed the child, and then, finding a comfortable spot near a window that looked out on her garden, she put the baby to sleep in the basket. From a distance she continued to observe her. She saw how the baby's eyes looked out the window to follow a passing bird, how she seemingly studied the roses that were beginning to bloom, watched intently as a fly bounced against the windowpane. This was surely no ordinary child, she said to herself and, going back to her, couldn't help but pick her up. Clutching the child in her arms, Doris felt shivers running up and down her spine.

"Baby, Baby, Baby," she murmured, rocking the child, bestowing on her the name that would never be erased.

"I told you," Charlie Oltz whispered conspiratorially to his wife. "There was a baby wrapped in that coat when she came back."

"I wouldn't have believed it if I hadn't seen it with my own eyes!" said Edna, who had sneaked around the Rumsey house and spotted the infant through the garden window. "She's got the thing stuck in a basket."

"What are we supposed to do?" Charlie scratched his bald dome, as he did whenever he was troubled.

"Well, we gotta do something."

"Maybe she's baby-sitting?"

"That baby's not even a couple of days old. I know a newborn when I see one."

"What are you thinking?" he asked, turning to look at her.

"You know what I'm thinking," she said, and together they quickly resolved to take action.

" 'Scuse me," said the young man standing in Doris's doorway. He was wearing a plaid sports jacket and maroon slacks and had a dark moustache.

"Yes?" asked Doris, pulling her robe tight around her neck. The young man looked clean-cut and reminded her of one of those Mormons or Jehovah's Witnesses who came around, except he didn't have a book in his hand.

"I'm Detective Iacovelli, Ithaca City Police," he said, flashing a set of papers.

"Oh," said Doris nervously.

"We have a report that you have a baby here," he said, looking at the woman who appeared disheveled, old, and run-down.

"And?" asked Doris suspiciously.

"Well,' began Iacovelli uneasily, looking down at his shiny shoes, "*do* you have a baby in the house?"

Doris paused and looked straight at the young man.

"Do you?" he persisted.

"Yes," answered Doris.

"How old is the child?"

"It's new," she said tersely. She would have liked to lie, but all her life she had always stuck to the truth.

"Whose is it?" asked Iacovelli.

"Mine," answered Doris, and before the man could ask another question she had closed the door.

"I checked the wire and there's no report of any missing baby anywhere." Iacovelli told Chief Lean when he made his report back at the police station behind Woolworth's.

"I don't see what you're bothering me with this crap for," said the chief, letting out a disgusted grunt. "Last night we had five break-ins, a gas station on Elmira Road was knocked over in an armed robbery, and a co-ed got raped just off the campus, and you're asking me about a simple case of a misplaced baby?"

"I just never ran into anything like this before," explained Iacovelli, stymied. "I don't want to go out and get a warrant."

"So don't! Why don't you talk to her?" Lean clamped his teeth down on the stub of an unlit cigar.

"I tried. I just didn't get anywhere."

"Try again. Make her produce a birth certificate." The phone on Chief Lean's desk rang. "How old did you say the lady was?" he asked, picking up the phone. "Lean here," he said into the receiver.

"Late fifties"—Iacovelli raised his voice to keep the chief's attention—"maybe sixty."

"Are you kidding?" Lean rolled his eyes to the ceiling. "No, not you," he said into the phone. "Look"—he covered the receiver and turned to Iacovelli—"I've got my hands full. Do the best you can, huh?" Then he turned back to the phone. "You got him?" Lean barked into the phone while Iacovelli continued to stand there, his hands at his sides. "Well hold the son of a bitch! That's right. Sit tight. I'll be right down!" Lean said, shoving his chair away from his desk and scrambling to his feet. "Come on, tiger"—Lean grinned and gave Iacovelli a playful punch on the shoulder—"go get her." He laughed around his cigar and then disappeared.

"I'm sorry to bother you again, Mrs. Rumsey," said the detective uncomfortably. "Can I come in?"

"No," said Doris flatly but politely.

"I can get a warrant if I have to," he said, and over the man's shoulder Doris could see her neighbors, the Oltzs, watching from down the block as they pretended to work on their lawn.

"OK, come in." She motioned and Iacovelli followed her into the house.

Iacovelli looked around. It was an old house, he noticed, one of those that had probably been built in the early 1920s. There was a large, wooden staircase that came down into the entranceway, hardwood floors in the hall and living room, faded linoleum in the kitchen. The oak trim and wainscoting that had originally been built into the house had not been painted over and the wood was still evident through layers of old varnish. The house seemed dark and smelled musty and sour. The inside seemed dirty, Iacovelli thought, but he had seen worse.

"I'd like to see the baby, please," he said, lifting up his dark eyebrows, and Doris took him to the wicker basket that stood by the garden window.

Baby was awake in her makeshift crib and, looking down, Iacovelli, a father himself, noted that she seemed alert and healthy. Instinctively he reached down and tickled her tummy. Baby smiled and Iacovelli smiled back.

"You say this is your child?" he said, still looking down into the basket.

"Yes," answered Doris, watching the detective.

The walkie-talkie on his belt burst out with a garbled message.

"May I ask if the father is around?"

"There is none," Doris answered evenly.

"Oh," said Iacovelli discreetly, opening his pad and beginning to write.

"Your age?"

"Do I have to answer that?"

"I need it for the records, ma'am."

"Uh-huh," she said and muttered something.

"Huh?"

"Fifty-something."

"Fifty what?"

"Fifty-eight," she said and knew it was just a small fib.

"And this is your child?"

"Yes, that's what I said," she answered firmly.

"Er . . . do you have a birth certificate you could show me?"

"No."

"No?"

"No."

"Where was the child born?"

"In Lansing."

"In a home out there?" he asked, realizing that there was no hospital out that way.

"No."

"Then where?"

"Out there. In the country."

"You mean *outside*?"

Doris nodded.

Iacovelli took a long breath and slowly exhaled. For an instant he felt like going out and throttling those neighbors down the block for dragging him into this stupid mess.

"Look, Mrs. Rumsey. Let's try to make this easier for both of us, OK?" The walkie-talkie barked again and he turned it down.

"I'll try."

"This all sounds a little unreasonable."

"I understand."

"If you could just in some way prove to me that this is your child or that—let's say—you're taking care of it for a granddaughter who maybe got into a little trouble. Or—"

"But it *is* mine."

"Then I could be on my way. I've got a lot of pressing cases."

"But it *is*."

Iacovelli nervously played with his walkie-talkie.

"OK. Fine. Could you take me to the place where you gave birth to the child?" he asked, deciding to call her bluff.

Doris paused for a moment. She weighed her situation, realized that this man had the power to take Baby from her if she didn't cooperate, and then finally relented.

"Yes," she told the surprised detective. "I'll take you."

Doris gathered up Baby in her blanket, and as the Oltzs watched, she got into the detective's car. Iacovelli called into headquarters, waited for a response, and then pulled away from the curb.

"This way," she said, directing him out Route 13, and by the time he reached the top of the hill he realized he was already out of his jurisdiction. What he was doing was definitely not by the rules, but neither was this case.

"Turn left here," she said, holding Baby protectively so that if he stopped short the child would not be hurt against the dash. The radio in the front seat crackled, and a series of calls went back and forth between a cruiser and the dispatcher as Doris pointed out the way.

"Stop there." Doris finally motioned as they came over a rise.

"Now where?" Iacovelli asked when he had parked the car. They seemed to be somewhere out in the sticks.

Doris got out, cradling Baby, and began walking into the field, stepping over the young stalks of oats as Iacovelli followed, a foolish look on his face.

"She doesn't cry much, does she?" he said, trying to make conversation. The sun was hot and he was beginning to sweat under his polyester sports jacket.

"Baby's an angel," said Doris, and Iacovelli could see from the gentle way she held the child that she loved it.

"Here," she said when they arrived at the shale rock that jutted out of the ground by the hedgerow.

Iacovelli looked around. The grass around the trees was, indeed, matted. Someone had been here recently. His eyes began to scan the area and almost immediately fell on a foul, bloody mess that was covered with flies. It was an afterbirth. He wrinkled his nose and looked away.

"That it?" he asked her.

Doris nodded with lowered eyes. Iacovelli quickly scribbled something in his pad and then they left.

"Jesus!" said Iacovelli through his teeth when they reached the car.

"What?" asked Doris.

"Nothing."

That evening when Detective Iacovelli came home from work he was still thinking about his encounter with the old lady on Willow Avenue. Later when his children were fast asleep and he lay in bed with his wife, Sandy, he told her about Doris Rumsey, the fifty-nine-year-old lady who had actually given birth to a child—and out in the middle of a field of all places. Sandy Iacovelli worked as a secretary in the engineering department at the university and, during the morning coffee break the following day, she told some of the other women in the office about it. Naturally each of the women couldn't help but relay the unusual tale to at least one of her friends. One of the women present that morning at the coffee break was Helen Scaglione, who was a good friend of Carol Place, who just happened to be an old school chum of Mary Sullivan. Mary Sullivan, it turned out, was a reporter for the Ithaca paper and it was precisely through these kinds of contacts that she got some of her best stories. It was therefore not at all odd that Mrs. Sullivan appeared at Doris's house the very next evening.

"Are you Mrs. Rumsey?" asked the woman standing on Doris's porch. It was dark outside, but Doris could see that there was a man standing behind her.

Doris said nothing.

"I'm Mary Sullivan from the *Ithaca Journal*," chirped the woman. "And this is—" She began to introduce the man, but as soon as Doris spotted his camera, she reached for the door. In one quick instant the camera suddenly came up, a blinding flash went off, and Doris slammed the door shut. Locking it tight, she stood leaning against the door, waiting for her sight to return. As soon as the white ball burning in front of her eyes began to fade, Doris hurried around the first floor pulling all the blinds. She carried Baby in her basket up to the second floor and there went around drawing all the curtains and blinds, resting only when she was sure she had sealed herself off from the outside world.

"Hey, will you look at this?" said Shockley the next evening.

He and Ruth were sitting around the table after dinner while Julie and Annette took their turn washing the dishes. From Randy's room upstairs came the irritating grate of hard rock, which Shockley tried to block out.

"At what?" asked Ruth, looking up from her section of the *Ithaca Journal*. She always took first crack at the section that held real estate ads, while her husband began with the world and local news.

"I know that old lady. I almost ran her down with my bike a couple of weeks ago," he said, holding up the fuzzy front-page picture. On top of the photo was the caption:

60-Year-Old Woman Gives Birth to Child

"That's really incredible," exclaimed Shockley. "Sixty years old!"

"Ah"—Ruth waved away the article— "the *Journal* always gets its facts screwed up."

7

When Doris picked up a copy of the *Journal* with her groceries and recognized the picture of the startled woman on the front page she suspected that her troubles had only just begun.

As she opened the front door, the phone was already ringing. Instinctively she grabbed for it.

"Hello?"

"Mrs. Rumsey?"

"Yes," she answered against her better judgment.

"This is Andrew Scott, Associated Press in Syracuse. I'm calling to verify a story that—"

Doris hung up. She went over and checked Baby, who was lying in her basket on her stomach, her eyes open, the child silent as ever. Doris turned her over onto her back, checked to make sure she was still dry, and smiled at her. Baby looked quizzically up at her with her wide, pale eyes, her fine wisps of golden hair pressed against the pillow.

Taking her groceries into the kitchen, Doris went about unpacking them, trying not to dwell on the call, on her photo in the paper, nor the way the checkout girl at the P&C had kept staring at her as she rang up her meager order, Pampers and all.

The phone summoned her again.

Doris let it ring. She lifted a container of skim milk out of the paper bag and put it into the refrigerator. Then cottage cheese. A couple of oranges. A small bunch of bananas. All as Markowitz had recommended. For Baby's sake she was determined to eat right, take care of her health, try to lose a few pounds.

The phone continued to sound. Finally she went and answered it. It was a woman from United Press International.

"Please, I need to be left alone," Doris pleaded.

"I won't take more than a minute of your time," began the woman, trying to wheedle her way in. "I'd just like to ask you—"

Doris broke the connection.

Later, while she was trying to breast-feed Baby, the phone rang again. It rang and rang. Finally, after ten rings, it stopped and Doris heaved a sigh. A few minutes later the phone started in again, but this time Doris no longer heard it. Her attention was completely absorbed. She was riveted to another sound. Baby, lying on her tummy in Doris's lap, seemed to be issuing a faint noise. Doris was almost sure of it. Anxiously she put her ear close to Baby, straining to ignore the shrill echoing of the phone. Nothing. But there had been something coming from Baby's lips. She had heard a muffled, cooing type of sound. She could have sworn to it.

Quickly she turned Baby over. The infant was smiling, a little bit of cheesy milk dribbling out of the corner of her mouth. Sliding her hands under Baby's armpits, Doris raised her up and, holding the tiny infant in front of her face, waited tensely. Baby looked around the room distractedly. The phone finally ceased, and the house became almost silent. All Doris could now hear was a large truck rumbling in the far distance along Cayuga Street. The noise faded and there was total silence. A moment passed as mother and child looked at each other. Then Baby took a short breath, opened her mouth, and a faint sound emerged, filling the void. Doris's own mouth fell open. It was not a cooing sound, she realized, listening in astonishment to the continuous utterance. No. Rather, it was a kind of—yes— music. Baby was singing. Actually singing. Coming out in the high voice of an infant was a faint though coherent series of notes, a melody of sorts. Holding her breath Doris sat spellbound, listening to the unearthly strain emerging from the lips of this child, who for the days since her birth had shunned all sounds, listened as Baby sang for her mother, her notes pure and crystal and perfect. Never had she heard such strains. It was the bell-like music of a flute, the high resonant notes of a plucked harp, the perfect strain of a violin. It was all of these and yet none of them. But whatever it was it caused the tears that welled in Doris's eyes to break loose as her soul became buoyant, taking flight as though the unspeakably heavy burden she had carried for so long was suddenly being lifted. And as Doris clutched her infant, holding Baby with great tenderness as if fearing she might crush the faint song, a radiant smile spread across her tear-stained face, a face that no longer looked quite as creased and haggard.

The phone rang again, but Doris could no longer hear it. Baby's song had already transported her far from the confines of her dreary house. In that moment, as the phone continued to urgently peal, a startling revelation was dawning upon her. Suddenly, in that span of an instant as wide as time itself and as short as the gap between those rings, the purpose behind all the trials and travails of the last months made sense. Baby had never been meant as a punishment or a curse. Baby had been intended as a present, a very special gift, she realized, weeping in open thanks, as Baby sang for her her unworldly, childish melody.

Each passing day Baby's voice grew gradually stronger, the notes of her mellifluous song surer, her crystalline sounds yet clearer. As the Oltzs could hardly fail to notice, other significant changes were also taking place in the Rumsey house. The blinds that had been kept drawn day and night were now open again, leaving the sunlight free to splash into the house. Doris even began to venture out for more than a quick dash to the supermarket down the street. On a number of occasions she was seen working in her garden, humming happily to herself as she tended her yard, pruning the forgotten roses planted by her father or weeding the unruly flowerbeds at the edge of the house. And the Oltzs, when by chance they met Doris on their walk, were mystified to be greeted by their neighbor with a sweet, benevolent smile.

After a stretch of balmy July weather, a week was marked by one of those bleak rainy spells endemic to Ithaca. The cold, damp air sent people scurrying back into their houses, where they lit wood fires to drive out the persistent chill. For that dismal week Doris was hardly seen by her neighbors. Then late one night the heavens secretly cleared and, the next morning when people arose to go off to work, they were greeted by the beginnings of a glorious day. Above the town the sky blazed a perfect dome of blue, extending cloudless so far as the eye could see; a rippleless lake sparkled in the azure of the sky; the green of the summer foliage sprang forth lusher then memory could recall, and a splurge of flowers filled the air with a heady, fragrant perfume.

It was on that day, that inordinately paradisiacal day, that Doris decided to take Baby on her first outing.Wrapping her child in a thin blanket, she wandered up Yates Street to Cayuga Street, and when she passed the public library she crossed the street and walked into Dewitt Park. There, finding an empty bench among the sunworshipers, she sat down and, opening the blanket, let the morning sun fall on Baby's delicate skin. Although it was still early, the park was already moderately busy. Two young boys on skateboards were zigzagging down the pavement practicing turns and nearly colliding. In the grass a group of young people lounged around a trio strumming guitars. An old wino sat backward on another bench, his feet pushed through the slats as he sipped from a paper bag. Two sulky-looking youths with long hair and army jackets sat propped up against a marble monument, rolling some suspicious-looking cigarettes.

Turning her face up to the sun, Doris closed her eyes and dozed for a few moments. She awoke, checked Baby to make sure she wasn't too hot, saw that her child was content, and then closed her eyes again. For a few minutes Baby lay still, soaking in the warmth of the morning sun. Then she let out a yawn, stretched her arms and, taking a long breath, began to sing. The two youths sitting on the monument across from Doris stopped rolling their joints and, looking up in sudden puzzlement, nearly dropped them. Couched in her blanket, Baby continued to sing, her melody now getting louder as it climbed and fell like water tumbling through a stream, her little voice sure and velvety. The drunk on the nearby bench sat up erect and gaped as a rivulet of red wine ran down his chin. The youths at the monument exchanged bewildered glances as Baby sang on. For a moment they continued to sit frozen and then, certain of the source of the music, they stuffed their paraphernalia into their pockets and went over to where Doris was sitting.

"Wicked!" mumbled the first one, spellbound, as the pair stood looking down on the old lady with her singing child.

"That's so fine it's pitiful!" gasped the other, shaking his dirty curls.

Doris opened her eyes and, looking up at the pair, gave them a knowing smile. Quietly they sank down and sat cross-legged on the walk by the bench.

The kids on the skateboards whizzed past and, catching a few of Baby's notes, nearly fell off their boards. Executing a sharp turn, they came back for a second pass. When they reached the bench and again heard Baby's song, they jumped free of their boards, letting them run off down the walk until they flipped over and lay forgotten in the distant grass.

The drunk on the neighboring bench disentangled his feet and stumbled over.

"Did you ever—?" he began, and the two youths sitting on the walk silenced him with their hands, their earlier glower now replaced with smiles of peace and contentment.

The crowd around Doris's feet grew rapidly as new people came past, stopped at he sound of Baby's song, and ended up sitting dwn to listen. What had started with a few people had now grown into a few dozen sitting in an awestruck circle around Doris's bench. Yet more people arrived until, suddenly and without explanation, Baby stopped singing. For a moment there was dead silence. Then a long, unanimous sigh went up in the crowd. The people who had sat in rapt silence began to slowly stir and fidget as though awakening from a trance. Patiently they remained seated waiting for more, but clearly the child had finished singing and the spell was broken. A few people moved away embarrassedly. Others lingered on, puzzled and uncertain just what it was they had heard. Doris tickled Baby under her chin; the little girl smiled, emitted a burp, an then, closing her eyes, fell asleep in her mother's arms. Doris closed the blanket, got up from the bench, and, weaving her way through the stunned throng, headed back home to give Baby her feeding.

Word of Baby's song traveled fast, especially among the younger people of Ithaca—the students and hangers-on, ex-students and teenagers—who frequented the park and Commons. Within a few days something of a ritual was established, Doris returning each morning to Dewitt Park to find a sizable crowd waiting expectantly. Not one to disappoint Baby's admirers, Doris would sit down, open Baby's blanket, rock her in the sun until, sure enough, Baby would draw that telltale long breath, open her little mouth, and begin to trill for her enraptured audience.

Ithaca now buzzed with tales of Baby. She soon became the number-one topic at school, surpassing sex, sports, and rock. The kids talked about her in the halls, passed notes during class, and discussed her animatedly after school in the game room at the Pyramid Mall, their voices raised above the whines and beeps and crashes of the electronic games.

"Did you hear her sing?"

"Who?"

"Why, Baby, you dink!"

"Where've you been living all this time? Under a rock?"

"A baby?"

"No, not *a* baby. Baby."

And it *was* hard to believe. Who had ever heard of a month-old child who could sing, actually *sing*? But she did, and what came from her lips was nothing short of incredible.

"Her music's sort of like a bird's chirping," some would say, trying to grapple with a description.

"No," others who were more poetically inclined might differ. "It's more like a brook babbling, or—"

"Or the wind whistling through the trees."

"Or glass chimes tinkling in the breeze," sighed a young girl still under the spell of Baby's song.

In Doris's mind, they were all correct. Baby's music seemed to be a distillation of all the mellifluous sounds of nature, of wind and songbirds, flapping geese, and rushing water. It was as if Baby, while still in Doris's womb, had absorbed all these colors of sound, for the lyrical melody that she sang could only be that of a wanderer.

As the news of Baby's music continued to spread, Baby's audience continued to swell, subtly changing in composition. Where once there had been mostly young people, there could now be discerned, sitting in the grass by the bench, older people—a smattering of retired folks, a few laborers, secretaries, even a well-manicured banker in a three-piece suit, who came by whenever he could pull himself away from business.

Once heard, Baby's sweet-noted song could hardly be resisted. It buoyed the spirits, enticed the soul, planted hope where before there had been fallow despair. That, and apparently more.

"You know those gruesome headaches I had," said a woman to her husband. "Well, they're gone. Vanished. That baby did it."

"I'd been depressed for months," confessed a widower with dark circles under his eyes. "I couldn't sleep. Nights were hell. Days were even worse. I considered ending it all by jumping in the gorge. Then I heard her. That little baby. And suddenly my perception of everything changed. Oh, sure I still hurt, but I can live with it. You ought to give it a try."

"There's this little, teeny-weeny baby," said Randy Shockley to his parents over dinner. Randy spent a good deal of his time hanging around the downtown area looking for girls and by chance had wandered past the park a few days earlier. "And she sings."

"Sings?" asked Ruth Shockley, tilting her head in puzzlement. As of late, Randy had been acting queerly. He seemed to have gotten unusually subdued, and Ruth secretly feared he was dabbling in drugs.

"What kind of baby?" asked Shockely, his curiosity pricked.

"A little one. A newborn."

"And she sings?" he asked, a smile stretching his lips.

47

"I heard her with my own ears. She's got this weird kind of song," said Randy, and he tried to imitate it, but it came out sounding wrong to his own ears and he shrugged it off.

"You're telling me that there's a baby that sings?" Shockley laughed aloud.

"No, it's true, Dad"—Annette came to her brother's rescue—"I heard it from Laura Epstein. She was down in the park. This old lady has this baby—"

"This *newborn* baby?" Ruth questioned. She prided herself on being a logical person and wanted to pass on to her children a smattering of that precision.

"Well, I don't know if she's newborn, but she's very little. Like this," she said, approximating Baby's size with her hands.

"And she holds a tune," said Shockley sarcastically.

"No, sings!" Randy flushed.

"I heard it too," Julie chimed in.

"With your own ears?" Ruth asked.

"Well, not exactly. Stevie DeFilipis told me."

"Oh, *him*"—Shockley rolled his eyes—"that kid's mother is a Bible-toting, certified looney."

"But *I* heard it!" Randy insisted, and then, giving up in disgust, went back to picking at his potatoes.

"And I suppose you heard it too, kitten?" Shockley gave his youngest a tickle under her arm.

"I didn't hear nothing," said Cindy with an innocent shrug.

"Anything," corrected Ruth.

"Huh?" said Cindy.

People soon found out where Doris lived, and what had begun as a morning affair now occurred twice daily—once in the morning as usual at the park, then again later in the early evening on Willow Avenue.

Emerging onto her porch with Baby in her arms, the gentle light of dusk casting long shadows, Doris was always sure to find each evening a crowd of local people waiting in front of her house. There, clustered in respectful silence, would be men, women, and children, mothers holding their own babies, others pushing strollers or carriages, laborers with coarse, grease-lined hands, bowlegged old folks leaning on canes. Lining the sidewalk they would patiently wait, their numbers

often growing so large that they spilled into the street, blocking
the road almost up to the edge of the creek. With the street filled,
passing cars would be forced to slow down and wait for the
crowd to part. And, if by chance Baby happened to be singing,
the drivers would inevitably leave their cars and end up joining the audience, causing traffic to hopelessly jam up.

"This is getting to be a goddamn circus!" Charlie Oltz had
fumed when once the crowd had swelled to such proportions
that they had trampled some of his shrubs.

Angrily he and Edna had charged over to complain.

"Hey, just one second here!" He had elbowed his way
through the crowd toward Doris, who sat with Baby on the front
stoop, Edna following in his wake.

"Hush!" said Muzzy, the realtor, who lived around the
corner. "A person can't hear with you shouting like that."

Oltz had stopped long enough to catch it. The baby. That little
baby that Doris Rumsey had stolen was singing. Actually singing.

"Edna. You hear it?" he said, his anger melting.

"I got ears," said Edna, a dreamy, youthful look coming into
her eyes.

"Hush," said Mrs. Muzzy softly.

"Holy shit," muttered Oltz to himself later as he walked away
after Baby had finished. He was so touched he could hardly
swallow. "If I hadn't of heard it with my own ears I wouldn't
have never believed," he said, his skin still tingling. "Not in a
million years."

"That woman's got a gold mine there," said Edna as they
watched the late show on television, the effects of Baby's song
having slowly worn off.

"And she doesn't even know it," echoed Charlie wistfully.

"See, I told you," Randy admonished his father. "You just
never believe me, do you?" he asked, but Shockley was too
absorbed in the *Journal* article to answer.

"Infant Sings to Ithaca Crowds" read the caption.

There on page one was a picture of that toothless old lady
Shockley had almost run down on Wait Avenue. She was grin-
ning and proudly displaying a tiny infant in her arms.

"Oh, this is getting screwier by the day." Shockley shook his head. "Here, listen to this, Ruth," he called out. Ruth was sitting curled up in a chair trying to grade some math prelims. "'The child,'" Shockley read aloud, "'who, the mother claims, is only five weeks old, is able to sing a continuous melody, which some Ithaca residents claim possesses curative properties.' My God, what a crock!"

Ruth looked up from her papers.

"Maybe it's true," she said, with a pencil still in her teeth.

"Come on, Ruth, do you really think a baby who's barely a month old can hold a tune?"

"Anything is possible, I suppose."

"Oh, yeah. Then listen to this: 'Ithaca-born Doris Rumsey, fifty-nine, purported mother of the child, alleges that there was no father involved in the conception of her child.'"

Ruth grinned.

"Not only do we have a month-old child that can sing. We also have a virgin birth on our hands! Now this is just absolutely ridiculous!" he said, slamming the paper down on the rug. "I really don't see why we keep subscribing to this rag!"

"And I don't see why you're so upset."

"She usually comes out around this time of night," said a man with gray stubble on his cheeks. The man talking to Shockley was at the far edge of the crowd by the banks of the creek and was standing on tiptoes, straining to see over the heads of the others. Though the throng was probably close to a hundred people, Shockley found it surprisingly subdued, people hardly speaking and then only in muted voices. Feeling awkward and a bit foolish, Shockley had selected a place far from the street lamp in the hopes of not being recognized. It was an unusually hot, sultry night with barely a breeze, the sourish odor of perspiration hanging in the air. Shockley was sweating profusely himself and could feel his shirt sticking to his body. The air in the valley basin was so humid that, sighting down the row of street lamps lining Willow Avenue, he noticed that each globe stood surrounded by an eerie halo of white.

"Hey, there she is now," said the stubbled man, and a sudden murmur went up in the crowd. Raising himself up on tiptoes, Shockley watched through a jumble of heads as a familiar hunchbacked lady emerged from the front door of the house. A tiny infant in her arms, the aged woman acknowledged the people with a soft smile and nod and, moving over to a rocking chair that stood on the porch, carefully took a seat. The buzzing in the crowd subsided. Feet that had been shuffling froze. Whispers died half spoken. The street fell absolutely still as the crowd held its breath as one. Shockley drummed his fingers on his thigh and waited, feeling sillier than ever.

"When does she—?" he whispered to the man.

"*Sh-sh!*" said the man, putting a finger on his lips.

Shockley grumbled silently to himself and felt like an idiot. He checked his watch.

A half hour passed and still there was no action from Baby.

"How long does it take?" he whispered to a pretty, well-dressed woman who stood with her arm around her young daughter.

"Be patient," said the lady, touching him softly with her hand, and, embarrassed, he shrank away.

Shockley was peering at his watch for the third time when, suddenly, he felt the people around him tense expectantly. He tilted his head to one side and listened. From the far distance at the head of the crowd came a faint sound. A voice of sorts, he thought. Getting up on his toes he craned his neck and strained his ears. A car roared by a few blocks away, blanking out all sound. When the noise finally faded, his hearing returned and with it that same curious, high sound. He stretched his neck upward trying to peer over the crowd. From what he could see the infant was moving its lips and, yes, yes, she seemed to be, sort of, sort of singing, he thought, dumbfounded, picking up bits and pieces of Baby's song. Inexplicable little shivers coursed up and down his spine. Shockley labored to hear, but was too far removed to catch more than just snatches. Carefully he began inching his way through the crowd, an ear cocked forward as he maneuvered between the tightly packed people, a look of intensity growing on his face as he neared the porch. Managing to wedge himself deep into the crowd before the bodies became too dense to budge, he came to a halt midway in the steamy press of people. Standing motionless, his hands at his sides, Shockley held his breath and listened. Listened and gaped.

"My Lord!" he muttered in astonishment, hearing the unearthly song issuing from the porch. "Is that actually coming from that little—?"

"*Sh-sh*," said someone behind him, putting a quieting hand gently on his shoulder.

Shockley pressed ahead a few more feet, his head craned intently forward. Closer to the porch, he was now in a position to see, unobstructed, both mother and child. Yet what he saw and heard defied the very foundations of all he knew and believed he knew. It was some trick. It had to be. Some electronic gimmickry, he thought, trying to shake off the music. Reaching into his shirt pocket he took out his glasses and put them on. For the longest moment he stood fixating on the child's mouth, carefully observing her lips. They were moving. Moving in perfect synchronization to the voice. And what a voice, he thought, barely able to contain his emotion. Whatever in the world it was, it was incredibly beautiful. Absolute perfection. In his entire life he had never heard the likes of this heavenly sound. Dumbfounded, Shockley listened as Baby swung through the sphere of her music, her voice cool and velvety in the low range, smooth in the middle, bright and birdlike in the upper.

He closed his eyes and let himself go with the music, feeling, as it tugged at the very root of his soul, the golden currents of Baby's song rushing in, cutting him loose and sweeping him aloft. Bathed in the melody of Baby's sweet song, Shockley could feel himself being lifted until he seemed to float on the undulating waves of her music, his absorption so complete that he was now oblivious of the hot, clammy skins pressed against his, unaware of the sour, stagnant breath of the crowd— Shockley engrossed to the point where he felt himself a solitary figure standing before this miraculous child, placed there as Baby sang for him and him alone, elevating him above all the adversities of life, moving him far beyond worldly cares and daily drudgery.

Lost in the midst of Baby's music, Shockley was caught unawares when the child reached the end of a passage and, without warning, stopped.

A single, audible sigh went up among the people and, opening his eyes, Shockley realized that his sigh had merged with theirs.

He looked back up at the porch and watched as Doris, smiling benignly, tucked Baby back into her blanket. The crowd stood mesmerized as Doris slowly rose from her chair. Gathering his wits, Shockley quickly nudged through the tight throng, fighting to near the porch as Doris headed for the door.

"Excuse me. Excuse me." He weaved his way forward through the unyielding bodies. "Wait," he called out as Doris reached for her door.

Doris turned. Shockley reached the steps to the porch.

"Mrs. Rumsey. I'm Irwin—" He began breathlessly to introduce himself.

"I'm sorry," said Doris, who thought Shockley was another reporter, "but I have to go." And she opened the door and went back into the house.

When Shockley got home that night, he was still under the influence of Baby's music. His nerves hummed. His skin tingled. The child's song was still ringing in his ears. Losing track of time, he paced the downstairs, stopping only when Ruth called to him.

"Are you coming up?" she asked from the top of the stairs.

"A little while," he answered absently and then, looking at his watch, saw that it was already past midnight. Baby's song, he thought. He should get her melody down while it was still fresh in his head, before it escaped him.

Taking a notepad from his study, he sat down in the living room and began to quickly jot down as much as he could recall. Although his memory was haphazard in everyday matters, when it came to music it was phenomenal. In a short while he managed to get down a good deal of what he had heard, making the direct transition from sound perceived in his brain to notes on paper. When he was finished, he went to the piano and, with one hand, began to play from his hasty scribbles. Over and over again he listened to the refrain he had transcribed, but as he concentrated on the melody, he felt none of the enthralling emotion he had experienced back in that Fall Creek neighborhood.

He stopped playing and got up from the piano. Something was bothering him and it wasn't Baby's music. Somewhere in the recesses of his consciousness, there was another song battling to come forth.

"Irwin?" Ruth called again.

From upstairs he could hear Julie's distinctive snoring.

"In a minute," he replied and went to get his pad. In his head Baby's music was suddenly vanishing and, as though a curtain were parting, in its place he was now listening to another song, his own song, melodic motives echoing in his brain, rhythmic patterns coalescing out of thin air. For the first time in ages he could feel fresh ideas beginning to flow.

Fumbling with his pad, he tore off the top sheets and, slumping down in his chair, began to set down a few tentative notes. He hummed them to himself, chewed on the pencil eraser, added a few more notes. Pleased, he went back to the opening, followed the line and then, without even humming, began to write feverishly, the music pouring from brain to paper, spilling out faster than he could record it.

By 2:00 A.M. Shockley was drenched in sweat, spent but exhilarated. He had finally broken the long, dry spell. He was composing again. He had started a tone poem, gone back to his point of departure and, in the heady rush of creativity, he was certain it was going to be better than *The Last Star* had ever been. Somehow, by some miracle, he had recaptured his youth, his exuberance, his lost optimism. His brain finally winding down, Shockley leaned back for a second and immediately fell into a deep, exhausted sleep, his pad in his lap, his pencil lost on the floor.

In the morning Ruth found her husband slumped in his favorite chair. He looked so peaceful that she let him sleep an extra half hour, awakening him just before she went off to work.

"Care for some coffee," she asked, holding out a steaming cup.

"Yes, definitely." He sat up, stretching and yawning. "Such service," he said, as he pulled her close and gave her a kiss. "Ugh," he grunted a few minutes later, staggering to his feet. His head throbbed and his face felt as though it had been run through a wringer.

"Why didn't you come to bed?" asked Ruth, gathering up her books.

"I meant to." He smiled sheepishly and, taking a few sips of his coffee, told Ruth about his experiences last night, about the crowd around the Willow Avenue house, about Baby, about his new work that had miraculously materialized out of thin air.

"So, the child sings?" she said, a grin forming on her face.

"You don't believe me, do you?"

"I didn't say that." Ruth laughed, sidestepping the question. What was uppermost in her thoughts was that her husband, for whatever reasons, was finally composing again. It meant that he would be happy and such contentment usually had a way of reflecting itself through the entire family.

After Ruth left, Shockley called up the departmental secretary and had her cancel his summer-school classes for the day. Now that he was composing again, he had no qualms about playing sick.

After a second cup of coffee Shockley went into his study. He opened his pad and began by reviewing his previous night's scoring. He changed a few bars, nervously fiddling with some notes and rests and then, approaching the point where he had left off, tried to pick up the pieces. He tried to concentrate, but the kids were in the kitchen making a racket. When he got there he found Annette and Julie squabbling with each other about who would get to pour milk first on their cereal—Annette with her round, saturnine features and pubescent body squaring off with spirited, sticklike Julie.

"Hey, what's going on here?" he asked.

"Annette's hogging the milk," said Julie, still holding on to the container.

"I am not. I had it first," Annette objected righteously, refusing to relinquish her own hold. "It's not fair."

"Girls. Please. I've got important work to do," said Shockley, who had gone through this same scene countless times before, always losing his temper and usually ending up by taking the milk away from both children. "I want a single, honest answer. Who had the milk first?"

"I did!"

"I did!"

The girls looked nervously at their father.

"This is silly," he smiled benignly and the girls exchanged a fleeting look. "In the time that you've spent arguing you could already have poured out enough milk for an army," he said sweetly.

"But it's the principle of the matter," insisted Annette.

"Yeah, and I had it and she tried to grab it away."

"Well, we can either cut the container in half"—Shockley

smiled—"or, better"—he went to the refrigerator and took out a fresh container and placed it before Julie—"let you each have your very own container."

"But—" sputtered Julie.

"But what?"

"But you've *always* told us we're not allowed to open a new one until we've used up the old one."

"When did I say that?"

"Yesterday, as a matter of fact," said Annette, mystified.

"Well, that was yesterday. And today is a different day," he said pleasantly and, giving each girl a pat on the head, went back to his study.

Awaiting him at his desk was his open pad, exactly as he had left it. He sat down and, hunching over it, tugged at his hair. He went back to the beginning and tried to recapture last night's inspiration. What, he asked himself, had he intended to do after that last bar? He should have left himself some scribbled reminder before dozing off.

Shockley pulled himself away from his desk and walked to the window. He looked out. It was going to be another beautiful, sunny day. A few faint wisps of clouds hung over the north end of the lake. He could tell by the number of sailing boats tacking across the blue waters that there was a stiff breeze up. For a moment he wished he were out on a boat knifing across the water instead of sitting in this room staring blankly at some squiggled pencil marks. He tried to clear his mind but, looking back at his desk, felt a sinking sensation overtake him.

Breakfast. That's what he needed. A good breakfast. He went into the kitchen. Randy was making his favorite: pancakes. The kitchen was a mess, full of spilled batter, the air heavy with oily smoke.

"Want some, Dad?" asked Randy cheerfully over his shoulder.

"Yeah. Looks good."

"How many?"

"Load up a stack."

"Sure thing. One stack coming up," chirped Randy, who, like his mother, was blessed with a naturally sunny disposition.

"When does she come to the park?" Shockley asked his son after the boy proudly served him a mound of partially burned flapjacks.

"Who?" asked Randy, who knew what he meant but just wanted the satisfaction of hearing it from his father's lips.

"You know, the old lady with the baby," he said with a full mouth.

"Oh, *her*," he said, biting his tongue to keep his freckled face from splitting into a grin. "I'd say around ten-thirty or eleven. If the weather is good. Hey, where are you going?" he called as Shockley headed out the door to his car, his pancakes half-eaten.

"They were excellent." Shockley stuck his head in the kitchen window an instant later, surprising his son. "I'll finish them when I get back," he said, trying to sound sincere. "I promise."

Randy laughed and watched as his father made a dash for his car.

By the time Shockley found an empty parking spot on the Buffalo Street edge of the park, he discovered he was already late. Through the windshield he could see people positioned on the grass around a bench on which sat a stooped figure holding an infant in her arms. Leaving his car without locking the door or putting a coin in the meter, he sprinted across the park. When he reached the crowd, Baby was already singing. Quickly, he scanned through the mass and, noticing an empty patch of grass not far from the bench, he cautiously clambered over the people, careful not to step on any outstretched hands or legs.

Sliding down into the vacant spot, his chest still heaving from his sprint, Shockley tried to still his panting. From where he sat, he could clearly hear Baby's voice. What she was singing, he noticed, was a variation on the melody she had sung the previous night. Slowly Shockley's breathing quieted down and, wiping the sweat that ran into his eyes, he began to concentrate. Her music, he thought, sounded even better than last night. Her voice seemed to have gained a measure of fullness, her notes struck him as even purer. Shockley closed his eyes and listened, listened with sheer pleasure as his body began to sway to her music, a fresh glow spreading from his stomach, extending outward until it caressed his thought and lightened his head.

Then Baby stopped.

Shockley opened his eyes abruptly. Baby let out a long yawn and stretched her little arms. She was finished, he realized, feeling vaguely cheated that he had been able to catch only the end of her song.

As the crowd began to stir and slowly straggle away, Shockley got to his feet. Looking over the array of bobbing heads, he watched as Doris rose and began to make her way through the parting crowd. As she shuffled away Shockley stood debating with himself.

"Mrs. Rumsey," he called, pursuing her long after she had left the park. "Please. I'd like to talk to you," he said catching up.

Doris turned to look at him and stopped. She was standing by the curb on Court Street waiting for the light to change.

"My name is Irwin Shockley. I'm a musician," he said hurriedly.

"Oh, that's nice." Doris smiled innocently, and when the light changed, she simply turned and walked off with Baby, leaving Shockley standing there baffled.

Shockley remained on the corner, watching as the old lady trudged up Cayuga Street, her back hunched protectively over Baby. Finally, shrugging to himself he turned and strolled back to his car. Halfway across the park, his nostrils were assaulted by an increasingly foul but familiar odor. He stopped and sniffed, trying to locate the smell that seemed to pursue him. He checked the soles of his shoes and then, turning at the waist and pulling around the seat of his pants, suddenly discovered why that prime patch of grass by the bench had been vacant.

"Ugh," he moaned disgustedly, looking at the crushed fresh leavings of a dog. Finding a stick, he cleaned off the mess as best he could and continued across the park.

When he got back to his car, Shockley found a piece of paper awaiting him on the windshield. It was a violation for overtime on the meter.

Normally, either one of the two distasteful events that had transpired might easily have sent Shockley into a fit. This morning, however, he accepted his fate with equanimity. Calmly pocketing the ticket and covering the driver's seat with a rag, he slipped into his car and drove home.

The next day it rained on and off. When Baby failed to appear in the park for her morning sing or on Doris's porch that evening, Shockley found himself unable to work on his new tone poem. The day proved a complete loss. It was on the second day, however, when he got up in the morning and saw it pouring again that Shockley began to panic. He knew from experience that once the wet weather set in, it could take interminable days for it to lift, sometimes weeks. Why, the previous July it had rained the entire month. And what was he supposed to do in the meantime? On the second day he realized that it was Baby's music he needed, if only a few notes, to keep him moving. Damn! he muttered in disgust, pounding his fist into his palm and pacing the house. Unable to work, Shockley knew he should return to school, but he was afraid that the demands of teaching might further snuff his spark of inspiration. He took off yet another day and passed the morning looking blankly at his earlier work, trying to push further the development. Whatever he did manage to write, however, came out tinny and contrived. Without Baby's euphonious song lingering in his ears, his own music refused to budge.

By ten the rain was coming down in sheets, and Shockley knew that Baby surely would not be out. He walked the confines of his study mumbling to himself and finally, against his better judgment, jumped into the car and drove down to the park. There, sitting in his car, his windshield wipers sweeping away the cascading torrents, he looked out forlornly on the soaked and deserted bench.

"You've got to hear this child," Shockley explained to his wife in the early evening as he alternately checked his watch and the weather. "Then you'll understand."

"After all this talk," said Ruth emphatically, "I *would* like to hear her."

"Come with me."

"In this beastly weather? But you said she hasn't been there in the rain."

"Tomorrow then."

"Sure," she said, and Shockley thought he detected a patronizing tone.

"Where are you going?" Ruth asked worriedly when he grabbed his trenchcoat and headed for the door.

"Out," he said, turning up his collar.

"I ran into Krieger today," she called after him. "He was very concerned about your health."

"Ruth, you didn't—"

"No, I didn't tell him you were playing hooky. But Irwin, this is a small town. Sooner or later you're going to bump into him. And what then?"

"So I bump into him."

"You can't do this. You can't take on a responsibility and then just chuck it."

"I have to. This is more important."

"You don't even have tenure. They can fire you on the slightest whim."

"All the more reason to take that chance. Do you think I want to spend the rest of my life at the mercy of their whims?"

8

Doris had been up in the attic rummaging through the family trunks when her doorbell chimed. Searching in the hope of finding some old baby clothes, she had inadvertently come across some forgotten photos. In the dim light of the attic she had curiously shuffled through the pile— pictures of grandparents and aunts and cousins now long dead or moved away—when, by chance, she had come upon a dog-eared snapshot of herself as an infant. Staring at the picture, she found she couldn't put it down. The resemblance was so striking she had to shake her head and laugh. The photo could have been that of Baby. As an infant, apparently, Doris, too, had had those blond wisps of hair, those big, pale eyes, those angelic features. Why, they could have been twins, she mumbled. Then the doorbell chimed, shaking Doris from her reverie. She sat motionless holding the picture and waiting. Sure enough, it rang again.

Gathering together the odds and ends she had managed to dig up for Baby, Doris closed the trunk and carefully descended the rickety wooden stairs leading back to the second floor. When she got to the landing and snapped off the attic light, the person at the front door stopped ringing and began rapping loudly. Doris checked Baby as she slept in her basket and then, as the knocking persisted, she resignedly went down the stairs. It was not easy getting accustomed to the endless stream of visitors, people who, at any hour of the day or night, would come by to sneak a peek at her child, to question Doris, to have their picture taken with Baby—there was always some request. Though Doris tried to be civil, it was very trying. Tonight, maybe because of the gloomy weather, she felt particularly tired and would have liked to pass a quiet evening reading or watching a TV program.

The knocking stopped.

Snapping on the porch light, Doris stared through a chink in the lace curtain on the front door. It was that man, she recognized, the tall one with a goatee who had tried to approach her twice before. She switched off the porch light and turned to leave, but the knocking began again, this time more frantically.

"Oh, dear," she sighed, realizing that he was not going to give up.

Doris went back, turned on the porch light and, leaving the chain on, opened the door slightly.

"Mrs. Rumsey, I beg you," began Shockley, who was soaked to the bone. His hair was plastered to his head, and water was dripping off his long nose. "I've got to speak to you."

Doris looked at him blankly.

"It's *really* important." He shivered, and Doris, seeing his desperation, finally took pity on him.

"OK, come in." She closed the door, took off the chain, and then opened it barely enough for him to squeeze through.

"Whew," he said, standing apologetically in a puddle and shedding his coat. "It's pouring outside."

"Let me take that," she said and hung his coat in the bathroom behind the kitchen.

"I won't take up much of your time," he began when she returned.

"I've got lots to do," she fibbed.

"I'll try to be brief." .

"You're not a reporter, are you?"

"No. I swear to you. I'm a musician. A composer. And I've been listening to Baby."

"Yes, I've seen you," Doris said, and Shockley noted she

seemed pleased when he indicated his interest in Baby. "Would you care to come and sit inside?" She said, leading the way.

Shockley followed her into her living room. It was a rather grim room with dark, flowery wallpaper that had been in fashion forty years ago. Her somber furniture, worn and old, seemed to match the period. Doris motioned for Shockley to take a seat. He sat down on the sofa beside a sleeping cat, who languidly opened her eyes, looked at him, and then went back to sleep.

"Mrs. Rumsey," he began cautiously, wetting his lips and swallowing, "Baby's had a very profound effect upon me."

"Upon many people." Doris smiled knowingly, her gums showing briefly.

"No doubt," he said a little brusquely and caught himself. For an instant his eyes fell on six photos taped to the living room mirror. They were pictures of young, dark-skinned children, four boys and two girls, all stiffly posed with their hair neatly combed and their scant clothes pulled straight. They were obviously foreign, and the pictures puzzled him.

"I'm working on a piece of music," he struggled to explain, looking back to Doris, who had been watching him.

"Yes, you mentioned you were a composer," she said, detecting the lofty tone in his voice and just wanting to let him know that, though she might be old and tired, she certainly wasn't senile.

"Mrs. Rumsey—" Shockley struggled with himself trying to find the best approach. Every time words came to mind, they seemed lame. Finally he threw up his hands, deciding on the truth. "Look, before I heard Baby sing I had come to the point in my life where—where—well, I just couldn't write. Sometimes I'd start to compose a new work, get maybe to the halfway point, but then run out of steam and not be able to finish it. Or, if I did, it would turn out to be garbage," Shockley confessed, and noticed that Doris was observing him intently with her pale, rheumy eyes.

"I don't know if you'll understand this," he said and then, despite himself, began the story of his life, the words springing from his mouth. He told her how as a young boy he used to wander by the shore of the bay near his parents' Long Island home singing to himself, composing in his mind, nurturing dreams of bringing to the world music more moving, more beautiful than had ever before been created. "It was a childish fantasy, I admit, but it was what drove me and sustained me." Doris listened and nodded. Shockley continued to talk about his early years as a violinist, about his harsh father, the conductor, who was convinced his children were prodigies, his cowed mother, his sister, who ultimately hanged herself in her room. He disclosed to Doris the pains of his life, the rewards, and confided in her things he realized he had never told even Ruth. He spoke of his first success, of his prize, of the seemingly endless grants that came to an end. With the old lady nodding sympathetically, Shockley opened his heart and told Doris of his deepest dread, that he was finished as an artist, about his growing sense of uselessness, of the gulf developing between him and his family that he loved.

Shockley stopped and looked straight at Doris. In the old woman's eyes he recognized a tender look of compassion that absolved him from feeling foolish for having made this confession to a total stranger.

"But," he said finally, brightening, "since hearing Baby it's all changed. I'm now working on the piece that I'm sure will give people everywhere as much pleasure as Baby has given us here in Ithaca. Mrs. Rumsey, I need Baby."

"Need her?" Doris suddenly went rigid.

"I mean, to hear her," he corrected himself. "Regularly. I can't lose precious days because it rains or you won't take Baby outside or—"

"Well—" she said thoughtfully.

"The piece I'm working on," he said, the words pouring out of their own volition, "I'm going to dedicate it to Baby."

Doris sat motionless, continuing to stare at him, but he could already see that he had struck a responsive chord.

"It'll be *her* piece as much as mine."

Silence. Shockley sat perfectly still, his eyes moving about as though searching for something. Doris sat staring down at her hands. A long minute later she looked up.

"I'll go get her," she said suddenly, surprising him. "I can't promise you that she'll sing, though."

"Your teeth have been sitting here waiting for you," said Markowitz amiably when Doris appeared at the dentist's for her long-overdue appointment. She was neatly dressed, he noticed, and her hair had been braided and rolled into a bun. "They had almost given up hope," he joked as the nurse took Baby and Doris sat down in the chair. Markowitz had read the stories in the paper about Doris and her "wunderkind" but decided not to mention anything about Baby unless she brought it up.

"Let's see now," he said, adjusting his light and peering in. "H'm. Looks like it's healed nicely," he remarked, and went to get Doris's upper plate from his little lab in the back room while his nurse cooed to Baby.

Checking the fit, Markowitz began to hum to himself as he put the finishing touches to Doris's new teeth. He ran his grinder over the pink plastic that would sit against her gums, checked for conformity, took out the plate, and filed down a high spot. He was still humming above the whine of his tool, when he realized that there was someone else singing in the background. Markowitz let his machine wind down to a stop and tilted his head. Lying in the nurse's arms and staring at the ceiling, Baby was singing to herself in a high but gentle voice, her dulcet song meandering slowly between notes. A smile appeared on the dentist's round face, growing wide until it stretched from ear to ear.

"Oh," said Markowitz with a sigh, "that's beautiful. Perfectly gorgeous." He was a music lover who traveled all the way to New York City once a month just to hear an opera at the Met. In his time he had heard some of the greatest singers. But this! This!

"My teeth," said Doris, reminding Markowitz, who was off in a reverie.

"Oh, yes," he said with an embarrassed grin and reluctantly went back to work, forsaking his machine for hand tools as long as he could.

Baby stopped singing, and in short order Markowitz completed the job.

"There," he said proudly, holding the mirror for Doris. "Now you look like a teenager," he laughed.

Doris grinned and her new teeth gleamed.

"That child has the loveliest voice I have ever heard," said Markowitz, taking the bib off Doris. "Funny, you know it reminded me of my mother, bless her soul. When I was a little boy, she used to sing these Yiddish melodies to me. I had almost forgotten them," he nodded to himself and then began to hum, his eyes turning misty.

When Doris opened her pocketbook to pay the nurse at the desk, Markowitz went to intervene, leaving another patient waiting in the chair with open mouth.

"Listen, there's really no rush," he said, holding up his hand. "Whenever you have it—"

"I have it," she said, fumbling with some bills.

"How much are you charging this fine lady?" he said, looking over his nurse's shoulder. "No. That's wrong," and with a stroke of his pencil he cut the amount in half.

"Dr. Markowitz?" Doris ventured before she left. Markowitz struck her as a worldy person—certainly more than she was—and her instincts told her she could trust him.

"Yes, dear!" He smiled.

"Do you know a man by the name of Shockley?"

Shockley? Shockley? he thought, scanning his brain.

"He's a professor," she said, motioning with a finger toward East Hill.

"Yeah. A musician. A composer. Writes crazy kind of music. Not that it's so bad. I mean, who am I to be a judge? He has all these kinds of electronic noises and banging." Markowitz shrugged indulgently. "My wife and I used to go to concerts a lot up on the Hill. Why are you asking me about Shockley?" he inquired, his curiousity piqued.

Doris hesitated for an instant and then opened up. She told him about Shockley, about their first encounters, his need for private visits in addition to the public singings, the daily visits that had now gone on for almost two weeks, how he brought Baby gifts, listened to her music, making copious notes, about his altogether consuming interest in every facet of Baby's life.

"And you don't want him to come?" Markowitz probed.

"No, it's not that."

"What exactly is it he wants?"

"That's what troubles me. I'm not quite sure."

"Well, I'd be very careful. Whatever you do, don't sign anything and don't make any commitments. You really ought to get some good legal advice," warned Markowitz. "You've got a very valuable little baby there."

9

Somewhat reluctantly, almost a full three weeks after Shockley had first seen Baby, Ruth finally let her husband drag her down to the park one morning and there, for the first time, she, too, heard Baby sing. Astonished by what she witnessed, Ruth then often joined her husband when he went for his private hearings at Doris's. Although Ruth found herself touched by Baby's music, the child's song had none of the all-encompassing hold that it had on her husband. She went along on these visits, she suspected, because she couldn't resist the chance to hold a little baby. Whenever she came, Ruth always made it a point of bringing along some useful gift for the child, and on this particular Saturday, when she and Irwin went down to the flats to visit Doris Rumsey, she brought along the little knit suit with matching booties that her mother had made for Cindy. In addition to his usual notepad, Shockley decided to lug along his tape deck.

"What's that for?" asked Doris when she saw the unwieldy machine.

"It's a recorder," he said, plugging in the device and putting on a large reel. "I want to record Baby's singing. It won't hurt her in any way. It's just a simple tape machine," he repeated.

"It looks very complicated," Doris said.

"It's like a run-of-the-mill recorder, except a bit more sophisticated. With it I can get reproduction with almost perfect fidelity," he said, and, noting her adverse reaction, realized he had been wise in delaying it these weeks. But the recordings were vital. With them, he reasoned, he would have Baby's song always close at hand, easily summoned forth by the push of a button. Too, Shockley felt it incumbent upon himself to amass as much material on Baby as possible—notes, transcriptions of her music, recordings, even a daily diary—though to what ends he was still not quite sure.

"Ah, here we are!" said Shockley, holding out his hands when Doris brought Baby into the living room. She was dressed in Cindy's pink suit and seemed actually pleased. Even Doris looked delighted. "And how's my favorite little singer?" he said, taking the child in his arms and holding her for a moment until she smiled. Shockley had a great fondness for small children, and holding Baby reminded him of the days when his own kids had been infants. As he held Baby against his body, feeling her respond to his little strokes and tickles, Shockley noticed through the corner of his eye the leery way Doris was watching him. Quickly he returned Baby. "Here we go, back to mommy," he said with a flourish, but felt a small twinge of regret.

Putting the microphone close to where Doris sat in her rocker with Baby, Shockley turned on the recorder and then joined Ruth on the sofa. Ruth took out some mending she had brought along, and as Doris rocked Baby, the three sat waiting patiently.

"I wonder what it is that precipitates her singing," said Shockley, breaking the silence.

"There doesn't seem to be any pattern," said Ruth, looking up, tearing a thread with her teeth.

"She knows," said Doris obscurely.

"Knows what?" asked Shockley, and as Doris opened her mouth to answer, Baby suddenly began to sing.

Ruth put down her sewing in midstitch. Shockley checked the microphone, pushed it closer, and then leaned back on the sofa to listen. Doris continued to rock Baby, looking down pleased as Baby opened her little bird's mouth and sang out to her, mother and child exchanging knowing glances.

Baby sang for a good ten minutes, her voice with its infant's coloring sweeping through her full range, her sweet tune folding back on itself like waves hitting the shore. When she stopped and Shockley was certain that she was finished, he snapped off the tape machine.

As Doris readied herself and Baby to go out for her morning stroll, the Shockleys continued to hang around, Irwin busying himself by rewinding his tape, taking more time than obviously necessary.

When Doris went out to the back porch to put Baby into Cindy's former carriage, which the Shockleys had brought the previous week, Ruth approached her cautiously.

"Baby's seven weeks old now," said Ruth gently, trying to approach her on a mother-to-mother level.

"Six and a half," corrected Doris. Somehow being with them,

she always felt the compulsion to let them know that she was on top of matters.

"I don't know if you noticed, but, well, she seems a little thin."

"She's OK," Doris mumbled, lowering Baby into the carriage.

"A baby that age ought to be a little, a little plumper. Just a little."

"What are you trying to say?" Doris looked up at Ruth.

"She may not be getting enough food," answered Ruth, treading carefully. She and her husband had discussed the matter for almost a week now before daring to bring it up. They didn't want to do anything that would jeopardize his access to Baby, but on the other hand, they genuinely felt that the child was not getting enough nourishment.

"What is it you want me to do?" asked Doris.

"I think it would be a good idea to see a pediatrician."

Doris remained silent.

"Baby has never seen a doctor. She should probably be getting some vitamin drops. Maybe—"

"No," said Doris obstinately.

"Look," said Shockley bluntly, joining the discussion when it was at an impasse. "You've got a responsibility to Baby. To make sure she is in the best of possible health. Now if you're concerned—"

"I am."

"Well, then you should take her for regular checkups."

Doris looked from husband to wife. Though she knew they were right, her instincts warned her.

"She's supposed to be growing now. It's critical that her progress be monitored," Ruth urged.

"If she's not getting the proper nourishment, she could get sick," Shockley warned, Baby's eyes on him.

"She's going to need vaccinations, too. She's—"

"Mrs. Rumsey," said Shockley, peeved by her thick-headedness. "You've got the life of a baby in your hands," he said with emphasis. "Do you *want* her to get sick?"

The Shockleys had already made an appointment with the pediatrician on Albany Street before they brought up the subject, and to their minds, it was only a matter of getting Doris to go along.

"But what about the people waiting in the park?" Doris asked, concerned, as they bundled her and Baby into their car.

"Let them wait," said Shockley. "This is more important."

"It'll take only a half hour," Ruth tried to soothe her as they pulled away from the curb.

"And don't worry about the bill. We'll take care of it," said Shockley, waiting at a red light.

"I can pay," she said, wondering if going to the doctor constituted a commitment, as Markowitz had warned.

"I'm sure you can, but please let me," said Shockley.

"You've already done too much," said Doris, only the faintest edge in her voice.

"For Baby, nothing's too much." Shockley smiled, pretending not to detect the double meaning. "Here we are," he said, a moment later pulling up in front of the old Victorian off Clinton Street that housed the pediatrician's office.

Ruth and Doris went in with Baby while Shockley waited in the car.

Inside, the place was busy, the waiting room packed with kids—lying on the floor playing with toys, thumbing through storybooks, or sitting listlessly in a parent's lap. There were children coughing, children sneezing, children waiting fearfully for shots. As soon as Ruth presented herself at the desk, one of the nurses ushered Doris and Baby directly into an examination room. Ruth followed behind into the small room, but when she saw the doctor approaching said, "I'll be out in the waiting room," and slipped away.

Doris watched nervously through the open door as Ruth moved down the corridor.

"Well, what do you know?" Dr. Waterhouse smiled after introducing himself. "Here we have our little celebrity." He was a short, middle-aged man with bifocals and a soft-spoken manner. From the loving way he took Baby's diminutive hand in his, Doris could tell he cared for children. She let him take Baby to the examination table and watched as he carefully unbuttoned her new pink suit. Observing Dr. Waterhouse as he systematically examined Baby, cooing comfortingly to her as he listened to her heart and chest, palpated her intestines, weighed her, peered into her ears and mouth, Doris began to feel foolish about all her misgivings. It had been downright silly of her to have delayed bringing Baby in for a checkup.

When the doctor finally completed his examination and had elicited from Doris some basic facts about Baby's habits, he was brief and to the point.

"She looks basically healthy, I'd say. But she's definitely underweight. She's also a bit short for her age," said Waterhouse, looking at Doris over the tops of his glasses. "I think we'd better take her off the breast and put her on a fortified formula immediately."

Doris looked questioningly at the doctor.

"Yes"—he nodded, responding to her unasked question—"it's important."

Obediently Doris went with Ruth Shockley to the drugstore on the Commons and bought the formula. She let Ruth, who was obviously experienced, help her prepare the first batch, show her how to sterilize the bottles and nipples. She even permitted Ruth to give Baby her first bottle-feeding, which Baby readily accepted.

Late at night, however, when Doris was lying in her bed listening to Baby sleeping in the basket at her side, she felt possessed by a queasy sensation. She sat upright and turned on the light and looked at Baby. For a few minutes she sat perfectly still, watching as her child's small, bony chest heaved and sank. Looking at Baby's tiny fists that lay on top of the covers, Doris reached over and worriedly caressed those perfect little hands. She tried to allay her qualms, telling herself that her fears were groundless, but her distress continued to grow, her worries feeding on themselves until she became frightened and her heart began to race. Deep down inside, Doris realized, what she really feared was that this formula business was just the first step, that they were conspiring to wean Baby away from more than just her breast. At that instant Baby suddenly awoke and, blinking her eyes, glanced up at her mother.

That night Shockley, too, was plagued by insomnia. He tossed and turned. He got up and closed the windows. When the room turned hot and stuffy he got up again and opened them. He threw off his covers, got cold, and pulled them back on.

Something was nagging at the back of his mind and wouldn't let go.

In the afternoon he had finished the initial sketch to his tone poem. It was now basically all down on paper, the fragments, the rhythmic runs, the melodic motives, the piece tentatively welded into a large first-draft conception. In the rush of inspiration that had come over the weeks, he had even assigned some of the notes to particular instruments, perhaps scribbling at the head of a passage when the insight came WW for woodwinds; or, backtracking on his previous notes he might think, This would be perfect for oboes and clarinet together with strings, and he would quickly jot it down lest he forgot. That afternoon, thanks to Baby's help, he had come to a point where he had finally tagged and committed to paper all the ideas that had flown through his mind. In essence, he had come to grips with the toughest part—to nail down the abstractions of the composition into a concrete form. All that remained now was that day-to-day task of craft, of hammering those whimsical notations into a unified and orchestrated form. Though it would take tedious months, Shockley was over the hump. He could return to his neglected grad students and private lessons at school while tending daily to the laborious but straightforward grammar of his tone poem.

When he had finished the sketch that afternoon, adding those final bars, rather than experiencing elation at the end of a good job, Shockley had felt let down. It was odd and it troubled him. Perhaps, he had mulled, it was the postpartum blues. Spurred on by Baby, he had driven himself relentlessly. He was thoroughly drained and exhausted—that was it. Maybe he should put the music aside? Go away with Ruth and the kids for a weekend. Have a good time.

Wearily Shockley had gone into the living room and, taking the tape he had made that morning, had threaded it through his deck. At that faltering moment Shockley desperately craved Baby's music to revive his spirits. Turning on the tape, he had hunted through the endless feet of silence until coming to the squeal marking Baby's song. Backtracking, he had put the machine into its normal mode and, lying on the floor, had positioned himself close to one of the speakers. With his head cradled in his arms, he had closed his eyes and waited as the

71

beginning of the song snaked its way toward the heads. Soon the hiss of the tape had given way to Baby's familiar sound, her light-voiced trilling echoing as it had in Doris's living room. Shockley had listened to the familiar melody, its simplistic line, those childish combinations of vowels and consonants that constituted Baby's other worldly language. He had let the music play over him, concentrating diligently as the tape ran on but—but could feel nothing—the effect from the tape giving little more than the flat, emotionless response he had gotten when he had tried her melody on the piano. Whatever it was in Baby's music, one couldn't capture it and hope to keep its effect. It was neither the notes, nor the melody, nor the language, nor all of these together that created that thrilling aura. It was Baby herself, he had realized, who held the magic.

"Are you sick?" Ruth had inquired when he refused dinner and just moped around the house.

"Me?" he had asked absently. "I'm fine. Perfect. I just finished the sketch today."

"How is it?"

"Good. As a matter of fact, great." He had tried to drum up his enthusiasm.

But at night he couldn't sleep—he who had always been such a sound sleeper. Shockley stared upward and watched the light from an occasional car play across the ceiling. Outside in the sticky August night the summer crickets chirped. Downstairs, he could hear the refrigerator humming. I need a rest, he told himself. And he resolved to stay far away from his music and Baby for a while.

Shockley knew of a quaint inn right in the heart of Pennsylvania Dutch country. It was a rather exclusive place set amidst miles of rolling, manicured lawns. The advertisements for the stately old mansion-turned-guest house boasted of golf courses, tennis courts, horseback riding, saunas, pools, and fine cuisine. It was a rich man's retreat, without a doubt, something they could ill afford—which is why he decided to splurge.

Shockley liked to spring surprises on the family and, without telling Ruth or the children where they were going, loaded the whole gang into the station wagon.

"But where are we going?" Cindy repeatedly whined. She didn't like surprises.

72

"Are we going to like it?" asked Annette eagerly.

"You'll hate it." Shockley laughed.

"Are there girls there?" Randy asked, combing his hair for the umpteenth time.

"Millions."

"Yeah, but are they good-looking?"

"Each one guaranteed to be a dream."

"I know," said Ruth when they got near Allentown and she guessed it. "But how are we going to afford it? We're still far behind because of the house and—"

"Plastic money," said Shockley with a wink.

"You have to pay that in the end, you know," said Ruth with a grin.

"You do? Gee, if I had known that—" Shockley feigned worry and announced to everyone that he was immediately turning around.

10

"Why didn't you tell me?" asked Olive Eldridge, leaning over Baby, who was taking her midday nap. Looking at this startlingly perfect baby it was hard for her to grasp that it had come from poor Doris. "Even though I was out of town, you could've reached me by phone."

"I was ashamed," said Doris.

"What's there to be ashamed about, woman?" she said, turning around and planting her feet squarely apart. "I'm a friend of yours. Don't you know what that means?"

"Yes—I do now," Doris admitted, embarrassed by Olive's effusiveness, yet touched.

"That is just one gorgeous baby." Olive shook her head in honest admiration. "What do you call her?"

"Baby," said Doris matter-of-factly.

"Yes. Sure. But she's got a real name, doesn't she? Like Olive. Or Doris. Or—"

The phone began to ring. It rang repeatedly, and when Doris made no move to answer it, Olive looked at her with puzzlement. "Aren't you going to pick it up?"

"It rings all the time."

"Who's calling?"

"Everybody under the sun," answered Doris. "I was thinking of having it disconnected."

"But who?" persisted Olive.

"Oh, folks from the newspapers. From television programs. Like these," she said, going into the kitchen and grabbing a handful from the stack of mail that lay on the table. To one side there were three opened envelopes with foreign stamps, letters from her foster children overseas.

"So, she really does sing?" said Olive, thumbing through the pile.

"You stay around until she wakes up and you'll hear it too," Doris couldn't help but boast.

"Most certainly will." Olive laughed uncomfortably. "Mind if I look at these?"

"That's just today's," Doris said as Olive went through some of the letters, her eyes nearly popping out.

"Do you know what's in here?"

"I've read some of them from before. They keep sending these letters. Calling. I even get telegrams. What I need is a secretary," Doris laughed good-naturedly.

"Look at this! They want you to appear on the "Donahue Show." And here's one from "Good Morning America." And another one from—"

"It's not me they want. It's Baby."

"And here's one from Warner Brothers. In Hollywood." Olive moved her lips as she read. "They want to discuss a film contract," said Olive, flabbergasted. "They want to put Baby in the movies!"

"I know," answered Doris.

"Look at this, will you? They're offering you here five thousand dollars for a one-time appearance on the "Tonight Show." Doris, do you know what this means?"

"Yes. It means that Baby's staying here. She's not going on

any television shows, and certainly not into any movies."

"But why? You could do it in such a way that it wouldn't hurt the child. And you could make a fortune. She'd be set for the rest of her life. And so would you."

"That isn't the point."

"What is?" asked Olive, who came from a poor family, and all her life, until finally being appointed principal, had had to scratch for a living.

"Baby was not meant to be used like that. She was not meant to be exploited for money. Don't you see?"

"No, I don't see."

"She was a gift from God."

"Phooey!" said Olive, who was a pragmatist.

"If I would do that—put her in the movies, put her on TV shows, sell her music—He'd take her away from me."

"You don't *really* believe that?"

"Oh, I most certainly do." Doris nodded her head. "And I don't think I could bear to lose her."

Shockley knew that he should be having fun. The resort more than lived up to the promise of its brochures. Nestled below the branches of high, ancient oaks, the inn sat encircled by sweeping lawns that undulated far off into the rolling hills. The interior of the old Victorian mansion proved as ornate as the scrollworked exterior. The rooms were lavishly appointed with Oriental rugs and fine period antiques. The cuisine was authentically French, the chef having been lured over from a renowned Paris restaurant. What they served for breakfast alone would have sufficed Shockley for an entire day. There were servants to attend to every whim—bellboys and waiters and maids, personnel to serve drinks by the pool, cabana boys to give out deep, fluffy towels that smelled of sun. Because it was costing him far more than he could afford, Shockley felt that he should be enjoying himself. He went through all the motions. He was visibly enthusiastic at dinner when the escargots, smelling of drawn garlic butter, were brought out on silver platters. He swam and played tennis with apparent gusto. He bantered with the other guests over cocktails. But, as much as he forced himself to indulge in his surroundings, he wasn't really enjoying himself.

For the first day of that three-day weekend Shockley had managed to keep up the pose for his family. By Saturday, however, after walking the same corridors of the inn, exploring the dining rooms, the gym, and the lounges, he realized that there was really only one thought in his mind—Baby. During lunch he spoke not a word.

"Daddy," said Cindy, sidling up to her father as he got up from the table. She took his hand and held it to her cheek. "Tell me a story."

"Not now, kitten," he said, slipping his hand free.

"Please," she pleaded. "You haven't—"

"I said, not now. Later, maybe," he answered and walked off.

"I thought we'd play a game of doubles with the Purcells," said Ruth, catching up with him. She was wearing a bathing suit, and her healthy suntanned skin was in marked contrast to her husband's pallor. "They seem like such a nice couple."

"Why don't you go ahead and play with them? I had something else in mind."

"Play doubles with them? But—" she began to object, but Shockley was already on his way.

Shockley wandered up over the hills behind the inn, crossing the golf course that sat on a plateau high above the mansion. Moving obliviously across the field of players, bright distant swatches of color standing out against the uniform green, he entered the woods that rustled and hummed with unseen life. Continuing to walk aimlessly mile upon mile, Shockley struggled to clear his head, but all he could think about was Baby, her and his own damned music and how they seemed connected. Here he was, living at the veritable pinnacle of luxury, the sketch for a promising new score on his desk, the prospects for the future getting brighter, yet—if he were to be reasonably honest with himself—he was utterly miserable. All he could do was dwell on Baby, long to hold her, and have her wondrous song fill his ears. If only, he thought, if only I could see her for just a few minutes.

Shockley pushed the image of the infant out of his mind. This craving was a form of lunacy. A passage from his new piece sang through his head, and loudly he whistled another tune to drown it out. He marched on, picking up his pace, but in a few minutes the woods came to an end and he arrived at a highway lined with fast-food joints, gas stations, and a muffler shop. It was a rather hideous strip and Shockley laughed to himself. Here he thought he had succeeded in leaving behind the realities of life, when, in actuality, just beyond a ring of woods it was all still there.

For a few moments he stood watching the traffic as it moved along the strip, cars snaking busily in and out of the parking lots. Then he turned and went back into the woods. Retracing his steps through the bog, the noises of the highway quickly lost, he was suddenly thinking about his childhood. To mind came the image of him sitting with his father on a stump in the woods by a hotel, oddly enough something like this place, and the old man was saying, "Remember, whatever it is that you do in life, just be sure that you're the best at it. Always the best." Shockley recalled the way his father, for emphasis, had raised one of his bushy eyebrows, fixing him with his hard, unyielding stare—the memory of which still to this day made him shudder. Too, he could still feel that same old frustration, that familiar anguish that he knew was making him so desperate about his own music.

Shockley crossed the golf green and saw the inn coming into sight. He felt himself sinking deeper into melancholy. Removed from Ithaca, he felt aimlessly adrift and, though it was only Saturday afternoon, he was already counting the hours.

Though he felt bone weary, Shockley managed to appear cheerful at dinner. That night he went to bed early and quickly fell into a deep, exhausted sleep. Within minutes he was dreaming. It was a strange dream in which he saw himself riding a long traveling belt of the kind used in airport terminals. He was being transported along the band in the direction of what should have been the departure gates, but instead of moving to the ramps where the planes took off, he was being carried toward a bright, blinding light. In his ears there echoed the singing of children, a chorus of a hundred infants, their mouths opening in unison as though appearing in trick mirrors, their voices fusing in an overpowering and peculiar harmony. The music grew louder and louder until it became deafening. The light brightened in intensity until he became totally blinded. Suddenly Shockley felt something placed in his arms. His chest was bare and the object felt pleasantly warm against his skin. The belt reversed itself. The light began to recede, and when his sight returned, Shockley looked down and saw that he was holding Baby against his chest. The music from the chorus slowly subsided, and he clung protectively to the infant, who glowed in his arms. That music, he was thinking, still clutching the warmth to himself, such odd harmony. Then he awoke with a start, awoke to find that he had Ruth's arm clasped against his bare skin.

Shockley opened his eyes and checked his watch. It was only two. He had slept at most a couple of hours. He got up and went to the bathroom to urinate. Groggily watching the tail end of his stream, he tried to recall the harmony of that dream chorus, but though it had been very real then, it now eluded him. He went back to bed and lay down next to Ruth, convinced that he wouldn't be able to sleep any more that night, that ahead of him lay a long, wearying six hours. He closed his eyes for a second. When he opened them again, Ruth was already long since up and it was nearly ten.

Shockley got up, dressed, shaved, and had breakfast. All through the morning he continued to think about the dream. After lunch he paid the bill while Ruth packed. They loaded the car and began the trek home, Shockley still plagued by that lucid dream and hardly speaking.

When they began to approach Ithaca in the late afternoon Shockley felt noticeably better. The depression that had engulfed him at the inn began to dissipate. His senses started to tingle.

"Slow down, please," Ruth warned, and he glanced down at the dash to discover that he was speeding wildly.

He drove in toward Ithaca on the Slaterville Road, and then, instead of turning north toward the Heights, Shockley continued down State Street right into town. Ruth looked at him questioningly as he cut down Aurora Street, took a left on Yates, and pulled up on Willow Avenue. Leaving the engine running, he slid out of the car and closed the door.

"Why don't you drive yourself and the kids up to the house?" He said through the open window to his flabbergasted wife, "I'll get a lift up later myself." And then he was gone, eagerly racing up the steps of Baby's house.

Shockley took a cab up the hill to his house. With Baby's music fresh in his ears, he felt he couldn't afford to waste a precious second.

"Irwin"—Ruth tried to stop him when he charged in the door—"what in the world is going on?"

Shockley raised his hand, begging indulgence, and wordlessly scooted past her into his study.

Going to the drawer where he had left his new piece, he took out the thick sheaf of papers and brought them over to the spinet. Hunched over and squinting at his notes cluttered with insertions and erasures, Shockley began to play his way through the work, filling small gaps with improvisations as he went, all the while disciplining himself to listen to his own music as though with a foreign ear. He played through the entire composition without pause and when he finished he sat looking at the keyboard.

"Well?" said Ruth, who was standing at the door.

He looked up to see her, a curious smile playing over his lips. "You heard."

"I heard." She nodded. "It's good. It needs work, but it's good."

"Yes," he agreed, that strange smile still present. "It's innovative, graceful, melodic. A bit romantic," he said as though he were a critic. "I'd say some of the passages are pleasingly infectious, wouldn't you?"

Ruth nodded again. She didn't like the look on his face. It worried her.

"Polished and orchestrated, it would probably be the best thing I've ever done."

"Would be?" she echoed, picking up the subjunctive.

"Come," he said, patting the vacant spot on the bench beside him, motioning for her to sit. Ruth came over and sat down.

"If," he said, lifting a finger, "if I had never heard Baby's music, at this point I'd probably be dizzy with joy."

"But," she prompted nervously.

"But—Here listen to this," he said and played through a short passage.

"Sounds wonderful to me."

"No, listen," he said, annoyed, his smile fading as he played the bars over again.

Ruth remained silent.

"Don't you hear? It's not my music. It's Baby's. It has her nuances. Her color. Her little twists and turns," he said. "Yet," he continued sharply, closing the cover to the keys, "yet it's got none of her depth. None of that soul-shaking power. I knew back at the inn there was something bugging me."

"I think you're being very harsh on yourself." Ruth tried to calm him, but saw that it only goaded him, and she stopped.

"Harsh? No." He shook his head. "Ruth"—he turned to her, and when she looked at him, his eyes seemed wild and frenetic—"it's *her* music, Baby's, not mine and a lousy imitation at that. Don't you understand?"

"I understand that you're tired. You've just had a long drive. Your nerves are still frazzled from all the work."

"That may well be true, but it's also true that hearing Baby has drastically changed my perceptions. Ruth, darling," he almost pleaded, "this piece, or any piece that I do in the future, will at best be a second-rate copy. Trivial."

"That's a rather depressing view."

"No. No, it's not. In fact, it clears up a lot, a hell of a lot. I finally understand," he said, taking the sheaf of notes and rolling it mercilessly into a tight roll, "after all these agonizing years of trying to compose, what it is that I *really* should be doing."

"Which is?" Ruth asked, her eyes on the roll as he continued to twist it, the skin on his knuckles turning white.

"Everything has been preparatory. I was being shaped—or shaping myself—being honed to the point where I would be able to recognize the profundity of Baby's music when I finally heard it. Somehow I feel—" He hesitated, perceiving how silly his thoughts might sound. The recollection of his dream suddenly sprang to mind and he decided to mouth his sentiments. "I feel as though—Well, I've been singled out to protect Baby, selected as the one to bring Baby to the world. Now, I know it sounds ridiculous." He laughed a little sheepishly.

"No," said Ruth uncomfortably. "It sounds fanatical."

"I'm no fanatic." He laughed and, putting an arm around Ruth, gave her a hug.

Disarmed, Ruth smiled.

"I just know what I have to do."

"And what's that?" she questioned, following as he got up from the piano with his twisted sheaf of notes and moved into the living room.

"First I'm going to put an end to this nonsense," he said, hesitating for a moment in front of the fireplace and then impulsively tossing the entire roll onto the grate. The papers landed with a thud and began to unwind.

"Irwin. No!" she said as he hunted on the mantel for a match.

"Where the hell are the—?" he said and went into the kitchen. When he came back with a book of matches, he found Ruth on her knees hurriedly gathering up his composition.

"Please. Don't." She looked up at him beseechingly.

"May I?" he asked, trying to take the papers from her grasp. She held to them firmly. "They're mine, you know," he said, tilting his head.

"Don't burn them," she said, reluctantly releasing her grip. "You'll regret it."

Wordlessly he spread the papers on the layer of cold coals that lay on the grate.

"Oh, Irwin," she gasped, watching as the fire licked the edge of the pile, layer after layer curling up and burning with a bright, almost blinding flame.

Shockley lost little time in approaching Doris with the plans he was formulating for Baby. Early the next morning, under the guise of bringing Baby some freshly pureed fruits, he paid her a visit. Doris was still in her kitchen preparing Baby's morning bottle.

"Baby's no ordinary child," he said when Doris was sitting quietly, Baby drinking in her lap.

"That's obvious," Doris replied guardedly.

"She's got an absolutely phenomenal gift."

"What is it that you want?" she asked, cutting to the heart of the matter, Baby pulling away from the nipple to take a rest.

"I want you to share her with the world."

"That's what I've been doing," said Doris. "I take her out to the park when the weather's—"

"Ithaca's not the world. It's only one little town in one little state. I'm talking about the *world*."

Doris looked a little overwhelmed and Shockley backed off.

"Let me help Baby," he urged softly.

"You've helped her already," she said as she held Baby against her shoulder and burped her.

"I meant in terms of her future. She has one, whether you want to face it or not."

Doris fell silent, her pale eyes troubled, and Shockley knew he had hit a tender spot.

81

"You won't be here forever." He followed his advantage.

"No, I won't," admitted Doris, putting Baby into her lap and looking squarely at her child.

"When Baby's thirteen, still a young girl, you'll be almost—almost seventy-three."

"If I'm still around," she said without looking up.

"Yes. That's exactly the point. She won't always be an infant. She's got a life ahead of her. She'll have needs—"

"I still don't understand what you're leading up to."

"What I'm saying is that the right moves now could guarantee her a secure future. She could have money, all the money she'd ever need. There could be emergencies, or maybe she'll want to go to college, or travel, or—"

"I'm not going to put her on TV shows or in movies," she said adamantly.

"I'm not talking about that."

"Then what?"

"I'm talking about letting her go on tour, letting her sing for others, letting her give concerts."

"It's the same thing."

"No, it's not. She wouldn't be displayed as an oddity. She would be a singer, singing for people who love music. There's a world of difference."

Doris opened her mouth to speak, but Shockley held up his hand.

"Hear me out, at least. Please."

Doris heaved a sigh.

"First I want to take her to meet some key musicians around the country. I'd like them to hear her sing. Get their endorsements. Then she could go on tour. It would be no big deal. She could sing for small groups just exactly as she does here. And you'd be with her. Traveling with her. We could have a nurse along to help. She'd be given the best of everything. For the rest of her life she would never want for anything."

"And what do you get out of all this?" said Doris with unusual acerbity.

"Nothing. Absolutely nothing but the pleasure of knowing that others have had a chance to hear her."

"No," said Doris tersely, getting up.

"What do you mean, 'no'?"

"Just that. No. She's not leaving Ithaca."

"You can't bury her here. Keep her under house arrest. It's criminal," Shockley flushed.

"She stays put. Right *here*," said Doris, plunking Baby into her basket by the garden window. "And that's that!"

By the time September rolled around and the university was in full swing, it was vexingly apparent to Shockley that there was an ever-widening gap between his plans for Baby and Doris's uncompromising and shortsighted view of her child's future. Each small concession had to be painstakingly wrung out of this old woman, who seemed to be getting more obstinate by the day.

Shockley wanted to take Baby to the Eastman School in Rochester just for the morning to present her to some colleagues there.

"No. She stays in town," said Doris obdurately. "I told you that before."

"Then let me at least take her up to a departmental meeting here at the university. There's one next week."

"I don't know—"

"You can even come along."

"We'll see." Doris put off the decision, and, of course, when the date rolled around, she nixed the idea without so much as an excuse.

In the month that followed, Shockley exhausted every conceivable approach. He tried pleading with Doris, threatening her, cajoling her. Sometimes he backed off and ignored her completely. In early October he again tried reasoning.

"Doris, please," he appealed to her. "Don't put me in the position where I have to badger you and coddle you and play all these games."

"You put yourself in that position. Why don't you just enjoy Baby's music and let it go at that?" she asked.

"Because I honestly feel that it's selfish. Doris, tell me, how long will she be able to keep singing like this? Will it be another year? Another five?"

"It might be forever."

"Or she might stop next month. Then it'll be all gone."

"I suppose it's in God's hands, isn't it?" replied Doris fatalistically.

"Perhaps. But what she does with her gift is in ours. Yours. Baby was meant to be heard. Can't you grasp that?" he pleaded.

"I can," she said evenly. "But it doesn't mean that I agree."

"Oh, you're like a stone wall," he muttered and, walking over to Baby's basket, peered in. Baby, who was lying on her stomach, lifted her head and, recognizing Shockley, gave him a big, toothless smile. Turning her over and holding out his hand, he felt her firmly grasp his finger in her fist. Well over three months, she was now rapidly developing. With Doris agreeing to feed her solid foods—the fresh apples, bananas, and cooked vegetables that Ruth pureed daily in her blender—Baby was finally putting on weight and growing. Her cheeks were round and chubby, her limbs plump, and she had a thick head of curly, blond hair. Baby released her grip on his finger, and Shockley stood by the makeshift crib watching in fascination as she reached out for the toys that hung above her head. Knocking a stuffed monkey on a spring, Baby laughed and cooed delightedly when the bells on its neck jangled. One of Doris's cats jumped up on the basket, following the bobbing toy with a paw. Looking in horror at the outstretched claws, Shockley shooed away the cat.

"If you could only give me one good reason," he said to Doris, containing the impulse to warn her about keeping those damn cats away from the child, "why, for instance, we can't take her to just a couple of schools."

"I know why," she said, looking over at the basket.

"Why?"

Baby lifted her head above the edge of her basket and looked at her mother. Doris smiled back at her child. "I have my reasons."

"I hate Baby," said Cindy bitterly during a Sunday morning brunch that the family had in a downtown restaurant.

"But how can you hate her?" asked Shockley, cracking off the top of a soft-boiled egg in a single stroke. "You've never even seen her."

"I don't have to." Cindy pouted, playing with a spoon in her cereal.

"She's a cute little baby and she—"

"I know. I know. 'She sings like an angel,'" Cindy mimicked.

Shockley and his wife exchanged glances.

"Why don't you come along with me this morning when Mommy drops me off, and we'll visit her together?"

Cindy shrugged her shoulders indifferently.

"Cindy's such a spoiled brat," muttered Julie in disgust.

"That's not nice," Ruth interceded quickly.

"But it's true," Julie answered and, shoving her chair back, got up from the table.

"Women," muttered Randy, trying for a laugh. Ruth fixed him with a stare and he became silent.

After breakfast Ruth drove her husband and youngest daughter to Willow Avenue. Holding the shopping bag containing the usual jars of freshly prepared food and other odds and ends for Baby, Shockley took his daughter's hand and led her up the walk to Doris's house.

"You're really going to like her," he said, extolling Baby's virtues as they climbed the stairs. "If you're very careful, maybe you can hold her."

"Can I feed her?" Cindy tested.

"I suppose so," said Shockley, smiling down at her.

As her father rang the bell, Cindy stood on the porch waiting, tapping her feet, and turning around to watch the creek that gurgled past the house. The door opened and Doris appeared. Greeting Shockley, she looked down with mild surprise to see his daughter.

"And how are you, young lady?" asked Doris, who always made it a point of paying attention to children.

"My father says I can feed Baby," Cindy blurted out as she marched in. Doris looked noticeably taken back by the girl's brusqueness and tried to smile.

"No, I said—" Shockley began to explain as they entered the hallway, but stopped abruptly when he spotted a well-dressed man sitting on the living room sofa. The stranger was holding Baby, and Shockley felt his heart begin to race.

"Who's that?" he asked curtly.

"Oh, let me introduce you," said Doris as they entered the room. "This is Dr. Nolan. He's from the Rochester—"

"Eastman School," said Nolan, returning Baby to Doris and rising to greet Shockley. "Mrs. Rumsey has been telling me about you," he smiled.

"What's he doing here?" Shockley challenged openly. Though he didn't recognize Nolan by face, he knew the musicologist by reputation.

Nolan stood with his hand still outstretched.

"He just came by to hear Baby. And I thought—" Doris stammered confusedly. Nolan took back his hand.

"You should have called me." Shockley turned a deep crimson.

"Hey, hold on one second," said Nolan, facing Shockley squarely. "You don't *own* the child."

Cindy's eyes darted from one tense adult to the next.

"Let's go," said Shockley, angrily slamming down his shopping bag, the jars inside clanking together dangerously. Grabbing Cindy's hand, he yanked her out of the room, passing Doris without a glance.

"But I didn't even get to hold Baby," Cindy protested, dragging her feet as they left the house.

The front door slammed shut, and Doris watched through the window as Shockley marched furiously down the block, his little girl repeatedly turning around. Perplexed and shaken, Doris remained at the window for a moment staring out at the maple leaves that tumbled from the trees onto her walk. She felt tangled in contradictions. Shockley had been badgering her to expose Baby. And here she was, finally complying with his wishes only to have him fly off in a rage.

"Maybe you'd better go, Dr. Nolan," said Doris a few minutes later, feeling weak and spent.

"But I haven't had a chance to—" Nolan started to object.

"Some other time," said Doris, her head starting to spin. She had been feeling poorly for days and was worried about it. "I just don't feel up to any more people today." She apologized, showing him the door.

"Well, you have to understand, Irwin's moody," explained Ruth the following day. Monday afternoons she had a three-hour gap between classes and decided to take advantage of the time to bring Doris some fresh jars of food and look in on Baby.

"I'd say that he was jealous," said Doris, who sat in her favorite chair rocking Baby.

"That's probably also true." Ruth smiled, noticing how wan Doris looked. "He feels that he discovered Baby and—"

"But he didn't discover her. He wasn't the first."

"No. But he was the first musician," said Ruth, trying to smooth over the situation. "And I think he's very concerned about her future and her welfare. In a very unselfish way, as a matter of fact."

Doris shook her head languidly and, rising with difficulty, made a move toward the kitchen, where her kettle was whistling loudly.

"Coffee?" she asked.

"Oh!" gasped Ruth and then quickly regained her composure. She was looking at the cushion on which Doris had been sitting. It was soaked with blood. Doris slowly turned, staring back at the chair, and out of politeness Ruth hastily averted her eyes. Doris paused for a long moment, her eyes going from the cushion to Ruth and then back to the cushion.

"I've been bleeding a little lately," she finally admitted with embarrassment.

"A little?" asked Ruth, looking back at the large, sticky stain.

"It wasn't this bad before. It seems to be getting worse," she said, holding Baby in one arm as she fumbled to untie the cushion with the other.

"Here. Let me," said Ruth, going over and unfastening the stained cushion. She noticed that the whole lower back of Doris's dress was drenched with blood. It became obvious to her that the woman was very ill. The flesh on Doris's face hung lifeless and limp. Her eyes had a distant glazed-over look. Every breath seemed to require a great effort.

"Why don't you see a doctor? I have a good gynecologist—"

"I've thought of it," Doris said, and she looked so weak that Ruth quickly took Baby from her arms.

"Here, sit down again." Ruth helped her over to the sofa. "Maybe you want to stretch out for a minute," she said, slipping a pile of newspapers under Doris to protect the couch.

Doris surrendered to Ruth's suggestion, and she lay back gratefully as Ruth fitted a pillow behind her head. Ruth looked down at the old woman and then, instinctively, lowered Baby into her arms.

"I was going to see a doctor," said Doris haltingly. "But I was afraid. Maybe I'd need an operation or something—"

"If you need it, you need it," said Ruth, who tended to be practical.

"But then what would happen to Baby while I was in the hospital?"

"We'd take care of her for you; you know that," said Ruth as though it were a foregone conclusion.

Doris opened her eyes and stared at Ruth. Ruth read her mind.

"We'd take care of her while you were sick and then, just as soon as you'd be well and strong enough—" she began to explain and then interrupted herself. "But this is silly! You don't even know what's wrong with you. Maybe it's nothing serious at all. Perhaps all you need is a simple D and C. And that's no big deal. It takes only a day."

"Yes," said Doris, brightening, the color slowly returning to her face. "You're probably right." She smiled and then laughed at herself. "I do have a way of making mountains out of molehills."

11

Please, ma'am," begged the man standing in Doris's doorway, his hat deferentially held in his hand. "We won't take much of your time. And we ain't gonna be much of a bother." The man's ears stuck out from the sides of his head, and from his clothes Doris could see that he was of poor countryfolk.

"I'm sorry. It's just not a good day for me," she said, gripping the doorframe.

"We came all the way from Ohio," he said, turning back to his junker, which stood parked in front of the house. It was an old, pockmarked Ford with its rusty fenders held on with straps. Doris looked out and could see the girl with glasses sitting in the car, watching expectantly, a wheelchair folded in the rear seat. "I know that if she could just visit up close with Baby, maybe let the little one touch her."

"Baby can't help you that way. She doesn't heal. She just sings. Please, I have to—"

"It can't hurt none to try," said the man desperately. "The doctors, why they've done just about everythin' and—"

"Please. I'm sorry," said Doris, closing the door. Immediately afterward she was stricken by guilt pangs. Leaning against the wall, she stood in the hallway debating with herself. She peeked through a chink in the curtain and watched as the man went back to the car and stood talking to the girl through the open window, motioning with his hands and looking back at Doris's house. The girl looked young, maybe fourteen or a frail fifteen. Doris nervously chewed her lip in indecision, then reached for the doorknob. By the time she opened the door, however, the car was moving down the street, a loose tailpipe dangling below the bumper.

Doris went back into the house, closed all the blinds, disconnected a wire leading to the doorbell, and took the phone off the hook. In a little while, she surmised, people would be gathering in front of her house for the customary listening. She had not been up to facing the morning crowd in the park, and she doubted she had the strength to face them this evening. She needed to conserve her energy for what lay ahead.

"I'd recommend a hysterectomy," Dr. Gaskins had told her. "The bleeding is profuse and it seems to be coming not only from the uterus but—"

"Is there a choice?"

"Not really," the physician had said in a businesslike manner. "Matter of fact, it should be done immediately."

"Can I be out in a day?" she had asked, knowing full well that it was a fatuous question.

The doctor had smiled indulgently. "You'll need some time to recover."

"Oh," she had said, fighting the tears forming in her eyes.

"It's not an unusual operation." He had put his hand on hers. "We do them all the time," he had reassured her, deciding to play down the possible complications.

"Can I think about it?"

"I'd like to reserve a bed at the hospital today," he had pressed.

"I need time."

"There isn't much," he had persisted. "You've lost an awful lot of blood. You shouldn't even be on your feet."

Sitting at the Formica table in her kitchen and looking blankly into a cup of tea gone cold, Doris tried for the umpteenth time to reason her way through her dilemma. She was afraid to leave Baby. Once out of her hands, there was no telling what might happen to her.

"I'd be very careful." Markowitz's words rang in her ears. "You've got a very valuable child there."

"We'd take care of her while you were sick," said Ruth, "And then, just as soon as you'd be well—"

Doris wrung her hands together. For an instant she saw before her Shockley's youngest daugher, and the image of that child impudently saying "My father says I can feed her" worried her.

Doris moved through the downstairs of her house toward the rear window where Baby's basket sat. The sun was getting low and the garden was couched in dark shadows. In her bones Doris could feel the first rawness of winter that was but weeks away. She peered into the basket. Baby was up, patiently waiting for her feeding, quiet and uncomplaining as always.

"You are such a perfect little angel," said Doris, tears welling up in her eyes. Baby looked up at her expectantly. "Mommy's a bit of a coward," she said, and a solitary drop rolled off her cheek and splashed on Baby's face. Doris took a finger and wiped it off her infant's smooth skin.

Reaching down, she carefully lifted Baby from her basket, holding the child's head in the palm of her hand. As she shuffled back to the kitchen, Doris could feel the warm dampness of blood moving threateningly toward the edges of her napkin, and she wished it would all just stop and go away. Outside her house she could hear the first murmurs of people.

"I have no choice, do I?" she asked, and Baby looked back at her, her delicate brow furrowing as though she grasped every word and desperately wanted to help. "If I don't go for the operation we'll lose each other forever. If I go, it'll be a long time. And who knows what will happen," she murmured, realizing how helpless she now was, and how utterly dependent she would be on the Shockleys. "Will you remember your mommy, huh?" She stroked the curls on Baby's head with two fingers as the child peered back searchingly. "Oh, how I wish you could talk," she said as Baby's eyes darted worriedly from side to side and then suddenly stopped as she stared fixedly at her mother.

Baby drew a long breath, her small chest swelling until it could grow no more. Her delicate lips parted and then, as she slowly exhaled, there emerged a song, a new song, a plaintive melody that Doris had never heard before, the child remarkably capturing and distilling the melancholy mood of the moment. It was as though Baby comprehended the impending trials that they would both face and through her song was urgently trying to convey that understanding to her mother.

Doris closed her eyes and listened to Baby's new song with its long-held elegiac notes and sorrowfully meandering melody, Baby's voice low and barely audible as if she had taken the measure of her audience of one.

"Baby, Baby, Baby." Doris sang along in her own creaky voice, weeping openly as her child's compassionate melody granted her comfort, giving her the fortitude to face the harsh realities that waited in the days ahead. "Baby, Baby, my angel Baby." Doris sang out from the depths of her heart, lost in the moment of the song.

Within the span of a single day Baby's presence rapidly transformed the tone of the Shockley household as all activity began to revolve around the new arrival. Shockley, who had never particularly troubled himself with the mundane needs of his own children when they were little, was now changing Baby's diapers, powdering her bottom, making formula, feeding her, and worrying about the ravages of diaper rash. Annette, who from the start fell under the spell of Baby and her music, eagerly took on the role of surrogate mother whenever she could.

"She's not a pet or a plaything." Shockley had joked when Annette started dressing her up like a doll for the third time that day.

"Oh, Daddy. She's so gorgeous," Annette gushed, holding up Baby in a frilly little nightgown and matching booties.

Julie appointed herself official walker and that afternoon, when she returned from school, she proudly pushed Baby's carriage up and down the sidewalk under the watchful gaze of her eldest sister.

Even Randy, loathe to partake in any domestic activity that

might endanger his *reputation*, volunteered in the privacy of his home to hold Baby while she drank, taking secret pleasure in watching the little girl as she eagerly tugged at the nipple. When Baby rewarded him with a song, he was tickled with pride.

Of all the children, Cindy showed the least interest in the new visitor, and Shockley correctly assumed that it was her closeness in age to Baby that made her so standoffish, though from the start he had scrupulously tried to head off any rivalry.

Bringing Baby home that morning after helping Doris to the hospital, Shockley had made it a point of letting Cindy be the first of the children to officially greet her.

"Wouldn't you like to hold her?" he had said, extending Baby to her.

"Well—" Cindy had pouted, swaying her hips from side to side with studied indifference. "Well, I suppose so," she finally conceded.

Shockley had put Baby into her arms. "Now, hold her carefully. And use your arm like this to support her head."

"I know!" Cindy had responded, piqued. "I'm no dummy," she'd said, peering down at Baby, a mixture of curiosity and suspicion crossing her face. Lying in Cindy's arms, Baby had suddenly become agitated, her eyes taking on a desperate look. And then, for the first time in Shockley's experience, Baby had begun to cry and struggle.

"I'd better take her," he had said shaken, unable to disguise his own distress. "You may be holding her too tight," he'd added as an afterthought. "It takes a little experience."

"Who cares, anyway?" she had muttered, sauntering off to her room. "She's just a stupid little baby who poops in her pants."

"Maybe you'd like to feed her," Shockley had worriedly called after her.

"Not now. Maybe later," Cindy had said, tossing her head back and slamming the door to the room.

Unsettling as it was, the incident with Cindy did serve to substantiate a suspicion that had been with Shockley for some time.

"Not everyone is affected by Baby's music," he said, sitting bolt upright in bed in the wee hours of the morning. "Ruth," he said, shaking his naked wife who had been snuggly curled up against him. "You awake?"

"No." She smiled sleepily at the ludicrous question.

"Until now we've only seen the people who're attuned to Baby's music. They're the ones who've made themselves evident. But not everyone is touched by it."

"Nor," said Ruth, yawning and then completing the thought, "to the same degree."

"Precisely! You can see it among our own kids," he said, but Ruth was already deep asleep.

The following morning after the kids went off to school, he excitedly continued the discussion.

"There seems to be a hierarchy of effect," he said, as he gulped his coffee and burned his tongue.

"There was no reason to think otherwise," said Ruth matter-of-factly. "In nature, in biological phenomena, there's usually a continuous, often Gaussian type of distribution. You know, a bell-shaped curve." And she drew it in the air with her hands.

"But this is not biology."

"Most certainly not," Ruth agreed, with a smile. "It's religion."

"Aw, come on," Shockley said with a mouthful of toast.

"And even in religion, there's probably some sort of distribution with a small collection of atheists, skeptics, and assorted disbelievers on one end, then a growing number of moderate people somewhere in the middle and then, finally, a diminishing number of zealots at the other extreme."

"Sounds like a good Ph.D. thesis," Shockley joked.

"It's all yours," said Ruth as she drained her cup and gathered up her dishes.

"Seriously though," said Shockley, stuck on the subject, "if you look at our kids, the erfect of Baby's music seems to go by age. Annette is the most profoundly affected, then come Randy, Julie, and finally Cindy, who's totally deaf to it."

"Now that's not fair!" Ruth objected defensively.

"I didn't mean it disparagingly. I love her as much as you do."

"She's not deaf to it. She hears it. It amuses her. She just isn't quite as moved."

"Because of her age?"

"Who knows?"

"What about us?" he probed thoughtfully, wiping his lips with a napkin and putting his dishes in the sink.

"I'd say that although I'm very touched by her music, you're far more profoundly influenced. I'd put you in with the zealots," she grinned.

"Hmmm," said Shockley, standing in the middle of the kitchen, rubbing his chin thoughtfully. He was still working on his theory, trying to plug others he knew into a slot.

"Now don't try to point out that I'm a year younger," she said, heading for the hallway, "and attempt to draw an inference from that."

"Now you're joking with me," he said, pursuing her.

"Oh, Irwin." She lovingly stroked his cheek and then, turning, hunted through the hall closet for her coat. "You'd make a hell of a scientist," she laughed.

"But what's wrong with—?"

"There's nothing wrong with your theory except that you're trying to draw conclusions from isolated observations. You don't even have a decent statistical sample."

"I'm grasping at straws, I'll admit it, but I'm trying to make sense out of it all."

"Isn't it possible that there is no 'sense'? That there is no physical correlation? That age or sex or height or even musical ability doesn't necessarily matter?"

"In some way people are predisposed to her music. In some way they are more or less open, more or less receptive."

"I'll grant you that," said Ruth, pulling on her coat. "And it could just be that that receptivity is not quantifiable, at least not in any earthly way. Do you find that so hard to accept?"

"From you, absolutely! I thought you were the pragmatic, scientific brain in this house and I the sensitive, emotional, whimsical artist."

"Turns things around, doesn't it?" Ruth gave him a wet kiss and, with an enigmatic wink, hurried off.

That very afternoon Shockley had another revelation about Baby's music.

It was almost five when Shockley was finally able to break away from his last class at the university, and by the time he came home Annette had already relieved Mrs. Holger, the helpful neighbor who had agreed to look after Baby during the day. Ruth was in the kitchen making dinner with Julie and Randy—Randy objecting loudly about getting stuck with the dull job of peeling potatoes. Annette sat in the living room doing her homework, one eye on Baby, while Cindy lay on the floor working on a jigsaw puzzle.

After spending a few minutes with Baby, Shockley began to wander aimlessly around the house. His offer to help fix dinner rebuffed, he took out his violin. He was scheduled to get together with his chamber group later that evening and he thought it a good idea to run through some of the pieces they would play.

"How much longer?" he called out to Ruth, tightening his bow. The house now smelled enticingly of frying meat and freshly baked bread, and he could feel the juices in his mouth beginning to flow impatiently.

"A bit," she answered vaguely. "Can't you entertain yourself for a while?"

"What's a while? I'm starved," he said, thumbing through his notes.

"Me too," said Cindy, hunched intently over her puzzle, her knees pulled up to her stomach.

"Me three," joked Annette.

Shockley picked up his violin and played a passage from a Haydn string quartet that had previously given him some trouble. He played through part of a Mozart piece and had just started a Bartók work when Ruth called them to dinner.

Annette and Cindy dashed off to wash their hands as Shockley hurriedly put away his violin. He was just closing the case when Baby began to sing.

"Ruth," he called out urgently after an instant. "Come quickly!"

She appeared, wearing her apron, the children coming from all directions.

"What's the—"

"Listen!" he said, pointing to Baby as she lay in her basket.

"Baby's singing," said Julie matter-of-factly. "She always—"

"No. Listen again," Shockley said, closing his eyes and tracing her notes with a finger in the air.

When Baby had finished he turned to Ruth, who stood with tears in her eyes.

"You heard," he said, beaming, and she nodded.

Annette had gooseflesh on her arms.

"It was a different kind of song," she said, filling the silence.

Baby turned to look at the collection of faces encircling her basket and smiled.

"A new song."

"It sounded a little like the Mozart you were playing," said Randy, who had a good ear.

"And maybe a touch of the Haydn," added Ruth thoughtfully.

"Are we ever going to eat?" asked Cindy, but she was ignored.

"Ruth, my God," said Shockley delightedly, "she's learning. She's picking up new ideas—a little of the whimsy of Haydn, a touch of Bartók's lyricism—and synthesizing them in her own way. She's taking from the masters and going beyond."

"Far beyond," admitted Ruth.

"What does it mean?" asked Julie, baffled.

"I'm not sure, but from now on we're going to give her a chance to hear other kinds of music. The best. There's not going to be a music-free moment in this house anymore." He reached over and pulled Baby's shirt down over her bare tummy. "Our little singer here is going to have a blitz course in music appreciation."

"That's great"—Cindy pouted,—"but what about dinner?"

"Don't you see?" Shockley said to Ruth late that night when he got back from his chamber group. "Baby's trying new modes of expression. She's moving beyond that same basic theme we've heard for weeks. She's actually developing a repertoire."

"Two songs don't comprise a repertoire."

"You're a cynic."

"A realist," Ruth shot back. "Why must you always jump the gun?"

Shockley tried to sleep but couldn't. His mind was in a jumble. He was thinking about Doris, who was scheduled for surgery the next morning; he was thinking about Baby, about the two of them together. He tried not to dwell on the future.

"The reason she didn't evolve any new forms," he said later to Ruth, who was trying her utmost to doze off, "is that in Doris's home she was never exposed to any music."

"Maybe she's just maturing, and tonight the time just happened to be ripe." Ruth stifled a yawn.

"In Doris's home she was deprived," he said, a little dog-matically.

"If that's what you want to believe—But I'm sure that Doris probably had the radio or television on at some time. There's always some—"

"I mean *music*, not junk."

A few minutes later Shockley was talking again.

"I was thinking—" he began.

"I really wish you'd stop thinking. It's late. I'm tired. I don't know about you, but I have to work tomorrow." Ruth got testy. "And I want to get some sleep."

"Oh. Sorry," he apologized innocently. "I was just think-ing—"

"So what is it already?"

"We can't let Baby go back to her, to that bleak house."

"There's no choice."

"There is," he said, chewing his lower lip. "I had an idea. We could let Doris move in here after she gets out of the hospital."

"Forget it," said Ruth and rolled over, turning to the wall.

12

Doris came out of the anesthesia in agony. The wound, which ran from hip to hip, was one white-hot, searing pain. Her insides felt torn and stretched, cut and twisted around. There were tubes in her arms and her nose, a catheter in her urethra. When she vomited, it felt as though she would burst her stitches, and all she could do was try to lie perfectly still on her back, which also ached. If she dared to make the slightest movement, perhaps turn to her side, her pain became torture. Doris found herself trapped in a living night-mare in which she moved between sleep and wakefulness, unable to differentiate between them, time marked by the short-lived relief of injections—the faces of the silver-haired surgeon, the Shockleys, the nurses and orderlies merging with the apparitions of her wild dreams until she was unsure whether those people had actually been there at her bedside or in her dreams. When the suffering became unbearable and the next injection seemed an eternity away, when she no longer believed that she was alive and was convinced she had landed in hell, Doris would cry out in a low, desperate moan for Baby. She would call for her child until her strength failed and then fall into an exhausted stupor, wondering if there really ever was a Baby or if that little, golden-voiced infant had also been no more than a figment of her dreams.

On the second day things didn't seem much better. Doris was still in torment. She seemed even weaker and hardly conscious of her surroundings. The ordinarily persistent nurses, who were instructed to get their patients moving the day after surgery, didn't have the heart to force her up. When they tried to merely roll her on her side to halt the developing bedsores on her back, Doris wailed in pain.

"How are you feeling?" asked Ruth on the third day when Doris opened her eyes.

"Bad," groaned Doris through cracked lips, and then closed her eyes again.

"Well, it's not healing quite as it should," Dr. Gaskins explained to Shockley a day later. "And she's running a fever."

"Which means?"

"She may have an infection. But don't worry. I've already put her on antibiotics. These things happen, but they usually re-solve themselves quickly. Though—"

"Though what?"

"She's not exactly young. And she was not in the best of shape when she finally came to me. She was torn apart inside. She had lost an enormous amount of blood. There was internal bleeding. She was anemic. She—"

"It sounds to me like you're hedging your bets," said Shockley bluntly.

"No. I'm just trying to give you a realistic assessment."

"Do you think she's going to die?" he asked straight out.

The doctor looked only mildly surprised. He paused thoughtfully and then finally said, "There is that possibility, though that kind of pessimism isn't warranted. Not yet."

"What is?"

"Caution," said the doctor. "We're going to have to watch her very carefully. I'm considering opening her up again to put in a drainage tube."

"Is there anything else we can do?"

"Hope for the best."

It didn't take long for Shockley to get an inkling of how Baby's presence was to disrupt his family's ordinarily quiet life. With Baby absent from her downtown home and word spreading of her whereabouts, Baby's followers now began to appear at the Shockley house in ever-growing numbers. They came on foot, by bike, car, and taxi. They arrived individually or in large groups spilling out of vans. They hung around the Shockley house, clogging the street and angering the neighbors, who lived in the Heights precisely because it was supposed to be private and excluded what they considered "town riffraff."

"What the hell's going on there?" Dr. Dusenberg, the Nobel laureate physicist, who was Shockley's neighbor on the north, called to complain.

"I don't care if Jesus Christ himself is living in your house!" fumed Mrs. Rifkin from across the street when a couple accidentally trampled one of the sprigs in a new hedge she had planted just last spring. "Get rid of them or get rid of the baby."

"There must be some law against it," said Dr. Garfinkle, the historian, conferring with Simpson, the famous economist and presidential adviser next door.

"Maybe there's a zoning ordinance against babies," quipped Simpson, who always found humor in everything, but later lost his temper when someone's car inadvertently blocked his driveway.

"I'm sorry." Shockley nervously confronted the crowd standing on his lawn. The last leaves of the season were drifting down from the ancient oak overhead as he spoke, and in the background he could hear the phone ringing in his house. He couldn't be sure if it were another neighbor, or the press, or God-knows-who. "Mrs. Rumsey is seriously ill and until she gets better there won't be any listenings. Please. I must ask you to leave. The neighbors are complaining."

Some of the people left with grumbles and resigned shrugs. Others were more insistent. They took to hanging around at all hours, leaning against their cars and smoking or sitting cross-legged on his lawn. One couple, who had come from Buffalo, even had the audacity to demand their rights.

"Look, you're just going to have to go," Shockley had insisted a bit more firmly.

"But when can we hear her?" asked a petulant girl, who was dressed in an army fatigue jacket and looked like a former student of his.

"If you don't leave, I'm going to call the police," Shockley warned.

"I don't want Julie taking Baby out for walks on the road anymore," Shockley later told his wife.

"Baby's safe. They just want to hear her, that's all."

"That was Doris's mistake. We're not running a circus here. Baby will be heard. At the right time and in the right place."

"When and where is that?"

"I haven't decided," Shockley answered perfunctorily. The demands on Shockley were growing, and he seemed to be getting progressively more short-tempered.

In addition to the people who hung around the Shockley house in the hope of catching Baby's song, the calls and requests that had previously besieged Doris were now being redirected to the Shockleys. In a single day a deacon from some fundamentalist church in Binghamton appeared, demanding to see Baby; two fanatical women describing themselves as born-again Christians tried to force their way in, claiming that they had been divinely appointed to exorcise the devil that had possessed the infant; a blind woman plunked herself down on their front step and refused to budge until her sight was returned. And at the university, Shockley's colleagues were hanging on his heels as if he were a dog in heat, begging for an invitation to his house; and, of course, the same television people who had been working on Doris were still trying to get their foot in the door.

"I'm simply not going to discuss any proposals on the phone," Shockley tried to put off a particularly insistent ABC news producer who was trying to finagle an immediate booking for Baby on "20/20." "All inquiries should be made by letter, setting forth the terms."

"But we've done that already," the man objected in frustration. "In fact, we've sent about six letters and I don't know how many goddamn telegrams to Mrs. Rumsey."

"Well, I'm not Mrs. Rumsey. Why don't you do it again, but this time address it to me? You may have better luck."

As the days passed and Doris's condition appeared to worsen, Shockley soon found it impossible to fuse in his mind the disparate worlds of Doris's misery, the meaningless drudgery of school, and his buoyant life at home with Baby. Encased in the sterile sphere of the hospital, there was the old lady, tubes running into her body, dark yellowish urine haltingly dripping into the bottle under her bed, life measured in sluggish drops. Awaiting him each day at the university were his new music-appreciation classes, so crowded that students had to sit on the floor of the lecture room, students and teacher locked in by requirement not choice. And at home was Baby, lying in her crib, the glorious sounds of Beethoven or Brahms or Britten filling the air, the little girl listening and looking expectantly as if she were waiting just for him. Moving from school to hospital to home, Shockley felt he was being torn into three distinct pieces.

Returning home from the county hospital one evening, a little more than a week after Doris's surgery, Shockley suddenly blurted out what had been in the works for days.

"I'm taking Baby for a trip," he announced.

"A trip? But where?" Ruth asked puzzled.

"She's going on a tour with me to see some people around the country."

"But why? I don't understand."

"Why?" he echoed as if it were self-evident. "To give her a little exposure. To let people hear her. Other people. People outside this town. People who know music. Baby was meant to be heard, not hidden. Too much time has already been wasted. I—"

"You can't do that!"

"It's all arranged. I made the reservations this afternoon. We're already expected. I'm going to USC, to Peabody, to Juilliard—"

"But what about Doris? You know how she feels about Baby being—"

"Doris? She doesn't even know what's happening."

"She's the mother."

"She's sick and dying, a crazy, old lady who in the last fifteen years hasn't ventured out of a five-mile radius, who—even in her best years—probably has always been out of touch. Look, Ruth, I feel sorry for her. Honestly I do. She's a sad shell of a human being. A tragic case."

"And you have a responsibility to her."

"Yes, I do. But I have a larger one too. I feel a moral obligation to make sure that Baby is heard, an obligation that goes far beyond the one to Doris."

"She entrusted us with her child."

"God Almighty! We're not boiling the kid in oil. All I want to do is take her to see some people. I'll be back in less than two weeks."

"Two weeks!" Ruth all but gasped. "But what am I going to tell Doris?"

"You don't have to tell her anything. If she asks, just say that Baby's happy and fine. And it'll be the truth."

"And what about your job? You can't just take off. If you lose it, then what?"

"God'll provide," he said with a confident smile.

"Sure," said Ruth sourly.

The phone rang.

"That must be for me," Shockley said, rushing off. "I'm expecting a call from Lenny Bernstein. I'm trying to set up a meeting. Keep your fingers crossed."

Almost from birth, Irwin Shockley was drawn into the world of music. Even before he was old enough to lift his own miniature violin and scratch out a tune, Shockley was being exposed to an impressive sampling of the most eminent composers, conductors, and performing artists in the business. Though Maestro Henry Shockley was never to attain the heights of fame he had always assumed were his due, he did nonetheless possess a savvy instinct for rubbing shoulders with the musical luminaries of his day. A list of the people whom young Irwin had come into contact with almost from the start of his life might read like a *Who's Who*. Aaron Copland, who used to stay weekends at the Shockleys' Long Island home had—according to Shockley's mother—changed baby Irwin's diapers during an emergency. Eugene Ormandy had gotten down on the floor on all fours to play horsey with Irwin. Arthur Rodzinski had once held a serious conversation with the promising five-year-old that Shockley could still recall today. Dimitri Mitropoulos had shown the fledgling violinist a nifty new way to finger strings. And on and on. Walter Piston. Samuel Barber. Fritz Reiner. Leopold Stokowski. Shockley had been exposed to his father's contemporaries almost without knowing who they were. They had all dropped by at one time to have a drink or chat with Henry Shockley—an outwardly warm, considerate, and affable man.

From the age of six and onward, Irwin Shockley's contact with the august world of music became more formalized. Observing the agility with which his son taught himself the violin, Henry Shockley had come to the conclusion that young Irwin had all the earmarks of a prodigy. Above the weak objection of his wife, he sent the headstrong six-year-old off to study with Ivan Galamian. Galamian, whose previous students included Itzhak Perlman and Pinchas Zukerman, was quick to spot not only the boy's inherent talent, but also his rambunctiousness, which could prove a problem. As a favor to Maestro Shockley he accepted the boy, assuming he could channel Irwin's energies into the violin. He was wrong. The young Shockley was no easy student. He cut classes, stubbornly refused to sepend the required five hours a day in uninterrupted practice, and was more interested in play than playing.

After a frustrating year, Galamian, sapped by the demands, threw up his hands.

"Listen, Henry," said Galamian, breaking the news, "he's a sweet kid. I like him. A competent violinist he can be, that's obvious. But a genius he's not. Take my advice. Don't push the boy. Let him develop. He's a wild kid who needs to have fun, to mature. He's got a good ear and a nice touch." Galamian had tried to soften the blow. "Who knows what direction he'll take? Maybe he'll become a great conductor like his father. Or another Mozart," he laughed.

Irwin's failure, however, was no laughing matter. Nor was it to be accepted. Galamian didn't know what the hell he was talking about. Off went Irwin to the next violin master. And then the next. Never one to learn from experience, Henry Shockley also discovered in his daughter the makings of a prodigy. A pianist, this time. Karen proved more malleable than her older brother. With her father's coercion, she practiced endless hours without a whimper or complaint, forsaking the carefreeness of childhood for the rigors of the keyboard. By the age of twelve, this high-strung, frail girl had been formed into an accomplished soloist. By fourteen, she was on the road giving recitals around the country. By sixteen, she had ended her life. With Karen's death the light went out of Henry's life. The house became cold and barren, devoid of visitors and music. Irwin Shockley fled to school and never returned. Henry's wife left him without warning. A couple of years later Maestro Henry Shockley died a lonely, disappointed, and impoverished man.

Aside from the debts against his estate, Maestro Shockley did, however, leave his son a legacy of sorts—the Shockley name. It was a key that, if not guaranteeing success, did at least open doors a crack. Just as Galamian had so astutely predicted, Irwin Shockley had moved in other directions. He put away his violin and became a composer. All those early contacts paid off handsomely in admittance to the best schools, scholarships, fellowships, grants, recognition. And today, thanks to the lasting image of his father, Schockley still had entré. All he had to do was pick up a phone. Which was what he had done for Baby.

"Zubin," said Shockley when Maestro Mehta finally returned his call. "How good to hear from you. The reason I called—"

On the morning of his departure, Shockley was the first one up. It was a crisp November morning with a layer of frost covering the grass and, after turning up the heat in the house, Shockley hurriedly packed. For Baby he filled up a large suitcase with diapers and extra bottles and blankets, her vitamin drops, a tube of ointment, and a sampling of her best clothes. For himself he packed a much smaller bag. After shaving and eating a hasty breakfast, he dressed in a new suit and went up to the guest room that had been converted into a nursery. Still deeply asleep, Baby was lying on her stomach, her hands placed by her head, her knees tucked under her, elevating her tiny bottom into the air. Reluctantly Shockley awoke Baby, rolled her over and changed her diapers as she stretched her mouth in a long yawn, her face still creased from sleep.

"We're going for a big trip," he told her after her breakfast, when the airport limousine pulled up in front of the house and honked.

Baby looked back at him confusedly, and laughing, he touched her nose and gave her a quick loving peck.

At the Ithaca airport Shockley checked the bags and boarded the waiting jet. The engines roared, shaking the cabin. Fastening his seatbelt, he held on tightly to Baby, muttering soothing words to the child, who seemed alarmed by the noise. As the massive machine plunged headlong down the runway, its shell quivering violently, Baby's apparent fear suddenly became infectious and a terrifying thought raced through Shockley's mind. What if the plane couldn't lift off and crashed at the end of the runway, trapping them in a fiery heap? Pressing his forehead against the cold plastic of the window, Shockley forced the vivid image from his mind as though that unmentionable thought had the power to shape events.

The plane lifted its nose with a groan, banked steeply, and started to climb. Shockley let out his breath. Distorted through the scratchy plastic of the window, he could see the roads and houses turn to doll-like proportions. A stretch of forest with bare-limbed trees merged to an even blanket of dark, cold brown. The choppy waters of the lake passed below, yielding to the neat squares of outlying farms.

Shockley pulled himself away from the window and, looking down at Baby, saw to his surprise that she was sucking her thumb. It was the first time in her life that she had done it, he thought, gripping her tightly as the plane continued to climb, bouncing through the thick, ominous clouds. The jet lurched and jolted. Finally it broke through the gloom, and they were now moving in an unobstructed field of brilliant, blue light, riding smoothly above a frothy, white layer cushioning them from the ground. The plane reached altitude and, as the noise in the cabin began to abate, Shockley noticed that Baby was singing, or trying to sing, her thumb still lodged in her mouth. Curious, he bent forward, bringing his head close to hers, his nostrils picking up her scent of powder and milk. She was not exactly singing, he observed above the drone of the engines. Rather, she was humming to herself, humming around that thumb. He pressed his ear tightly against her curled fist and strained to pick up the bits and pieces of her slow, melancholy song. How I wish Ruth were here to witness this, he thought, touched by the pathos of this new melody. He had been right.

Baby had it in her. Another new song, he muttered jubilantly to himself. And though it was a new song to him, it was, in fact, the same elegiac melody that Baby had sung for her mother on parting, one that she had, unnoticed, come to sing to herself in her moments of distress or longing.

By the time they reached Los Angeles, Baby was clearly exhausted. She had not slept a wink on either the first flight to Chicago or the connecting one to the coast. She was tired and irritable and refused to eat. Afraid that Baby might balk at singing, Shockley debated delaying the scheduled appearance before the USC music department. If he did, however, it would foul up the entire itinerary and, worse, might start raising suspicions.

"Are you going to sing tonight?" he asked nervously, and when Baby finally took her bottle he decided to push ahead with the appearance.

"You may have to be patient," he explained to the gathering of academics and musicians.

"Is this a joke?" asked one of the men peering into Baby's portable crib that sat on a table at the front of the rather large and austere lecture room.

"She doesn't sing on cue," continued Shockley uneasily, ignoring the comment. "You're going to have to sit very quietly and just wait."

They all sat and waited. Overhead the fluorescent lights hummed noisily. Outside on the street a siren wailed. A dog barked. After half an hour some of the people in the room started fidgeting in the hard, wood-backed chairs. Forty minutes later people started drifting out of the stuffy room.

"Please," said Shockley, almost angrily, to those who were getting up. "Give her a chance."

Looking over at Baby, who was lying there inertly staring at the cold ceiling lights, Shockley felt a wave of resentment sweep over him.

After an hour and a quarter, with the audience dwindling down to less than half, Shockley was beginning to feel like a fool. His nerves were ragged, and he knew that if Baby didn't sing, he would never live this down.

"Maybe she's tired," he suggested, preparing for his downfall. "She's been traveling all day. Let's give her another quarter of an hour," he pleaded, and the remaining audience grumbled but stayed.

Then, moments before the time was up and Shockley was at his breaking point, Baby suddenly relented. Opening her mouth she drew a long breath and began to sing. It was a variation of her earliest melody, and though she sang barely loudly enough for the assemblage to hear, Shockley fell back in his chair in exhausted relief. A murmur of surprise went up, then quickly subsided as people strained to hear, Shockley delightedly observing their faces, which registered the full range from rapt attention to startlement to blissful tears. When Baby finished, there was dead silence.

A man at the rear started to clap tentatively. Someone else joined him. An instant later the assemblage burst out in loud, unanimous applause.

"Hurrah!" someone shouted.

"More!" cried a woman, as though she were at a concert.

The people rose to their feet as one and for three long minutes gave Baby a standing ovation.

With a grin Shockley took a bow for Baby's benefit.

"Thank you. Thank you," he said when the applause finally began to subside. "Please inform your colleagues about what they missed."

13

Zubin Mehta was still in town and Schokley took a cab over to his house to catch him before he left for a concert in Tel Aviv.

"So you're the little singer." Maestro Mehta laughed, spreading apart the blanket and peering curiously down at her face.

"I have to warn you," said Shockley, hedging his bets, "it's not always easy getting her to sing. It took almost two hours at USC today."

"For me she'll sing," said the swarthy man, holding out his arms and accepting the infant. "Come, darling, sing for Uncle Zubin," he coaxed gently, and without a moment's hesitation, Baby began to open up. She sang basically what she had sung earlier that evening.

"Divine," said Mehta, shaking his head. "Can you do more?" he asked, puckering his lips in the form of a kiss.

"She's got another song," Shockley started to explain, and Baby interrupted him by singing her plaintive song, singing out loud, and finishing by sticking her thumb into her mouth.

"What a sad song!" said Mehta, obviously stirred. "What's she trying to say?" he asked.

Shockley shrugged.

"What are you going to do with her?" questioned Mehta when Shockley was getting ready to leave.

"I want to share her with the world. I want everyone to hear her."

"Yes, of course. But you must be careful," said Mehta sagaciously.

"Don't worry, I am," said Shockley, meeting his dark eyes.

"I've never seen anything like this. But I do know that with children you have to be exceedingly careful. Talent can be burnt out," he said with a raised eyebrow. Mehta had heard the tale of Shockley's sister and knew he didn't have to say more.

The next morning Shockley flew with his protégé to the State University of Arizona at Tempe where Baby—in noticeably better spirits after a good night's sleep—performed without a hitch. From Tempe they went east to the University of Indiana. The grapevine was working at high speed and, when they landed in Bloomington, they were greeted at the airport by a contingent of eager musicians.

A day later the pair arrived at West Texas State. Baby's reputation had apparently preceded her here, too, because, though she stalled for a good two hours, not a single person in the packed auditorium wiggled so much as a toe. While at the Peabody Institute in Baltimore a week later, Shockley received a long telegram from Pierre Boulez, the former conductor of the New York Philharmonic, requesting a private audience. Boulez was known for his interest in avant-garde music, and Shockley was exceedingly pleased by his request. It just added further credibility to an already accepted Baby.

"Shockley's Find Is the World's Find!" raved a critic for the *Los Angeles Times* who had waited out Baby's performance at USC, knowing that, no matter the outcome, he would have a good story.

"Composer and Infant Hitch Teams," read a large headline in *Music World* over an article replete with pictures of Shockley and Baby—eight pages of the normally staid journal devoted to the infant prodigy and her impresario. Scattered throughout the article were shots of Shockley standing over the makeshift crib taking notes, Shockley holding Baby aloft before an overflow audience at West Texas State, even a photo of Shockley feeding Baby her afternoon bottle.

At the New England Conservatory, Shockley was mobbed outside the building where Baby was to perform, and mounted police had to be called in to clear a path through the crowds for Baby's limousine.

"You wouldn't believe what's going on," Shockley breathlessly told Ruth in a short phone conversation they had one night. He was trembling with excitement and had to grip the phone with both hands.

"I believe it," she said dully, having just read about Baby in *Newsweek*.

They talked for a few brief minutes and then, as Shockley was saying good-bye and was about to hang up, she said to him, "You know, Irwin, you haven't even asked me about Doris."

"Oh. Doris. Yes. How is she?" he asked, still flushed with success.

"Feeling better?" inquired Dr. Gaskins, leaning over his patient.

Doris opened her hooded eyes a little more and tried to swallow. Her throat was parched. Sensing her thirst the physician lifted her head and held to her lips a paper cup filled with ice chips. Doris took a mouthful of the cold chips and, pressing them against the gums where her upper teeth had once resided, felt the soothing, melting water ease down her throat.

"You had us all a little worried," he said, taking out a blood-pressure sleeve. Pumping it tight, he rolled his eyes upward, concentrating on the stethoscope plugged in his ears. "H'm," he smiled a little too cheerfully. "It looks good."

Doris swallowed the remaining ice that had turned to slush, her eyes searching the doctor's face.

"The worst is over," he said, meeting her gaze. "Your fever's down. Your red count's improving. By tomorrow I want you up. OK?"

Doris gave a weak nod. She tried to smile, but the muscles in her face refused to obey.

"I know what hell is like," she said when the doctor was leaving.

He turned and laughed. "Well then, you can warn all us sinners," he grinned and turned on his heels.

"Up to the bathroom," said the nurse the next morning, a few hours after Doris's catheter had been removed. "Doctor's orders."

"Oh, please." Doris protested feebly as a team of nurses disconnected the tubes and hoisted her up despite her moans.

"Now that wasn't as bad as you thought it would be, was it?" said the young nurse when they led her back to bed and covered her.

"Worse," said Doris, and they were sure she was joking.

She wasn't. What did they know with their young bodies that had never been sliced in two?

In the afternoon Doris ate her first meal: Jell-O, a half slice of toast, and a cup of tepid tea. It all tasted faintly like plastic, but she knew that if she were ever to get out of this place—and not in a pine box—it was vital to eat. For Baby's sake. When they took her tray away, Doris lifted the covers and for the first time peered down at the drainage tube that emerged through the gauze and tape of her bandage-covered wound. Quickly she covered it up again and tried not to dwell on the fact that it ran deep into her body.

In the evening Ruth came by with a smile and some flowers.

"You're looking much better," she said, and Doris had the feeling she was hiding something. Maybe she was dying and they didn't want to tell her the truth?

"How's Baby?" was the first question she asked.

"Oh. Baby," Ruth blustered. "She's fine. Happy. Well."

"Why do you seem so surprised that I asked?"

"It's the first time you've asked anything." Ruth shrugged nervously.

"Where is she?"

"With Irwin."

"I'd like to see her."

"They don't allow children to visit the surgical wards," Ruth said and realized that her answer had come out a little too quickly.

"Maybe you could bring her tomorrow. Outside the window," Doris said, motioning behind her head to the long window that looked down three stories into a grassy courtyard.

"Maybe." Ruth smiled. She suspected that Doris had been thinking about it all day.

"She wants to see Baby," Ruth explained to her husband when she finally located him. He was on the way to New York. "Tomorrow!"

"Stall her."

"I can't. I tried."

"You have to. Tomorrow I see Boulez and Bernstein."

"Why am I stuck with the disgusting and utterly onerous job of lying?"

"I didn't say lie. I said stall."

"Why should *I* be the one?"

"Because I need you to. Look, a few more days. What the hell difference will a few lousy days make?"

"Plenty."

"I can't stand here and argue it now. I've got to catch a flight that leaves in less than—than half an hour." He checked his watch. "And it takes almost that to get out to the airport, even with an escort."

"A what?"

"Can't explain now. Listen, darling, I've got to be at a meeting tonight. Tomorrow it's Juilliard."

"Now *you* listen."

"A few days. What's a—Wait! I've got it. They don't allow children to visit patients in the surgical ward," he said, frantically rushing his words. "Tell her that."

"I did already. She wants me to bring Baby to the window."

"What floor's she on?"

"Why?"

"What floor?"

"Third."

"Great! Wrap up a blanket and parade it down in front of her window. It'll work out perfectly. Doris'll be tickled. You'll be off the hook. And everybody'll be happy."

"I will not!"

"You will."

"Why carry on this charade? Sooner or later she'll find out."

"Maybe. But let it be later."

When Doris saw somebody standing below in the courtyard holding a pink bundle, she fumbled for her glasses. Seeing that it was Ruth holding Baby, she burst into tears.

Forcing herself up in her bed on an elbow, she moved closer to the window and waved, dabbing at her eyes with a tissue.

"Baby, Baby," she called from behind the sealed panes, pressing her hands against the icy glass.

Ruth tipped up 'Baby' and pointed her toward her mother. Doris laughed through her tears.

"Just seeing her," Doris confessed when Ruth came upstairs later, "makes me feel well already. I feel like hopping out of this old bed and charging home," she laughed exuberantly. Ruth swallowed uncomfortably. "But if you're up here"—Doris suddenly stopped, her smile fading, lines of worry registering on her face—"then who's with Baby?"

"Cindy's sitting with her in the lobby. She's OK," Ruth said reassuringly and felt like strangling Irwin for putting her through this.

"It's not that I don't trust you," Doris quickly apologized.

"I understand," answered Ruth, wanting to leave.

"I'm always worried about her."

"That's normal."

"I suppose when you have a child this late in life and with so much trouble you get to be silly and overprotective," she said, looking down at her white hands that were splotched with freckles and lined with blue veins. "I've always been afraid that if I let go of Baby even for a minute I'd lose her forever. It's ridiculous, I know, but that's why I acted the way I did when I left her with you. But you've taken good care of her. I can see that," Doris said, becoming uncharacteristically loquacious, her hand coming to rest on Ruth's. "How can I ever thank you people?"

"You don't have to," Ruth said and with a mumbled excuse finally rushed from the room. She took the elevator down to the main floor and met Cindy, who was sitting in the lobby, one of her lifelike dolls held in her lap, the pink blanket trailing to the ground.

"I don't get it," said Cindy, probing her mother's face with her dark, deep-set eyes.

"There's nothing to get. Come on. Let's go," she said, taking her by the hand. "We're late for your lesson."

"Was Mrs. Rumsey supposed to—?"

"Will you mind your own business!"

"I was just asking."

"Well, don't!"

When they moved Mrs. Skibinski into the empty bed in Doris's room, Doris knew it was a sign that she was recovering—though she wished that they would have found anyone but Mrs. Skibinski. The thirtyish woman with owllike features had undergone removal of a tumor in her right breast and from the moment she awoke from anesthesia and learned that the lump had been benign, there had been little peace for Doris. Mrs. Skibinski chewed gum, talked incessantly, and was visited by an endless string of friends, relations, and co-workers who crowded the tiny room and stayed for hours. Worst of all, Mrs. Skibinski's husband had rented a television set for her, which blared unabated from early morning to late night. In vain, Doris had once requested Mrs. Skibinski to turn down the set, please.

"It's down as far as it'll go. If I turn it down any more," said the woman testily, "I won't even be able to hear it."

Doris resigned herself to the television, trying to concentrate on the books that the hospital volunteers brought her, aware that her irritation was a healthy sign. Before, they could have dropped a bomb in her room and she wouldn't have noticed it. On and on the television ran as Mrs. Skibinski whimsically changed the channels, giving the tube no more than a cursory glance. Sometimes Doris would look at the oblique screen, catch snippets of a dull soap opera or gameshow or the shrill commercials that vied for her attention. Mostly the programming filtered into the background of her consciousness, returning to haunt her in her sleep in the form of jingles that looped over endlessly in her head.

The second night of TV, as Doris was finishing her dinner, a news report coming over the cable from New York abruptly broke through the wall of her consciousness.

"And, coming up," the newscaster was saying, "Mayor Koch calls for yet another cut in city workers. A tragic fire in Brooklyn. And a baby who can sing takes the city by storm. All after these brief messages."

Doris dropped a spoon into her rice pudding.

"What's that!" she gasped, her heart standing still.

"It's the news," said Mrs. Skibinski, lighting up a forbidden cigarette.

"What did they *say*?" Doris asked, feeling the blood drain away from her head, her chest tightening as she fought for breath.

"The usual." Mrs. Skibinski shrugged.

Doris's mind began to race. A baby that can sing. Takes New York by storm. That's what he said. She was almost positive. And how many babies in this world can sing? she wondered, throwing off her covers and shuffling barefoot across the icy floor.

"What's the big deal?" asked Mrs. Skibinski, who thought Mrs. Rumsey a pain but was curious to see her suddenly interested in something on television.

Doris moved up to the set.

"You're blocking it," said Mrs. Skibinski, who didn't want to miss whatever it was that excited her roommate.

Standing hunched in front of the screen, her eyes riveted to a bleach commercial, Doris didn't budge. After the first ad there was one for toothpaste, followed by an interminable dramatization about floor wax in which two women were arguing about who had shinier floors. Doris was still worrying about what she thought the man had said. Feeling woozy and weak, she took a step backward and leaned against Mrs. Skibinski's bed for support.

"Make yourself at home while you're at it," said Mrs. Skibinski caustically.

The newscaster came on again. There was a story about

Mayor Koch. Some sanitation workers were interviewed. Angry faces threatened the city with mayhem in the form of uncollected garbage. Then there was a scene of flames shooting out of a brick tenement, and Doris tried not to let her imagination fly as she saw bodies wheeled away on stretchers.

The newscaster came back on and introduced the next story. The picture switched to a black reporter standing on a city street holding a microphone.

"Well, John, we weren't allowed in, nor for that matter were our cameras, but we have it on reliable advice that there's a most unusual three-month-old baby in town. And she arrived quietly in New York about two days ago."

The picture cut to a shot of a man emerging from the rear of a limousine. The car was flanked on either side by police holding back an eager crowd of reporters and onlookers. Doris, who berated herself for not bringing along her glasses, moved back to the set, bringing her face close to the tube until the picture became distorted. She turned up the sound.

"The baby, who goes by the name of 'Baby' "—the newsman let a chuckle slip into his voice,—"has been on a tour of . . ."

The camera was being jostled, and Doris held her breath as it searched through the confusion of people, found an opening, and slowly started zooming in.

"According to our sources, this three-month-old little girl can actually *sing*."

The camera was now closing in on the man and child.

"Oh!" cried Doris in anguish.

". . . discovered by music Professor Irwin Shockley of Cornell University, this little girl is causing quite a stir around the country. Purportedly . . ."

The newscaster came on screen again and the report was over before it had hardly begun.

"Well, a baby that croons," said the announcer with a laugh and a wink, wrapping up the program on a light note. "That's a new wrinkle. And that's it for this evening. Chuck Bates will be back at eleven with the final roundup. From all of us here at TV 10."

Doris slumped down on the corner of Mary Skibinski's bed.

"Hey, Mrs. Rumsey. Are you *the* Mrs. Rumsey who—Oh, wow!" she exclaimed, realizing that her roommate was a star.

"Wait till I tell Hank about this!"

Doris sat in bed the entire day waiting in turmoil for Ruth to appear, rehearsing in her mind what she would finally say to her. In her lap sat a copy of the *New York Times* opened to a second-page article headlined "Infant Prodigy Stirs Juilliard." Under the headline was a picture of Shockley holding her Baby. Doris had read the article over eight times and there were phrases she could quote verbatim:

"After a hectic cross-country swing . . ."

"Experts at the University of Southern California . . ."

"At Baltimore's Peabody a group of eminent . . ."

"Shockley was purposely vague about his plans to. . . ."

Doris tried to reason through her predicament, her thoughts torn by anger and despair and bitter fury. Ruth had lied to her. Straight to her face. Had tricked her. How in this world could one human being do such a heartless, deceitful thing to another? How could one mother, who had given birth to children of her own and knew the feelings it engendered, be so callous to another mother? Shockley she could understand. He was pushy, arrogant, self-centered. But his wife. How could she have taken part in this heinous deception?

Ruth never appeared that day, and the speech Doris had so carefully prepared went unused. That night, feeling wretched and helpless, Doris cried herself to sleep. She awoke early the next day before the morning shift of nurses had arrived, feeling as though she hadn't slept a wink. At lunchtime she looked up over her tray to see Ruth standing in the doorway. The television was squawking loudly, but all Doris could hear was the thunder of blood in her own ears. Ruth remained framed in the doorway, giving a tentative smile, the corners of her mouth twitching nervously. The instant her eyes met Doris's she realized that the old woman knew.

"I'm terribly sorry," she said, aware that it was a lame apology.

Doris stared at her with narrowed eyes, her fists bunching up the sheets, her nostrils flaring with each breath. She tried to speak, but the words she had prepared failed her.

"I can't tell you how bad I feel. You're angry. I understand. I would be furious too."

Doris continued to stare fixedly at her, her features frozen and hard, her expression going beyond anger or pain. She swallowed with difficulty and then, finally, the only words she could muster issued from her lips.

"You betrayed us," she said succinctly and turned her back to Ruth.

"Don't be rash," said Dr. Gaskins, who had learned of Shockley's deceit. "Stay at least until you're strong enough to cope with the situation."

"You can't keep me here against my will," said Doris firmly.

"No. I can't," he admitted. "But if you go, I won't be responsible for what might happen."

"I didn't ask for that."

"Give yourself a few more days. You've made a splendid recovery. Why ruin it?"

"I want to go now."

"Wait at least until the morning."

"Now."

"There are forms to be filled out," he stalled. "The business office needs time to—"

"Now," she said obstinately.

"You'll have to sign a release and waiver."

"Whatever."

"It was a stupid thing to do," said Ruth, breaking the silence as she drove her husband home from the airport, Baby dozing in his lap.

"It was and it wasn't, Ruth." He turned to her in the darkness, the headlights from a passing car harshly chiseling the lines of his face. "I had to grab the chance. If I hadn't done it now, I might never have had the opportunity. Now they all know. The child exists."

"And to do it you duped Doris and you used me."

"I don't deny it. I admit it."

"And you're not contrite."

"No, not especially."

Ruth stopped at the intersection to Route 13 and waited for the long lights to change. The motor idled noisily and Shockley thought about getting the car tuned.

"How are the kids?"

"You should ask first how Doris is."

"I'm afraid to."

The light flashed green and Ruth turned onto the highway. She drove down the long incline, passing the malls flanking both sides of the road, their parking lots busy with cars. The sign of a Holiday Inn glared to one side. An electronic sign alternated numerals, 35°, 8:45, 35°, 8:45.

"OK, OK. It was wrong. Morally despicable. What else do you want me to say?"

"Nothing," she said, but her words belied her meaning.

"Look, I couldn't help myself," he burst out after a moment. "Whenever she sings, I have no choice. I feel impelled to do something. I can't just sit on my hands and let this magnificent child get buried alive. Do you understand?" he asked, looking down on Baby's placid features and noticing that her thumb was again in her mouth.

"No"—Ruth glanced away from the road for an instant—"not really. I don't understand."

"Boy, I'm glad you're the one who has to confront her now, not me," Ruth said as they pulled up the driveway to the house. "I don't think I could ever look her in the eye again. Or for that matter myself in the mirror."

Ruth got out of the car, but Shockley remained in the front seat, holding Baby.

"Would you mind driving us to the hospital?" he ventured meekly.

"Right now?"

"I'd rather face her now and get it over with. I don't like things hanging over me."

Ruth got back into the car.

"Maybe," he said as they passed through the octopus exchange at the far end of town and began the climb up West Hill to the hospital, "maybe I can reason with her."

"Fat chance," said Ruth.

"Checked out this afternoon," said Mrs. Skibinski, with a smile on her face and a fresh wad of gum between her teeth.

"Left?"

"The doctor told her she was nuts." Mrs. Skibinski shrugged. "I'm getting out myself tomorrow morning. None too soon for me. I work up at the—Hey, you're the professor we saw on television, aren't you?" she called out as Shockley left.

"We called a cab for her," said the head nurse when Shockley found her. "I assume she went home, because the doctor arranged for a nurse to visit her daily and—"

Shockley hurried to the elevator and pressed the button. The elevator was in the basement and seemed to stop at every floor. He grew impatient and hurried down the stairs two steps at a time.

"She's left," he said, getting back into the car and taking Baby, who had dozed off.

Ruth looked stunned.

"But where to?"

"Home," he said tersely.

Ruth started the car and drove back toward town. She cut through the west end of the city, drove over the small bridge on Cascadilla Creek, and turned on to Willow Avenue. The lights were on in Doris's house, and Ruth and her husband exchanged worried looks.

"You can wait here," he said, getting out with Baby, who was waking up.

"I'll go with you."

"You're not responsible for what happened."

"I know what my responsibilities are. I don't need you to define them," she said going along.

Shockley rang the bell. No one answered.

He rang again. Still no sign.

He peered in through a parting in the curtains of the front door. Looking into the hallway, he could see no one. He rang again, holding the button. Suddenly Doris's face appeared framed in the curtain opening and for a moment the two stood fixed eye to eye, Shockley feeling himself wilt under her slitlike gaze. The door slowly opened. Doris stood planted in the doorway, her body blocking the way.

"Give me Baby," she said, holding out her hands.

Shockley hesitated.

"Doris, I want to explain—" he began.

"Give her the child," said Ruth emphatically.

Obediently Shockley handed over Baby.

Doris took her child and looked down at her as though examining Baby for damage. When she was finally satisfied, she lifted her face and directed her words to Shockley.

"You're never to come around here again, or see Baby again," uttered Doris in a low, quaking voice. "No one is. Forget about Baby," she said and with that slammed the door.

"Come on," mumbled Ruth, going back to the car.

Shockley remained on the porch, stunned. He stood there staring blankly at the door, watching as the downstairs light went off, shivering from the chill of the evening, from trip fatigue, from the incisive awareness that Doris Rumsey truly meant what she said. The door was to be closed. Forever.

TWO

14

Shockley busied himself raking leaves in the yard. Ordinarily it was a task that he enjoyed, relishing the smell of crisp leaves and deriving a certain satisfaction from the orderly swathes of lawn that followed in his wake. Today, however, it gave him little pleasure, and he did it only to kill time.

Leaning his rake against his shoulder Shockley anxiously checked his watch for the third time. By the time he glanced up, a stiff gust had done a good job of scattering his neat pile. He tried to round up the tumbling leaves, but the wind tricked him, picking up speed and repeatedly switching direction. A frigid blast swooped up from the valley, cutting him to the bone and turning his fingers numb. Helplessly he watched as the last leaves on his pile scattered over the expanse of dormant grass.

The sky turned dark and for a moment there was a rush of wind-driven snow. The heavens lightened, the sun peeked through a blue chink above the rim of West Hill, then disappeared. A few vagrant snowflakes fluttered to the ground, as low, boiling clouds charged recklessly overhead. Turning up his collar, Shockley thought about the desolation of the incipient winter, a winter without the consolation of Baby. In his mind's eye he could already picture the snow dunes blowing blindly across the roads, see the deep, rutted piles of salted slush clogging the city street. Shockley shivered at the prospect. In Ithaca it was always the weater, the damn weather. It governed conversations, moods, needs, the condition of the pocketbook, the outlook on life, even sex. Looking into the skies one could almost forecast the state of the day's events. A cluster of snow stuck to his eyelashes and, wiping it away, he tossed aside his rake and went inside to the phone.

Picking up the receiver, Shockley waited for a dial tone, but none came. He jiggled the button, but still there was no signal. It was then, hearing the static in the receiver, that he realized that someone was on the line.

"Hello?" he questioned the hiss.

"Hello," echoed a distant female voice, sounding surprised. Apparently he had picked up the phone an instant before it was going to ring.

"Professor Shockley?"

"Yes?"

"One moment, please," said the woman and, before he could even inquire who was calling, the line was switched and a man with a familiar foreign accent was on the line.

"This is Jacobsen. Ivar Jacobsen," said the man with the guttural pronunciation.

"Oh, Mr. Jacobsen," said Shockley, taken off-guard. "I'm terribly sorry. I meant to get back to you."

"I was waiting for your call," replied Jacobsen rather brusquely.

Ivar Jacobsen was a powerful booking agent with offices in New York, London, and Rome. Representing some of the most distinguished opera singers, performing musicians, and conductors, he flew around the country in his private jet replete with communications equipment and staff, and Shockley had no idea where he might be calling from. While in Texas, Shockley had been contacted by an associate in Jacobsen's New York office. The famous Mr. Jacobsen, he was informed at the time, wanted very much to speak with him. Shockley was flattered, and an appointment of sorts had been arranged. At the appropriate time, he was told by the caller, Mr. Jacobsen would find him. Ultimately Jacobsen had caught up with him in New York.

Emerging with Baby from the auditorium at Juilliard after her performance, Shockley had been getting ready to run the gauntlet of reporters awaiting them outside the hall when he spotted a tall man with regal bearing standing discretely off to one side of the crowd. His head towering over all the others, he was a strikingly ugly man with long, exaggerated features, a heavy brow, thick jaw, and long strands of whitish blond hair encircling his bald dome. The man's eyebrows were nearly transparent and his skin so light he looked almost albino. Though Shockley had never met him in person, had only seen pictures of him, he immediately recognized Jacobsen. Before Shockley realized what was happening, three of Jacobsen's assistants had encircled him and Baby and were deftly whisking them past the reporters and into Jacobsen's waiting limousine—a small contingent of cooperative police holding back the onlookers who pressed close. It was, in fact, that very limousine that Doris would later see on Mrs. Skibinski's television.

Holding Baby, Shockley had silently ridden with Jacobsen and his crew to Central Park South, the limo pulling up in front of the Pierre Hotel. Until they reached Jacobsen's top-floor suite not a word was exchanged, Jacobsen's aloofness and stern bearing cowing the normally irrepressible Shockley.

Jacobsen's suite was lavish. A pair of large crystal chandeliers hung from the vaulted ceiling of the main room, the gleaming furniture was solid mahogany, and on the floors were rugs that appeared to be authentically Persian. Shockley was staying with Baby in a rather ordinary motel on the West Side and, gazing around in awe at the splendor of Jacobsen's rooms, he promised himself—and Baby—that the next time they visited New York they would also live in style like this.

"I don't have much time, so let's get right down to business," said Jacobsen bluntly after they were seated in armchairs facing each other. Lighting up his fifth cigarette since they had met, the Dane exhaled a flood of smoke. Baby coughed and wrinkled her face, but Shockley didn't dare object.

"What sort of business did you have in mind?" asked Shockley, his attention caught by a Teletype chattering away in the next room.

"I'm talking about Baby, of course. I had a chance to hear her today."

"She is remarkable, isn't she?" Shockley beamed.

"Yes," replied Jacobsen without emotion, "but what you're doing with her is certainly less than remarkable. In fact, if you'll pardon me, I think it's a disaster."

Shockley's smile fell.

"I think you ought to realize that if you're trying to set up a career for her, you've gone about it in the worst possible way," he continued, snuffing out a half-smoked cigarette.

"I'm not sure that I do want to set up a career for her," said Shockley defensively.

"Well then, what is it that you're trying to accomplish?"

"Frankly, at this point, all I'm trying to do is to give her an opportunity to be heard."

"By the greatest number of people?"

"Yes. Of course."

"Well," said Jacobsen, his mood suddenly shifting and turning cordial, "in that case it looks like you need some help, doesn't it?"

"Perhaps," Shockley hedged.

"Come on, Dr. Shockley, let's not beat around the bush. I want to put Baby on tour." Jacobsen absently fumbled for another cigarette. "But I'm talking about a *real* tour, not this half-hearted farting around with music schools. I'm talking about a tour that can draw big box office, big money," he raised a hand. One of his gold cuff links caught a gleam of light and Baby strained forward to get a better look.

"I'm not interested in money. That's not my motivation."

"Fine. But what about her?" said Jacobsen, motioning to Baby, who sat in Shockley's lap attentively watching the agent's every move. "Did you ask her?"

Shockley laughed.

"Sure," said Jacobsen, "she's only a little baby now. But one day she'll be big and her gift could be gone. This might be her only chance in life and it could end up being squandered. Have you given her future *any* thought?"

"Well," Shockley stumbled. "Not really. I'm taking this one step at a time."

"Yes, that's obvious. But maybe you should be looking ahead. Five, ten steps. Not one. With an extraordinary child like this you have to think big, really big," he said, the near-transparent flesh on his face flushing. "If for no one else then for *her* sake."

"I suppose you may be right," Shockley conceded, suddenly feeling his own inadequacy in the face of this man who had shaped the lives of countless performers.

"I *am* right," he said, not mincing words. "Look, let me make a proposal," Jacobsen wet his lips. "I want to put Baby on tour. I want to put her in the biggest, most prestigious concert halls in this country and overseas. You want her to be heard? She will be heard. That I can guarantee you. And she'll make money. Bundles of it, which we'll put away in a trust fund for her. Then, when she's old enough, she can decide whether or not she wants it. If not, let her give it away to charity!" He laughed. "Dr. Shockley"—he suddenly turned serious—"you know as well as I do that I can get her bookings anywhere I want."

Shockley swallowed and nodded.

"Well? Do we have a deal?"

"I have to think about it."

"Well, think."

"Right now? You want an answer this instant?"

"No." Jacobsen chuckled. "Take a few minutes."

"You're joking."

"I'm serious. I want an answer before you leave. If you don't want to do business, that's fine with me. We'll shake hands and part friends. It was a pleasure to have met you. If you want to do business, then we'll get right down to brass tacks."

"Only one go-around."

"You've got it," Jacobsen looked at him squarely, his face taut and etched with deep furrows.

"I see," said Shockley, looking down at Baby. Nervously he stroked her hand with his finger. Baby turned abruptly and looked up at him.

Silence.

"There are other booking agents in the business," said Jacobsen helpfully, but implicit in that suggestion Shockley knew was the affirmation of Jacobsen's supremacy.

Silence.

"OK," said Shockley hoarsely a long minute later. "OK. You'll take care of her bookings. But that's all."

"Good," said Jacobsen affably, his face turning magically

smooth and bright. "Good man. You've done the right thing," he said and, motioning for his secretary, he began dictating a letter of agreement.

"She is yours, isn't she?" Jacobsen suddenly interrupted his letter and turned to Shockley.

"Yes. It looks that way."

Jacobsen arched an eyebrow, paused, and turned back to his dictation.

After Jacobsen finished the agreement and his secretary had gone to type it, he turned back to Shockley.

"You heard my terms, didn't you?"

Shockley nodded.

"There's one more thing we have to understand, and that's reliability."

"Pardon?"

"Is she reliable? Will she perform on schedule?" he asked, irritated by Shockley's apparent thickheadedness.

"So far she has. Sometimes it takes a little while."

"I noticed."

"Generally, I'd say yes."

"Are you reliable?"

Shockley laughed, then looked offended. "Yes. Of course."

"Good," said the Dane, rising to his feet. "Hans," he called out to his associate, who had been awaiting his cue.

"Mr. Jacobsen," said the man deferentially.

"We're ready to roll." He nodded, and clasping his hands behind his back and looking up at the ceiling, Jacobsen began his litany, reeling off names that made Shockley's head spin. "Try Symphony Hall for the fifteenth, Severance for the twenty-sixth," he said, pacing the floor and scanning a mental list. "I think we have a hole there, but you'd better double-check." The man looked up from his pad and then went back to scribbling. "Try—"

"So soon?" interrupted Shockley nervously.

"You said you wanted a tour. So I'm setting up a tour," Jacobsen said, fixing him with a hard stare that made Shockley wilt.

"Yes, of course. It's just that I didn't think it would all go so—so—"

"So?"

"So fast!" He forced a smile.

"Is she ready or isn't she?"

"She is," Shockley said, trying to sound determined. "I just have to clear up a few matters back home."

"I was waiting for your call," repeated Jacobsen. "You said you'd call to confirm as soon as you returned. It's now—"

"I'm sorry," he apologized lamely. "We've had some minor problems on this end."

"I've already set up the dates."

"There's been a hitch."

"What kind of hitch? You gave me the go-ahead," snorted Jacobsen.

"That was subject to my clearing up certain matters. Besides, Baby's got a cold."

"A cold? I asked you if she's a reliable performer."

"My God, how can we control a—?"

"Hang on a second," mumbled Jacobsen distractedly, and Shockley could hear another voice in the background. "I've got an urgent call from London. Could you hold on for a couple of minutes?"

"Why don't you call me back when you're finished?" suggested Shockley, trying to put off the man. At the moment, uppermost in his mind was another call.

"OK," said Jacobsen, abruptly breaking the connection.

Shockley hung up for an instant and, checking a number he had carried around all day, hurriedly picked up again and dialed.

It rang on the other end.

"Come on. Come on," mumbled Shockley as it repeatedly rang. Finally the ringing stopped and a woman answered. "Mrs. Rudd? Shockley here."

"Oh, yes, Mr. Shockley," said the visiting nurse, sounding cheery, her false gaiety rubbing him wrong. "I just got in the door this second," she said breathlessly. "Some weather, isn't it?"

"Did you see her?" he inquired, hardly able to go through any pleasantries.

"Yes. I changed her dressings and—"

"The baby? How's the baby?"

129

"I couldn't spend much time staring at the child. Mrs. Rumsey was watching me like a hawk. Wouldn't let me hardly near her. The best I could do was sort of casually take a peek—like you suggested."

"And?"

"She looked OK, I suppose," she said circumspectly.

"What do you mean?"

"Mrs. Rumsey's awfully weak. Matter of fact she can hardly move. She's barely strong enough to care for herself much less her child. And the place—Well, it's not what I'd call exactly neat," said Mrs. Rudd.

"And the child?"

"She seemed healthy."

"You sound hesitant," he tried to draw her out.

"Well, I am. I took a look in the fridge when Mrs. Rumsey wasn't looking. Heaven knows what they're eating. It was just about bare. And she's certainly in no condition to go shopping. Why, she can barely make it to the bathroom."

Shockley remained silent for a moment, assailed by visions of Baby hungry.

"You still there, Mr. Shockley?"

"Yes. Look, do you think you could go shopping for her?"

"It's not exactly my job, but—Yes. Sure I could."

"I'll bring some money right over. I want you to get whatever you think they might need. Especially for the baby. I'll pay you for your time and trouble."

"That won't be necessary."

"I insist."

"Well, if you—"

"It's important they have anything they need. Spare nothing. I don't want them suffering in any way."

"You're a very kind man," said Mrs. Rudd warmly.

"Just don't tell her where it's coming from."

"If that's the way you want it."

"It is," he said and, as an afterthought, added, "Please."

Shockley put down the receiver. The phone rang almost immediately.

"Mr. Jacobsen calling for Dr. Shockley," said a young male voice.

"He just stepped out."

"When is he expected back?"

"Not till late tonight. I'll have him return the call."

"What does she see?" asked Cindy when the screen filled up with the terrified face of the actress.

"Huh?" asked Shockley, turning to his daughter in the darkened theater. He had been sitting there for almost an hour, staring blankly at the movie, without anything registering. He had been thinking about Baby.

"I said, 'What does she see?'" Cindy repeated.

"I don't know." Shockley shrugged distractedly. "Why don't you wait and see?"

An instant later Cindy's question was answered. It was a decapitated body covered with blood, and Shockley was wondering why he'd let her talk him into taking her on a sunny Saturday afternoon to such a morbid film. He suspected he had gone along in the hopes of occupying his own thoughts but, here he was, dwelling on Baby, vexed at how Doris was undoing all he tried to accomplish, and at how damn helpless he was to do anything about it. He tried to push Doris out of his mind. Tried, but she was like a festering sore.

"What's she going to do now?" asked Cindy a minute later, again breaking into Shockley's thoughts.

"Don't ask me," he snapped irritably.

"OK," mumbled Cindy hurt, turning back to the screen and reaching deep into a near-empty bag of popcorn to dig out a few stray kernels.

A minute later, however, Cindy was again bugging him with questions.

"What's going to happen now?" she asked, gripping his hand.

"How should I know? I didn't make the damn movie!"

"Quiet!" hissed someone behind them.

"I was just asking," Cindy whispered. She was glad to have her father back again, doing things with her, like going to a movie in the middle of the day. It felt good, even if he was grumpy.

"I think she's gonna be murdered," she explained a few minutes later.

"Maybe," said Shockley, guilt-stricken for snapping at the child and wanting to apologize.

"See!" Cindy crowed delightedly when the woman fell over

dead, a knife in her back. "Gross, isn't it?" She grinned, wide-eyed.

When the movie was over they filed out of the theater. The brightness of the afternoon was blinding, and Shockley felt a dull headache throbbing at the back of his skull.

"Where are we going?" she asked when they didn't go directly back to the car.

"I've got to take care of something," he said, a dime already in hand as he stepped into a phone booth on State Street.

"Not Baby *again*," she muttered to herself as her father dialed a number.

"This is Shockley," he said into the mouthpiece, covering his free ear to block out the sounds of passing traffic.

"Oh, I'm glad you called," said Mrs. Rudd.

"How is she?"

"Getting stronger."

"The baby. The baby."

"The diaper rash is worse. Mrs. Rumsey's hardly ever changing her diapers. And now it's getting ulcerated. I tried to tell her not to use the rubber pants, but she keeps doing it anyway. I gave her some salve, but the baby looks very uncomfortable. I told her it's almost better to leave everything off, but she doesn't trust me. She's a strange woman, very strange."

"Is she taking the baby out?"

"No. Not at all. I told her that a child needs fresh air, but it's like talking to a wall."

Silence.

Shockley stood by the phone thinking. For an instant his eyes shifted to Cindy, who stood waiting, her hands on her hips in an expression of impatience.

"You know, Mr. Shockley, somebody ought to do something," said Mrs. Rudd. "That's just not a good situation. That woman should be back in the hospital, and that baby should be getting proper care. I know it's not really any of my business, but, well—"

15

It all happened so fast that Doris hardly knew what hit her.

"Mrs. Rumsey?" questioned the woman standing on the porch and rudely trying to peer past Doris into her house. Actually, she was more a girl than a woman, Doris judged. She looked almost like one of those college students with her longish, straight hair and stern, wire-rimmed glasses. "I'm Miss Cassaniti"—she introduced herself as Doris held a ready hand on the door—"I'm from social services."

Doris felt her heart stop.

"What do you want?" she asked, swallowing dryly.

"I'm here to investigate a complaint."

Doris's eyes widened. The veins at the side of her neck bulged.

"About a possible child neglect—"

Before the woman could complete her sentence, Doris shoved the door closed, locking it with the dead bolt.

Neglect. Neglect. Neglect.

The words exploded in her ears, keeping beat with the deafening thud of her pulse.

The woman knocked on the door. She knocked again. Gave the bell a few perfunctory jabs. Surrendered.

A scant few minutes after the investigator left, Doris began to worry that she had made a serious mistake. Watching through the upstairs window as the woman questioned her neighbors on either side, Miss Cassaniti motioning with her pencil toward Doris's house, Doris was plagued by second thoughts. Her instincts told her to summon back the woman, explain her first, frenzied reaction, show her Baby, how happy she was, perhaps even let Baby sing for her. Logic was one thing, her panic another. It was real, palpable, and left her paralyzed. The next hours were fraught with fear as she tried to guess just what was in store for her and Baby. If only she had had the presence of mind to handle the situation, she cursed herself. Twice in the span of those hours she started to call Olive Eldridge, but never completed the call. She even went so far as to look up the number for social services and sat for a half hour staring worriedly at the listing in the telephone directory.

By late afternoon Doris's forebodings materialized in the form of a lumbering deputy sheriff mounting her porch. The man was so enormous and looked so fiercely determined that Doris feared that if she didn't instantly open up, he was likely to come crashing right through the door, dead bolt and all.

"Doris Laura Rumsey?" he asked, filling the doorway.

"Yes," she responded meekly, looking up at the square-jawed, humorless face.

"Sign here," he said, handing her an official-looking document and pen.

"What is it?" she asked, holding the pen in abeyance.

"Subpoena," he answered tersely.

"What for?"

"I'm not a lawyer, lady," he said, motioning impatiently with his chin toward the pen. Obediently Doris signed.

Long after the patrol car left, she remained riveted in the doorway. Finally she opened the document, bringing it close to her eyes to read, the wind shaking the paper between her fingers as if trying to tug it free.

Halfway through, a cry escaped her lips.

"Oh, my!" she moaned, rereading the words. The paper was not just a subpoena. From what she could gather she had been served with something called a show-cause order from the family court. She was to show cause within five days why the court shouldn't terminate her custody of Baby.

The next days were an unsettling mixture of despair and anxious waiting punctuated by brief glimmers of hope. Somewhere in that period Doris managed to gather her strength, enough at least to consider looking for a lawyer—though she really didn't quite know where to begin. She had never been in need of an attorney, nor for that matter had her parents. All their lives the Rumseys had lived a notably quiet existence, never getting into any squabbles with anyone, much less any legal entanglements.

Doris knew she had to seek help from a lawyer. Olive Eldridge had once mentioned Frank Kiely. Doris had seen his picture in the local paper more than once. No doubt he was as good as any of them, and probably just as expensive.

Counselor Kiely turned out to look just like his picture. He was a robust, portly man with jowls, double chin, and a wide, outgoing smile. Dressed in a pin-striped suit with a bright red tie and diamond stickpin, he struck Doris as an intelligent and sophisticated man.

"Mrs. Rumsey. How are you?" said the lawyer, stepping out of his office and greeting her with his rich baritone. "This way, please," he said cordially. He motioned her into his office and followed behind as she shuffled painfully toward his desk, which was piled high with papers. It was a sturdy early American model, and the rest of his furniture also seemed to be antique. The walls were lined with leather-bound volumes, there were hanging plants in front of the window, and some paintings of local country scenes hung on the wall. Entering the room Doris felt as though she were taking a comforting journey back into the past.

Kiely pulled up a chair for Doris, and when she was seated he sat down behind his desk.

"Now, how can I help you?" he said, and Doris handed him the subpoena.

"Oh, my," he said, glancing at the order and invoking the same words Doris had. "This is not good. Not good at all," he muttered, and then his phone rang. His phone, in fact, kept interrupting every few minutes until, sensing Doris's exasperation, he had his secretary hold all calls.

"Now I want the whole story," he said, fixing her with his stern eyes and exuding such a strong sense of confidence that Doris's misgivings started to vanish.

"Where do I begin?" she asked.

"Start at the beginning," he said coaxingly, his features softening, and taking up a legal pad began to make notes.

Doris told him about Miss Cassaniti, who had come from social services. She tried to explain how, in a moment of terror, she had foolishly locked the woman out. Kiely muttered something about impeding an investigation, shook his head sternly, and told her to continue. Doris explained about the deputy serving the paper.

"Where is the baby now?"

"At home."

"With whom?"

"She's alone," she conceded, but explained that Baby was

sleeping safely and that, because of her recent operation, she didn't quite yet have the strength to push her carriage or carry her.

Kiely pressed for details. What operation? Who was the attending physician? Why had she left the hospital early? What was the name of the visiting nurse? Did she feel her child was getting proper care? Could she in any way document it? Were there friends? Family? Priming her with questions and continuing to take copious notes, he let Doris talk, her pent-up frustrations pouring out. In the matter of a scant half hour Doris had managed to span the entire story of Baby, of her birth, her talent, Doris's experiences with the Shockleys, her own physical condition. When she had finished, Kiely sat for the longest time chewing thoughtfully on the rubber eraser on the tip of his pencil, his eyes fixed on the pad. Then he slowly looked up at her, a smile spreading across his face.

"I think we can take care of this," he said, tapping his pencil on his pad, and Doris heaved a long, relieved sigh. Here was someone who apparently knew just what to do, who could take this mess off her hands.

Kiely sat silently looking at Doris, drumming his fingers on the desk, his head tilted back expectantly as though waiting for Doris to say something. Doris looked at him blankly. Kiely cleared his throat.

"I'll need a retainer to take on this case."

"Oh, yes, of course," she said, embarrassed.

"It may get expensive," he warned her.

"Whatever it costs," she said ingenuously. "I certainly don't want to risk losing Baby."

"A thousand dollars," Kiely said. "That's my minimum fee," he added as an afterthought.

Doris already had her checkbook out and was filling in a check.

"Do you think you could call me a taxi?" she asked, handing over the check. She would have to go to the savings bank to cover that big a sum and doubted she could make it on foot.

"Why certainly." He smiled.

"Now remember," said Kiely as he left her in his outer office to wait for her cab. "Be sure to be on time at the family court on Friday."

"You don't have to worry about that," she said absently, thinking about her dwindling savings.

"You know where it is?"

"In the courthouse?" She checked.

"Right. Second floor. Ten sharp. And please bring the child."

Doris arrived an hour early all keyed up for the hearing. She came to the courthouse dressed in a freshly pressed suit. Her hair had been washed and set, she had put on lipstick and a touch of rouge, and hanging from the lobes of her ears were small earrings studded with imitation diamonds. For the hearing Baby had been bathed and powdered and dressed in one of those new frocks with matching hat she had once gotten from the Shockleys. Even her blanket had been scrubbed the night before in the tub.

Leaving nothing to chance, Doris had arrived at nine sharp, and in the intervening hour she sat expectantly on the hard wooden bench with Baby on her knee, watching people file in and out of the courtroom. Each time someone passed, Doris would look up searchingly, hoping to see Mr. Kiely's familiar face.

Ten o'clock arrived, yet there was no sign of counselor Kiely. By ten-thirty Doris started getting nervous. The frightening thought suddenly occurred to her that she might have missed her lawyer—that the hearing might at this very minute be going on without her. Raising herself with effort, she cautiously moved over the marble floors to the swinging doors marked Family Court.

"I'm Doris Rumsey," she said softly when a uniformed man appeared on the other side of the doors, blocking the closed hearings. "I'm supposed to appear this morning." Through an opening in the door she could see into the courtroom. A woman was sitting on the stand holding a handkerchief to her face, and the sight gave her a sinking feeling.

"One second," whispered the court assistant, and he let the doors close. A moment later he returned.

"You're not on the docket today. It was changed to Tuesday," he said, reading from a clipboard.

The doors swung shut and Doris stood in front of them, baffled. Turning, she descended the long arch of stairs leading to the lobby and went to the pay phone. Propping Baby against the shelf next to the phone, she searched through her change purse for a dime and then called Kiely's office.

"Oh," said Kiely, his voice booming on the other end. "Didn't the court call you? They were supposed to. Your case was delayed. It was moved to Tuesday. Eleven-thirty. Be sure to be there on time. We don't want to keep the judge waiting."

When the brick exploded through the picture window, showering the room with glass shards, Ruth felt as though it had crashed through the brittle shell of her life. For a moment, too stunned to move, she just stared at the missile that lay in front of her on the glass-strewn rug, then at her husband. By the time she had gathered her wits, Shockley was already on his feet racing out the front door. Ruth stood and shook the glass out of her lap and then, closing her eyes, carefully brushed her face for splinters. She opened her eyes and looked down at the brick. It was wrapped in a piece of paper. Bending down she untied the paper, her hands trembling.

"Free Baby," read the note scrawled in childish block lettering.

"There are some people out there as usual," said Shockley, returning, looking flushed. "But they insist they didn't hear or see anything. I'm calling the police," he said and then, turning to go, stopped abruptly. "Are you OK?"

Ruth nodded and he hurried to the phone.

In a couple of minutes the police were there, questioning everyone and clearing the street. The neighbors stood watching from the safety of their houses.

Picking off the stray shards of glass that lay on the far side of the sofa, Ruth cleared a place for herself and sat down. Staring in disbelief at the gaping hole, at the mess of glass at her feet, she felt a wave of nausea rise from her gut.

"Don't worry about it," said Shockley when he came back. He looked harried and frightened. "The insurance'll pay for the damages," he explained, trying to cheer her up, and immediately realized he had said the wrong thing.

"I don't give a damn about the money," she said hoarsely.

"It's the fucking principle of the thing," he agreed readily and knew that he had again put his foot in his mouth. It seemed that no matter what he said to Ruth it came out wrong.

"Here. A little message for you," said Ruth in disgust, handing him the note.

"Free who? Are they nuts? She's not even here!"

"If Baby had been here, would it have made more sense?"

"Don't be ridiculous," he said irritably, watching as Ruth got up.

"Baby's brought us nothing but trouble," she said, stooping down and carefully gathering in her hands the bigger fragments of glass.

"How can you say such a thing?" he uttered, looking down at her, troubled.

"It's the truth," she said, controlling her rage, her face turning a deep crimson.

"You mean because a rock comes sailing—?"

"I don't mean just this," she said, standing up to face him. "Since this whole damn thing started, it's been hell living with you."

Shockley stood with his hands at his sides, facing her.

"I've been difficult, I know," he admitted.

"You've always been difficult. I knew that when I married you. That was part of the package. It also came with the redeeming fact that you cared for me, for us, all of us."

"But I *do*."

"It's not like it used to be," she said, dumping the pieces with a crash into the wastepaper basket. She went to the hall closet to get the vacuum.

"I love you and the children," he said, following on her heels. "Nothing has—"

"Everything's changed. The most important thing in your life is Baby. It's the only thing!" She spun around accusingly.

Shockley tried to reach for the vacuum, but Ruth blocked him.

"Since the day you saw her she's ruled your life, our lives. Admit it."

"She's important. Yes."

"The most important."

"I wouldn't say—" he hedged.

"At least be honest!"

"OK, OK. Right now she's the most important. She's on my mind. I'm not going to deny that."

"You're deserting your own children for someone else's."

"Why must you always speak in absolutes?" he shot back,

and knew that they were at each other because there was no other culprit to blame for the brick—knew it but was still helpless to control his own anger.

"Because absolutes are all you understand."

"I'd better put some plastic over the window," he mumbled, turning to leave.

"Coward!" she called after him, and though Shockley pretended not to hear, the word stung.

16

When Doris returned on Tuesday for her rescheduled hearing, the edge was off her fear and she was now more resolute than timid, convinced that with forceful Mr. Kiely on her side the truth would be out and once and for all she would be free of all these meddling people. The last days had taken their toll in anguish and sleepless nights, she thought, taking a seat on the now-familiar wood bench. Even Baby was tense and restless these days, prone to upset stomachs and fitful sleep. How she wished that people would just let them alone and let them live in peace.

Doris awoke from her thoughts to find a man standing in front of her. He had a large shock of light hair that covered part of his forehead, and with his wide, chubby cheeks and big grin he looked like a young boy. He introduced himself as Robert Bennett.

"Mr. Kiely's associate," he added by way of explanation.

"Where's Mr. Kiely?" asked Doris, puzzled. Baby's eyes moved from her mother to the young man and back again.

"He's asked me to take over your case while he's out of town."

"Out of town?" she echoed.

"Mr. Kiely's on another case," explained Bennett a bit sheepishly.

"Another case? I paid him a thousand dollars to represent me!"

"I'm a lawyer too," said Bennett sympathetically. He was dressed in a three-piece suit that seemed to accent his round, boyish face, and when he spoke there were deep dimples in his cheeks. If this kid is a lawyer, thought Doris, giving him a second look, then he must barely be out of law school.

"I'm sure you're a lawyer," said Doris, trying to control her frustration. "But how can you help me? You don't know the case." In the back of her mind she was wondering how in the world, in just a few minutes, she could possibly go through all those explanations again.

"I've consulted with Mr. Kiely and tried to familiarize myself with your case."

Though he fixed her with his clear eyes that looked honest, the word *tried* stuck in her mind.

Bennett nervously checked his watch. "Shall we go?" he asked tentatively.

"I don't have much of a choice, do I?"

"You do. You could try to request a delay and retain another lawyer."

Doris debated. She saw herself forking over another thousand dollars.

"One way or the other, you have to decide fast," he said, as Doris's thoughts raced around in her head.

Doris nodded reluctantly.

"How old are you?" she asked as they went together through the doors.

"Twenty-eight." He grinned.

"You look a lot younger," she said, but seemed mildly relieved.

"That's Tony Tribble. He's the assistant county attorney," Bennett whispered to Doris as the lanky man with wavy hair approached the judge sitting behind the raised oak bench. Doris and her young lawyer were seated together at a table toward the front of the small courtroom, Baby quietly taking her late-morning bottle, the sounds of Baby's drinking punctuating the momentary silence of the high-ceilinged room. "Tribble is

going to act in the capacity of what you might call a prosecutor—though he's not really a prosecutor. This is supposed
to be something of an informal hearing."

Doris was listening to her lawyer with one ear as she watched
the presiding judge. His name was J. S. Warren, she could see
by the nameplate in front of him. He was a man with gray hair,
deeply set eyes, and hollow cheeks that gave his face a sepulchral look. Beneath his robes, Doris could see that he was bony
and small, but it was his eyes that gripped her attention. They
struck her as cold and distant, as though they had seen too much
misery and anger, as though a wall had been constructed
blocking out all emotion. His manner, too, seemed abrupt and
impatient, rushed.

When Doris turned her attentions back to the proceedings,
county attorney Tribble had already made a short statement and
was requesting permission to bring in a first witness. When the
social services caseworker marched through the door and took
the stand, it came as no surprise to Doris. After being sworn in
and asked a few preliminary questions, the woman was requested by Tribble to summarize her report.

"After receiving the complaint, I attempted to question Mrs.
Rumsey," said Miss Cassaniti, glancing up from her notes to
look at the defendant's table, her eyes falling on Baby for an
inordinately long moment. Tribble cleared his throat to catch
her attention. "I attempted to question the mother," she said,
quickly returning to her file, "but she refused to cooperate with
the investigation. I was also denied access to the premises. I
interviewed a number of the neighbors in an attempt to
corroborate—"

"Your Honor!" Bennett was up on his feet to object. "If we're
going to introduce hearsay—"

"Counselor"—the judge rapped his gavel—"let me remind
you, this is just a hearing, not a trial."

"But an adverse decision from this court has the power to
remove Mrs. Rumsey's child—"

"Continue, please," said the judge, turning back to Miss
Cassaniti. Bennett sank down deflated. He mumbled something apologetic to Doris, noticing how the baby in her arms
had been fixedly watching him. He tried to shift his attention
back to the stand but could hardly wrench his eyes away. There

was something uncannily adult about the child, he thought, and it made him uneasy.

Miss Cassaniti continued to read from her report. From what she had been able to see through the doorway of Mrs. Rumsey's house, she explained, the place appeared to be in a state of disarray and neglect. The outside of the dwelling seemed in general disrepair. There were weeks' worth of garbage on the back porch, uncovered or improperly bagged—an invitation to roaches and rodents. She went on to testify that she interviewed four different neighbors, all of whom expressed serious questions about the infant's welfare. Citing the names of three additional city residents, people whom Doris had never even known existed, Miss Cassaniti indicated that they, on their own initiative, had approached her to state their concern that the baby seemed grossly neglected.

"That's a lie! A horrible lie!" Doris objected loudly to her lawyer.

"Quiet! I want you to warn your client to refrain from any further interruptions," the judge snapped.

Bennett muttered something inaudible.

After a brief and fruitless cross-examination by Bennett, Miss Cassaniti was dismissed from the stand and, at the behest of the county attorney and despite the strenuous objections of Doris's young lawyer, Judge Warren accepted into evidence Miss Cassaniti's entire file.

Following the testimony by the caseworker, Tribble began what seemed an endless parade of witnesses.

He brought in Detective Iacovelli.

"On the twenty-third of June I was called to investigate what was an alleged kidnapping," explained Iacovelli in response to the county attorney's query, the detective looking down at his hands as they wrestled each other.

"And would you tell us what you found?" pressed Tribble.

"What do you mean?" asked Iacovelli, flushing when his eyes met Doris's.

"Would you tell us about the conditions in which this child was living?"

"Well, like I told Mr. Tribble, the place wasn't exactly neat."

"Would you call it unhygenic? Adverse to the health of a newborn infant?"

"I'd seen worse," Iacovelli tried to soften his remarks.

"Please answer the question," ordered the judge.

"I'd call it messy."

"Would you say that it was the proper environment for a newborn—"

"Your Honor!" Bennett was on his feet again, Baby's eyes still on him. "Counsel's leading the witness!"

"Overruled!" Judge Warren brought down his gavel with a bang.

Doris looked over at Bennett and tried to smile encouragingly. He wasn't so bad after all. He was really trying his best, she thought, but Doris couldn't help but wonder how Kiely would have done.

Iacovelli went on to describe the alleged site of the birth.

"It appeared that she had given birth in the hedgerow," he explained.

"In the hedgerow?"

"Yes, sir."

Attorney Tribble looked meaningfully at Judge Warren, who gave a noticeable shudder.

"Thank you," said Tribble, turning away from the stand. "Counselor?" he addressed Doris's lawyer.

"Mr. Iacovelli," said Bennett, rubbing his chin intently as he approached the witness. "You said that you had seen messier homes. Could you elaborate on that?"

"Your Honor!" Tribble was now on his feet. "This is completely irrelevant. The question in point here is whether Miss Rumsey's house was a suitable place for an infant."

"Sustained."

"Isn't it true, Mr. Iacovelli," continued Bennett, "that there are homes in this county, in your experience, housing infants, that are in far worse—?"

"Objection! Counsel is rephrasing the same question."

"Sustained."

Bennett took a long breath and wet his lips. Beads of perspiration were forming on his forehead.

"From what you could see, Mr. Iacovelli, of the interior of Mrs. Rumsey's home, didn't it strike you as one adequate for bringing up a child?"

"Well—" Iacovelli shuffled his feet nervously. "Well—it wasn't *that* bad," he admitted.

144

"And didn't the mother seem loving?"

"Yes. Very definitely so."

"Thank you. No more questions," said Bennett, stopping while still ahead.

Tribble called in his next witness.

"Well," said Mrs. Oltz, drawing a long breath as Doris sat in stunned shock. "After I knew that there was a baby living there, I just took a walk over to have myself a look. I took a peek into the house and, let me tell you, she had that poor little baby stuck into a basket. A dirty, old laundry basket. She didn't have any clothes on. The baby, that is. And it was cold then, damp. Her place was a mess too. For the last months," volunteered Mrs. Oltz, "before she got hold of that baby, Miss Rumsey was sick. You could see it. She could hardly walk. Her clothes were in rags. Why, she didn't even have hardly a pair of shoes on her feet, they were all broken down. And then she got that baby— don't ask me how. I still think she stole it. I mean, did you ever hear of a fifty-nine-year-old woman—"

"Mrs. Oltz, would you please limit yourself to your observations?" said Tribble, bringing her back on track.

Baby, sitting up in Doris's lap, let out a loud yawn. The judge looked over, annoyed.

Mrs. Oltz then went on to explain how the baby looked malnourished, how the mother was exploiting her singing ability, keeping her up to all hours of the night and forcing her to sing for folks, how people would crowd around the house and make nuisances of themselves in the neighborhood, how—

"Mrs. Oltz," said Bennett when his turn came to cross-examine the witness with the birdlike countenance. "You've never had a child, have you?"

"Well, no, but—"

"Please just answer the questions," said Bennett, trying to impeach her testimony.

"Have you ever cared for a child?"

"I did baby-sit for the Muzzys when their mother went to the hospital."

"When was that?"

"Oh, 'bout year or two ago."

"Isn't it true that you don't have any recent and real experience regarding the care of an infant, that you are in no position to judge whether Mrs. Rumsey is an adequate mother?"

"Objection!"

"Overruled."

"Well—I mean, I am a woman." Mrs. Oltz flushed.

"Isn't it also true," he probed, hoping to show preconceived prejudice, "that you think there's something disgusting about a fifty-nine-year-old woman having a baby?"

"Sure is strange, isn't it?" She chuckled.

"Mrs. Oltz, do you drink?"

"Objection! Counsel is—"

"Overruled."

"Do you drink, Mrs. Oltz?" he pressed.

"I have taken an occasional little nip. You know, when we have company or—"

"Had you taken an alcoholic drink before you went over to spy on Mrs. Rumsey through her window?"

"Objection!"

"No! Absolutely not! I was as sober—why, as sober as the judge here sitting on the bench!" she snorted indignantly.

"No more questions," uttered Bennett, turning his back.

After Mrs. Oltz had left the courtroom, Bennett approached the bench.

"Your Honor," he said in a subdued voice, "this is ridiculous. So far, counselor Tribble has not brought in one valid, expert witness."

The judge looked at Tribble.

"Be patient," replied the county attorney, pushing his glasses back up on his nose and, with a confident nod, motioned to the court assistant. The doors opened and Dr. Waterhouse, the pediatrician, appeared.

"Why are they doing this to me?" asked Doris forlornly when Bennett returned to her side.

"Well, the child was underweight," admitted Dr. Waterhouse under questioning. "Yes, I'd say so," said the doctor, taking off his glasses and cleaning them on his handkerchief. Without his spectacles, his eyes looked small and tired.

"Why was she underweight?" pressed Tribble.

"From what I was able to gather, the mother was trying to feed the child solely from her breast."

"On whose advice?"

"On her own."

"Had she ever consulted you before?"

"No."

"Had she ever consulted another pediatrician?"

"Objection!" Bennett jumped to his feet.

Doris, afraid that he was going to blunder into dangerous water, grabbed his sleeve.

"I never did," she warned him in a low whisper, and withdrawing his objection, Bennett slowly returned to his seat.

"Let me amend that," said Tribble magnanimously, looking at his colleague with undisguised sympathy. "Had she ever consulted another pediatrician so far as *you* know?"

"No."

"Did you specifically question her on this point?"

"I did."

When the county attorney was finished, Bennett strode to the witness stand.

"Would you say, doctor, that the child was malnourished?"

"As I said, she was underweight for her age."

"Does that constitute malnourishment?"

"Not necessarily."

"Is being underweight an unusual occurrence among children?"

"It happens."

"Is it always caused by neglect?"

"It can be."

"But you can't specifically say—"

"We've gone through this line of questioning already," said Judge Warren, who wanted to move the case along. He had a long, jammed schedule of hearings, other cases of neglect, child abuse, custody battles, orders of protection for wives whose husbands beat them, women seeking another twenty dollars in child support, men fighting for denied visiting privileges.

"I'm being railroaded," said Doris to her lawyer when the next witness was called. It was Mrs. Rudd, the visiting nurse. "Can't we stop this?"

"You'll have your chance to tell your side of the story," said Bennett, putting a comforting hand on hers. "After their last witness. I promise."

Doris looked at Baby and felt like crying.

Mrs. Rudd began her testimony by substantiating Mrs. Oltz's contention.

"It's certainly no place to raise an infant. Nor is Mrs. Rumsey up to the job. And I base that on my years as a registered nurse. Let me give you an example," said Nurse Rudd all too eagerly. "The child had been suffering from a severe rash, which, because of inattention, had turned into ulcerated sores. I tried to advise Mrs. Rumsey about the child's condition, suggest treatment, but she refused to listen," she continued without prompting. "To top it all off, there was no food in the refrigerator and, until I took the initiative, no way for her to get it. Mrs. Rumsey was in no condition after surgery to administer to her own needs, much less those of a small child."

"And you'd say, without reservation, that this was a case of child neglect?"

"Without reservation," said Mrs. Rudd emphatically.

"Any more witnesses?" asked Judge Warren, who couldn't help but wonder why the county attorney was going in for overkill.

"The people have no further witnesses, Your Honor."

"Do you have any witnesses?" the judge addressed Bennett.

"The defendant, Your Honor, will offer testimony on her own behalf," said Bennett. Trembling, Doris made her way toward the stand, her child clutched possessively in her arms.

"This is all unfair," she said, her lips quivering. "You've all made up your minds. This trial is a sham." Then tears welled in her eyes, and despite her best efforts, she broke down and wept.

"This is a hearing, Miss Rumsey, not a trial," the judge corrected her, apparently unmoved by her tears. "If there's something you wish to say on your behalf you're free to say it," he explained, fixing her with his steely eyes. "Please take a seat."

Doris's lawyer approached the stand and began to question his client gently. He asked her if she knew how to care for a baby, eliciting from Doris the fact that she fed her child regularly, kept her clean and dry and warm. He questioned her about her experience with children, with Doris indicating how she had spent her entire adult life working with children.

The judge sat listening to Doris's testimony and after a few more queries finally interrupted.

"Would counsel have any objection"—he addressed Bennett—"if asked a few questions?"

Bennett nodded his consent.

"Miss Rumsey," said Judge Warren, shifting in his chair and leaning toward Doris as she dabbed at her eyes, "there are a couple of matters this court would like clarified."

Doris blew her nose, snuffled, and looked at him.

"Miss Rumsey, did you have any prenatal care at all?"

Doris shook her head.

"You have to answer with words," he said referring to the stenographer.

"No," she replied, her voice cracking.

"Other than your single visit with Dr. Waterhouse, did you have any postnatal care for the baby?"

"No," she answered again.

"Where is the father?"

Doris mumbled something.

"I'm sorry, what did you say?"

"There is none," said Doris, stroking Baby's cheek.

The judge cocked his head to one side.

"You mean you don't want to identify him, is that it?"

Bennett was hurriedly approaching the bench. The judge held up a warning finger and Bennett obediently froze. Holding his breath Tribble stared at the witness, his eyes narrowing as though sensing a kill.

"No," said Doris hoarsely.

"Let me understand this," said Warren, confused. "You're saying that there *is* no father."

"That's right. That's why I didn't go to any doctors. I didn't even know I was pregnant. And when I realized it I was too ashamed. How could anybody ever have believed me?"

"You maintain," interrupted the judge leaning farther over the bench toward her until she could almost feel his breath flowing past her, "that this is a *virgin* birth?"

Doris hesitated. She looked at Bennett, who was frantically trying to warn her off with his eyes. She glanced at Tribble, who stood to one side of the room, poised. She looked down at Baby. The room became utterly silent.

"Yes," she answered, raising her head and breaking the silence. "Yes. I do."

The judge's face blanched. He fell ominously silent, and only a telltale twitch tugged at the corner of his lips. What this woman was saying was absurd, insane, and it made all the reports and testimony offered this morning suddenly superfluous.

"Counselor"—the judge addressed Bennett—"do you wish to continue?"

Dutifully Doris's lawyer approached the stand and tried to pick up the threads of his previous line of questioning. He asked Doris about where the child slept, if the house had adequate plumbing and heat. He tried to raise the matter of why people might, in view of the child's unusual talent, want to have her removed from Doris's custody. Though he went through all the motions, Doris knew they were already beaten.

When Bennett finished, Doris sat on the stand, drained and empty.

"Thank you, Miss Rumsey," said the judge, dismissing her, but Doris remained rooted in the chair, her eyes dry, her jaw set.

The judge sat at his bench, uneasily fingering his gavel, avoiding the sight of the old woman and her child. Bennett stood waiting at the defendant's table. The stenographer sat at her machine, her hands in her lap, her gaze lowered. The court assistant stood slouching against the outside door. Tribble busied himself closing the notes on his desk. The air seemed to crackle with tension. Baby's eyes began to dart around the room, moving from adult to adult. Deep furrows formed on her forehead. Restlessly she squirmed in her mother's lap. Judge Warren started to speak again, but before he could utter a complete word Baby drew a quick breath and, opening her mouth, began to sing. Mustering her strength she sang out into the courtroom, her notes emerging in an urgent rush, her desperate and compelling plea filling the air.

Tribble looked up from his papers. The court assistant straightened himself. Bennett stared at the child with undisguised bewilderment.

"Quiet that child!" snapped the judge, banging his gavel, "She'll have to be quiet or be removed from the court!" he shouted irritably, loudly rapping his gavel as though trying to drown out her music.

Doris pressed her fingers onto Baby's lips and instantly she stopped.

"Later," whispered Doris, giving her child a kiss, "later."

"We'll have a recess," said the judge, rising abruptly from his chair. "Ten minutes," he said, stalking out through the oak doors that led to his chambers.

After the short recess Judge Warren appeared again from his chambers. Everyone rose and waited for him to take the bench.

"I'm issuing a temporary order of removal pending a dispositional hearing," he said in a noticeably calm voice. "In that period Miss Rumsey will be required to meet the following conditions," he paused and, putting on his glasses, lifted a paper from his desk. Doris's grip tightened on Baby.

"That she undergo a thorough psychiatric examination," read the judge, clearing his throat. "That, following that examination and in the event she receives an evaluation confirming her competency, she radically alter the living conditions in her home so that they are conducive to the raising of a child and meet the standards to be set by the Department of Social Services. That, further, Miss Rumsey obtain assistance with childcare as well as clearly demonstrate her own competency in that area."

"How long is temporary?" Doris asked her lawyer when the judge had finished.

"That depends," said Bennett, poker-faced, determined to leave before they wrenched Baby from her arms.

Andrea Cassaniti turned out to be a blessing of sorts. That such a cooperative young lady came to the position where her judgment would be instrumental in determining Baby's fate was, oddly enough, a direct consequence of Baby's musical gift.

A recent graduate of the university, Miss Cassaniti had been hanging around Ithaca trying to figure out what to do with her life and new degree when, one morning in late August, she stumbled across a crowd assembled around Doris's bench in the park. Edging up to the outside of the mass, Andrea Cassaniti picked up the strains of Baby's music and before the child's song was completed knew that her fate was foreordained: it was here in Ithaca, close to this miraculous child, she was meant to stay.

Hunting around for work, Andrea Cassaniti accepted one of the rare but poorly paying jobs available and in early October became a caseworker for the Department of Social Services.

Shortly thereafter Doris was taken to the hospital for surgery, the Shockleys took over the care of Baby, and the child that had kept Andrea Cassaniti in Ithaca became inaccessible. When Miss Cassaniti was assigned to investigate a complaint alleging Baby's neglect, there could not have been a more fortuitous turn of events, and Andrea Cassaniti was determined not to let the opportunity slip by. In return for placing Baby in the legally sanctioned foster care of Professor Shockley and his wife, Miss Cassaniti extracted a number of small concessions for herself. For her efforts in securing Baby's fostership for the Shockleys as well as appearing before the court, which was to appoint Dr. Shockley guardian *ad litem*—a cozy arrangement empowering him to execute contracts on Baby's behalf—Miss Cassaniti was to be granted the privilege of private audiences with Baby. Further, according to another agreement privately reached between Miss Cassaniti and Professor Shockley, in return for a guarantee of only *pro forma* interference in the matter of Baby's custody (leaving Baby free to travel outside the state), Miss Cassaniti would receive a modest monthly "consultant's fee" intended to supplement her present low wages—said payment to be derived from Baby's future earnings, skimmed before insertion into her court-directed trust fund and to be kept off the books. What had initially seemed like a dull and unrewarding job dealing with the dregs of Ithaca society turned out to be a golden opportunity for Andrea Cassaniti.

"It stinks," mumbled Shockley to himself when Miss Cassaniti finally delivered Baby. "But it's got to be done."

"As soon as things settle down," he later told Ruth, "I want to let Doris move in. We can put her in the guest room."

"To soothe your conscience?"

"Yes. As a matter of fact, I don't enjoy being a bastard. There's no reason to punish her more than necessary."

"Necessary?"

"She's a crazy old lady who backed herself into a corner. Now that the rules are established and she knows she can't bury Baby, as far as I'm concerned she can spend every minute of the day with Baby. It was never my intention to deprive her of her child. Never!"

"Tell it to Doris," said Ruth.

"I will. As soon as the time is ripe."

"Hello. Jacobsen?" he said later on the phone. "Shockley here."

"Professor Shockley," said Jacobsen. "What a pleasure finally to hear your voice."

"We're on," said Shockley, ignoring the snide tone. "We've had some difficulties on this end, but we're all set now."

"Are you sure?"

"Positive."

"Well, that's fine, because I'm not!"

"Look, I'm sorry about all—well, all the back and forth."

"I'm not interested in your sorrys, Shockley. What the hell do you think you're doing? Do you think you can dangle me on a string? Jerk me around any time you want? I don't play games like that!" he shouted.

"We've had problems on this end."

"*You've* had problems!" he whined. "Do you have any idea of the chaos you've created? What you've cost us already? The liabilities we've incurred?"

"Listen, I'm sorry, but it was unavoidable. If you're trying to tell me that you don't want to represent Baby, then just say it."

"I want to represent her all right," said Jacobsen, slowing down. Shockley could hear him puffing furiously on his cigarette on the other end. "It's *you* I don't want to represent."

"What are you talking about?"

"Shockley, if I'm going to take on the child it's going to be under *my* terms."

"Which means?"

"I want a binding agreement with you."

"That's certainly reasonable. I don't—"

"A booking *and* management contract."

"But I'm Baby's manager."

"Not if I'm going to represent her. If you want me, then we tear up our previous agreement, which you've already violated, and start anew. From now on I make the sole decisions as to when and where Baby appears and in what format. I call all the shots."

"That's not acceptable."

"It's got to be."

Shockley sat in stony silence.

"Shockley"—Jacobsen took a long pause—"I understand

you're a good musician. Quite a composer, I hear. You probably are. But let me tell you one thing, you're a hell of a lousy businessman."

"That's never been one of my goals in life."

"Precisely! And at the rate you're going, you're going to end up burning yourself out and getting nowhere. You didn't know what you were doing when you first tried to start a tour, and you don't know what the hell you're doing now when it comes to managing."

Shockley didn't respond.

"Come on, let someone who knows the business take care of the child's affairs," said Jacobsen soothingly.

"You?"

"Exactly," said Jacobsen. His other phone buzzed and for an instant he covered the mouthpiece, then returned. "Look, the pie is big enough for everyone to have a nice, fat slice."

"I'm not after money. I've told you that before."

"Who's talking about money? Here's my suggestion. It's very simple. I'll be her manager; you'll be her impresario. I'll take care of her tours; you'll attend to her artistic needs. As a businessman, I'll direct the course of her business life. As an artist, you will attend to her artistic life," explained Jacobsen, his voice all sweetness.

Shockley swallowed uneasily, his mind racing. Although there were other booking agents, none even approached Jacobsen. His major concern, he reminded himself, was to ensure that Baby had an audience. What difference did it really make who her manager was? When it came to Baby's music, he could not allow his own feelings to interfere.

"She'll always be your find," said Jacobsen, breaking into Shockley's thoughts. "No one can ever take that away from you. And through me she will have access to places you could only hope for in your wildest dreams."

Shockley sat at the phone, playing with a pencil.

"Well, what's it going to be? In or out? I don't have all day."

"OK," said Shockley tensely. "I'll go along with it."

"In writing."

"I'm a man of my word."

"One thing I've learned in this business is, always get it in writing from an artist," he said, his lips caressing the word *artist*. It flattered Shockley. "You'll get a contract in the mail tomorrow. I want it all in writing."

"In writing."

"It'll protect you also."

"What do you mean?"

"Nothing. Just that," he said offhandedly. "Someone could grab Baby from you too," he said and laughed loudly.

"Too?" asked Shockley, but the connection was already broken.

17

Olive Eldridge sat on the edge of her seat, her purse in her lap, both hands planted squarely on it. Uneasily she looked around the sterile fourth-floor visiting room of the Willard Psychiatric Center. Green cinderblock walls. Barred windows looking out on a gray, snowy day. Near her sat a woman with thinning hair and drooping features, absently fingering the seam of her gown, oblivious of her husband's imploring voice. A teenage boy with wild eyes swimming in their sockets stood in front of his mother, giggling hysterically into his hands. An old man on the other side of the room was rocking his body back and forth, peering over his shoulder at Olive as he whispered conspiratorially to a visitor.

When Olive saw Doris coming down the corridor with the attendant she immediately rose to her feet, watching anxiously as her friend approached. As Doris moved toward her in a slow, shuffling gait, Olive couldn't help but see that there was something decidedly truculent and determined in the way she proceeded. Though hunched over as Olive had always known her, Doris seemed to move like an aging, wounded cat, threatened, poised, and ready to spring.

"I came as soon as I heard," she said, hugging Doris. "Oh, dear, I'm so sorry."

"I'm glad you came," Doris said, and characteristically there was no self-pity in her voice. "I didn't want to call you, but I really didn't know who else to contact at this point."

"Hush!" said Olive lovingly. "Now why don't you just tell me what's going on?"

"There is nothing much to tell." Doris pulled her hospital robe tight around her. "Somebody complained that I was neglecting Baby. Before I knew what happened I was in court, they were taking her away from me, and they stuck me here because I'm supposed to be nuts," she said angrily.

"Why didn't you get yourself a lawyer right away?"

"I did," explained Doris, and she went on to tell Olive the story of Kiely, how he had seemed so competent and optimistic and how, in the last minute, Mr. Bennett had appeared in his place.

"Did you say Kiely?" asked Olive, as though disbelieving her ears.

"Frank Kiely. On Tioga Street. I had heard you mention his name once and I figured that—"

"Oh, dear Jesus!" said Olive, putting her hands to her graying temples and shaking her head.

"No?"

"No. Absolutely no. The reason I had mentioned Kiely was because my sister-in-law, you know Frieda, had gone to him because of a lawsuit. He ended up botching the whole case and sticking in one of his 'associates.' If anything, I was warning you away from the creep. Not recommending him. Kiely? Why, he's absolutely worthless. A bum. A slumlord up in Collegetown."

"Oh my," said Doris, now suddenly remembering the connection in which she had seen his picture in the paper.

"He's the one who's been accused of all those building violations. It was in one of his hovels that those four students burned to death last year. Doris, honey, he wasn't on another case. He just took your money and sent in one of his flunkies, that's all."

"I've got to get out of here," said Doris, searching her friend's face.

"We'll get you out. We'll start by getting you a lawyer. A good one, this time."

"Then I want Baby back," said Doris, getting up her pluck.

"I'm with you."

"Olive, I'm so tired of being such a soft touch, of being pushed around."

"Good girl!" Olive beamed.

"I'm going to fight this thing to the end. If it takes every last penny and every last ounce of strength I have, I'm going to get Baby back. I'll get justice even if I have to go all the way to the Supreme Court," said Doris, getting carried away.

"Heavens!" said Olive. "Maybe you *are* crazy." She slapped Doris affectionately on the knee and laughed. She had been afraid to come here and find Doris a vegetable. "There's a young lawyer I know," said Olive, drawing close to Doris.

"Not another young one," said Doris apprehensively.

"Oh, but he's a fine young man. His name is Harry Terkel. From what I hear he's one of the best in town. A real fighter. Brash and hard driving—and that's what you need."

"Is he expensive?"

"Probably. But you get what you pay for. That's what my Al always used to say. Don't worry about the money. It'll come from somewhere. It always does," said Olive, taking Doris's hand. "Now, let's just concentrate on getting you out of here and getting Baby back to her mother, right?"

Doris nodded but looked at her askance.

"Are they giving you any pills here?" asked Olive suspiciously.

Doris lifted a flap in her gown and with a guilty grin showed her a pocket full.

"They try," she said.

"Lord!" Olive exclaimed. "How did you do that?"

"It wasn't easy," said Doris proudly. "But they're not going to mess me up. I know what I want."

"Good for you," said Olive, standing up and retrieving her coat. Olive had always been a quiet rebel herself, and Doris's gumption was certainly impressive.

"You know, Olive," said Doris, her courage waning and her mood turning melancholy as she watched her friend buttoning her overcoat, "I've spent a lot of time here thinking about all that's happened. And it's funny," she laughed sadly to herself.

"What's that?"

"The more I think about it, the less I understand. I bring something beautiful into the world and—what happens to

157

me?—I'm crucified for it. I don't understand it. Just don't understand. Why, Olive?" Doris shook her head.

"Doesn't make any more sense to me, honey. But for that matter, most everything these days doesn't make sense," she said, tying a scarf around her neck and putting on her fur hat. Outside it was still snowing, and Olive didn't relish the slippery trip back to Ithaca. "These are wicked times," said Olive, as much for her own sake as Doris's. "And it seems as if all the junk's floating to the top instead of sinking. Well, got to take care of some business for a friend." Olive winked and, giving Doris a peck on the cheek, hurried down the corridor to the locked steel door.

"What do you mean 'strange'?" Shockley questioned his eldest daughter when he came home from work on Tuesday. "Either Baby sings or she doesn't."

"Well, she sings," Annette explained uneasily. "I mean, she starts to sing," she corrected herself. "But then just stops after a couple of notes. She just sort of runs out of steam."

"Baby's been acting funny ever since she came back," said Julie, taking Baby's hand in hers as Baby sat propped up, listless, in her seat on the kitchen table, her dish of food getting cold.

"I think she's sad," said Annette, stroking Baby's face. Baby looked up at her, her appearance decidely dejected. Her cheeks were slack, her mouth slightly open, her forehead wrinkled like an old person's.

"Maybe she misses her mother," said Randy, joining the group.

"She's been with us before," said Shockley, trying to stem the panic that was edging closer. In four days Baby was scheduled to make her first gala public appearance in Cleveland's Severance Hall. Everything was set. Jacobsen had taken care of all the publicity, pouring a small fortune into advertisements. The media had been primed, the papers full of stories. Tickets were being sold. Another couple of days and it would be impossible to halt the juggernaut without lawsuits and losses and irreparable damage to Baby's image. The word *reliable* rang through Shockley's brain and he trembled.

"Maybe she was starved and didn't get enough food," said

158

Julie, looking compassionately at Baby with her own serious eyes. "And now she doesn't have enough energy."

"Put some music on," ordered Shockley. "Here, heat up her food again," he said to Annette. "Come on, sweetie," he tickled Baby under her chin, trying to elicit a smile. "Gee, she seems cold," he said, touching her cheek, then forehead.

"Maybe she's sick and dying," said Cindy, sauntering by casually and driving a stake into Shockley's heart.

"Don't talk like that!"

"It was just an idea. Ideas don't hurt. You've always said—"

"Not now!" Shockley snapped. "Please. Come on, Baby. Sing a little song for us. La la la," he tried to induce her with his own voice, but Baby just turned away and stared out the window off into the snowy distance. "Shit!" he muttered. "Hell, don't put on Wagner!" Shockley called out when the music came blasting over the speakers in the kitchen. "Put on something light. Try Vivaldi. Or even some pop music. That's it. Put some junk on. Maybe that'll bring her out of it."

But it didn't.

"I knew I shouldn't have gone to classes today!" said Shockley to his wife, passing back and forth in the kitchen while dinner cooked. "The first day she's back and look what happens."

"I doubt if your being here would have made any difference. I don't think she's sick. She doesn't have a fever. She looks well to me. She's just a little confused, probably. It's not good to shuffle a little baby back and forth," said Ruth in her usual levelheaded way.

"Do you think her singing's winding down?" he asked later, fear creeping into his voice.

"Who knows?" said Ruth. "If it is, I doubt if there's anything you could do about it, anyway."

"She's got a concert on Sunday. That's only four days away," he said, visions of Jacobsen's skull-like head appearing before him.

"She *may* have a concert on Sunday."

"I'm quitting the university. This is the end. The last straw. I'm not leaving Baby's side. Not for a minute."

"I was waiting for that," said Ruth fatalistically.

"It was inevitable. I warned you."

"You didn't have to warn me. You just have to figure out how to pay the mortgage and the orthodontist and the car payments. The peanuts they call my salary certainly won't keep this production on the road."

Shockley went upstairs to check on Baby. She was lying fast asleep in her crib, her thumb in her mouth, her little rear raised. He turned on a small light and brought his face close to hers, the milky smell of Baby reaching his nose as he listened to her breathe. As she slept, he noticed, her eyebrows were busily knitting, her lips tensely moving about her thumb, her cheeks working away.

"Please, Baby," he whispered forlornly, stroking her tiny back, "don't stop singing. We love you so much. We need your music. Don't let us down," he murmured, and suddenly realized that he was weeping, large tears careening down his cheeks and falling onto her curled-up little form.

Doris turned sixty on the Friday she was released from Willard. She has spent a scant four days undergoing "observation," but it might easily have gone on to be four weeks or even four months had not Harry Terkel deftly pulled a few strings. Considering her ordeal, the indignity of being held with all the other crazies, real and suspected, Doris looked remarkably fit. For the first time since her operation she had a chance to eat regular meals, get nursing help as well as some direly needed rest, and it showed. Her incarceration also produced a report for Judge Warren and the family court, a copy of which was already in Terkel's possession. He was, in fact, reading it when Doris arrived at his office. Basically, what the evaluation—a consensus report by three resident psychiatrists—stated was that "Though Miss Rumsey was capable of holding rational and logical discussions, was cognizant of her surroundings, aware of her actions and how they affected others, she still suffered from religious delusions; Miss Rumsey persisted in the belief that she had given birth to a child through a virgin birth brought about by divine intervention. Exhibiting certain paranoid tendencies, she nonetheless impressed the observers as being, for the present at least, lucid, responsible, and capable of caring for herself in a noninstitutional setting."

"That's damning you with faint praise," said Terkel, putting down the report. "What they're saying is that you're as sane as the other nuts that they've been turning loose lately because of state cutbacks."

Doris looked back at him in surprise.

"*I'm* not saying that," he said, pointing to himself. "I'm just reading between the lines," he laughed loudly. Terkel was a little man, probably in his early thirties, who had dark, curly hair, a pug nose, and seemed to bristle with energy. Whenever he spoke, his hands were in motion, pointing, gesticulating, waving in the air, and Doris wondered if he were doing it for her benefit. "A noninstitutional setting," he repeated and laughed, shaking his head. "That's big of them. Listen, Doris—can I call you Doris?—don't feel bad. If they put me in there, I wouldn't get half as good grades," he laughed again, and Doris nodded her head in agreement. "Sending you for psychiatric evaluation—what nonsense!" Terkel snorted. "Jack Warren should have been thrown off the bench years ago. He's totally incompetent. And "—he took a breath—"if you had had decent counsel, you would have known from the beginning that you didn't have to identify the father."

"But there was none."

Terkel's smile faded.

"Oh," he said and stood up and walked over to the window. From his office on Court Street he could see the brick building that was the sheriff's office and jail. On the third floor a prisoner, one of his clients, stood with his face pressed against the barred, snow-encrusted window. The man was awaiting trial for the rape-murder of his mother. Terkel knew all about sanity—sanity and insanity. It was getting to be his specialty in Tompkins County. That and criminal law. From the vantage point of the cases that staggered through his office, the county seemed to be crawling with crazies, crooks, druggies, or a combination thereof. Eccentric old ladies didn't throw him.

"First of all, let's lay down some ground rules, OK?"

"Depends," said Doris cautiously as he turned back. She was struck by how small Terkel actually was when he stood. He was about the height of a large midget or a small teenager.

"If you want me to represent you, you have to agree to them."

"Well?" she said, wanting to hear him out before making any commitments.

"First of all, if any question arises in any further hearings, 'examinations' "—he lifted the psychiatric report and dropped it back on his desk—"court proceedings, depositions— whatever—you will neither mention not make any allusions to a virgin birth."

"But—"

"I don't care if it's true or untrue. For all we know the good Lord himself came down out of the skies and—and—well, whatever." He cleared his throat. "If you're ever asked again in court, just say that you refuse to identify the father. Period."

"I don't want to lie."

"It's not a lie!" Terkel tore at his hair as Doris watched imperturbably. "It's an evasion. If you had done it to begin with, you wouldn't be in quite such a mess today. Please."

"OK," sighed Doris, who was not used to lying *or* evading.

"Next thing. Make sure that your person and living premises are immaculate." Terkel stopped short, recognizing his unfortunate pun. "You know, buy a couple of new dresses. Get in a cleaning lady. Scrub the place down from A to Z. Hang up some bright curtains. Go to the beauty parlor. Get your hair and nails done. And let everybody know it."

"What about Baby?" questioned Doris, trying to bring the lawyer back on base.

"That's exactly what I'm talking about. I'm getting to the gist of the matter. What I'm trying to do is establish that, first"—he raised one finger—"you are not only a fit mother but also a loving, competent, and totally sane one. For that we're going to send you to two psychiatrists of *my* choosing for evaluation." Terkel paused to let it sink in. When Doris didn't object, he continued. "Second," he said, adding another finger forming a victory sign, "we are going to attempt to substantiate collusion."

"All that time I had to myself back at Willard," said Doris, catching the spark of Terkel's enthusiasm, "all that time I kept wondering, of all those witnesses they brought in—"

"Noticeably absent was Mr. Shockley. Yes. Funny, isn't it?" Terkel grinned, pleased with his client. "Equally odd is the fact that Mr. and Mrs. Shockley were given custody of your child. I did a little snooping around yesterday and I learned that it was Miss Cassaniti, the young lady who testified against you at the hearing, who conveniently arranged for the Shockleys to have foster care. Which brings me back to my second point. We're going to try to show collusion between this Shockley character and our Miss Cassaniti—whoever the hell she is. Also, if possible, I'm going to try to establish some connection between Shockley and the other witnesses."

"I wouldn't want him to go to jail," said Doris worriedly.

"Oh!" Terkel slapped his head dramatically. "He can steal your child, stick you in Willard for an indeterminate sentence, and you don't want him to go to jail? Miss Rumsey, Doris," he brought himself close to her, his hands outstretched, his head thrown back.

"I just believe that two wrongs don't make a right."

"I wish I had you for an adversary," he said, rolling his eyes heavenward.

"I don't think Professor Shockley really meant evil. I think he just couldn't help himself. And, in his way, he felt he was doing it for Baby's sake."

"You're a true Christian," said Terkel, who wasn't.

Doris just shrugged.

"Now. Where were we? Yes. Our attack," said Terkel, checking his watch and beginning to speak quickly. "Point three"—he resumed with his fingers—"I'm going to file a notice of appeal today with the family court. Four, I'm also immediately filing a brief with the appellate division in Albany."

Doris smiled. She liked Terkel's forthrightness. Particularly, she liked the word *immediately*.

"How long will it take?" she asked. "Until I get Baby back, I mean."

"That depends."

"On what?"

"It can take some time for the appellate court to get to our brief."

"How long?"

"Well"—he hedged—"they're swamped. I suspect, it could take a few months. Four, maybe five," he said, almost timidly.

"Ooooh," said Doris, letting out a pained sigh.

"I'll try to petition the appellate court that your case be given preference. We'll get it moved up if I can convince them it's a critical case."

"But it *is*," insisted Doris.

"Yes. To you and me. But we have to convince an appellate judge," explained Terkel, watching Doris's initial enthusiasm start to wilt. "Look, I'm going to attempt something else," he

163

said, hoping to buck up her spirits. "But I don't want you to hold your breath."

Doris nodded.

"Before I do anything else, I'm going to petition the appellate court for a stay of the lower court's order pending review. To get the stay, I'd have to show that we'll prevail in the ultimate decision. If we got it, Baby would be returned to you prior to any rehearing."

Doris smiled at the prospect.

"I said *if*," cautioned Terkel uneasily. "It's a long shot. You've got to understand that. I don't want you getting your hopes up and then have them dashed. With the child already removed from your custody it's going to be an uphill fight. It's going to take some time though we *will* prevail. I just want you to try and be patient. Please," he said, touching her gently with his hand. "I know what you've been through and what you're going through."

"Do you?"

"I'm a father. I can understand." He glanced again out the window at the brick prison. "But look at it this way. You *do* have visiting privileges. You're *out* of Willard. And we've got a heck of a good chance to win this case. Try to look on the bright side of things."

"I am, but it's not very bright without Baby."

"Go see her."

"I don't know if I could bear to see her and then have to leave."

"Take each day at a time."

"I do. I will. The days are OK. It's the nights, Mr. Terkel, the nights."

"I'll be in your corner fighting for you."

"I'm counting on it."

There was a silence. It filled Doris with a sense of déjà vu, except that this had actually occurred before. In Kiely's office. And at about the same time in the course of the conversation.

"And your fees?" asked Doris, saving Mr. Terkel the trouble.

"It's going to run into money."

"I thought you'd say that."

"I understand your circumstances. But you must also understand that there are going to be out-of-pocket expenses to meet.

For an appeal there have to be twenty printed copies of a bound brief. I'm going to have to go to the appellate court in Albany. Maybe a few times. You're going to have to pay for the private psychiatrists' evaluations. There'll probably be a few visits to each one. These men are highly respected, the best in the profession. Their word carries weight in this state. I'll see to it that they give you a break, but they're not cheap."

"How much?"

"You'll have to travel to Rochester and New York to see them. There'll be overnight lodgings. Bus or plane fare," he continued his litany. "There's—"

"Altogether. What do you think?"

"Then there are my fees," he continued obliviously. "I'm very expensive. In your case I'll make an adjustment. I'm interested in your case," he said, sounding sincere.

"Well?" she pressed. "I have to know."

"I'd figure if I were you probably—in the neighborhood of a few thousand, minimum."

"That much?"

"If you want to protect your rights, you're going to have to pay for it."

"I don't think I have that much."

"You mean to say that after all these years of working you don't have any savings?" he asked puzzled.

"Well, I was never much of a saver," Doris admitted reluctantly. "Being alone, whatever extra I had I, well, I usually sent away."

"To whom?"

"Till now I was sending money to my children."

"Your children?" he asked, flabbergasted, his eyes nearly popping. "You didn't tell me anything about—"

"They're not really my children." She smiled. "They're foster children, overseas. You know. Here," she said and, opening her purse, took out pictures of the same children whose photos sat taped to her living room mirror.

Terkel rummaged through the stack.

"This is wonderful!" he exclaimed. "How long have you been doing this?"

"Well, these six for the last four, no five, years, but before them there were others."

"Doris Rumsey! This, this," he said, holding aloft the pictures, "is what, in the end, is going to save you. When the court finds out that you've been supporting six other children, that—" Terkel drew a breath. "We're going to win back Baby. That I can assure you—I think."

"If I can solve the money problem."

"Yes," he said, rubbing his chin thoughtfully. "But there must be a way. Your salary?"

"I'm on leave without salary. The earliest I could go back is next fall. I'm still too young for early retirement."

"You could"—Terkel thought to himself—"go on disability. You were ill, you had a—"

"No!" said Doris firmly. "If I applied for disability that would be just one more reason not to let me have Baby back."

"Good. Good thinking."

"I do have a house."

"Yes." Terkel nodded and waited.

"I suppose I could sell it."

"You could."

"And rent somewhere," she said, blinking madly to hide the tears that threatened to come.

"It'd only be temporary," said Terkel firmly. "After, when you get Baby back and you're feeling better, you could return to your old job."

"Yes," said Doris. "I was hoping to."

"Look, Doris. I'm not worried about my fees," he said, sensing her distress. "If you can just cover the real, out-of-pocket expenses, I'll help you with the rest. If things weren't quite so tight on my end, why, I'd cover the whole—"

Doris cut him off. "I wouldn't think of it. I'll get the money. I'll manage," she said stoically.

"Now, there's only one thing more," said Terkel.

"Yes?"

"I want you to promise that you're not going to worry, that you'll let me do the worrying for both of us."

"I promise." Doris smiled confidently, knowing that she had finally found one terrific lawyer.

"It's not going to be easy. It'll be a hard, protracted fight."

"I understand."

"But we'll take it step by step. Cross one bridge at a time." He smiled, and a minute after she left, he rushed off, late, to the

166

criminal court, where a jury selection awaited his ministrations.

"She's singing! She's singing!" rejoiced Shockley, waltzing through the house with Baby.

"Ruth! Baby's singing again!" he exploded over the phone after having a secretary summon his wife out in the middle of class.

"Thank goodness," said Ruth, relieved. She, too, had been worried that something was wrong with Baby, but for different reasons from her husband's worries.

"She sang two complete songs already. Two songs," he bubbled. "And—listen!" He held Baby close to the receiver. "You hear that? It's another one. A new one! Do you hear it?"

"Yes, I do," she said, and through the line Ruth could hear the makings of a joyous song that seemed to echo Shockley's sense of deliverance.

"She's happy! She's chirping like a happy little bird! You can pack your bags; we're off to Cleveland."

"Count me out," said Ruth quietly.

"You still mad at me for making you trick Doris?"

"That and all the lies I had to tell."

"I'm sorry. How many times do I have to say it? It's past. Let's forget it. I just want you to come along to Cleveland, to be with me for the gala opening. Please. You'll have a swell time; you'll see."

"I doubt it."

"Oh, come on, darling, give it a chance. Give me a chance. And Baby needs you too."

"Well—"

"I swear to you, Ruth, I'll never again in this lifetime ask you to do anything that goes against your own scruples."

"Is it *really* so important that I come along?"

"Yes. For me it is."

"It's just going to cost more money."

"I don't care. I can't worry about money at a time like this."

"Money is exceedingly tight right now," explained Mrs. Cornish, the real estate lady from Futterman's Showcase of Homes, surveying the downstairs of Doris's home. "Interest rates are skyrocketing. Mortgage pools are drying up. The banks have even stopped giving conventional mortgages," she said, stepping into the first floor half-bath.

Mrs. Cornish peeked into the hall closet and jotted a note on her clipboard.

"I'm telling you all this, Mrs. Rumsey, so you don't get your hopes up for a quick sale. We're by far the best in the business," she said, moving briskly over to the staircase, "but even for us it's not going to be easy. If we put it on multiple listing maybe we can sell it by spring. I say maybe. Mind if I go upstairs?"

Doris nodded and was about to speak, but Mrs. Cornish was already heading up to the second floor.

"I really can't wait until spring," said Doris, tagging behind the skinny woman with horn-rimmed glasses as she tramped up the stairs.

"Being a college town, this is a seasonal market," said Mrs. Cornish, checking out the bathroom. "Oh, you've got one of those old tubs with feet. I just love those," she remarked, noting on her form the absence of tile. "Now, with winter here, there just isn't much movement in the housing market. Is that another bedroom there?"

"I need the money now," explained Doris as Mrs. Cornish breezed through the second bedroom.

"Well," said the real estate woman, standing in the middle of the small room and turning full circle. "If you'd be willing to sell on land contract or hold a mortgage, that might expedite matters. You know, a small down payment to cover the commission and closing costs. Amortized, it would give you a tidy little something for retirement."

"I don't need a retirement, Mrs. Cornish. I need cash. Immediately."

"Oh, I see," said the saleslady. "Is that the attic up there?" she pointed with her pencil.

"Yes," said Doris, exasperated, as Mrs. Cornish went up by herself into the icy attic to check for roof leaks.

"That could be finished off into a nice study," she said, coming down the stairs and writing it down. "With a little spiffing up, a little modernization, this would make a very nice starter home for a young couple."

Doris followed her back down the stairs as she went back into the kitchen.

"Those cabinets and the sink would have to be changed. The

floors redone. The walls stripped," recited Mrs. Cornish, letting her imagination run.

In her mind's eye, Doris could see the young couple moving in, ripping out the cabinets and sink and walls. Too, she could see the reproving looks of her dead parents. She tried not to dwell on the agonizing task that lay ahead, of moving, of going through two generations of belongings and deciding what was to be eliminated forever.

"It's all a function of price," Mrs. Cornish explained later, when they were seated in Doris's living room. She took a small, cautious sip of her coffee and finally looked Doris in the eye. "If you're willing to lower the price so that it becomes sufficiently attractive, there are always people with cash watching the market and ready to step in."

"How low and how fast?"

"Tomorrow," said Mrs. Cornish, offering a strained laugh. "For instance, I know a gentleman with just oodles of ready cash. He's a lawyer here in town. All I have to do is give him a call."

"His name isn't Kiely, is it?" asked Doris.

"Why—Why, yes!" Mrs. Cornish, admitted, taken aback. "But how did you know?"

18

"What's going on?" asked Shockley.

"Let me explain. There isn't much time," said Jacobsen, anxiously checking his watch.

Dressed in a new tuxedo Shockley was standing in the stage manager's office in Severance Hall clutching Baby and looking bewildered. On stage, behind the curtain, the Cleveland Symphony was tuning up as the last of the audience were taking their seats in the cavernous hall.

"I don't get it. What's the orchestra for?" asked Shockley. "This isn't the way I planned it."

"That's what I'm trying to explain. If you'd just listen for a second." Jacobsen gritted his teeth. "Look, there are two ways of doing things. You can either throw Baby out on that stage cold with the audience unprimed and hope for the best. Or"—he paused, wetting his heavy lips—"or, you can—Oh." Jacobsen spun around as a man in powder-blue tux and garishly frilled shirt peeked his head into the office. "Jud!" he exclaimed, waving him in. "Just the man I was looking for. I want you to meet Dr. Shockley and, of course, our little star here." Jacobsen smiled at Baby, who was all spiffed up for the occasion in a red dress.

"Well, well," said Osgood in the deep, resonant voice that was his trademark. He chuckled. "This is certainly a great pleasure for me," he said, pumping Shockley's limp hand and chucking Baby under her chin. Shockley looked at the man with unveiled surprise. He didn't need any introduction. Anyone who had ever watched television in America could spot that high-cheeked countenance a mile away. With his toothy smile and self-assured manner, Judson Osgood was a household name, a living piece of broadcasting history who over the last decades had hosted innumerable variety shows, celebrity awards, and television specials. Trying not to stare, Shockley took a second look at the man. Though Osgood was getting on in years, he looked remarkably trim and vigorous. Standing next to him, Shockley was struck by how much shorter he seemed in real life and, despite the layers of makeup, Shockley could see that the taut, masklike skin on Osgood's face was pockmarked like the surface of a meteor-impaled planet. Nonetheless, Osgood impressed Shockley as a strikingly handsome man, as good as or better looking than he appeared on the tube—the performer filling the room with his notable presence.

"Well, shall we get on with the show?" said Jacobsen, sounding deliberately cheery.

"Fine. I'll take Baby now," said Osgood, stretching out his arms and flashing his famous smile.

"Take Baby?"

"Yes."

"No!"

"I'm not going to keep her." Osgood laughed good-naturedly. "I'm just going to introduce her, that's all." He smiled at Baby, who was watching him curiously.

"She stays with me." Shockley hung on to Baby.

"Shockley, let's be sensible. You're not a performer," said Jacobsen, trying to ease Baby from his arms. "What do you know about showmanship, huh? This thing calls for a professional. Now give me the kid and let's get this show on the road."

"I understood that *I* was going to take Baby out on stage."

"There was never any such understanding. I would hardly have agreed to such a thing."

"Come on, Professor Shockley." Osgood smiled patronizingly. "Be reasonable. What's the difference who takes her out, huh?"

"Shockley, we've got to hurry," insisted Jacobsen tensely. "You're being very difficult and I can't stand here arguing with you. It's too late. It's all been carefully rehearsed."

"For two days we've been busting our asses preparing for this show," said Osgood, looking hurt.

"The program's printed and the audience is out there now, reading it."

"Do you want to screw up everything in the last minute?"

"I've got to think about this," said Shockley, perplexed and outgunned.

"Don't worry. You'll get to take more bows than your back can stand," said Osgood, trying to sound comforting. He was beginning to sweat, large drops running through his makeup.

"Three minutes to curtain!" A stagehand popped his head into the office. "We've got a packed house out there, Mr. Jacobsen. S.R.O.!"

"Look. If this thing is to come off without a hitch, everyone has to do the job he's best at," said Jacobsen, speaking in a rapid-fire manner. "I'm the manager. You're the impresario. And Jud here is the showman," he said, pointing in turn to each of them, his finger trembling. "And, of course, Baby is the star. We should never forget that." He touched her cheek with his bony hand. Baby opened her mouth wide and burped.

"One minute!" called the stagehand.

"Shockley. For God's sake, let him have the baby!" said Jacobsen, turning a deep crimson, his voice low and controlled and tense.

Shockley's gaze swung from one to the other.

"Let him have her. Trust him. He's not going to *eat* the child."

"Relax," said Osgood, massaging Shockley's shoulder with his hand. When he smiled, his makeup began to crack at the crow's-feet around the eyes.

"Shockley, if you go out you'll fuck it up permanently. Let Osgood do it; he's the best in the world. Stop bucking everything."

"Go with the flow," urged Osgood soothingly.

"Do what's best for Baby, not what's best for yourself."

"Forget your own ego, man."

"It isn't ego," Shockley objected.

"Then what is it?" asked Osgood, fixing him with his hard eyes.

"I don't want Baby out of my sight."

"She'll be in your sight." Jacobsen held out his hands. "You'll see her. It's as simple as that."

"You can't use microphones. Remember, no microphones. It won't work with them."

"No microphones," Jacobsen echoed indulgently. "I promised you and I'm a man of my word."

Slowly Shockley released his hold on Baby.

"Good," said Jacobsen, sighing in relief. "Good," he mumbled, taking out a handkerchief and wiping the beads of perspiration from his upper lip as Osgood dashed from the room with Baby.

By the time Shockley reached his seat, the curtain was up and Isaac Popov, the famous Russian exile conductor/composer was mounting the podium to the loud applause of the audience. On stage the orchestra had risen to its feet, the violinists vigorously tapping their bows.

"You're here?" asked Ruth, surprised as her husband pulled an extra chair in the box next to her and sat down.

"Change of plans," he said in a clipped, lowered voice barely audible over the dying applause.

"So I see," she said, looking at her program.

Putting on his glasses, Shockley took the program. Quickly he scanned it, his eyes picking up on the first sweep the names of Popov and Osgood. In bold letters at the top of the bill stood:

BABY IN CONCERT

At the bottom in small caps was:

A JACOBSEN/SHOCKLEY PRODUCTION

Shockley went back over the program and began to read. For the occasion, explained a short paragraph, Isaac Popov had been commissioned to write and conduct an original work called *Ode to Baby*. After the orchestral piece there would be an introduction by Osgood and then, finally, Baby was to sing.

"How's Baby," whispered Ruth.

"Calm," he said, looking out from their box over the vast hall. Searching among the sea of elegantly dressed humanity, Shockley couldn't locate a single empty seat. "Jud Osgood's going to present her," he said, trying to sound upbeat.

"Yes. I saw his name on the program," she answered woodenly.

"I'll introduce you later." He gave an uneasy smile.

Without reply Ruth turned back to the stage.

After a few stray whispers the audience fell silent.

Popov stood frozen at the podium, waiting, baton poised, his eyes ranging over his players.

The orchestra tensed. The violinists raised their bows. The horns glistened in the overhead lights. A drummer behind the kettles took a last-minute squint at his notes.

Popov brought down his baton in a swift stroke, and the orchestra broke into a deafening thunderclap rocking the hall—the explosion quickly followed by the violins bowing furiously. The opening reminded Ruth of the brick bursting through her window. To Shockley it brought to mind the explosive birth of a planet.

The violence of the opening soon gave way to a melodic strain as the music moved into a cloying passage that to Shockley sounded like the worst of Mozart, Brahms, and Strauss rolled into one sticky ball.

Ruth watched as the Russian went through his theatrics—Popov leaning into the music, gyrating his torso, jumping up and down on his stubby, little legs, his long mane of graying hair flying behind him.

The music became more ethereal, taking on a cosmic, eerie tone—the violins following a tremulous line, the horns growing in the distance, promising revelation. The music set Shockley's hair on end, giving him chills. It was having the same effect on the audience. Maybe Jacobsen really did know what he was doing, it occurred to him as the theme began to fade and the lights on the orchestra slowly dimmed.

"Ladies and Gentlemen," announced a disembodied voice. "Mr. Judson Osgood!"

There was a brief flurry of applause, but the clapping failed to break the spell of the music that continued to issue from the darkened stage. A lone light reached out from above the rear balcony and caught Osgood as he marched solemnly out onto the stage approaching a microphone that rose out of the floor, his powder-blue tuxedo blazing brightly in the spotlight.

"Once in a small eternity," he intoned, his deep voice filling the hall and reverberating off the walls, "the earth is blessed with a miracle." The violins began to pick up. "A miracle of such profundity that humanity, people everywhere, must stop." The drums were now picking up, thudding ominously in the background. "Stop!"

The music stopped short, and the audience, as though dangled on a thin filament, seemed to hold its breath lest the string snap. A lone flute began to play, penetrating the stillness with haunting refrain.

"Stop and behold."

The oboes and violins began to join in behind the high flute. Shockley felt himself sweating. His shirt was damp, and perspiration seemed to ooze from every pore.

"And I saw an angel standing in the sun," quoted Osgood from the Book of Revelation, "who cried in a loud voice to all the birds. . . ."

Shockley's throat felt parched, and he swallowed tensely. For an instant he glanced over at Ruth, who sat stiffly in her seat, then quickly shifted his eyes back to the stage as Osgood's voice began to rise compellingly.

"The miracle is *now* and it is *here*," cried Osgood, as the kettledrums thundered deafeningly and a pair of beams suddenly shot across from opposite ends of the hall, training their lights on the pit at the forefront of the stage.

An audible sigh traveled up over the audience, moving from front to rear like a surging wave.

"For us to *behold!*" exclaimed Osgood, as Shockley glimpsed something bright rising up from the blackened pit.

Shockley leaned forward against the railing of the box and stared. There, sitting in a nest of white satin ruffles, was Baby, slowly rising out of the dark. The child's face was rouged, her lips painted, and in that satin-ruffled seat she looked as though she were entombed in a sarcophagus. Looking on in stunned silence Shockley noticed that instead of her red dress, she was clad in a pink gown trimmed with lace and dotted with sequins. On her head was an outlandishly large, pink bonnet. Continuing to rise up as the music swelled and pounded, Baby was squinting out into the glaring lights, the sequins on her dress and bonnet shooting out a myriad of tiny, dazzling beams.

The music came to an abrupt halt.

"Ladies and Gentlemen. We must now ask for your undivided attention," said Osgood with chilling firmness. "For your complete and utter silence."

The light on Osgood flashed off and, in the darkened hall, there remained only Baby, sitting alone in her nest of satin, her eyes peering out curiously at the flood of ghostlike humanity that sat there holding obediently still, stifling their coughs and sneezes and restless feet, two thousand people holding their breaths for a single infant.

"Quiet. Please. Perfect quiet!" reiterated Osgood from the darkness, and the hall became yet stiller.

Shockley sat pressed forward against the railing, chewing tensely on his knuckles. The ventilation that had been running in the hall was abruptly shut off, leaving an emptiness filled by the blood pounding in his ears. Inhaling in slow, controlled breaths, he could feel himself breathing in unison with the multitude around him. As he watched as Baby sat there in her nest, now elevated above the stage, her eyes trying to penetrate the blackness, a single worry raged through Shockley's mind: Would she sing?

The air in the hall became heavy, damp with breath and the smell of humanity. Someone in the balcony stifled a cough. A spring in a seat squeaked deafeningly. An infinity of eyes focused on the little head encased in the oversized bonnet.

"Baby," said Osgood's voice returning from the depths of the darkness, "sing for the people!"

A careless hand rubbed across the string of a violin and gave off a brief cry and the audience stiffened, thinking it was the child.

"Sing for us, Baby. Sing!" Osgood commanded.

Baby sat there lost in the converging spotlights. She tentatively lifted her thumb to her mouth, and Shockley was ready to burst out of his seat, run onto the stage, and pick up Baby in his arms. With him, he was sure she would perform.

"Sing! Sing!" urged Osgood, his voice echoing.

Baby let her hand fall back into her lap. She fidgeted with the lace on her dress, shook her head with the big bonnet, trying to free it.

"Sing!" cried Osgood, as Baby wrinkled her forehead in obvious suffering. "Sing! Sing! Sing!"

From the box Shockley could see her eyebrows knitting in conflict.

Slowly he rose from his seat. Ruth turned to look at him and just as she did Baby also turned and looked up as though spotting him. Gripping the back of his seat, Shockley froze and watched as Baby, cocking her head to one side, suddenly took a large breath. Noting it, the audience also caught its breath. And then it came. The voice. A small point source of music, a high rapturous sound emerging from that little mouth on stage, faint yet clear, note after note diffusing through the crowd, her uncanny melody drifting out and enfolding the waiting multitude, her crystalline, flutelike song distilling the essence of humanity's love and aspirations and longings—a solitary voice calling out in an unearthly language that all could grasp.

His heart thumping, Shockley gaped and listened as Baby's tentative music began to grow in confidence, her voice now a chorus of fine small voices, harmonies within harmonies. She was taking long deep breaths of the dank air and proudly singing out her music, her songs merging into one another as she weaved in and out of themes, her medley going from passages of hope to elegy to passion. In the audience people were weeping, men and women alike, swollen tears coursing unchecked down their cheeks, their faces set in rhapsodic expressions of devotion, their hands clasped tightly as though in prayer. Baby continued to sing, going long beyond Shockley's wildest expectations as though she were drawing strength from the packed crowd, sensing their needs and giving all she could muster. Lungful after lungful, she exhaled in a loud determined voice, her face damp with sweat, the fringes of hair peeking out from under her hat, plastered against her skin.

Enough. Enough, thought Shockley, wanting to spare Baby, but she seemed unable to stop, and he began to fear that she would exhaust herself and sing herself out. Enough, enough, he called out to her in his mind, but she continued to trill, her music rising to unattained heights, her voice promising to rid her listeners of despair and anguish, her optimism rising to a fever pitch. Higher and higher she climbed until, reaching a crescendo, her voice began to fade, her music wound down, her strength began to ebb. Finishing with a short birdlike strain, she came to a stop and her thumb went into her mouth.

The audience remained suspended.

Suddenly the lights flashed onto the orchestra. As though caught in a dream, the musicians fumbled for their instruments. Popov, looking obviously shaken, brought up his baton and, robotlike, led the orchestra through the closing section of his piece—Baby's music still ringing in his ears.

A moment later the cymbals crashed, the trumpets blared, and the audience broke into wild cheers and applause as Osgood, beaming his smile and proudly holding Baby, took bow after bow.

The audience rose to its feet.

Extending a hand to Maestro Popov, Osgood signaled the Russian to take a bow amidst a deafening ovation. Popov motioned for the musicians applauding him to take a bow themselves.

A spotlight swung over to Shockley's box catching him unawares and confusedly he, too, took a bow to the thunderous applause. The light swung back to Osgood. The curtain went up and down and up and down, the applause continuing unabated. Shockley left the box and joined Popov and Jacobsen on stage, joining hands, and took a rousing new round of cheers, Osgood holding Baby aloft to the crowd.

"Well," said Jacobsen out of the corner of his mouth, as he took a long, last bow, "do I know my business, or do I?"

177

Squinting in the bright light, Shockley looked up at the box where he and Ruth had been sitting. It was empty. Ruth had left.

That evening, for the first time since his college days, Shockley got drunk. It happened in the grand ballroom of the Shockleys' hotel at the celebration honoring Baby. Thrown by the Friends of the Symphony, the party was an extravagant affair mobbed by jet-setters and the cream of local society, and overflowing with catered delicacies. Long tables stood brimming with imported caviars and exquisite cheeses, smoked salmon and oysters, and endless mounds of jumbo shrimp piled high on ice. Uniformed waiters edged their way through the tangled crowds, serving champagne and canapés. Two bands took turns entertaining, vying with the din of hundreds of excited voices that filled the hall. There was barely enough room to move as people pressed up against one another, the men dressed in dinner jackets, the women in long evening dresses, their faces flushed, all animatedly discussing Baby. And, it seemed, everyone wanted to meet Professor Shockley.

"Oh, so you're Dr. Shockley," said an elderly man with flapping jowls, elbowing his way into a group encircling Shockley. "My wife's just been dying to meet you," he said, a lithe, blond girl in tow.

"How *ever* did you discover Baby?" asked a woman with bluish gray hair, her ears and wrists heavy with diamonds.

"I understand you won a Pulitzer Prize," said a famous film actor trying to squeeze a word in edgeways.

The drinks came in endless rounds. They appeared on the passing trays, at the four strategically placed bars, and they were slipped into Shockley's hands by considerate guests eager to hear anything about Baby.

"Well, it hasn't exactly been easy," said Shockley to a rather attractive steel heiress as he searched the crowded room in the hopes of spotting Ruth. Since the performance she was nowhere to be found, not in their suite or apparently anywhere in the hotel. "We've had our ups and downs with her. Why, tonight," he said, downing something that tasted like a martini, "Baby had me really frightened."

"When did she first start singing?" asked a man who introduced himself as a local music critic.

"What a gold mine you've got," said Isaac Popov, giving Shockley a playful poke in the ribs before he was whisked away to meet someone important.

"I'd like to have a serious discussion with you," said a toy manufacturer. "Not tonight, of course." He forced a loud laugh. He was hoping to get Baby's endorsement for his new line of educational toddler toys.

"When are we going to see Baby?" asked a double-chinned matron weighed down in gold.

"Yes," agreed her escort. "Where is that enchanting child?"

"Well, we thought we'd bring her in for a flew minutes later," Shockley slurred.

"She's sleeping and we don't want to disturb her," injected Jacobsen, appearing suddenly from out of the depths of the crowd. "I just checked with the baby-sitter," he added for authenticity.

"Well, if she's seeping we slertainly don't want to—" said Shockley, leaning up against Jacobsen for support.

"What a pity," sighed another woman in a tantalizingly low-cut dress.

"Shockley." Jacobsen pulled him aside. "A hard and fast rule: Nobody sees her without paying. Get it?" he said, and then disappeared into the crowd.

Shockley continued to drink, occasionally popping into his mouth a cracker heaped high with caviar or a lone slice of rare roast beef that tasted like fur, his perceptions of the party becoming progressively more obscured by a strange fog. Despite his inebriation sometime during that night, something caught Shockley's eye. He was standing with Osgood at the time, struggling to appear sober when he spotted it. It was a pendant that one of the more chic women guests was wearing around her neck, a minuscule gold charm cast in the shape of a pair of oval lips. Shockley tried to point it out to Osgood, but before he could speak, it was gone. Later on he thought he saw the same pendant on another woman, but by that point he neither trusted his powers of observation nor cared.

There was something else, too, that Shockley noticed that night at the party. It was a woman. He had spotted her early in the evening talking quietly with a man. She was tall and svelte. Young. Early twenties, he had guessed, unable to take his eyes off her. Her cheeks were high and broad, almost Slavic-looking, and her skin was smooth and flawless. Her beauty was so extraordinary that she had caught his eye almost from the moment he had entered the crowded ballroom. Once, later that night, while he was engaged in small talk with a television newsman, their eyes had met for a fleeting second. She was watching him. He was sure of it. And then she was gone. As he drifted through the party that night, yanked from one group to the next, he had kept searching for her, hoping for the chance to speak to her. At one point, when he discovered her close to where he stood, he had been tempted to pull away from a conversation and go over to her, but finally hadn't dared. She was so breathtakingly gorgeous that Shockley found himself intimidated by her beauty. Yet, as he drank his way through the party, his eyes continued to scan the crowd, still hoping to find her.

Around midnight, when the celebration began to wane, Shockley queasily took the elevator up to his rooms.

The woman who had been installed to watch over Baby rose quickly to her feet when he entered the suite.

"She's just been a perfect little angel," she gushed, as Shockley groped in his wallet to pay her. "I brought along some sewing, but I just couldn't take my eyes— Oh, heavens, what's this?" she asked, looking at the wad of bills. "I couldn't take that," she said, and Shockley noted as she put on her coat to leave that she, too, was wearing a pair of those golden lips around her neck.

After the woman had left, Shockley went into the bedroom and checked Baby, who was fast asleep in her crib. Looking over at the double bed, he could see that it was still freshly made, untouched. Shedding his clothes, he wearily pulled aside the covers and slid into the large, cold bed. He closed his eyes and immediately dozed off. A short while later he was briefly awakened by movements next to him. It was Ruth coming to bed.

"The lips," he uttered groggily.

"What?" she asked distantly.

"The lips," he mumbled, trying to concentrate, but his brain refused to pursue the thought and he fell back into unconsciousness. After that he slept only fitfully, waking up repeatedly, dreaming in short, vivid bursts, dreaming about Baby in a sarcophagus, about that dark, svelte woman who had looked at him, about those golden lips. In the early morning he awoke, sick to his stomach, nausea churning in his guts. He tried to stem it by pushing all thoughts out of his head, but the nausea just grew. He tried sleeping on his back, on his stomach, on one arm. Finally he surrendered and, dashing from the bed, hung over the toilet, vomiting repeatedly and swearing to himself that he was not going to get drunk again for at least another decade or two.

The following morning Ruth flew back to Ithaca, and for the next five days Baby continued to play Cleveland. Almost from the outset it became clear to Shockley that things were changing. To begin with, the character of the audience was altering drastically, shifting for each performance from that chic, opening-night crowd to more ordinary folks. Tux and evening dresses gave way to suits, which, in turn, were being infiltrated by jeans and sweat shirts. The audience, which had started out with the wealthy and powerful, now consisted of laborers and school teachers, drop-outs, aging hippies, and street people.

"I don't like the way the audience is changing," said Shockley after one of Baby's performances.

"Christ, Shockley, stop being such an elitist," said Jacobsen. "As long as they pay, why give a damn who they are?"

"You wanted exposure, didn't you?" said Osgood, handing Baby over to Shockley. "Well, that's what you're getting."

"You don't understand. That's not what I'm talking about."

What Shockley objected to was the program itself. It had taken yet another turn that made him uneasy. The change had occurred after the second performance when Osgood, according to plan, had commanded Baby to sing.

"Sing! Sing for us, Baby!" Osgood had called out from the darkness. Looking a bit overwhelmed, Baby had sat in her nest, silent. "Sing for us, Baby!" Osgood had tried again and again.

Then in the growing tension someone in the first balcony, losing control, had suddenly cried out, "Sing!"

Heads had abruptly turned to locate that lone cry, but a second later another voice coming from the mezzanine had punctuated the darkness.

"Sing!" called a high voice.

"Sing!" called a baritone.

Soon the entire audience was chanting in unison, stopping only when Baby opened her mouth to finally sing.

"Keep it in the show," said Jacobsen after the incident as Osgood, looking shaken, waited in the wings for Baby to end her performance.

"What?"

"It's perfect, don't you see? It puts the responsibility for the performance squarely on the audience instead of you. When Baby sings, it leaves them the feeling that they've elicited the song."

And from that point on, Osgood made a practice of encouraging the audience.

"It's hokey. It's rowdy. It's even worse *schlock* than that first night," said Shockley the next night in Baby's dressing room, taking off her bonnet and drying her sweat-soaked hair. "And I want it stopped."

"Do me a favor," said Jacobsen, watching as Shockley undressed Baby. "Please limit yourself to your own area of expertise. I have control over the format of the programs. You read your contract before you signed it, didn't you?"

"Contracts can be broken," said Shockley, turning and coming eye to eye with the Dane.

"Try to break it," said Jacobsen, a cigarette locked between his teeth.

"And?"

"You'll find out," he said, stalking from the room.

There were other points that also irked Shockley. Those tiny golden lips, for instance. They were becoming more and more prevalent, appearing on fine chains around people's necks, on lapels, in earrings. They made Shockley uneasy.

Then there was the matter of the media. What had started out as an exclusively positive press was now turning mixed and often vicious. In particular, Felix Lyons in his nationally syndicated column was coming out with almost daily attacks on Baby.

"If there ever were a good old-fashioned hoax," he wrote in one of his assaults, "it's being perpetrated on the masses by a team of sharpies and hipsters using an innocent infant as a front." Lyons went on in that article to accuse Jacobsen and Shockley of employing "electronic chicanery" to make it appear that Baby was singing; that Baby by some gimmick had been taught to move her lips to some decidedly weird-sounding music. It was the old back-tent circus con, and anybody shelling out twenty-five dollars for a ticket would fare better spending it on a psychiatrist.

"Why's Lyons doing this?" asked Shockley, handing the newspaper over to Jacobsen as they flew in the agent's private jet to Boston for Baby's Symphony Hall show.

"Maybe he's got some share in a psychiatric clinic," quipped Osgood, giving Baby her late-morning bottle.

"Let him say what he wants. What's the difference?" said Jacobsen, tossing the paper to one of his assistants. "Besides" —he took a tentative sip from his snifter of brandy and rolled the liquor around his tongue—"he's giving Baby enormous publicity. People are going to buy tickets just to see for themselves if Baby is a fake. They're not going to take Lyons's word. Would you?"

"Does everything boil down to money?" asked Shockley, as the plane banked and began to make its approach to Logan.

"Ultimately," said Jacobsen unabashedly. "Look, this is a stupid discussion. The trouble with you," he said, zeroing in on target, "is that you're on this morality kick that says that making money is evil. Well, I don't think it's necessarily so. I make money. Lots of it. But I also give most of it away to very worthy causes and people who need it. I've supported many a starving performer until they made it. And some who never did."

The engines on the plane cut back and the flaps came down.

"Stop trying to be all things to all people. You want to be loved by the whole world. Forget it. It's impossible. And forget this asshole Lyons," continued Jacobsen, as Shockley took Baby back into his lap. "He's not worth a second thought. He's doing it because he's one of those born-again Christians."

"What's that got to do with it?" asked Shockley, as the landing gear locked into place with a loud clunk. Jacobsen gave an enigmatic shrug.

"We're late as usual," he said, glancing at his watch and changing the subject.

Holding Baby tightly, Shockley looked out the window and saw the ground rising up to greet them. As the beginning of the landing strip came into sight the thought of Doris suddenly popped into Shockley's head. Then the tires hit the runway with a squeal, the plane lurched, and the thought was jarred from his mind.

After two days in Boston, Baby looked exhausted.

"She needs a rest," warned Shockley.

"She'll get a rest," said Jacobsen, trying to concentrate on the itinerary. There had been a last-minute cancellation for their Seattle date and he was trying to plug in a substitute in nearby Vancouver.

"When?"

"When the first part of the tour is over. We stick to the schedule. No deviations."

"Jacobsen, you're pushing your luck."

"And you're pushing me! Now be a nice guy and take care of Baby and see that she's ready."

Later, Jacobsen apologized.

"Hey, I'm sorry. I didn't mean to be rude. I've been a real son of a bitch lately, I know it," he said, putting his arm around Shockley. "It's the pressure."

"Yeah. It's getting us all," said Shockley, taken off balance by his candor. Just when he was convinced that Jacobsen was a cold-hearted, hard-driving businessman, he would surprise Shockley in some small way.

During the shows in Boston, Shockley took to nervously pacing around the theater to kill time. Secretly he was glad that Osgood was up there on stage taking the strain. It was no easy job and Osgood, too, was beginning to show the signs of fatigue.

On the night of the third performance, as Baby's ruffle-enclosed nest was rising up out of the pit and the audience was chanting for Baby to sing, Shockley was wandering around the theater when, by chance, he walked out into the lobby. There, where they were setting up for a last-minute sale of refreshments after the show, amidst the cold orange drink and wine and plastic-wrapped sandwiches, Shockley spotted a case holding a display of golden lips. There were lips that could be fastened to chains or bracelets. Discrete miniature lips that might almost disappear on the lapel of a suit, big obtrusive lips that could be worn on a ponderous chain. Together they formed a chorus of a thousand infant mouths opened in song.

"If you don't see what you want," said the old woman behind the counter, "just ask."

"What are they?" he asked.

"They're lips," said the lady matter-of-factly.

"I can see that."

"Baby lips."

"Oh."

"We've got them in all price ranges. We've got them, like these here, in pure gold," she said, unlocking a glass case and holding them out to Shockley. "Aren't they darling? And then we have them in gold plate, like these."

"Are you selling many of them?"

"They're selling like crazy. Why, I must have sold eight dozen tonight alone. Boy, I wish I owned this concession."

"You don't?"

"Oh, heavens no!" said the lady, waving him away and smiling, the lines on her face folding into deep gorges. "If I did, I'd be in there listening to that wonderful child, not out here working." She shook her head. "Heavens no"—she laughed—"I work for the Jacobsen outfit."

Following the Boston concerts, Jacobsen ferried Baby's entourage across the country for a West Coast swing, kicking off the tour with a three-day appearance before packed crowds in the Los Angeles Civic Center.

After L.A., Baby and Osgood did a one-night stand in San Diego, where Jacobsen experimented with yet another twist to the program. He had asked his old friend and pop lyricist Jay Kramer to see if he could come up with some lyrics to Popov's *Ode*. Excerpting one of the melodic refrains from the Popov piece, Kramer managed to hone a very catchy, moving tune, and Jacobsen decided to give it a whirl in San Diego. Before the orchestra began the Popov number, Jacobsen had a local choir troop onto the stage and sing Kramer's song.

> Baby, Baby,
> Our voice from heaven,
> Easing our pains
> Our hope you do leaven.
> Lifting our burdens with your sweet song,
> When you sing, the world can't be wrong.

Baby, Baby,
Baby, Baby.

By the time the choir was into its encore, the audience was on its feet. Joining hands and swaying to the infectious rhythm, the audience sang along in perfect harmony, and Jacobsen knew he had a hit. The song, recorded then and there in San Diego, was pressed and hurriedly put into production. In less than a week it was in retail stores and being played on radio stations around the country. On the flip side was the orchestral overture of Popov's *Ode* recorded live at the Cleveland opening. Hopes were high that the record would do a brisk business as a single. If initial sales were any indication, it looked as if the song would be up on the charts in a matter of days.

After San Diego the company flew to Vancouver, Kramer's song already an integral part of the program. Vancouver gave way to Dallas, Dallas to Chicago, Chicago to Detroit. Through all the travels, Felix Lyons continued to take potshots at Baby, his vitriolic attacks joined by a number of other journalists. Picking up a stateside paper in Vancouver shortly before the second show, Shockley read one of Lyons's more recent columns and finally understood the source of the man's virulence.

"There are those," Lyons wrote, concluding his column, "Babyists among them, who would have us believe that a messiah has arrived, who would have us cast off two thousand years of religious belief for a passing gimmick, who . . ."

It was the first time that Shockley had actually heard the word *Babyist*, and it confirmed his suspicions and made the connection between the fervor of the audience and those golden-lipped pendants. They were obviously more than just souvenirs.

"Looks like we've got an honest-to-goodness religion on our hands," said Osgood breezily, studying the article from the wings as the orchestra moved toward his cue.

"Here, let me see that," said Jacobsen, taking the paper and scanning the column. "What the hell's Lyons crusading about now?"

"You know very well and you've known all along!" said Shockley, his temper suddenly flaring.

"Lower your voice," Jacobsen whispered back. "They can hear you all the way out in the audience."

"I don't give a good goddamn if they do hear! I know what you've been up to all along. You're the one who's been feeding the fires. You're the one behind those damn lips. You're the one who's been selling them."

"Now hold on just one second!" Jacobsen's face burned a deep crimson. "I've been marketing them. I don't deny that. But I think you're confusing cause and effect. I just responded to a need, that's all. I certainly did not start these people going. My people sell the lips. Nothing more. Period!" he said, turning on his heels and marching away. A few feet later he stopped. "And by the way," he added, raising a finger, "the profits from those trinkets are not just going into my pockets. They're going into Baby's earnings as well!" And with that he spun around and stormed off.

"Christ Almighty, how many times do I have to tell you I don't care about—," Shockley shouted after him, but Jacobsen was already out of earshot.

"Jud, she's a singer, not a messiah," Shockley insisted in a firm whisper as he watched Baby being taken to the pit below.

"I think you're being a little unfair to Ivar," said Osgood, his hand poised on the curtain. "He was telling you the truth. He's not behind it. I know that for a fact. You've got to understand, the man's a businessman. His mind doesn't work like yours and mine. If he sees an opportunity to make some money and it's not illegal or immoral, he'll take it. Try not to be too judgmental. I learned that a long time ago in this business. It makes life a lot easier. And don't worry about these Babyists. They're OK. Relax," he said, touching Shockley's arm and smiling reassuringly. "Relax. Oops," he said, missing his cue from the conductor and, leaving in a hurry, he solemnly marched onto the spotlighted stage.

After Vancouver, Shockley heard the name Babyists again. He saw them mentioned in Dallas and Chicago papers. At the end of the week, *Time* magazine carried a brief article on the Babyists in its section on religion, including a photo of Baby in her costume, the picture credited to the Jacobsen outfit. In the lobby of one theater Shockley was handed a pamphlet by a matronly woman who had tried to hit him up for a donation. Around her neck she wore an enormous pair of golden lips dangling on the end of a thick chain. She introduced herself as Sister White, a member of the lay clergy. Fortunately, she didn't recognize him, and he was able to escape before she got too far into her sermon on the goodness of Baby and the pressing need for a temple. Later in Baby's dressing room, as the wardrobe lady was putting the finishing touches on Baby's makeup, Shockley took a moment to study the pamphlet. It was published by something called the Assembly of Babyists. He began to read:

For the fleeting moments in eternity that we hear Baby we become one with our great Master, who created her song. Through her we receive his message, fathom his intentions.

He tried to read further, but the booklet contained a lot of gobbledygook and biblical references to the new messiah. He soon got bored and crumpling the pamphlet, tossed it into the trash.

"What absolute drivel!" he said to Baby.

Baby smiled back at him, then scrunched up her face as the woman carefully dabbed it with a puff of powder.

When Baby was ready, Shockley lifted her into his arms and headed out the dressing-room door. In the hallway he hesitated, turned around and going back, extricated the pamphlet from the trash. Smoothing it out, he folded it into his pocket.

"I tell you, this Babyist business spells trouble," warned Shockley during a quick huddle before the Atlanta performance.

"Take it easy. You've nothing to worry about," said Jacobsen, trying to calm him. "They're absolutely harmless."

"I've been talking to some Babyists and they're really *good* people," Osgood added, noting Shockley's agitation. "Sometimes they come backstage to speak with me and—"

"They do?" This was all news to Shockley.

"All they really want is to listen to Baby and, if they can, serve her in some way," explained Osgood compassionately. "Where is the harm in that?"

"I don't like any of it," Shockley eyed him suspiciously.

"You can't tell people what to believe," said Osgood logically. "It's a free country, man."

"Don't cut them off," said Jacobsen sagaciously. "You never can tell."

"They might come in handy some day," echoed Osgood.

"How?" snorted Shockley. "By selling more tickets?"

The Dane smiled indulgently, and Shockley could see the wheels spinning in his head. He was looking for dollar signs in Jacobsen's eyes, but saw them only in Osgood's.

"I don't care what you two think," said Shockley, taking Baby after the show and heading directly to his hotel. "But I'm not taking any chances!"

"Nobody's saying you should," said Jacobsen, accompanying him to the door of his hotel room. "Take good care of her. That's fine with us. Just don't get paranoid about the whole thing."

From that moment on, Shockley made a strict point of always keeping Baby within sight. He had all his and Baby's meals sent up to his room. He no longer ventured out onto any of the city streets either with Baby or by himself, which would have meant entrusting her to another person. At night when she slept, he kept her crib close to his bedside, guarding his little singer jealously, often waking in the night to check her.

The strain of the shows, the endless travel, the new cities, the strange hotel rooms, the crazy hours and odd meals, his growing worry about the Babyists, all were slowly beginning to take their toll on Shockley. In everything he began to see the portents of imminent danger. The plane, while parked on the ground, could be sabotaged and they would crash. The food could be poisoned and Baby would be lost. The audiences, packing the poorly ventilated theaters, were infusing the air with potentially lethal bacteria. Before every performance he always checked the exits, outlining in his mind an escape route for Baby. The lips, which began to appear in profusion, greeting them as they arrived in each new city, chilled Shockley to the marrow. The Babyists who repeatedly tried to make appointments to speak with him regarding Baby were denied access. The less he had to do with them the better. The country was crawling with nuts and assassins, and he was not taking a chance with any maniacs who might want to martyr the child.

The mounting pressure became so intolerable that Shockley felt he was starting to see things. Driving in from the Atlanta airport, he thought he caught a glimpse near his hotel of that dark, svelte woman he had fleetingly seen the night of the Cleveland party. Now that he thought about it, he suspected he had spotted her once in Los Angeles and another time early in the tour on Boyleston Avenue near Symphony Hall. He knew his mind was playing tricks on him, but he felt helpless to stop it.

I don't know how much more of this any of us could take, he thought to himself on the night of the last performance. They were scheduled to return to Ithaca for a short break preceding the big New York City opening, and it was none too soon. Baby was tired, sometimes cranky and, as of late, she often had an upset stomach. Spontaneous songs had now become a rarity as though, calculatedly, she were saving her singing for the rigors of the show. When she did sing for him in private, Baby's songs struck him as morose and lonely. She was now sucking her thumb almost constantly, refusing a pacifier, her eyebrows knitting frequently. Shockley tried to cheer her up, with new toys, by talking to her, singing her lullabies, even telling her fairy tales. Nothing seemed to help. Baby seemed distant and preoccupied.

The tour had been too long. Osgood was showing the signs too. Without makeup his face looked old and haggard, and his hands were developing a small but perceptible tremor. Jacobsen was smoking up to four packs a day. He had gone through three assistants, two had been summarily fired, and one had collapsed in exhaustion. Every time Shockley boarded the plane, he seemed to be greeted by a new face on the staff. They all needed a rest. Badly. Ithaca came as a welcome relief.

It felt great to be back in Ithaca. The minute Shockley's feet touched the macadam at the airport, all of his fears and forebodings seemed to vanish. Even Baby looked suddenly happier.

"Have you heard anything from Doris?" he asked, hardly in the door.

"Not a word," said Ruth, accepting the child from his arms. "Boy, Baby really looks pooped."

"Nothing that a good few days' rest won't cure," he said, slumping down into a couch, putting up his feet, and swearing that nothing could make him budge.

A few minutes later, however, he was on the phone, calling Andrea Cassaniti.

"Oh, Dr. Shockley, you're back in town. I'll be right up," she said and hung up before he could object.

"Baby's sleeping now," Shockley apologized, letting Cassaniti in. "She's awfully bushed."

"Oh. I was really hoping—"

"Tomorrow. I promise you. She'll sing."

Cassaniti brightened, her eyes sparkling behind her glasses.

"One reason I called you was to inquire about Doris Rumsey. Ruth hasn't heard anything from her, and I was wondering, well—if you had?"

"Nothing." Cassaniti shrugged, slouching in her seat. "She's got visiting privileges," she said, twirling a strand of hair around her finger.

"I know," he said, watching her. "That's why I find it odd that she hasn't contacted us."

"I don't find it so odd. We deal with a lot of strange cases, a lot of strange clients. You wouldn't believe some of the weird parents we encounter. When we try to remove their children, they fight like crazy. They lie. They try to steal the kids. Try to smuggle them out of town. Then, once they're removed from their custody, the parents are actually glad. This job is better training in human psychology than any course I ever took up there," she said, motioning with her chin toward the campus.

Shockley nodded and smiled indulgently.

"Well," said Cassaniti, moving to get up. "Gotta be going."

"Yes," said Shockley, his eyes caught by a sudden gleam that appeared low in the front opening of her blouse. Subtly maneuvering his head, Shockley peered down into the fissure between her breasts and saw what it was. It was a small set of lips hanging on the end of a chain.

"As long as Baby's in town for the week, I was thinking of asking Doris to come and stay here," said Shockley that night while brushing his teeth.

"Is that a request or a statement of fact?" asked Ruth, appearing behind him in the bathroom doorway.

"It's both," he replied, a ring of white foam encircling his mouth. "I'm asking if you'd object," he said, looking up into the mirror to see her reflection.

"We're getting very considerate these days, aren't we?" she said quietly.

"Ruth. Please," he rinsed his mouth and turned to her. "Do we have to fight?"

"We're not fighting," she said, skirting around him to get at the sink.

"Can't we talk?" he asked, coming up behind her and wrapping his arms around her waist. Through the sheer nightgown he could feel her stiffening under his grasp.

"That's all we do, talk," she said, slipping away from him. "I'm tired of all the words."

"I feel very bad about Doris," he added a little later when they were together in bed. "The thought of her being deprived of Baby keeps haunting me."

"Obviously you feel guilty."

"Of course I do."

"Well then, instead of having her come here to be with Baby, why don't you let Baby stay with her?" she asked, sitting up on an elbow and facing him.

"Because we can't. According to the custody decision she's supposed to stay in our house, under our supervision."

"Irwin," she said, looking deep into his eyes, "how did we really get Baby?"

"I've told you. When I heard about the action, I quickly volunteered our names. I certainly didn't want her going to God-knows-what other family. Did you?" he asked, avoiding her penetrating look.

"Is that the whole truth?"

"Basically."

Ruth heaved a long sigh and lay down.

"OK," she said a few minutes later, staring up at the ceiling. "Ask her if you want. It's fine with me if Doris wants to stay here."

"I was sort of hoping that you'd ask her," he ventured tentatively.

"No," said Ruth flatly, snapping off the light on her side. "If you want her to stay, *you* ask her. Don't ever use me or put me in a position between you and Doris again. Ever!"

Shockley's first full day in Ithaca turned out to be a busy one. There were loose ends to be tied up at the university as well as a multitude of legal and financial matters that required immediate attention. Baby's first check from the Jacobsen organization had just arrived, and a trust fund and corporate shelter had to be established. Shockley didn't quite know where to turn. Fortunately, while picking up his last paycheck from Krieger's secretary, he ran into Burt Marra.

"Oh, I saw you and Baby in the Sunday *Times*," said Marra, greeting him like a long-lost friend. "How's everything going? Are you in town for a while? Why don't you and Ruth come over to the house for drinks tonight?"

Although he made a polite inquiry about Shockley's composing, professing a newfound eagerness to perform some of his latest works, it was obvious that all Marra really wanted to talk about was Baby.

Shockley took out a few minutes to talk to the rotund, little conductor. Marra, he knew, had inherited a small fortune from his wife's family and, when he wasn't rehearsing the university symphony, he was actively orchestrating his portfolio of stocks, bonds, options, and commodity contracts. He was obviously the right man to ask about Baby's financial needs. At the appropriate moment, Shockley slipped in a question about business.

"Sounds to me, what you need is a good lawyer," said Marra. "A man who knows tax laws, contracts, annuities, setting up trusts—the whole *schmeer*."

"Got any suggestions?"

"Matter of fact, I've got just the man for you." Marra's tiny eyes lit up. "Does all my work. He's absolutely the best. Knows the angles."

"What's his name?"

"Kiely. Frank Kiely. He's a real bullet, if you know what I mean." Marra gave a knowing wink.

"Thanks," said Shockley with a grateful nod.

"Always glad to help a friend. By the way," Marra called after him, "you can mention my name."

"I will," said Shockley, who was already thinking of his next stop.

When he wheeled around the corner on Willow Avenue, Shockley was immediately struck by the appearance of the Rumsey home. Devoid of curtains and blinds, the house looked hollow from a distance. Climbing onto the porch, he peeked in and discovered that not only were the windows bare but the front rooms were totally empty. The place looked as if a bomb had hit it. The wallpaper had been peeled off the walls, and the floors were littered with debris. Hurrying around to the side of the house, he anxiously checked a rear window. Then another. The dining room was bare. The kitchen had been stripped of its cupboards, and all the plumbing had been ripped out. Someone had started to spackle the deep cracks in the ceiling, and the only thing in the room was an old kitty-litter box abandoned in one corner of the desolate room.

"Where's Mrs. Rumsey?" he finally asked one of the neighbors, who had been scrutinizing him as he looked into the vacant house.

"Moved," said Mrs. Oltz tersely. "An' none too soon."

"Where to?"

"Been pulling down the whole neighborhood," grumbled Charlie Oltz, coming up to her side.

"Good riddance to bad rubbish," added Mrs. Oltz.

"Where'd she go?" Shockley persisted.

"Moved out to the trailer park," explained Charlie, blowing on his bare hands to keep them warm. "Leeming's Trailer Park. Up by Etna. You know," he added, noting Shockley's confused expression. "Hang a left by Gas and Electric."

Shockley jumped into his car and drove out onto the highway that angled up over the east lip of the lake. Climbing to the plateau above the city, he passed the shopping malls and then the airport. He took a turn off the highway and, checking his map, began a zigzag shortcut through the countryside. He had never ventured out this way in all his years in Ithaca and what he saw surprised him. After a short span of squat ranch houses built in the middle of what had once been hay fields, he began coming upon stretches of road lined with dilapidated houses and ramshackle trailers with tacked-on additions. They looked as if someone had slapped them together and missed. Between them were pockets filled with squatters' shacks that had been built of scrap lumber and corrugated steel. They were so small and shabby that Shockley was sure that no one could be living in them, except that there were TV antennas on the roofs and wood smoke curling out of chimney pipes. Everywhere there seemed to be piles of junk: old car carcasses that had been turned over and scavenged for parts, abandoned washers and mowers, trash galore.

After three wrong turns Shockley finally found Leeming's Trailer Park. Driving in on the rutted, muddy road he found the place worse than anything he could have imagined. "Park" was a euphemism carried to the nth degree. The place was crowded with old, crumbling trailers that looked as if they had been stolen from the junkyards. They were wedged together so tightly that a person could almost step out of one and into the next without setting a foot on the ground. As he rounded a turn, Shockley saw a child dressed in ragged clothes playing desultorily in the frozen dirt in front of a peeling green trailer. The boy's face was pale and smeared with grime, his expression vacant. A dog chained to the trailer barked relentlessly as he danced about at the end of his chain, his paws ankle-deep in piles of frozen turds.

Cutting a wide circle around the snarling dog, Shockley went to the trailer and knocked on the door.

An obese woman holding a child against her billowing hip answered the door. Her face was bloated and round as a ball, and her breasts were so large that they lay against the top of her protruding belly. Both she and her baby had the same pale look of abject vacancy as the child playing outside in the dirt, and both were lacking teeth, though for different reasons.

Shockley asked her if she knew Doris, as the dog continued to yap.

"Shadup!" she snapped at the unrelenting mutt. "Ya mean tha' ol' hunchback lady?" She turned back to Shockley, her eyes lost in the flesh of her face.

Shockley nodded uncomfortably, watching through the corner of his eye as two mangy dogs rummaged through the garbage oozing out of a pile of plastic bags.

"Just 'round there. Third one in," instructed the woman, and Shockley left his car where it was parked and walked on. As he cut across through the cluster of trailers, he came upon more of the same. Small children dressed in rags, without gloves or hats despite the biting cold, their faces hollow. Strewn trash. Lone dogs snapping viciously on their lines. He could hardly believe that this was just a short spin outside allegedly civilized Ithaca, home of an Ivy League university.

Shockley saw Doris about the same moment that she spotted him approaching. She was seated by the window inside a small pink-and-aqua trailer, staring out at the leaden day. When their eyes met, the muscles in her face went taut, the bones in her jaw jutting out through her transparent skin.

"Well?" she asked, coming to the door. There was an edge in her voice that Shockley had never heard. A blue vein at the side of her head pulsed with each beat of her heart.

"Baby's back in town—" he began falteringly.

"I know," she answered tersely. Her cat jumped up on the window ledge and looked curiously at Shockley.

"I thought—maybe—you'd like to see her."

Doris stood impassively. The dogs that had been scouring the garbage near the fat woman's home had trailed Shockley and stood eyeing him at a respectful distance.

"Ruth and I thought you might care to move in for the week," he continued uneasily, filling the silence. "That way," he went on, "well, that way you could be with Baby."

Doris fixed him with her pale eyes. Her cat continued to stare at him. Shockley swallowed.

"You want to see her, don't you?" he asked.

Doris stood tensed, her body rigid, as straight as she could hold it. A telltale finger at her side twitched nervously.

"Actually, it's not just for the week. I was hoping that, ultimately, you could move in and live with us," he ventured unsurely.

"Move into *your* house?" she asked, her upper lip quivering.

"Yes," Shockley nodded, trying to sound enthusiastic. "That was the general idea."

"Move in with you to condone your theft? Is that the idea?"

"No, that's not it at all," said Shockley defensively.

"Move in until you felt like throwing me out? Is that your plan?" Doris asked, her gnarled fists clenching at her sides.

"I was—"

"Mr. Shockley," she said, holding up her head. *"Professor* Shockley, I would rather be dead and roast in hell than set a foot in your house!"

Shockley swallowed, his heart thudding in his ears.

"I want to see Baby. I want to hold her more than anything in the world," she said, tears flooding her eyes. "But the next time I see Baby she'll be mine," she uttered, biting her lips.

"Doris, come on. Be reasonable," Shockley pleaded. "You're only hurting yourself."

"I have been reasonable," she said, a lone tear coursing down her cheek. "That was my big mistake. I should never, never have opened my door to you!"

"Look, I'll bring Baby to see you. Here, if you wish. I can—"

"No! Don't! How many times do you have to crush me?"

"Doris, please," he begged.

"Please nothing!" she uttered. "The next time I see her, it'll be for keeps. If it takes every last penny, every last drop of my blood, I'll get her back. She was given to me, not you. Now, for God's sake, go away and leave me in peace!" she said, slamming the door, her cat fixing Shockley with an unblinking stare.

Although the tour had stopped, the attacks on Baby continued to mount, and for each passing day there were fresh assaults, new slurs, and accusations disputing her gift and denouncing Shockley's motives. The mere existence of the Babyists was polarizing sentiment, and Shockley could sense the situation rapidly deteriorating to the point where one either worshiped Baby or viewed her as an insidious threat—which had absolutely nothing to do with Baby's music.

Picking up the lead from Felix Lyons and his cohorts, a reporter on the "Nightly News" did a scathing report on Baby. Using some unauthorized footage of Baby in concert, the correspondent broadcast the sound of the child's singing to prove his point that Baby's so-called music was nothing more than a case in point of mass hypnosis and hysteria. Included in the highly biased report was an interview with some academic type from the Harvard Medical School, who, even though he had never heard more than the recording of Baby's voice, felt free to pontificate at length on the hazardous powers of mind control manifested by this "child worship" and the progressive erosion of the country's moral fiber by the burgeoning number of cults.

Following the TV coverage, Shockley was deluged with bags full of hate mail, his phone service was flooded with calls, and the newspapers went into high gear, feeding the flames with even more pulp about Shockley's alleged scam. On the weekend, a group calling themselves Clergy United to Reject Babyism (CURB) took out a full-page ad in the Sunday *New York Times*. Warning of the perils inherent in worshiping a false messiah, the coalition called on the members of their congregations and faiths-at-large to reject the idolatry of this paganism and to boycott the upcoming Lincoln Center concerts. The list of endorsees on the CURB petition filled four columns, eight-inches long with fine type. Included among the signatories, Shockley noted, was the archbishop of the New York diocese, a number of prominent Lutheran, Episcopal, and Baptist clergy and lay-people, as well as one lone rabbi.

That petition was the final straw. Armed with copies of the accusatory articles and a videotape of the television report, Shockley went to see his new lawyer. This whole thing had gotten out of hand and the time had come to put an end to it.

"The accusations against Baby are insane," he said, plopping the pile on Kiely's desk. "It's not a case of gimmickry or hysteria or hypnosis. There's never been any attempt on my part to represent her as a messiah or any other kind of religious figure. I want to stop this thing right in its tracks. Now."

Kiely rummaged through the pile, glancing at a few of the articles.

"How about initiating a libel suit?" Shockley suggested.

"That's a possibility," said Kiely, turning an unlit cigar in his mouth. "But it's slow and cumbersome. What you want is something fast and effective. A sharp, swift cut."

"Yes."

"Something that will pick up the challenge. Nip this damn thing in the bud."

"Exactly."

Kiely thoughtfully licked the end of his cigar.

"Why not fight fire with fire," he suggested, a self-pleased smile forming on his ruddy face.

"How?"

"Use the media. Turn it on the bastards," said Kiely, the springs squeaking in his chair as he leaned back, his head cradled in his arms. He was thinking about his own ongoing war with the housing authority and how he had deftly managed to muddy the waters in the press. "Find yourself someone in the media who you think will give you a fair shake. Then use him."

"It's not a bad idea."

"Think about it," said Kiely, who had yet to hear Baby sing. As far as he was concerned, Baby's music was essentially a matter of indifference. His job was to handle the vast sums flowing in, administer her trust, pay her expenses, file for incorporation, minimize taxes, buy off people like Cassaniti and others, grease the wheels. Between his tenements in Collegetown and the lucrative work brought about by this singing kid, he had his hands full. The last thing in the world that he wanted was a protracted libel suit. There was no real money in it, just hassle.

Later, when other news programs started carrying a series of less-than-flattering items on Baby and her entourage, Shockley finally became galvanized into action. He decided television was the answer. He needed network coverage. If he were going to get a good audience for a single shot, he knew his best attack. Picking up the phone, he called Jim Fowler. The "On Line" producer had been eagerly seeking an interview for the last four months, and in a few minutes an appointment was firmed up for the following day in Ithaca. After the arrangements were finalized, Shockley felt an immense sense of relief. He was convinced that he had made the right choice. Almost everybody in the country watched "On Line," and the program was bound to give him the fairest shake. Once and for all he would make it clear that his intentions were solely musical, not religious. He'd nip this damn thing in the bud, just as Kiely had suggested.

19

Early the next morning, preceding the arrival of the camera crew, the Shockley home was in a minor uproar. The house was a mess and needed to be cleaned from top to bottom if it were going to be shown on national television. The children had been allowed to stay home from school so that they might be included in the program and, though they had all vowed to help, in the end they did little but add to the general pandemonium. There was furniture to be polished; there were rugs to be vacuumed, piles of magazines and books and papers to be put away; the broken blinds in the nursery had to be temporarily tied up; Randy's coin collection that littered the den had to be removed; Cindy's doll carriage and dolls had to be taken out of the living room and lugged back up to her room; Julie's bike had been left right smack in the middle of the front drive and the first car in would probably crush it. Through all the last-minute tidying up the kids expended most of their efforts horsing around, Julie and Annette getting into a knock-down, drag-out fight over a record they had found, each vehemently insisting it was hers.

Shockley ran the vacuum and tried to straighten up in the living room while Ruth attended to the kitchen. She had initially objected to letting the network people into her house, but realizing that her husband was under attack, she had grudgingly relented.

"I want everything to look shipshape. This program has got to go off without a hitch," he had warned the troops at breakfast. "This is Baby's big moment and we don't want to do anything to spoil it. And please, Cindy, when you're on camera, no dirty words."

"Yeah, and don't pick your nose." Randy grinned.

"Oh, screw you," said Cindy, giving her brother the finger. Annette giggled. "And screw Baby too," said Cindy, sulking, when her father had grabbed the offending finger and given it a small but painful twist.

"I mean it, Cindy," said Shockley, still holding that finger. "Just answer the questions, if there are any. And try to say nice things about Baby—for a change."

Outside it was beginning to snow heavily as they made the final preparations.

"Gee, I hope they don't get snowed in at the airport," said Shockley, peering apprehensively out the window. "There's already a good three inches on the ground and it looks very slippery. Do you think they'll close down the runway?"

"I wouldn't worry," said Ruth, preparing a lunch for the visitors. "They'll be here. They want this interview as much as you do. Probably more."

"We've only got this one day." He continued to fret. "I should have taken their advice and waited until we had a couple of full days for the shooting. I knew it." He worriedly looked out again at the dank day. "If we could only make more time. If only we didn't have to leave for New York tomorrow. Damn!" he muttered to himself, a sense of foreboding nagging like an itchy rash.

Shockley checked his watch a little later.

"They should be landing in fifteen minutes," he announced.

"Take it easy. The planes are never on time," said Ruth, and in her voice Shockley detected a note of reconciliation. They were over the worst, he told himself. Time would heal all.

"I want to go out and shovel the walk. Do you think you could get Baby up and ready?" he asked, giving her an appreciative hug. "I'm all thumbs today."

"Sure," said Ruth and, drying her hands on a dish towel, went up the stairs to the nursery. When she got there, she discovered Baby sitting up in her crib, a proud smile on her face. It was the first time she had sat up by herself, and Ruth was tickled to discover it.

"Look," she said to Cindy, who had tagged along. "Our little television star is sitting up all by herself."

"You want to give her an Oscar for it?" asked Cindy cuttingly. Ruth let the comment pass.

"Well, how about you and I giving Baby a bath, huh?"
Cindy shrugged.

"We'll get her all spruced up and smelling like a rose." Ruth lifted Baby and nuzzled her bare tummy with her nose as Cindy looked on in unveiled disgust.

"Can you keep a hand on her?" asked Ruth after she had put Baby on the changing table and taken off her diapers. Keeping her eye on Baby as Cindy held her, Ruth went to the closet to get Baby's plastic bathtub. "She rolls around a lot by herself, and you have to be *very* careful she doesn't slip off the table."

"I know. I know," said Cindy, pressing her hands down on Baby's hips. Baby's skin felt soft and rubbery, almost like warm plastic. Cindy looked down at the cheese dribbling from the corner of her mouth.

Ruth went out and Cindy could hear the water running in the bathroom.

"Drooling little creep," she muttered to Baby.

Baby looked up nervously at the little girl pinning her to the table.

"Keep your eyes on her at all times," Ruth called out over the sound of rushing water.

"What do you think I'm doing?" Cindy shouted back, but she was looking intently out the window at her father, who was hunched over a shovel in the driveway. Red-faced and puffing, he was intently cleaning line after line of asphalt. The snow was falling so rapidly that his hair and beard were already covered with white.

Ruth came quickly back into the room to find Cindy standing there obediently holding Baby, her eyes fixed on the infant.

"Good girl," said Ruth, patting her with a damp hand.

Double-checking the temperature of the bath, Ruth took Baby from her daughter.

Cindy watched as her mother cautiously lowered Baby into the tub, the water lapping her chubby legs and back and then stomach. Baby cooed and laughed and started flicking the water with her hands, making happy little splashes. Ruth let Baby sit against the rim of the tub as she lathered her with a soft cloth, starting at Baby's neck and working under her arms and down to her toes. Baby wrinkled her face as Ruth gently washed it. She stuck out her tongue and tried to lick the soapy water. Just as Ruth finished washing her, the phone rang.

"Why doesn't somebody downstairs pick it up?" Ruth turned distractedly as the phone beckoned loudly from the bedroom.

"Could you pick up the phone?" She started to dispatch Cindy, but then suddenly changed her mind. "No. Wait. I'd better get it. It could be important," she said. It occurred to her that it might be the television people trying to get through.

"Cindy, can you hold on to Baby again for a second?" she asked, and Cindy, dutifully putting her hands under Baby's arms, watched as her mother dashed from the room.

Holding Baby upright in her bath, Cindy glanced down at her for a moment, then looked out the window at her father, watching, absorbed, as he puffed behind his shovel. She noticed the snow was now coming down hard, as Baby slipped from between her hands and slid down under the surface of the water.

Outside, Shockley was now at the far end of the driveway, putting the finishing touches to the last neat patch of snow. Though his back and arm muscles ached, it felt invigorating to be working outdoors in the fresh air. The exertion was a welcome relief after all those tense weeks on the road, being cooped up without exercise in hotel rooms and conveyances.

Shockley shoveled clear a last, long line, touched up an area of newly fallen powder and then, with pleasure, straightening his back, let his eyes trace the cleared driveway and walk. A man needs a routine of hard physical work, he was ruminating philosophically when something at the nursery window caught his attention. He turned up to look. It was Cindy. Cindy with her face pressed against the sealed window.

Cindy smiled and waved at him, and instinctively Shockley realized that something was wrong, terribly wrong.

"Ruth," he cried out. "Ruth! Ruth!" he called into the wind. "Cindy, where's Mommy?" he shouted up at her.

Cindy shrugged.

Dropping his shovel, Shockley started toward the house, inexplicable fear suddenly gripping him. He broke into a trot, then began to race forward, his feet skidding on the slick pavement.

"Ruth!" he bellowed, bursting through the front door and starting up the stairs.

Halfway to the second floor landing he heard Ruth let out a shrill scream. As he dashed into the nursery, Ruth pulled Baby from the water.

"Oh, my God! Oh, my God!" she gasped.

"Baby!" uttered Shockley aghast.

"She's not breathing!" Ruth wailed, holding the limp infant in her arms, her sleeves soaked from the water that ran off Baby's inert body.

"Call an ambulance! Call a doctor! Call somebody!" sobbed Shockley, looking down at Baby in horror. Her eyes were open and she was staring blankly up at him, her pupils wide.

Frantically seizing Baby, he opened the child's mouth and, putting his lips to hers, began to blow.

"It's Baby!" wailed Annette, arriving at the room. "Cindy's killed her."

"That little brat drowned her!" cried Randy, afraid to look at his father and Baby.

"She's dead," Julie buried her face in her hands and wept. "Poor Baby's dead!"

"Wait, said Shockley, pulling his mouth away, his body trembling uncontrollably. "I think—I think she's breathing."

Baby's chest started to heave. She gasped for breath. She took a second frantic gulp, coughed, and emitted a short bleat. Then she took another breath and started coughing weakly.

"She's alive," uttered Shockley, almost afraid to hope.

"Quick!" said Ruth, grabbing her purse and keys, her face streaked with tears. "The hospital."

Taking Baby, she hurriedly wrapped her in two large towels and bolted with the child to the garage, Shockley right behind her.

Fumbling with the keys, Shockley got the car started on the second try and, throwing it into gear, lurched blindly backward down the driveway. At the end of the drive he wrenched the wheel, spun the car in a half circle and sped off, skidding and fishtailing down the street.

"Cindy's going to catch hell," said Randy, as the three Shockley children stood huddled at the front door watching the wheels kick up a tail of snow.

Doris realized she was breaking her vow but couldn't help herself. In the early morning she had been stricken by a sudden painful tightness in her chest that was forcing her to fight for each gasping breath. No matter how deeply or how often she inhaled, she felt as though she couldn't get enough air and was slowly but surely suffocating. At first Doris was sure it was her heart giving out. Then she realized that the pains were actually lower down, in her diaphragm, as if someone had hit her in the gut and knocked the wind out of her. It was anxiety, she belatedly recognized, panic, not a heart attack.

Doris had been thinking about Baby when the seizure struck and, as she quickly dressed in layers of clothes, wrapping two scarves around her head, her sense of alarm continued to mushroom. Something was amiss with Baby. She was lost. She was hurt. She was sick. She was dying. Doris was sure of it, as sure as of the pain in her chest. Baby needed her and there was no time to waste.

Once outside her trailer in the icy air, Doris found that she could breathe with less difficulty, though that looming dread continued to plague her. Taking her bearings, she headed out of Leeming's Trailer Park, the snow swirling around her in blinding squalls. She struggled through the deepening drifts on the unplowed country road and, in minutes, her coat and head scarf were thick with white. She reached the large plowed highway and, cutting onto it, began to trudge the long straight miles to town.

As Doris lumbered through the ankle-deep slush at the edge of the open highway, the relentless wind drove the snow into her face, filling her neck with dripping ice. Passing cars showered her with briny slosh. Her boots became waterlogged, her feet numb. Once she slipped on an icy spot, wrenching her arm and soaking the back of her coat. Determinedly she picked herself up and pushed on. As she made slow but steady progress into the vicious headwind, Doris tried to keep from thinking, tried to take hold of that insistent fear. She counted steps. Measured the miles by paces. Sang a childhood song to herself while flapping her arms to keep warm. Nevertheless, in her mind's eye Baby's face kept returning, the infant crying out, crying for her, her mother.

"Baby. Dearest little Baby," she mumbled, shuffling on now in an almost hypnotic gait, oblivious of the storm, her frozen feet clumping down in a monotonous rhythm that seemed to keep the worst of her horrors at bay.

"Baby, Baby, Baby," she continued to chant. "Baby, Baby."

Three frigid miles later Doris passed the airport road. Another mile and she reached the outlying shopping malls, their plethora of bright lights emerging suddenly out of the screen of snow. The traffic was now getting heavier as she neared town, and to avoid the dirty spray she was forced to squeeze farther onto the shoulder of the road, often having to climb up on the steep piles of compressed snow left by the early plows.

Doris crossed the highway on the overpass just beyond the Howard Johnson's and waded through the snow-choked peripheral roads leading into Cayuga Heights. Following her instincts, she negotiated the inner winding streets of the Heights. Here it was quieter, seemed warmer, the houses more protected from the storm, the snow less hostile, the tall pines beautiful under their crushing burden of snow. When she reached the street she had sought, her body began to quiver uncontrollably, her bottom row of teeth chattering against that lifeless upper plate. Her back ached, her hands throbbed, her feet felt like leaden stalks.

At the head of the street she came to an abrupt halt. A half block farther and across the street, through a veil of snow, she saw the imposing stone house that was the Shockleys' home. As she looked at it, her heart began to leap and her chest tightened.

The large house stood shrouded in a halo of white. The driveway and walk had been recently cleared. The garage stood open and abandoned and, though there was no car, she could see the shadow of the fishtailed tracks gouged through the snow. Doris riveted her attention on the stone facade of the building, stared and stared as if with her rheumy eyes she might penetrate its formidable opacity. She moved closer until she was almost across the street. The snow began to pick up, falling in large, wet clumps, striking with an almost audible splat, covering the Shockleys' drive and filling in the fishtailed sores. Doris remained fixed and waiting, planted in her spot, her solitary vigil unrelenting. The storm waxed and waned. Shafts of wind gusted through the street, driving up clouds of white that whistled through the wires. A big tree dropped its load of snow and shuddered in relief. Doris remained at her post, a lone figure engulfed by the storm, white and as unseen as the heavy-laden pines in the Shockleys' front yard.

Annette picked up the phone.

"How is she, Daddy?" she asked tremulously.

"Perfect," exclaimed Shockley. "It's nothing short of a miracle. No water in her lungs. She didn't even swallow a drop. No injuries of *any* kind. She had nothing but a nasty scare. She's even smiling a little now," he explained, and listened as Annette relayed the message to the cheers of Randy and Julie. "As a matter of fact, your mother and I are in worse shape than she is." He forced a chuckle, his body still trembling. "Have the television people come yet?" he asked a moment later.

"No," answered Annette, her voice noticeably subdued. "Wait!"

Shockley could hear Randy in the background running to the door.

"They're here. They're just coming up the drive. A whole mess of cars. What should we do?"

"Annette. Listen." Shockley's mind began to race.

"I'm listening."

"Tell Randy to come back. Not to open the door."

He waited as Annette repeated the message.

"OK," she said when Randy was back by the phone.

"I'm going to need the help of all you kids."

"Yes?"

The doorbell chimed.

"I don't want any of you to breathe a single word of what's happened. Do you understand?"

"Yes," she replied submissively.

"Now, tell that to Randy and Julie." He waited. "Where's Cindy?"

"Upstairs hiding. I think she's in the attic."

"I want you to go to her, stay with her and tell her Baby's not hurt. That's very important."

"I understand."

"And don't let her out of your sight. Try to comfort her. Tell her we're very upset but not angry."

"I don't particularly feel like talking to that little murderer," said Annette disgustedly.

"She's just a baby herself. She didn't know what she was doing."

"Oh, I wouldn't be so sure," she said bitterly. In the background Shockley could hear the doorbell chiming again.

"Let's get something straight. It's not for you or your sister or brother to judge her. I want you to make that clear to the others," he explained. "Now."

Annette repeated the message.

Shockley's throat felt tight and parched and he tried to swallow. His saliva felt like sand going down his gullet.

The doorbell chimed for the third time.

"All right," he continued tensely. "Let the television people in and let them set up. Just pretend that everything is perfectly normal. Tell them we got delayed somewhere. We're going to go through this as if absolutely nothing had happened. OK?"

"Sure, Daddy."

"The show must go on," he said, a trace of sadness in his voice.

"If you say so."

20

When Shockley and his wife returned home with Baby; the TV crew was already set up in the living room. The furniture that had been so carefully arranged earlier in the morning had been dragged away, and the lone couch shuffled to one side of the fireplace was being lit with kliegs. The rugs had been rolled back, and a sound man was taping down wires on the bare floor. A large camera perched on a tripod was having its magazines loaded with film while a man with a light meter circled the couch. The room was a jumble of boxes and wires and lights and people.

"Hi. I'm Jim Fowler," said the producer with the dark, droopy moustache approaching Shockley. "We spoke on the phone," he smiled cordially, holding out a hand.

"Sorry to be late. We had an unexpected problem," said Shockley, forcing a smile. Behind him stood Ruth holding Baby, who was resting flaccidly in her arms, the child still occasionally shuddering and emitting a residual sigh. "Baby's feeling a bit under the weather," he continued uncertainly. "I really don't know if she's up to going on for very long," he said, motioning to her. Annette stood in a far corner, fixedly watching her father as he spoke.

"In that case we'll try to make her part as quick as possible. Mrs. Shockley." He greeted Ruth, taking her hand, which was cold and limp. There were dark circles around her reddened eyes, and to Fowler she looked weak and ill.

"Well, it looks like we're ready to go," said Fowler loudly, catching the attention of his people, and it was then that Shockley noticed Joel Webster sitting off in a corner of the dining room with a woman, the two of them going over some last-minute notes. "Joel?" Fowler called out to him.

The woman looked up. Webster turned and, taking off his reading glasses, smiled toward the group. Although Shockley had never met him, Webster's angular and intense face was so thoroughly familiar that it felt as though he had known him all his life. Webster gathered up his papers in a neat sheaf and ambled over, his walk heavy-footed. Fowler introduced him. Webster mumbled some pleasantries to each of the adults and grinned at the infant in Ruth's arms. His manner was polite and polished and definitely businesslike. Webster's aloofness made Shockley uneasy.

"Shall we?" asked Webster, motioning toward the sofa after some strained small talk.

"Don't you want to outline with me beforehand what we're going to discuss?" asked Shockley puzzled.

"No. I don't think it's necessary. Actually, I think we'll just start rolling, if that's OK with you, Jim?" He checked with Fowler, who readily nodded, as though it had all been pre-arranged.

"Let's have all the kids in this opening shot," suggested the woman who had been sitting with Webster. She waved the three over, and Shockley excused himself as the family gathered by the couch. In a few minutes he returned with Cindy in tow. She looked pale and terrified and was unusually tight-lipped.

Shockley himself felt unsteady, and faint waves of nausea periodically rose and ebbed in his gut. He looked over at Baby, who lay passively in Ruth's arms, her eyelids heavy with exhaustion. Reaching out, he soothingly stroked her head, thinking to himself how lucky they were, how incredibly lucky. Furrowing her brow, Baby shifted her eyes and glanced over at him, a pained expression on her face.

The cameras started to roll.

They began with the kids, taking individual close-ups of each of the children for later cut-ins. Webster talked with them, asking them how they liked having a famous star like Baby living with them, what they thought of her music. Cindy answered with terse yeses and noes and nods of her head while the others tried to carry the ball. Watching them, Shockley felt pride at seeing how they behaved in the face of calamity.

Ruth went on camera. Haltingly she spoke about Baby's general routine in the home, how she fitted in, how the children had come to love and accept her—her eyes fleetingly meeting Shockley's.

The kids were then dismissed. The cameras were reloaded with fresh film and then Webster, moving a chair directly across from Shockley, started to question him.

WEBSTER: You're aware, Professor Shockley, of the skepticism, of the furor that's arisen since you've taken Baby on her latest tour around the country.

SHOCKLEY: Yes, Joel, I am. In fact, it's because of that skepticism, because of the attacks on Baby, her music, and even on me, that I've consented to this interview.

WEBSTER: You claim that Baby can sing.

SHOCKLEY: Yes.

WEBSTER: And she'll sing for us today?

SHOCKLEY: I hope so, though I can't guarantee it. She's her own master. [*Looking down at her.*]

WEBSTER: When did she start singing?

SHOCKLEY: Shortly after her birth.

WEBSTER: Which was?

SHOCKLEY: In June. [*Vaguely.*] Late June.

WEBSTER [*Sensing his reluctance.*]: I understand her mother was a fifty-seven-year-old woman.

SHOCKLEY [*Tersely.*]: Fifty-nine.

WEBSTER: Who claims the birth was a virgin birth.

SHOCKLEY: I really don't know anything about those claims. [*Trying to slough over the point and shift the line of questioning.*] That has never been my concern. The important point is that the child can and does sing.

WEBSTER: Do you attribute this to [*Struggles theatrically with his hand in the air as though probing for the word.*] to the hand of God? Is this child [*Looks down at Baby, who yawns loudly.*] the daughter of God?

SHOCKLEY [*Firmly.*]: Maybe this is a good time to set the record straight.

WEBSTER [*Giving a magnanimous smile, one eye directed toward the camera.*]: Be my guest.

SHOCKLEY: The fact that Baby can sing, could in fact sing almost from birth, is a marvel. To listen to her music is to be raised to lofty heights. With her songs she can stir the soul as I, as a composer—

WEBSTER: I understand you won a Pulitzer Prize for one of your works.

SHOCKLEY [*Modestly.*]: Yes. That's right. As I was saying, she can move people's emotions in ways that my music, or the music of other mortals, could never, ever, aspire to.

WEBSTER: Baby's a miracle.

SHOCKLEY [*Correcting.*]: A prodigy. A wonder, if you like.

But—But that's where it stops. She is not the daughter of God. Nor is she a messiah. Nor a messenger or what have you. Neither I nor Ivar Jacobsen, her manager, nor anyone else connected with her has ever maintained anything of that nature.

WEBSTER: Then how did this whole thing start?

SHOCKLEY: You mean the Babyists?

WEBSTER: Yes. Among others.

SHOCKLEY [*Surprised.*]: Others?

WEBSTER [*Firmly.*]: Others.

SHOCKLEY [*Heaving an audible sigh.*]: I don't know how it got started. I truly wish it hadn't. It can only make public access to Baby's music more difficult. As far as I'm concerned, these people, whoever they are, are misguided. [*Pauses.*] They're a bunch of fanatics and zealots. They're making it hard for Baby to function in the role that she was meant to function in.

WEBSTER: And that is?

SHOCKLEY: As a singer. As a performer.

WEBSTER: As a freak show?

SHOCKLEY: I resent that.

WEBSTER: Dr. Shockley, you launched Baby's career by first visiting a number of music schools around the country.

SHOCKLEY: Yes. That's correct. I anticipated a certain measure of skepticism and felt that she needed acceptance by some of the most prominent people in music today. That tour struck me as the best means to that end.

WEBSTER: Did you have permission from the mother to take her child on that tour?

SHOCKLEY [*Taken aback and unprepared.*]: Well, tacitly. Er, I suppose you could say so. There were many factors involved—including the mother's health. [*Clears his throat.*] The woman was very sick and apparently dying. Yes. I would say that there was a tacit understanding.

WEBSTER: Let's go back to her birth.

SHOCKLEY: I really don't know much about it.

WEBSTER: How did you discover her?

SHOCKLEY [*Reluctantly.*]: The way others did in Ithaca.

WEBSTER: And how was that?

SHOCKLEY: She was taken out by her mother to a local park, and she would often sing there. For small audiences. Er, there, or in front of her house. But this is really not germane to the—

WEBSTER [*Pointedly.*]: Why don't you let me decide that?

211

SHOCKLEY [*Looking at the cameras as they continue to whirl, unabated.*]: I'd really prefer limiting our discussion to Baby's present tour.

WEBSTER [*Oblivious of the objection.*]: Who is her mother?

SHOCKLEY [*Vaguely.*]: Er, Doris Rumsey.

WEBSTER: How did you get the child?

SHOCKLEY: She was put in our foster care by the Department of Social Services.

WEBSTER: Why?

SHOCKLEY [*Swallows uneasily.*] Why? [*Shrugs and tries to appear nonchalant.*] Apparently she was being neglected in her previous home.

WEBSTER: Was she?

SHOCKLEY: Well, according to the people at social services and according to the courts and whoever else was involved, it was determined that she was not getting proper care. I really don't know much more about it.

WEBSTER: Come now, Dr. Shockley. You don't mean to say that you didn't know the mother well *before* the child was placed in your custody.

SHOCKLEY [*Reddening.*]: I saw her singing. I listened to it. I was taken by it. If you're implying in any way that I was instrumental in her removal from the mother's custody, the answer is emphatically no! When I learned of the court decision my wife and I offered our services. Period.

WEBSTER: And not before?

SHOCKLEY [*Irritably.*]: I said *no*. If you want to know more, why don't you talk to the authorities? This is not a line of questioning I'm interested in pursuing. I thought you came here—

WEBSTER: Just what was your relation to—

SHOCKLEY [*Continuing.*]:—because you wanted to learn more about Baby.

WEBSTER: Were you in any way involved in the court procedures that led to Baby's removal from her home?

SHOCKLEY [*Vehemently.*]: I don't wish to pursue this line of discussion any further. It serves no purpose. Now is there anything more you'd like to know about Baby herself?

Shockley moved uncomfortably in his seat. His eyes strayed

212

from Webster, and looking beyond the glare of lights, he briefly caught sight of a snow-clad, hunched figure moving past his window and up the street.

21

Shockley fervently hoped that the New York City performances would go off without a hitch. After New York, Baby's next appearance was to be a series of Christmas concerts in Miami, and Shockley was looking forward to having Ruth and the kids join him there for the holidays. He figured that if he could just squeak through the New York shows without incident they could all celebrate Christmas together in the Florida sunshine and try to mend some of the rifts that had come between them. Almost from the start, however, his hopes were quashed.

When Shockley checked into the Plaza with Baby, he was met by a slender young man with blond hair and effeminate ways who introduced himself as Rolf Pettersson, another of Mr. Jacobsen's ubiquitous assistants.

"We anticipate a *little* bit of trouble tonight, sir," he said deferentially, after the bellboy had left and they were standing in Shockley's suite. Baby sat in the middle of the Oriental rug in the living room. Overhead a glittering chandelier caught her eye, and bending her head all the way back, she reached out her tiny hand as if she could grasp it.

"What kind of trouble?"

"Mr. Jacobsen wanted me to assure you that it's nothing."

"Well, what is it?"

"The CURB people are planning a demonstration outside of Avery Fisher. You know, the usual sort of thing."

Shockley shook his head. What was the usual?

"In order to avoid any kind of incident, we're going to use two cars as a diversion."

"Oh, Lord," said Shockley anxiously.

"This evening when you leave the hotel to go to the concert you'll, as usual, get into the limousine we'll have waiting in front. Instead of driving directly to Lincoln Center, it's going to head east to Third Avenue. There you'll change to a regular passenger sedan. The limousine will turn and take the regular approach to Lincoln Center. Inside will be someone who looks like you and he'll be carrying a bundle. Meanwhile, you and Baby will come in through a special back route."

"How do I know which sedan to get into?"

"That'll be easy. I'll be driving it. It's an old red Volvo. My car," he smiled sheepishly.

"And how the hell do I know that you really work for Ivar Jacobsen?"

Pettersson lifted up his eyebrows in confounded surprise.

"Well—Because—I—," he stumbled. "Why don't you just call up Mr. Jacobsen?" he said, finally gathering his senses.

"I will," said Shockley.

After Pettersson left, Shockley locked the door and went to change Baby, who was soaked from the long trip.

He scooped her off the rug and laid her on the bed in the adjoining room. First taking off her snowsuit, he slipped off her dress and unfastened her wet diapers. Baby lay quietly on the bed sucking her thumb, her knees brought up into a fetal position, her eyes peering expectantly up at him.

"Such a little troublemaker," he said, lovingly stroking her soft, pliant flesh. For a moment he stopped and studied her. Now, almost six months old, she was beginning to look more like a little girl than an infant. Her eyes were still as large and luminescently blue as ever, but some of the early baby fat from her face had melted away, giving it a slightly more mature appearance and defining the bones that formed her high cheeks. In the intervening months, her wispy hair had grown thick and dense and ever curlier, forming a blond halo that encircled her head. With her features more clearly defined, her babyish pug yielding to a thin and rather elegant nose, her chin emerging with a well-cut curve, Baby promised to be one very beautiful little girl—far more striking than she had ever been as an infant. Shockley searched her face and tried to match her features with those of Doris, but try as he might he could discern no resemblance and was secretly glad. He gazed down over her body. It was sturdier and plumper now than at any time since he had first seen her. From the length of her legs, her chubby but elongated fingers and her arms, he could see that she would ultimately be tall. No doubt, one day she would grow into a beautiful woman. It was hard for him to fathom that one day she would be a woman, imagine that she would have a lover, a husband. The thought made him shudder with a kind of fatherly jealousy. Somehow, previously, he had never thought of her in those terms. In his mind her image had been frozen, unyielding, as if she would always be just as she was now, just Baby.

Shockley took her into the bathroom, held her red and wrinkled rear under a stream of lukewarm water that gushed from the sink spigot. Carefully he patted her dry and carried her back into the sleeping quarters of the large suite. As he went about dressing her, he was reminded of his own Cindy when she was little like this, a pretoddler. And then he was thinking about Cindy as she was today.

"I didn't mean to do it! Really! I swear! " Cindy had shattered into tears as soon as the television people had left.

"I know," Shockley had said, trying to comfort her, touched by how she had fought back her emotion until this moment, and battling back his own tears. "I haven't been paying much attention to you lately, have I? " he asked, cuddling his daughter on his lap as Baby lay in Annette's arms intently observing it all.

"I was just bathing her with mommy," she said, as emotionally spent as they all were. "And the next thing I knew she was under water."

"It's OK," he had said, and Cindy looked at him with puzzlement. Then she had buried her head in her father's chest and wept bitterly.

That evening they had given Cindy dinner in bed, and after telling her a story, Shockley had tucked her in and turned out the light.

When Ruth was sure Cindy was fast asleep, she had finally broken her own silence.

"We can't take a chance again. No matter what she says."

"I really think it's going to be fine," he had said in a lowered voice.

"It's never going to be *fine*," Ruth spat out his words. "We'll never know for sure. I don't ever want to go through that again. Never ever!"

"What am I supposed to do?" he had asked worriedly. "Move out with Baby?"

"I've thought of that."

"I'm certainly not going to break up this home for Baby," he had replied determinedly. But he was also not going to give up Baby. Though he hadn't said it, he knew Ruth tacitly understood.

"Are you putting me to a choice?" he had finally asked after a long silence.

"No," Ruth had replied cautiously. "Not yet."

By six o'clock there was already a mass of noisy pickets concentrated in front of Avery Fisher Hall. By seven, still a good hour before Baby's concert, the ranks of the pack had swollen to an ugly, shoving mob barely containable by riot-equipped police.

From the safety of a window in Baby's dressing room Shockley watched the milling horde, their strident cries mingling and echoing up garbled from below. With a pair of opera glasses he tensely began to scan the waving placards.

"DENOUNCE THE PAGAN PROPHET" read one.

"THE LORD PUNISHES HEATHENISM" said another, bearing a large red crucifix.

He caught a momentary glimpse of a third that made his heart skip a beat. It read

"DEATH TO BABY"

He tried to read it again, but it disappeared from sight. Anxiously he kept searching the maze of signs, and when it popped back into view, he read it for a second time and saw that it actually said "DEATH TO BABYISM." He checked again, and though he was now sure that it read "Babyism" instead of "Baby," it seemed a paltry consolation.

Everything leading up to this show seemed to foreshadow disaster. Although he and Baby had been quietly ushered through the service tunnel running below the complex, the decoy car arriving a few seconds earlier had not fared as well. From what Shockley had learned, the limousine supposedly carrying Baby had been attacked by the crowd, people throwing themselves at the car, kicking it, and viciously smashing at the windshield with the poles from their signs. When the limousine had finally escaped under a rain of bottles and bricks, the mob had given off a unanimous cheer, certain that they had succeeded in aborting Baby's concert.

Shockley pulled himself away from the window and turned back to Baby, who sat in a portable crib in the darkened room. He picked her up and was about to shut the window when suddenly a deafening hue went up from the crowd, the sound expanding contagiously and building like the rumble of thunder. Holding Baby, he quickly went back to look. Below him he could see a contractive wave spreading over the mass and focusing on a single point at the periphery. Shockley picked up his binoculars and, following the wave, trained them on the point. From what he could make out amidst the pandemonium there were people scuffling with the police. With horror he watched as a cop lifted his club and brought it down on the head of a man. Then again on another man. Then a young girl. Shockley gagged in horror. Then he saw what was going on. A short distance away someone was being engulfed by the crowd at a point where the barricade had been breached. A man carrying a sign bearing the oval-lipped emblem of the Babyists had haplessly ventured too close and was being lunged at by the mob. Shockley heard piercing screams, the cries for blood going up. From across the avenue there came the wail of sirens as the pack tore at the man. Incredulously Shockley watched as the Babyist, covering his head, stumbled blindly under a rain of blows, men and women viciously tearing at him from all sides, kicking and stomping their crumbling victim. A phalanx of police was trying to break its way in to extricate the fallen man now consumed by the crowd, the cops swinging their clubs and driving a wedge through the unyielding cluster. Above the wail of sirens, the screams and bellows, the sounds of multiple explosions punctuated the air, echoing dully between the buildings. Shockley saw the clouds of gas billowing. The choking crowd pulled back as a team of gas-masked cops swept into the gap and dragged away the limp body of the Babyist, his face a bloody mass. From a block away there came the loud wail of an ambulance, its flashing red turret cutting through the haze.

Sickened, Shockley turned away as Baby, clinging to his

shoulder, maneuvered her head trying to look out. He pulled closed the window with his free hand and, drawing the blinds, turned on the lights in the dressing room. Baby blinked in the brightness, still straining toward the window. Shockley checked his watch. Another half hour until showtime. He wished Jacobsen were here. Osgood, who was doing a series of commercials in a downtown studio, would be arriving at the last minute. Shockley felt isolated and vulnerable alone with Baby. Three shows, he told himself, and we'll be out of this insane city and in the warm Florida sunshine. Already he could feel the healing rays soaking into his skin, see Baby tanned and content sitting with him in the hot sand at the edge of a surf-licked beach.

Osgood arrived still wearing his television makeup, and seemed hardly fazed by the crowds outside.

"Just a bunch of nuts," he said breezily. "It'll pass."

Once the orchestra started up and Osgood had the audience in control, the people singing along to Kramer's song, Shockley began to relax for the first time since arriving in New York. He smoked a cigarette he had bummed from one of the stage crew and stood in the wings listening to the audience as the wardrobe lady went through her last-minute preparations, tying on Baby's head the oversized pink bonnet.

> Baby, Baby,
> Our voice from heaven,
> Easing our pains . . .

Shockley took a peek through the space in the curtain. Compared to the frenzy outside, the audience seemed safe and civilized as they stood holding hands, swaying as they sang.

> Lifting our burdens with your sweet song,
> When you sing, the world . . .

Almost everywhere Shockley looked he could see those golden lips.

> Baby, Baby,
> Baby, Baby.

"Dr. Shockley?" said an elderly man, catching Shockley unawares as he took a fresh puff on his cigarette.

Shockley spun around and coughed.

"I'm sorry to startle you," he apologized softly, a benign smile creasing his ruddy-complexioned face. "I'm Thomas Fitzgibbons," he explained and waited.

Shockley looked at him puzzled. The man had a striking head of snow-white hair combed straight back from his high forehead, accentuating a big, broad smile. Though he had heavy jowls that weighed down his features, there was a distinct youthful bounce to his manner, and when he spoke, he had a distinguished air that reminded Shockley of an aging stage actor. Though he couldn't immediately place the face, Shockley knew that he had seen him somewhere before.

"Thomas Fitzgibbons," the man repeated seeing his confusion. "Father Tom."

"A Babyist?" Shockley inquired warily and then saw the heavy gold lips that hung from a chain partially hidden by his tweed jacket.

"Yes, I'm one of them," he admitted openly. "I've wanted to talk to you for some time, but, until now you've been unreachable," he said candidly. "Matter of fact, I had to sneak back here." Fitzgibbons smiled, his eyes twinkling. "So if you wish, you could easily have me thrown out."

"Why would I want to do that?" asked Shockley, disarmed by the man's frankness.

"Well, we've tried to contact you before—" He shrugged, and it was then that Shockley suddenly recognized him.

"Weren't you?" said Shockley, trying to put his finger on Fitzgibbons's past. "Weren't you involved in the antiwar movement?" he said, finally placing the face. "Yes. Fitzgibbons." Thomas Fitzgibbons. The activist Catholic priest. Very early on in the war he had heard Father Tom—as he was called by the students—speak on campus. It was ancient history now, but Shockley could remember being in sympathy with the man from the start, admiring his guts and determination and ultimate bravery. "So, from Jesuit to Babyist," said Shockley without a trace of malice. "That's quite a leap, isn't it?"

"Yes," agreed Fitzgibbons rather matter-of-factly.

The ineradicable image of the Babyist outside the hall being mauled by the crowd popped into his head. It now all made a bit more sense. With defections from people of Fitzgibbons's stature, it was little wonder the established churches felt threatened.

"A Babyist," Shockley repeated to himself, as though letting it sink in.

"Some of us have seen the light," Fitzgibbons said, and then, with a touch of humor, added, "or heard the song."

Shockley grinned. The man had a seductive way about him, and considering his record, the years he had sat in prison for what he believed in, he would be a hard man to simply discount.

"From what I understand, you think that we're a bunch of nuts."

"Well, I've"—Shockley searched for words—"I've never said quite that," he hedged.

"The reason I've been so eager to see you is that I'd like to dispel that image."

Shockley remained silent.

"I think it's important, now more than ever, that I tell you a little about us, about our beliefs, about how we feel."

"I think I know. You think she's the messiah, right?"

"Yes. In a sense. We feel that Baby is a gift from God."

"You could say that of all children, couldn't you?"

"Certainly."

"If you believe in God," Shockley added, quickly setting the record straight.

"For us—and we believe in a Supreme Being—he is speaking to us through the song of this child, his child, his daughter, just as he did through his son Jesus Christ." Fitzgibbons paused. "Her music," he continued, closing his eyes and going off into a reverie, "her music is the distillation of life itself, each precious drop bringing us closer to heaven, bringing order to chaos around us." He opened his eyes and looked directly at Shockley, who seemed unaffected. "Her music taps the springs of earthly human experience, compelling the spirit to burst forth. When I listen to this child, I am listening to all that is pure and good and heavenly."

"Well, you've got no argument there," said Shockley, recognizing that Fitzgibbons's words were so close to what he had once read in a Babyist pamphlet that he suspected Fitzgibbons to be the author. "But what you're talking about is the role of art, of music, not the direct hand of God."

"Well, if you want to call it art, fine. It's the Creator's art. Ultimately all art goes back to God—if you believe in him," said Fitzgibbons, gently backing off.

"You're not going to convert me to Babyism, you know," said Shockley defensively.

"It never was my intention. There's no need. Baby makes her own converts," he said succinctly. "All I've wanted to accomplish is to let you know we're here to protect Baby, support her. Whatever it is that she needs, we're here to provide."

Shockley looked at him, a glimmer of suspicion growing in his eyes.

"We're here to serve her," he repeated emphatically, sensing Shockley's skepticism and wanting to leave no room for doubt. "To give. Not to take."

"But there is something you want. Otherwise, why would you be talking to me now?"

"Just to keep the lines of communication open. That's all."

"OK, they're open." Shockley nodded.

"We just wouldn't want anything—" said Fitzgibbons, almost as an afterthought, "anything to occur that might interfere with our being able to hear Baby," he said and, without elaborating, clasped his hands together and turned to the stage as Osgood finished his introduction and Baby came rising up from the depths of the pit.

"Sing, Baby. Sing!" cried the audience in eager anticipation. "Sing!"

Outside, the crowds were assembling again for a new confrontation.

Shockley had reservations on the midnight flight to Miami, and when Baby completed her last concert in New York, he made a dash with her through the back tunnel to Rolf Pettersson's waiting Volvo. Their bags were in the car and everything was set.

Shockley and Baby, however, never made it to Miami. It had been snowing all afternoon, and by nightfall the highways were so bogged down in deepening snow that Pettersson was forced to turn back when they reached the expressway in

Queens, the Volvo narrowly making it back through the thickening maze of stranded vehicles clogging the roads.

"Consider yourself lucky," said Pettersson, heaving a sigh when they finally pulled up in front of the Plaza. He knew what the city roads were like, and had it not been for Shockley's insistence, he would never have ventured even as far as Queens. As it turned out, all flights in and out of the city were ultimately canceled as of midnight. Up and down the Atlantic Coast from Bangor to Norfolk airports were being shut down as a sprawling blizzard that had been brewing in the Ohio Valley began dumping a record three feet of snow along an eight-state-wide swath. Following on the heels of this storm, according to the ominous forecast, was another deep, low-pressure system, carrying with it the promise of yet more snow.

By the time Shockley checked back into the Plaza, the city was at a virtual standstill. Bus service had long since ceased, subways were stalled, phones malfunctioned, and there were many areas in the boroughs without power. Though thwarted in his quest for sun, Shockley realized that he was more than lucky to get back his familiar suite at the overflowing hotel.

As city crews began to tackle the overwhelming task of digging out amidst freshly accumulating mounds of snow, Jacobsen was on his Teletype attempting to reshuffle Baby's bookings, Osgood's agent was racking his brains seeing if he could fill in his client's downtime with some quick commercial spots, Shockley was trying to get through to Ithaca to let Ruth know the trip was temporarily off, and Mayor Koch, frantically manning his crisis center, was declaring a state of emergency and pleading with the governor to call out national guard troops.

It looked as if it were going to be one long siege.

22

S hockley tried to make the best of the coming days. Keeping to his suite of rooms, he had all his meals sent up. He read, watched television, and tried to entertain Baby. To break the monotony, he repeatedly called Ruth to get an update on an equally snowbound Ithaca. Inactivity never wore well with Shockley and by the end of the second day he finally understood the term *cabin fever*. From that point on he was constantly on the phone to the airlines, booking and rebooking space on phantom flights south. Concert or not, he and Baby were going to get out of this miserable cold for at least a few days, and he was damned if the family was not going to be reunited for Christmas. Dealing with the airlines was exasperating. The phone lines were forever busy. When he finally got ticket agents on the line, they usually gave contradictory information. Yes, there would be flights by the next morning. No, the airport was snowed in and, because of the blowing drifts and an approaching new storm, it was likely to stay that way until the end of the week.

Shockley felt himself in a state of suspension, which unnerved him. He felt the overwhelming need to utilize the time profitably, but that dangling sense of expectancy kept him from doing little more than reading the novels he had gleaned from the racks in the magazine stands in the lobby. Those and some of the Babyist literature that Fitzgibbons had insisted on leaving with him. Only once did it occur to him to try his hand at composing. He immediately dismissed the notion. It was, he told himself, a closed chapter.

But there it was, that nagging need to *do* something, to be active, to fight against the restraints of inertness. Secretly he envied those who knew how to let loose, to have a grand time, to have—fun.

After three days of confinement, Shockley knew he could not look at another paperback or television show or crossword puzzle or Babyist brochure without letting out a shriek. He had had it. He and Baby were going out that night. For dinner downstairs, and afterward—afterward a show, or something—anything! The hell with the Babyists and CURBISTS and all the other damn *ists*!

With Baby in one arm, Shockley passed the Palm Court, the strains of a violin fiddling some schmaltzy Viennese waltz drifting out between the palms. For an instant he considered going into the lobby restaurant with its plethora of rich desserts displayed on a cart by the entrance, but then he changed his mind and headed toward the Edwardian Room. There in the vaulted dining room with dark oak paneling and white pillars, red walls above the dark wood and ponderous chandeliers, he and Baby were shown to a small corner table. The maître d' lifted a finger and instantly a waiter appeared with a high chair. In a moment they were seated and Shockley was scanning the menu.

"Tonight you and I are going to have some fun for a change," he told Baby, handing her a piece of pumpernickel to nibble on. Baby bit down on the hard crust, kneading it against her bottom gums, where her first teeth were just starting to cut through. Desultorily she glanced around the sparsely populated dining room, then tilted her head back and stared up at the high ceiling. A small rivulet of drool mixed with crumbs cascaded down Baby's chin, and Shockley, putting down the menu, wiped it off with his napkin. As Shockley turned back to the bill of fare, his attention was suddenly caught by someone being shown to a distant table across the dimly lit room. Pretending to busy himself with his choice, Shockley peeked over the top of the card. His eyes nearly popped out. Being seated there by herself at a red-curtained window was, he could have sworn, the woman he had seen at the party the night of Baby's opening in Cleveland—that Slavic-looking beauty with the wide, high cheeks and svelte body. It had to be. After ordering, to make doubly certain, he put on his glasses and let his eyes drift over in her direction. Yes, it was. Not his imagination, as had happened before. He was positive. How could he ever forget a face like hers! What a coincidence! What luck!

Nervously he sipped his water, put down the glass, and watched as the waiter, who had been hovering attentively in the background, came forward and filled it again to the brim.

Baby dropped her piece of bread. The waiter picked it up and with a smile gave her a new piece. Another waiter appeared from the kitchen with a tureen of steaming soup. After he was served, Shockley poured off a little of the clam broth into a separate dish, careful to strain out the pieces. Blowing on each hot spoonful, he fed Baby, who noisily slurped up the liquid, half of it running down onto her chin and bib.

When Baby finished her portion, Shockley began to work on the remaining soup, his eyes perpetually shifting back to the woman by the window. In fact, as the meal progressed through the filet mignon, the asparagus tips in sauce Béarnaise, the tossed salad, even through the strawberry soufflé, coffee, and Grand Marnier, Shockley found that he could hardly take his eyes off the woman. She was, as he had first realized that drunken night in Cleveland, one of the most gorgeous women in his memory.

With coffee he requested a pack of cigarettes and lit one up. He inhaled and watched the smoke drift upward from his lips. He toyed with his cigarette, knocked off some ash, took another puff, his thoughts obsessively returning to the woman.

Shockley glanced over again to her table. She, too, was finished with dinner, and he realized that if he didn't talk to her now, get up and introduce himself this instant, he might never again in his life have the chance. He looked over at Baby, who was playing with the remains of her meal, moving crumbs and strands of noodles around the tray of her high chair in busy patterns. It was now or never, he told himself. He tried to lift himself from his chair but was gripped by fright.

When the check came, Shockley signed it and finally rose. Sliding Baby out of her chair, he stood by his table and felt the veiled gaze of the waiters upon him. He could hear his heart pounding in his chest, and he cursed himself for being such a coward. Slowly he headed for the dining room exit. Nearing the door, he suddenly stopped and, as if just discovering her, turned and approached her table.

"Excuse me," he said, as she looked up at him for the first time, her green almond eyes meeting his and causing him to melt. "This may sound silly," he began tremulously, "but I think—I think we've met before."

She smiled, her eyes flashing.

"Aren't you—Aren't you?" She wiggled her long fingers in the air as if trying to extricate his name.

"Irwin Shockley," he coaxed.

"And this is Baby," she said, reaching out and taking Baby's small hand in hers.

Baby looked down at her with bored disapproval.

"We met—?"

"In Cleveland"—he jogged her memory—"you were at Baby's gala in Cleveland."

"What a memory you have," she said, her voice having the faint tinge of an accent.

"I always remember faces," he lied.

"We didn't even have a chance to speak."

"But we do now," he said, a glint in his eye.

Would she mind if he and Baby joined her?

Of course not. It would be a pleasure.

Would she care for an aperitif? Perhaps some more coffee?

Waiter, a little more coffee for the lady. We'll also have Cointreau. No, just for the two of us, he joked. The baby isn't drinking tonight.

What fantastic luck meeting her, he thought. These days in New York were not going to be a waste, after all.

Her name was Irina, she told him in nearly faultless English.

"When I first saw you, I was certain you were Russian," he bubbled.

"Well, that's almost right. My father was Russian. My mother's Italian. But my father's parents were partly Polish and Hungarian. I'm a real mutt." She laughed, biting down delectably with her sharp teeth on her tongue.

"Well, despite all the handicaps, you seem to have turned out remarkably well," Shockley joshed exuberantly.

She told him that she lived in Cleveland, that she was in New York on business. A pending divorce. Sorry, he commiserated. Oh no, she said, she was happy. Now she was finally free, and rich, she laughed naughtily.

Baby sat momentarily forgotten in the high chair that the waiter had carried over from Shockley's table, her head moving from one adult to the other, watching the ongoing ritual.

Would Irina care for another drink?

Would she, Shockley ventured unsurely, care to join them in their suite upstairs? These days, what with all the publicity and troubles, it was best not to be out in public too much. Perhaps she'd care for some champagne? Yes, a bottle of champagne.

226

After all these days of being holed up in his suite, he was feeling in a festive mood, he explained to her.

In the elevator up, he hinted at how, after spotting her at that party in Cleveland, he had not been able to forget her.

When they toasted each other in the sitting room, toasted her divorce, Baby's future, Shockley confessed that he had noticed her as she came into the dining room but had been afraid to approach her.

"Silly man," she said, her eyes locking with his and then drifting down his face to his lips.

I can't believe this, he muttered to himself. When he put Baby into her crib in the bedroom, he noticed that his hands were shaking. For a fleeting moment he thought about Ruth, thought about her and pushed her from his mind.

He came back into the sitting room and found Irina waiting on the sofa with an empty glass. Eagerly, too eagerly, he poured it full. It foamed over and ran onto her dress. Nervously he apologized, patting her lap dry with a handy diaper, his face feeling as though it were on fire.

"I—I—" He started to speak, but his voice failed him.

"Yes?" she asked, looking up at him, her face alive and glowing from the champagne.

"I know this is going to sound ridiculous."

"We won't know until you say it, will we?" she said coaxingly.

"I want you," he finally blurted out, looking hungrily at her. "From the first moment I set eyes on you, I've wanted you." He swallowed and, taking quick, shallow breaths, waited.

"I know," she said matter-of-factly. "Is that so ridiculous?"

"Oh, God, no," he blustered, relieved to finally have it out. "That's not what I meant. It's just that I had to say it," he apologized. "I've never been very good at keeping things in." He rushed over his words.

"Don't explain," she said, sitting there expectantly.

The smile on Shockley's face froze. Cautiously he moved toward her. He sank down next to her on the sofa and paused as though waiting to be rebuffed. She remained motionless. He brought his face close to hers. They looked at each other for a short eternity. She was young, so very young, he thought. Her skin flawless. Her eyes luminescently green. There was an exotic appeal to her face that drew him ever closer. Awkwardly, he pressed his lips against hers. Her lips parted. He felt her arm caress his neck and gently pull him close. Her tongue touched his and he began to tremble, his entire body shaking in anticipation.

It's a dream, said one side of his mind over and over. The other side was trying to remind him that she was just a woman, an exquisite one, certainly, but just a woman. No more, no less. The tug-of-war, however, was an uneven one, and knowing it, he surrendered and eagerly led her into the bedroom.

In her crib Baby was lying on her back, her thumb planted in her mouth. Her knees were flexed up to her stomach, and with her free hand she was idly playing with her toes. Her eyes shifted to the pair when they entered the room.

Shockley began to undress Irina, fumbling with the front buttons on her dress. She saw his trouble, smiled, kissed him, and helped. Overwhelmed, he watched as she slid out of her dress, out of her slip, out of her pantyhose.

"Did anyone ever tell you you're beautiful beyond words?" he said, beholding her long silky legs, her narrow waist, her firm breasts, which stood pertly by themselves. His eyes again traveled down the length of her, stopping at the light patch of pubic hair incongruous with her long black tresses.

"Never," she said disingenuously. "Now it's your turn." She laughed and began unbuttoning his shirt.

Shockley took off his shirt. Confronted by the youth of her body, he felt unequal. He undressed and pulled himself close, his throbbing groin pressed hard against her belly. He reached around her and stroked her body almost too carefully, as if afraid that if he touched too firmly she might evaporate.

He flung off the covers to the bed, and they melted into the cool, fresh linens, which smelled fragrantly of soap. Shockley tried to think, to make sense of what was occurring, but pressed as he was against the smooth warmth of her body, his mind refused to cooperate. Then, almost without knowledge, he was sliding into the very soft core of her body, an audible cry emerging from deep within her throat. She was so beautiful that, as they made love, he felt compelled to keep his eyes open. Pulling back, his hips moving in an hypnotic rhythm of their own, he drank in her being, her lanky legs that were brought up around him, her arms that reached out to stroke him, her narrow pelvis that undulated under him, her face frozen in a distant, ecstatic smile, her teeth gleaming through her warm lips, the mounds of her breasts capped by bright, taut nipples. He soaked in her image, savoring it, burning it indelibly upon the memory of his brain so that he could never in a lifetime forget her. He tried to hold himself back, delay this flashing instant in the continuum of time, the days and months and years that made a man's life, preserve it, store it. His eyes caressed her body, and then, for an instant, he caught a glimpse of Baby in her crib. Holding on to the bars, she was standing and watching them. Blindly he groped out for the covers, trying to pull them over, but it was too late. The tension had mounted in his loins until he could bear it no more; his body quivered, his eyes slammed shut with an explosive force, his cries mingled with hers, and there was nothing in the world but the two of them.

When Shockley got up out of bed, Baby was still standing there, holding on to the edge of her crib, her eyes following him as he padded across the room and into the bathroom. Irina lay curled up in bed, asleep.

As he adjusted the water gushing out of the spigot, clumsily alternating between the the extremes of burning hot and freezing cold, Shockley was wondering about her, the woman in his bed. He was wondering if she had been attracted to him or if she were no more than a groupie of sorts. He hoped to hell she wasn't a Babyist. Though it was unlikely. If she were, she would have been wearing a pair of those fool lips, would have paid more attention to Baby.

Shockley washed and then dried himself. He looked at his face in the mirror. Under the harsh light above the medicine cabinet it looked old to him, old by comparison to hers. There were lines on his forehead, crow's-feet by his eyes, a deep furrow running between his eyebrows. Where was all this going? he asked. What was it leading to? He stood staring at his reflection. He knew that by all rights he should feel ashamed and guilty, yet he felt preponderantly guilt-free. Happy, in fact. For the first time in ages he felt invigorated. Young. Only those damn lines on his face contradicted his feeling of rebirth.

Shockley wrapped a towel around his waist and sauntered back to the bedroom. He found the covers drawn back, the bed empty. Irina's clothes, which had been lying on a chair, were gone. Instantly his eyes shot over to the crib expecting to see Baby's curious little head still peering over the bars. No head. No Baby. The crib was empty.

He rushed into the sitting room. It was deserted. He ran back into the bedroom, then back again into the sitting room. He even looked into the bathroom.

Frantically he raced from window to window, checking each one. He went to the door of the suite. It was unlocked. Clad still in only his towel, he sprinted out into the corridor. He charged up and down the intersecting hallways, then raced over to the bank of elevators. The arrows were pointing up and down in a confusion of signals. Bolting for the fire exit, he raced down ten flights of stairs, checking each level. He reached the lobby and ran toward the main entrance.

Hitting the bronze front doors, he burst through, nearly bowling over the astonished doorman. He was flying bare-footed down the snowy steps when he saw the car pull away— Irina sitting in the front seat holding a blanket-clad bundle against her as the car skidded off through the deep snow.

"Baby!" cried out the voice rising from the depths of his soul. "Baby! Baby!" he bellowed forlornly, the snow rising up over his ankles.

THREE

23

N ow let me get this here straight," said Detective Feldman to Shockley, his Brooklynese tinged with suspicion. "You never met this woman before in your life, right? Yet she just waltzes in here and takes off with the kid?"

"Well—I—I saw her at a reception in Cleveland, and I think I may have spotted her after that a couple of times. I'm not sure, but I never talked to her before this evening," said Shockley, hunched in his chair. As he ran his hands nervously through his hair, his gaze fell on one of Baby's toys that lay abandoned on the sitting-room rug, and a sharp pain stabbed at him. He looked back up at the cop, who was hovering impatiently above him.

"Look, if we're going to get your child back you're going to have to cooperate a little—level with us," said Detective Hoover, standing with his hands in his pockets and looking out the window at the traffic that crept along the south rim of the park. He was a barrel-chested man, whose clothes seemed almost too small to contain him. Wearing a perpetually somnolent look, he had until this moment remained silent, seemingly content to listen. "With all due respect," he continued, "this sounds like a lot of bullshit to me."

"Was she a hooker?" asked Feldman.

"No, of course not!" said Shockley, pressing his hands together to keep them from shaking. "Listen, I've given you a complete description of the woman. The waiters downstairs can corroborate it. I've told you the car was an older Ford, maybe '70 or '71."

"But you have no license number."

"No. I didn't get it. I've told you that. Why the hell don't you check with the doorman? He must have seen more than I did. That car was probably waiting for her out there all the time. Look"—he gritted his teeth—"I've told you everything I know."

"Have you?" asked Hoover, and his apparent insouciance rattled Shockley.

"If she's a known hooker we could probably have her picked up in less than an hour," Feldman persisted.

"But she's *not* a hooker! Can't you get that straight?"

"How can you be so sure if you don't know her?" asked Hoover, zeroing in.

The phone rang. Both cops suddenly jumped to life.

Feldman grabbed Shockley's hand as he reached for the phone and held it for a moment.

The muscles in Hoover's face tensed, tight strands of tendon protruding through his skin as he moved away from the window. On the third ring he motioned for Shockley to pick it up. Again reaching for the receiver, Shockley felt his heart race.

"Hello?" he said anxiously, and listened.

The cops looked at each other.

"It's for you," said Shockley a moment later, and he could see the detectives sinking back into their lethargy, punctured, Feldman gravitating down on the arm of the sofa as his partner took up the phone.

Hoover mumbled something, his lips barely moving, then hung up.

"That's Franken over at the Bureau," he said. "They're coming in on the case. Now"—he turned menacingly on Shockley—"you're sure it's a kidnapping?"

"No, I gave her Baby!" Shockley spat out angrily.

"There'll be hell to pay if it isn't," warned Feldman.

"Tell us about the woman again," said Hoover, forever circling the same point like a vulture sensing carrion. His gaze drifted around the room, taking in the ornate fixtures and furnishing, and in his eyes there was unveiled contempt. He never particularly liked rich people, folks who lived their lives sealed in their fancy hotel suites and penthouses, moving in air-conditioned limousines between safe points in a rarefied space, insulated from the everyday dirt and mayhem of the street.

"Again?"

"Again. And start at the beginning."

"There's nothing more to tell. I met her in the dining room. She came up for a drink. I went to the bathroom. When I returned she was gone and so was Baby. That's it. Period," he said. He recalled Baby's innocent little face, how she stood up in her crib for the first time in her life, and he felt a pang of emptiness as though a hole had been permanently punched out of his life.

"You been sleeping?" asked Feldman, looking into the bedroom.

"Huh?"

"The bed," he said, motioning with his chin. "It's all mussed up." He strolled into the room, walked first over to the crib and then the large double bed. "Hey, this your long, dark hair?" he called, lifting a strand from the pillow and, coming back into the room, dangled it in front of Shockley before slipping it into an envelope.

Shockley stared down at his hands.

"Come clean," said Hoover irritably. "Shit, man, we weren't born yesterday."

"You're insulting our fucking intelligence," muttered Feldman.

"Are you in on this in some way? Is this a con?"

"Was she a partner?"

"What?" Shockley asked astounded.

"What's the scam, huh? Insurance money on the kid? A publicity stunt?"

"Scam? My child has been kidnapped and you're standing here accusing me of a scam?" he said, livid. "You should be out looking for her, not standing here hassling me."

"Yeah? Well, tell us where."

"You got any hot tips?"

"Maybe," said Shockley, looking up, a rim of red underlining his eyes. "I'm not sure."

"Who?"

"It's only a hunch."

"Who?"

"The Babyists."

"Huh?" asked Feldman.

"You know," explained Hoover, "the ones with the lips."

"Why them?"

"Why not?" said Shockley, warming to the idea. The more he thought about it, the surer he became. It was a setup right from the beginning in Cleveland when he had first spotted Irina and those lips. He struggled to remember if she had been one of those wearing a pair of lips that first evening. "They've been dying to get their hands on her."

"That don't mean they took her."

"This guy Fitzgibbons, Thomas Fitzgibbons, approached me during one of the shows here in the city—"

"And?"

"It's what he said."

"Yeah?"

"He said"—Shockley racked his brain to recall the words—"he said, 'We just wouldn't want anything to happen to Baby that might interfere with us being able to hear her.'"

"Doesn't sound very incriminating to me."

"It's not really what he said; it's how he said it."

The cops looked at each other for a moment.

"Why don't you question him? He must know something."

The buzzer to the suite sounded, and Feldman opened the door. Behind it stood two men dressed in squarely cut dark suits. Rushing up the corridor directly behind them were a television crew and a group of reporters. The detective let the two men slip in and held the others back with a raised hand.

The door closed on the newsmen, and the four conferred in a quick huddle.

Shockley sat and watched, helpless. He was thinking about Baby. He just hoped to God that Irina—or whatever her name really was—hadn't already sneaked Baby out of the city or, worse, out of the country. He hoped that she was taking good care of her. That Baby was being fed, kept warm, that she wasn't terrified by the strangers. If only he could just get his hands

236

on that lousy woman, he'd strangle her pretty neck with his bare hands. Shockley stared morosely out the window. It had stopped snowing, and the dark night sky was beginning to clear. Above the illuminated haze of the city he could make out through chinks in the clouds the light of a few solitary stars. The storm had run its course. His had only begun.

"There's more to the story," Shockley muttered.

The cops all turned around.

"Good," said Detective Hoover, with a glint in his eye. "Now we're finally going to find out what you were doing running around outside with just a towel on."

"Let me start at the beginning," he said, and knew that he had fooled no one but himself.

Once the FBI took over the case, they decided that the most prudent approach would be to keep a low profile. Attempting to simulate the appearances of minimal police intervention, they immediately pulled back the city police as well as their own agents, keeping a tight but invisible surveillance on the hotel.

That night, Shockley sat by the phone in his suite hoping against hope for contact by the kidnappers. The line was coupled to the Manhattan field office of the FBI, where an agent also sat vigil, waiting for the ring that would give the investigation its first substantive clue. As the long night wore on and no attempt for ransom was initiated, Shockley became more convinced than ever that it was the Babyists. They had stolen Baby, so his reasoning ran, because they feared that he might end Baby's tour as a result of the continuing violence at the concerts. Fitzgibbons's concern about access to Baby, suddenly voiced after all these weeks, solidified Shockley's conviction.

Going on Shockley's lead, the FBI began rounding up for questioning prominent Babyists across the country. One of the first to be pulled in was Father Thomas Fitzgibbons.

"That's not the way we operate," Fitzgibbons told his interrogators, appearing genuinely distraught. "A kidnapping is contrary to everything we hold sacred. It's a vicious, deplorable act."

What was he doing backstage?

"I was hoping to initiate a dialogue from which we might develop a way for us to serve her."

Why suddenly then, just two scant days before her kidnapping, had he made his approach?

"Pure coincidence. The time was ripe. The opportunity presented itself."

They showed Fitzgibbons the sketch of the alleged woman kidnapper done by a police artist. Fitzgibbons studied it carefully for a long minute.

"To the best of my knowledge," he said, "I've never set eyes on her in my life."

"He's lying!" Shockley told the agent, who called at 4:00 A.M. to inform him of the questioning. "If Fitzgibbons is not behind it, then it's one of the other Babyists," he injected as an afterthought.

After the call Shockley tried to catch some sleep, but his conscience gave him no peace. Over and over he replayed the evening's sequence of events, hunting in vain for a clue. Repeatedly he berated himself for not having the presence of mind to take down the license number of the car, cursed himself for ever having left the suite, for ever having gotten involved with that damn woman.

As he lay tossing in bed, Fitzgibbons's reply to the police began to bother him, too. As he recalled the Babyist literature he had read, Fitzgibbons's response did have the ring of truth to it. The Babyists, from what he had been able to glean, were Christians—neo-Christians, as they called themselves. They accepted the Old and New Testaments as part of their faith, the appearance on earth of Jesus as the son of God. Although their prayers and liturgy now recognized a new trinity—the Father, the Son, and the Daughter—they did preach a return to fundamental Judeo-Christian morality, to purity, honesty, and goodness, all that they heard in Baby's song. Could they really steal a child without violating their own tenets?

Shockley gave up sleep and continued to wait by the phone, watching the sky turn bright as morning broke over the city, the sun filtering in shafts of red through the gaps between the buildings lining the east side. The day promised to be clear, cloud free, and bitterly cold. A sanitation truck with plow moved noisily up and down the street, pushing back the high banks of still-clean snow.

Just after seven, Shockley notified the FBI man by means of the newly installed auxiliary phone that he was stepping out for a minute. He rode the elevator down to the lobby, went into a phone booth, and, granted that modicum of privacy, called home.

"Ruth, darling," he said hoarsely, feeling spongy and wrung out.

"Irwin?" she said, surprised to hear from him so early in the morning. "Is something wrong?"

"Matter of fact, yes," he said, and knew that she hadn't yet turned on the radio. "I wanted to talk to you before you hear the story from somewhere else."

"Oh, my God," she said. "Something's happened to Baby."

"Yes," he said tersely. "She's been kidnapped."

Ruth gasped.

"The police are on it. The FBI. The New York police. Don't panic. I'm sure we'll get her back," he tried to sound reassuring, but his voice belied the message.

"Oh, Irwin, can I help? Should I come in?"

"No, not right now," he stalled. "Listen, there's something else you should know."

"What?" she asked, short of breath. "How did it happen?"

"That's what I wanted to talk to you about"—he hesitated—"before you hear it from other sources." Shockley struggled to recall how he had planned to break the truth, but his rehearsed lines evaded him.

"Is it bad?" she asked, sobbing quietly.

"There was a woman," he said.

"I don't understand," she questioned, but knew she did.

"I got—involved—with a woman. A stupid thing."

Silence.

Shockley waited for her voice, but all he could hear was the faint, indistinguishable background of cross-talk riding the waves of static.

"She took Baby," he struggled to explain.

Still silence.

"I'm sorry," he said lamely, hearing her cry on the other end. "Terribly sorry," he lamented when her silence became unbearable. "I just had to tell you," he continued, but the connection had already been severed and he was speaking to a dead line.

"Oh, good. I'm glad you called," said Harry Terkel, standing by the desk. He had just stepped in his office and was still wearing his overcoat. "I've been trying to reach you."

"I haven't got my phone yet," said Doris, standing in her neighbors' trailer and trying to hear Terkel above the racket of their five small children.

"Well, I've got good news and I've got bad news," he quipped. "Which do you want first?"

"Whatever," answered Doris. She was in no mood this morning for jokes. All last night she had had trouble sleeping and had awakened with an excruciating headache and chills. She wondered if she were coming down with a flu.

"The good news first. The appellate court has granted your case preference. That means they're going to move it up on the calendar," he added when she gave no response.

"When are they going to hear it?" she asked. An infant was crying loudly in the background, and as she stuffed a finger into her free ear, Doris was thinking about her own Baby, that sweet angel who had never cried, never complained.

"I can't get a straight answer out of the clerk, but, I'm only guessing now, I think it'll be sometime after New Year's, probably in the latter part of February."

"But that's two months away!" Doris objected. "And that's the *good* news?" she asked testily.

"Very good news," Terkel responded defensively, surprised by her ingratitude.

"And the bad news?"

"The stay we requested for the family court order was denied."

"Oh," said Doris, trying to think through the haze of her throbbing head.

"But I told you that was a long shot. Remember?"

"Yes. I know you did," Doris answered wearily, heaving a long sigh.

"Don't worry," Terkel tried to cheer her up. "We'll get her back. It's just a matter of time. Hang in there."

24

Hey, Fay, she's starting in again!" called the man standing guard at the shattered window. Peering out over the line of plastic that had been hastily tacked up to cover the missing lower panes, he nervously scanned the empty street, trying to ignore the singing that issued from the far-rear room. Though his face was covered with a growth of thick stubble, he was a ruggedly handsome man. With chiseled features and a square jaw, clear, piercing brown eyes, and carefully cut dark-blond hair, he looked noticeably out of place in this condemned South Bronx tenement. A car moved down the snow-clogged street, and quickly he hid to one side, watching as it disappeared around the corner. "Come on," he called out as the singing continued. "Shut her up, for Chrisake!"

"I can't," answered the woman from the other room—a room that had once been a kitchen before repeated fires and scavengers had mercilessly gutted the building. "I've got my head in a bucket of water. You're closer, Sloan. Why don't you?"

Pulling tight the collar of his overcoat, Sloan moved through the cold, cavernous apartment littered with broken glass and plaster and went into the room where Baby lay shivering under her thin blanket on a stained and grubby mattress.

"Shut up, kid!" he growled just as she opened her mouth to emit another desperate stream of song. "And I mean it," he warned, standing menacingly over her. Baby closed her mouth, and muttering to himself, he stalked back to his post by the window. Hardly had he sunk down on his mat and begun to roll a joint than Baby started in again.

"Oh, shit!" he cursed, spilling the weed in his lap. Angrily he marched into the kitchen and confronted his girlfriend. "Look, I've got to watch the window, and you've got to watch the kid," he said to the woman, who stood leaning over a pot of water, giving her hair a final rinse. The stove and plumbing had been rudely ripped from the room, and all that remained of the fixtures was a section of jagged counter that dangled from the crumbling wall. Precariously balanced on it stood two lone bottles, peroxide and dye.

"I can only be in one place at a time, Sloan," she said, squeezing dry her newly shorn hair. Blindly she groped out for a towel as water dripped on the shoulders of her elegant coat.

"Screw the hair," he said, handing her the towel. "You can always play with that later. Listen to what's going on out there," he said, motioning with his head toward the other room, where Baby lay singing. "If she keeps up like this, we're going to have the whole goddamn world in here buying tickets."

"I thought you said that this place was safe," she asked, wrapping her head in the towel.

"It is. It is. But there's other people here, too. They may be junkies and winos, but they sure as hell aren't deaf. What do you want to do, advertise that we've got the kid?"

"Jeez," she mumbled, exasperated but, then, looking at him, her eyes meeting his, she suddenly relented. "OK," she said and obediently went to the rear room.

Sloan headed back to his post by the window, stopping momentarily to warm his numb hands by the small portable kerosene heater near the window. When the feeling in his hands returned, he slumped back down on the mattress and picked up his cigarette paper. He rolled a fresh joint and lit it. Taking a deep drag, he held it in as long as he could before finally letting the smoke burst out between his lips. He closed his eyes and tried to relax, but the damn kid was still singing. Scrambling to his feet, he stormed back into Baby's room. There, sitting on the edge of Baby's mattress was Fay, stroking the child's white face as Baby trembled under her blanket, still trying to sing.

"I said shut her up, not play with her," he snapped.

The woman who had once called herself Irina but whose real name was Fay Dworkin and who was of midwestern heritage rather than Russian, looked up at her boyfriend.

"She's cold. Can't you see that? And I'm freezing, too."

"This is not supposed to be a picnic," he said as Baby kept struggling to sing out. "Quiet!" he snarled, and reaching down, he grabbed Baby's arm and shook her violently.

"Sloan!" the woman screamed, grabbing his hand and wrenching it free. "What's the matter with you? Have you gone crazy?" she asked, hanging on to his arm, her eyes wide. He threw her hand off his and charged out of the room.

Dumbfounded, Fay watched as he left. Then she looked down at Baby, who lay stunned on the mattress, her jaw trembling.

"He didn't mean anything, sweetie," she said, taking off her coat and covering the child. "You try to sleep a little," she said, tucking the coat tight around Baby's body. "You go to sleep, and before you know it you'll be right back home," she murmured softly and thought again about Sloan. In the two years that she had known him, had worked with him in that Off-Off-Broadway showcase, had gone to all those auditions with him, those cattle-calls, even these last three months they had lived together, she had never witnessed this side of him. Though he was an intense man, strong and determined and unswerving—which is what attracted her to him in the first place—she had never seen him mean like this. Realizing what it was that she had done, how by a single act she had irrevocably committed herself to Sloan, she became frightened. It had been one thing letting her imagination fly, splurging their last money on clothes, travel, and finally that extravagant dinner, becoming for a few hours Irina, the exotic divorcée with the foreign accent. The consequences, however, were another, and now they were painfully dawning on her. Rubbing her arms, she rose to her feet and went into the front room and stood by the smelly kerosene heater watching Sloan as he leaned up against the wall near the window nursing his ill-humor. Grudgingly he looked at her for an instant, then, taking a toke of his joint, turned back to the street below.

"I've never seen you act like this," she said, unwrapping the towel and shaking her head to fluff up her damp hair.

"It's the pressure," said Sloan, taking another drag and holding the joint out to her.

Shaking her head, she waved it away.

"Take it," he insisted through his teeth, holding his breath. "You need it."

Ignoring him, Fay took out a mirror and looked at herself. All traces of the black dye were now gone from her hair and in its place was a clipped version of her original flowing chestnut red. For the first time since leaving school it was short and felt strange, as though she had cut away more than just a length of hair.

"You know," she said, slipping the mirror back into her

purse, "you're not the only one under pressure. And even if you were, it wouldn't give you the right to bully me around like this and beat up on that little baby."

"Oh, please, spare me."

"The reason I went along with this," she continued, enunciating her words through her sharp, even teeth, "was that I felt we were building a future together."

"We are. We are," he said, watching through the milky plastic as a black man staggered past the front entrance of the building four stories below.

"That it was a way for us to get out of this rattrap of a city and start a new life.

"Brazil," he said. "Now tell me, doesn't that sound like a new life to you?"

"It doesn't matter really where we go, it's what's going on between us now that counts. And I don't like what's happening."

"Look, Fay, honey," he approached her and held her about the waist. "This just isn't the time to start discussing our future. In fact, it's the worst possible time," he said, as she looked searchingly into his face. He moved his head close and kissed her on the lips.

"I did something—a number of things—I don't really like myself for. I went to bed with—"

"Come on. Don't start playing the blushing virgin. I was not the first man in your life and—"

"But you are the only one—" She turned in his arms.

"I understand," he said soothingly.

"Do you? Do you really?"

"Sure. Of course. But it's the feeling that counts, not the act itself. I mean, do you think I feel so great about having my girl—well— Look, let's just forget the whole thing." He waved his hand and went back to the window.

She watched him as he maneuvered his head to get a better view of the cross street down the block.

"How long is this going to take?"

"Not long," he said. "Not long at all. Just don't start getting antsy and pressuring me. OK?"

"I just want to know, that's all."

"We've got to wait this thing out. Let them stew for a while. The longer we wait, the bigger the stakes, and the less likely this guy Shockley will be to cooperate with the police. We want him desperate, at his wit's end. So eager to deal that he'll even cross the cops."

"Sure, but how long do we wait?"

"Till the vibes are right," he said, evading her eyes.

"How many hours has it been?" asked Jacobsen, even though he had a watch and was perfectly capable of making the simple calculation.

"It's five-thirty now," said Pettersson, his eyes following Shockley as he again circled the room restlessly. "That makes it—almost twenty hours, Mr. Jacobsen."

"Twenty hours," Jacobsen repeated to himself, strumming his fingers on the arm of his chair.

"The longer it goes, the worse it is," worried Osgood.

"That's not necessarily true," said Jacobsen and then interrupted himself. "Damn it, Shockley! Will you stop marching in circles? You're making me dizzy. Try to come up with some ideas instead of wearing out the carpets."

Continuing to pace, Shockley looked over at Jacobsen and mumbled an obscenity.

"I've got an idea," said Osgood, who had been staring out the window at a Santa Claus who stood on the street ringing a bell. "Let's offer a reward."

"Yes," agreed Shockley, stopping in his track. "I've thought of that too. It's not a bad idea." He had spent half the day looking through mug shots of women, and to his sleep-deprived, addled brain, any suggestion of action seemed better than the endless waiting.

"It stinks," said Jacobsen.

"No, it doesn't," replied Shockley obstinately. "Offer a large reward, say ten thousand dollars, for information leading to the return of Baby."

"Dead or alive," added Jacobsen cuttingly, still rankled at Shockley for succumbing to the oldest trick in the world.

"That's vicious," said Shockley, whose guilt didn't need stoking. A moment earlier, before Osgood had come up with his suggestion, he had been thinking miserably about Ruth, his kids, about the Christmas that would be coming up in two days and their planned holiday together that would never be.

"Use your head," said Jacobsen, dismissing the notion of a

reward. "If someone kidnapped her for money, you'll be hearing from them. Don't worry. If it wasn't for money, no reward is going to bring them out of the woodwork."

"But someone may have seen something," Osgood persisted. The more he thought about it, the more he liked the idea. "It might be just the impetus needed to bring someone forth."

"OK. You want to offer a reward, offer it. But out of your pocket," said Jacobsen, hoping to stop Osgood short.

"That's all right," said Osgood evenly. "It's the least I can do for Baby."

Shockley looked at him, surprised.

"I really appreciate that," he mumbled.

Osgood shrugged, embarrassed.

"I'll call the papers," Pettersson volunteered.

"It can wait another hour until this evening's press conference, can't it?" Jacobsen stopped him.

Shockley nodded and went back to pacing.

Osgood turned back to the window. With his hands clasped behind his back, he watched as the street lamps began to flicker on up and down the streets encircling the park. The snow that had inundated the city only a day earlier was now a filthy mess lying in oozing humps along the gutters. Under the harsh glare of the arc lamps, the piles took on the sepulchral appearance of funeral mounds.

"You know," began Osgood a moment later, his eyes searching the approaching night, "I have this feeling—"

"Oh?" said Shockley.

"This odd feeling that—well, not only Baby's life is in the balance," he continued earnestly, "but that we're being tested, as well. We, as people."

Shockley stopped and looked at him squarely.

"Please," said Jacobsen, who was staring at the phone. "Please spare us the religion. We've got enough headaches as it is."

"I don't believe this!" said Sloan, slamming his fist into the wall when Baby began to sing again. As he stumbled to his feet, Fay caught him, putting a hand on his shoulder.

"Let me," she said and hurried to Baby's room.

Sloan got up and followed her.

"She's blue with cold," she said, hunched over the child and turning to see Sloan standing framed in the doorless jamb. "Can't we at least move her to the front room where she'll be closer to the heater?"

"So everyone can hear her better from the street? Is that the idea?"

"If she's warmer she'll probably be quiet," said Fay, holding Baby tightly against her as the child looked up at her beseechingly.

"This is utter bullshit! I've had enough. Put a gag on the kid already!"

"What?"

"I said, put a gag on the kid," he repeated. "You know, take a handkerchief or something and stuff it in her mouth."

"Are you absolutely crazy?"

"Then you can move her anywhere you want," he said logically.

"If you put a gag on her, she could spit up her bottle and end up choking."

"Nah." He waved her away.

"You could kill her!"

"Chrisake, stop getting hysterical," he grumbled, and in his eyes Fay saw a ruthless look that in a single glance obliterated all her hopes—of escape, of riches, of a new life with this man. Frantically her eyes searched his face, looking for familiar landmarks, something to connect with the man she had loved, or thought she had loved. There were none.

"It's Father Tom," said Shockley, covering the mouthpiece to the auxiliary phone. "He's downstairs with hotel security and wants to come up."

"Is he carrying a ransom note?" asked Jacobsen sarcastically, crushing a butt into his brimming ashtray.

"He just wants to talk."

Jacobsen shrugged his indifference.

"It can't hurt," said Osgood, who believed that there was strength in numbers.

A few minutes later Rolf Pettersson let Fitzgibbons in.

Osgood, who was slumped in a chair, looked up and gave Fitzgibbons a smile and a polite nod.

247

Jacobsen, following his usual tactic, remained silent and waited for Fitzgibbons to make the first move.

"Well?" said Shockley.

"I was horrified to hear what happened," he said, addressing the room, his eyes moving over to Shockley, who looked old and haggard. There were dark circles under the man's eyes, and deep lines ran across his face. To Fitzgibbons he looked as though he had aged ten years.

Silence.

"There's been an enormous outpouring of concern from our people all around the country."

Silence.

Jacobsen groped in his pocket for a fresh cigarette. Pettersson got up, yawned noisily, and stretched.

"Have there been any developments?"

"We were hoping that *you* might have some word," said Shockley, trying his best to sound mistrustful, but Fitzgibbons's demeanor undercut his suspicions. As he looked at Fitzgibbons, with his upright bearing, his open, honest eyes, it was hard for Shockley to continue nursing his suspicions about the former Jesuit. True, he had once doused a draft-board office with blood. True, he had once broken in with some of his followers and burned government records. But in those actions there had been a clear-cut, moral forthrightness. Kidnapping, Shockley had to admit, was just not up Fitzgibbons's alley. If he had been part of a conspiracy to take Baby, he would have owned up to it, just as he had done during the war.

"I know what you've been thinking," said Fitzgibbons, drifting over to Shockley.

"I've been thinking a lot of things lately," said Shockley wearily.

Father Tom smiled at him.

"No," he said finally. "I don't think you were involved. I'm sorry."

"You don't owe me an apology," said Father Tom. "You only did what was natural. I was a logical suspect." Father Tom looked at him. The two men were of nearly the same height and as their eyes locked, Fitzgibbons detected a sadness in Shockley's eyes that verged on tears. "We're only flesh," he said quietly, reading Shockley's thoughts and giving him the first words of consolation since the kidnapping. "If they hadn't gotten Baby this way," he said, his hand touching Shockley's arm, "they would have gotten her another."

Shockley swallowed with difficulty.

"I appreciate that," he said, clearing his throat uncomfortably. "Even if it's not true." He smiled wistfully.

The phone rang.

Shockley looked up abruptly.

It rang again.

"It's the hot line," gasped Pettersson, pointing at the table holding the two phones.

The phone rang again.

"Hell, man, answer it!" said Jacobsen, on his feet and ready to leap at the instrument.

Shockley held up a hand, let it ring one more time, and then reached for the receiver. Tensely he put it to his ear. From the other end he could hear above the faint, crisp static the sound of distant traffic.

"Hello?" he said, his eyes darting nervously from side to side, his nerves humming.

"Dees da professor?" asked a high, nasal male voice with a distinctly Hispanic accent.

"Yes, it is," answered Shockley, his heart racing.

"You wan' dee baby bock, meester?"

Shockley's voice failed him and he nodded mutely.

"You wan'?" repeated the high voice.

Shockley felt the blood draining from his head. Dizzily he lowered himself until he was perched on the edge of the low table.

"Is she all right?" he asked hoarsely.

"Do like you tol', understan'?"

"Yes, but is she *OK*?" Shockley persisted. The police had warned him to keep any callers on the line as long as possible, but though their advice was lost in the terror of the moment, Shockley's own needs made him stall.

"She fine—for dee time being."

"What do you want? Please, we want her back.—"

"We wan' dee money, meester."

"Yes. Yes. Whatever. Just—"

"Three million dollars. Cash. No marked beels. Meexed beels. Understan'?"

"Yes. Yes. I understand."

"No bait money. No serial numbers. Or she one dead baby."

"Yes. Of course," agreed Shockley, who would have agreed to anything.

"Tomorrow."

"But where? I mean, to whom do I give it? Who—?"

"You' find out," said the voice, and then the connection was broken.

Dazed, Shockley surrendered the phone to Fitzgibbons, who put it into its cradle. An instant later the auxiliary phone began to ring and Jacobsen grabbed for it.

"Did you get it?" he shouted to the Fed on the other end and then waited tensely. "Shit!" he muttered a minute later, slamming down the receiver. "It was a phone booth. They didn't have enough time to dispatch a car."

It was then that the enormity of what he had done began to dawn on Shockley. He had just blithely agreed to deliver an enormous ransom.

"Three million dollars," he muttered forlornly. "Where the hell are we going to get that kind of money?"

"Fay babe, we're in!" said Sloan, winded from racing up the flights of stairs.

With Baby slumped in her lap, Fay looked up.

"By tomorrow we'll be on our sweet way, three million smackeroos richer," he crowed. He grabbed her shoulder, but she pulled away abruptly. "I can't believe it's going this easy," he continued as she rocked the listless infant in her arms. "I could have said eight million and that professor would still have jumped," he beamed. "Hey, come on honey. Cheer up. What's with you? I thought you'd be tickled."

"Did you really?" she asked sullenly and went to the heater, where a bottle was sluggishly warming in an old dented pot. "Where's the baby food?" she asked suspiciously.

"Oh shit!" He slapped his head dramatically. "In all the excitement I forgot."

"I'll bet you did."

"OK, OK, so I didn't. She's got milk, doesn't she?"

"She needs food, not just milk. She's a child, not a calf."

"Look, I can't walk into a grocery store and start buying up scads of baby food. Now how would that look, huh? Use your head," he said, glaring back at the infant, who followed him with her glazed eyes. "We'll give her some of our stuff."

"Oh sure, popcorn, pizza, beer—"

"Listen," he warned, raising his eyebrows, which joined in the middle, "I don't want you to get stuck on the kid." He had been watching the way Fay had taken to the baby, cuddling her and rocking her, holding her close and letting her quietly sing to her. And he didn't like it. Not one bit.

"Don't worry about me," she said determinedly. She thought about the money. Sloan could have said thirty thousand or three hundred thousand and it would still have sounded like a fortune to her.

"Look, honey," he cajoled, "We're almost over the hump. In no time we'll be rich and on our way to paradise. We'll start a new life, a good one," he said, sensing the direction of her thoughts. "I promise," he added, trying to fix her with his eyes.

"Don't bullshit me, Sloan," she said, busying herself with the bottle, shaking it up and testing it on her wrist.

"Would I—?"

"You lied to me. And you keep lying to me. Every second word out of your mouth is a lie. I should have known I could never trust you."

"Oh, come off it! Why must everything with you—you—" He stopped short. He was going to say women and managed to catch himself in the last minute. Fay knew what he was going to say even before it came out, knew what was going through his mind. For the first time in two years she knew she was seeing him for what he really was. A callous con man, a go-getter. Just as he had screwed friends out of bit parts with his shenanigans, he was trying to pull a fast one, run circles around her. He was the kind of unscrupulous creep who used people, and she was damned if he was going to steamroller her.

"As far as I'm concerned," she said, avoiding his eyes, "from now on this is strictly a business arrangement."

Sloan scratched the stubble on his chin.

"Well"—he shrugged—"it's not what I had planned, but if that's the way you want it."

"Sloan, will you, for God's sake, cut the crap?"

"Crap?" he asked, innocently wide-eyed.

"You haven't heard a word I've said, have you?" asked Jacobsen.

"Huh?" Shockley looked up blankly at Jacobsen, as if rousing from a dream.

"Do you have any idea how much money that is?"

"Yes. But we've got to get Baby back," said Shockley, wetting his parched lips. "I don't care what it takes."

"Fine. I understand your sentiments. But try to be logical about this thing."

"You shouldn't have given in to everything right up front," said Osgood, with the clarity of hindsight. "You should've tried to hold out, bargain."

"I'm not bargaining with Baby's life."

"But where the hell are you going to get three million dollars? And by tomorrow?"

"I don't know. I was hoping—well, at least some of it might come from Baby's future earnings." He looked over at Jacobsen.

"In other words, you were counting on *me*," said Jacobsen.

"Well, partially, yes," he said, feeling himself plummeting into despair.

"Forget it," said Jacobsen, but seeing the wretched look on Shockley's face, he finally took pity on him. "Look, friend," he began in one of his unexpected turnabouts, "if I could help you, I would. Believe me. But if I had that kind of cash, do you think I'd be in this business?"

"Then what the hell are we going to do?" asked Shockley, rubbing his hands over his face, trying to clear his mind.

"Don't ask me," said Jacobsen. "My experience in the ransom business is very limited. Fortunately."

"By agreeing to their demands, Dr. Shockley may have locked himself in," said Pettersson, echoing the thoughts of most of those in the room.

"Maybe," said Father Tom. "But Irwin did the right thing. Any of us would have done the same in his shoes. He'd have been crazy to try and haggle at this point. I think we should look at it on the positive side. The important thing is we've made contact."

"If they really have her," injected Pettersson.

"They probably do," said Jacobsen. "If they have any brains in their heads—and these people have probably been planning this for some time—they know that we're going to demand proof before any payoff."

"I feel she's safe," said Father Tom. "For the time being, at least. And I think we should concentrate on raising the money."

"Father Fitzgibbons," said Jacobsen, his mind working, "how about your people? Your church? Is there any chance—? "

"Three million? Not a ghost of a chance." Father Tom shook his head. "We're not the Catholic Church," he said with a smile. "We're a young church. A loose federation at this point. And without any money to speak of."

"Damn," muttered Shockley miserably. "There's no way we're going to raise that kind of money."

"There probably is a way," said Father Tom, who wasn't easily defeated. "It's just that we haven't come up with it, that's all. If we put our heads together," he said, fighting to dissipate the gloom that was settling down on the room, "we can lick this thing and get Baby back. The important thing is to have faith."

"Yes," snorted Jacobsen, who naturally fell into the role of iconoclast. "To get down on our knees and pray."

"Right," said Father Tom, but before he could seize the opportunity, the auxiliary phone rang. It was the FBI again. Just as Shockley had expected, they had no new ideas to offer, just consolation.

"Stall," said the agent. "Keep them dealing. We'll get them, don't you worry. It's just a matter of time. Let them think that you're really trying to raise the cash."

"We are," said Shockley, and the agent wasn't quite sure which way he meant it.

"Ruth, please. Don't hang up on me," pleaded Shockley from the phone booth in the hotel lobby. "We've got to talk."

"So talk," she said perfunctorily, and Shockley tried, but the words didn't quite come. He had planned to tell her about the kidnapper's call, about the depths of his despair, about his regrets at hurting her, how he felt himself being dragged helplessly along in a current that threatened to drown him. He wanted to tell her about Father Tom, who was now up in the suite with the others, all of them racking their brains, trying to come up with the ransom. He wanted to confess how he now longed for the old life, for those relatively simple days when he had taught at the university and composed, how he missed her, their children, the familiar surroundings of their home, which they had so lovingly restored with their own hands. He wanted to tell her that and much more, yet he felt overwhelmed as though sensing the futility of the task.

"I'm scared," he finally blurted out. He swallowed and waited.

"Yes," she said a long minute later. "I figured you would be."

"Of what's happening to us through all this."

"Has happened," she corrected, but there was no malice in her voice only a profound sense of disappointment and weariness. The anger she had first felt when she had read the papers and seen the news reports that seemed to rub her nose in the lurid details of the kidnapping had now yielded to melancholy, to the point where she could almost empathize with her husband.

The phone line fell silent again, and Shockley knew that she was reviewing their lives together as he himself was doing, running through the tape of their existence at high speed, picking out discrete spots, images that seemed to distill their lives into its very essence: The birth of Annette, their first child—Shockley present as his little girl was born after fourteen hours of labor. His Pulitzer Prize—the heady excitement, the whirl of parties and congratulations, and the promise of seemingly unlimited happiness. Ruth getting her doctorate. Julie born. Annette's ruptured appendix—the ghastly fear of losing their child. Her recovery. Their tears. Through Shockley's mind in that short instant of time there flashed other quick shots, small but meaningful events that seemed at this moment filled with content. A dinner with Ruth's father days before he died. A walk along Park Avenue with Ruth one warm summer evening. Another summer the two of them lying together in bed, exhausted from making love, outside the surf pounding on a beach—a vacation somewhere. Cape Cod? Spain?

"Too much has gone on between us for it to end just like this." He struggled to clear his thoughts.

"It's over," she said.

"It can't be. Not like this. Just because of—"

"Not just because of—of her," she said, meaning the woman in the Plaza.

"Then why? Why?"

"Because of everything. Because you've changed. Because you're not the man I married. Because you made a choice without ever thinking about us, about me."

"You mean Baby?"

"Exactly!" she said bluntly.

"I had to."

"Yes, I understand. You had to. I don't blame you. But you also have to live with the results."

"You mean to say we're breaking up because of a little baby girl?" he asked, trying to sound incredulous.

"You're trying to simplify it. It's not because of her per se. It's because of all the misery and trouble she's brought us. You called her a blessing."

"She was. I mean"—he corrected himself—"she is. *Is*," he reemphasized.

"She's been a curse," said Ruth harshly. "To our lives, at least."

"Ruth—"

"She's damaged Cindy. That poor child still goes around crying all day. And now she's convinced she's somehow responsible for Baby's kidnapping."

"Ruth—"

"You've given up composing, quit your job. And for what? To become a promoter. A hipster. Irwin, you're the laughing-stock of this town."

"So that's it!"

"No, that's not it. I don't give a damn what anybody else thinks, not really," she said, but he suspected that she did. "It's what *I* think. Irwin, you've changed. And I don't particularly like what you've become. Can you understand that?"

"No," he objected. "Not quite. Look, Ruth, I can change again. You think I like what I've become? I'm not any happier than you are."

"Because you're miserable, why should I be?" she went on, and suddenly Shockley understood that she was talking not only about the last six months since Baby; she was thinking about all the years she had passed with him, supporting him with her life tissue as he struggled to compose, bouncing through the highs and lows of his roller-coaster existence. Baby, he realized, was but a catalyst. Ruth was tired. Tired of him. The ups and downs.

"What a holiday this turned out to be," he said forlornly before hanging up.

"Merry Christmas," she said to herself long after he had gone.

Subdued, Shockley rode the elevator back up to his suite, keeping to the rear of the car. The elevator was crowded with guests, jovial people, their faces still red from the cold, Christmas gifts tucked under their arms. They joked, bantered, laughed, all of which seemed to drive home Shockley's sense of isolation. Without his family, without Baby and her song, he felt cut loose from the world. As the elevator stopped on the second floor to disgorge a noisy couple, he tried to imagine life without Ruth, but it eluded him. As far as he could see, the future was a blank, and he knew that he had reached the lowest point in his life.

Seventeen years together, he thought as the elevator slid open at the next stop and the remaining people spilled out, leaving him finally alone. Seventeen years in which they had shaped each other, fitting together like matched pieces of a puzzle, a single, fused, living unit that breathed in unison. Yet—yet now all that was out the window, and the prospect of facing life alone made him shudder.

What was odd, he thought, leaving the elevator and advancing over the soft carpets to the door of his suite, was that this was happening to *them*. In recent years he and Ruth had watched from the safety of their marriage as many of the couples they had known in Ithaca—friends and neighbors, colleagues and acquaintances—people like the Stearnes and the Pompilios, the Halperns and the Todds and the Millers, steady, solid couples, had dissolved their homes and marriages. They had watched it all from the sheltered distance of their union, safe and secure. Theirs was an island of stability in a turbulent sea of recriminations and custody battles and property squabbles. Yet here he was being sucked into the same morass, aware of what was transpiring, but utterly helpless to stop it. And the catalyst? he thought to himself, reaching for the doorknob. A baby of all things. An infant, sweet and innocent as the morning dew, a child blessed with song.

After calling Terkel in the early morning, Doris had gone directly back to her trailer. The chills she had awakened with had gotten worse, and no matter how much she turned up the heat or put on extra clothes her skin was still covered with goose bumps.

Piling all the blankets she could find onto her bed, Doris had crawled under the covers in an attempt to warm up. Hardly had her head hit the pillow than she fell into a deep sleep. For hours she lay beneath the layers of blankets, lost in a dark, dreamless pit, her body quivering with shivers. Toward nightfall her sleep was suddenly invaded by a ghastly vision. In her dream she saw Baby naked and wandering, lost in an icy blizzard. Her lips were blue with cold and she looked as though she were freezing to death. Above the merciless howling of the wind Baby was trying to sing, calling out to Doris in a tremulous and fading voice. Doris reached out her hand but couldn't quite grasp ahold of Baby. She lunged forward toward her child, but Baby kept retreating back into the storm, still frantically crying out for her mother.

Doris suddenly awoke and realized that she was sitting up in bed. Dazed, she looked around, her heart thumping, her body cold as ever. She glanced out the window. It was already dusk, and the people in the neighboring trailer had turned on the string of colored Christmas lights lining their doorway. Sliding her feet into her slippers, Doris wrapped herself in her coat and turned on a light.

What a horrible dream, she thought, shivering by the furnace duct as the warm air streamed past her. The headache she had had in the morning was still with her. Her bones ached and her back was acting up again. She was sick, Doris realized, probably one of those viruses that were going around the trailer park. She went to the medicine cabinet and swallowed two aspirin. She took her temperature and, to her surprise, found that it was normal. If only she could shake this darn headache, she thought, as she put on some water for tea. While waiting for the tea to steep, she sank down at the kitchen table. That dream, she thought, running her fingers over the Formica pattern on the table, her mind drifting back. She couldn't recall ever having had such a vivid or frightening dream. She knew it was silly. Baby couldn't walk. She was barely six months old. But Baby's plea in that dream had been startlingly real.

Doris poured herself a cup of tea, and taking a sip, she suddenly felt ravenously hungry. Busily she set about making herself a meal, her stomach churning in hunger. She boiled two eggs, dropped some bread into the toaster, poured herself some milk as Markowitz had recommended—even took out the orange juice she had been rationing for a week. What was odd, however, was that when her meal was all prepared and she sat down to eat, she could hardly stomach a morsel. Though her belly was knotted in hunger, she could only manage to swallow a bite of toast.

It was all crazy, she told herself, as she bent down with pain to feed her cats. Chills without fever. Hunger without being able to eat. And that terrifying nightmare.

She watered her plants and went about tidying up her trailer. She felt so sick, however, that after a few minutes she gave up and slumped down in her chair by the window, closing her eyes for what seemed a moment. When she opened them again, it was already late at night and someone was banging loudly on her door. It was Mrs. Schooley.

"They're asking ransom!" said the fat woman, breathless from the short walk, a toddler tucked under one arm. When she spoke, her words issued out into the cold night in a stream of smoke lit by the light from Doris's trailer.

"Ransom?" asked Doris confused, trying to shake off her lethargy. She had just had that same dream over again, and she couldn't comprehend what her neighbor was talking about.

"It's supposed to be on the news again. Johnny thought you'd want to see her. Hurry," she urged.

The cold was pouring into the open door, and rather than questioning the woman, Doris grabbed her coat and followed Mrs. Schooley over the trampled path of snow.

"They're asking three million dollars!" said Johnny Schooley by way of greeting. He was a skinny man, as bony as his wife was fat. His ears stuck straight out from his head like wings, and the creases of his neck and hands were always lined with mechanic's grease. Getting up from his recliner in front of the color set, Mr. Schooley motioned toward Doris to sit in his place.

"What are you all talking about?" she asked, rubbing the sleep from her eyes.

"Why the kidnapping, 'course!" said Mrs. Schooley.

"Of Baby," echoed her husband.

Doris turned white as a ghost, and the couple suddenly became scared that she might pass out right then and there in their double-wide trailer.

"Oh, cripes!" said Mrs. Schooley, slapping her hand over her mouth. "And we thought you knew! Why we never would—"

"She doesn't know?" asked Mr. Schooley, baffled. How could she not know? The whole freaking world knew.

25

I think I've got it," said Father Tom, looking up with a full mouth of lasagna and breaking the deadlock. By that time the four men had spent the entire day brainstorming. Trying to come up with a scheme for freeing Baby, they had gone through and dismissed everything from raising the ransom by levying a tithe on every Babyist on Father Tom's mailing lists (too slow and clumsy) or floating bank loans (Jacobsen: "On what collateral? On a star we might never get back in one piece. Bankers are businessmen not philanthropists.") to stuffing a suitcase with paper and letting the police nab the person who made the pickup (Osgood: "By the time he—or she—spills the beans, the others will be miles away and Baby might be dead.").

Up until the evening press conference, the four repeatedly consulted with the FBI man on the other end of the auxiliary phone. One after the other he effectively punctured all their schemes, suggesting instead that Shockley continue to stall, holding off the consummation of *any* deals until their officers had exhausted every possible lead. What kind of leads? The FBI wasn't telling.

"If you give in to their ransom demands," explained the gravel-voiced Fed on the other end, "and on a prominent case like this, then you can be sure as hell we're going to have a rash of these kidnappings around the country."

"Obviously you're more concerned with the fallout than freeing Baby."

"Oh no, we want to get her back, Dr. Shockley," the cop objected. "But we also have to deal with the wider implications. We have responsibilities. And so do you. You don't want this thing happening to other people, do you?"

"Does that mean you're going to interfere if we try to make a drop?"

"No. We gave you our word on that. But we're certainly not—at least at this time—going to encourage you to give in."

"I think I've got it," said Father Tom, looking up from his plate, his eyes brightening.

The men in the suite held their forks in abeyance, looking at him expectantly.

"A way," he continued, swallowing eagerly, "of raising a large quantity of money, relatively fast."

"Go on," said Shockley. With a warm meal in his belly, he was ready for a new surge of hope.

"Well?" pressed Jacobsen.

"A benefit."

"A what?" asked Shockley.

"A benefit performance. A Christmas benefit for Baby," said Father Tom.

"Yes. A concert. A show," said Osgood, immediately picking up on the notion. "Big names. A variety show of sorts. Singing. Dancing. Acting."

"Exactly!" Father Tom grinned.

"With the right people," said Pettersson, wetting his lips thoughtfully, "you could pack them in, run performances head to tail."

Jacobsen sat expressionless, his eyes following the speakers, absorbing what they were saying.

"There are lots of show people who really care about Baby," said Father Tom, turning his attentions to Jacobsen. "Why, off the top of my head I could name a half dozen," he said eagerly, hoping to ignite Jacobsen.

"Name them," said Jacobsen coolly.

'Well—Well—For instance, Joan Baez," said Father Tom, grabbing at a name. "And Barbra Streisand. And Redford. Robert Redford. I know they'd help."

"That's three."

"Wayne Newton," Osgood chimed in excitedly. "I'm positive we could count on him for a good cause."

"Lenny Bernstein," piped Shockley enthusiastically. "He's in town. And I'm almost sure he'd lend a hand."

"How about McCartney?" added Pettersson, looking at his boss. "We could fly him over from London. On the Concorde he could be here in a matter of hours."

Jacobsen still didn't react.

"Baryshnikov," Fitzgibbons tossed in as the room became electric. "Now he's absolutely crazy about Baby. And Dolly Parton. Pat Boone. How many more do you need?" He laughed happily.

Jacobsen sat silent, an unlit butt dangling from his lower lip.

"It's not a bad idea," Pettersson cautiously prodded.

"Bad idea? It's one hell of a good idea," exclaimed Osgood, congratulating Fitzgibbons. He could already envision the show, see himself as master of ceremonies.

"If you could take care of arranging a theater and ticketing"—Fitzgibbons faced Jacobsen—"we could probably in less than a day round up the stars."

"No," said Jacobsen, shaking his head.

"No?" asked Shockley, his smile fading. "What do you mean 'no'?"

"No theater," answered Jacobsen.

"No?" echoed the other men.

"No," answered Jacobsen, rising to his feet, and there was the hint of a smile on his lips. "Television," he continued tersely, nodding his head to himself.

"Yes," uttered Osgood in a near whisper, catching the spark.

"A telethon for Baby," said Jacobsen, pointing a single finger skyward.

Shockley watched him, holding his breath, almost afraid to hope.

"Look at it logically," said Jacobsen, now himself, and busily pacing the floor. "A theater has a limited capacity. What can it hold? Five hundred seats? A thousand? Assuming you can get one quickly, by the time you've paid the rent and security and ads and God-knows-what-else, your net is down to nothing. Theaters, even bowls and stadiums, they're all finite, all regional. But, on the other hand, television"—he beamed—

"blankets the country, the world. It's essentially infinite. It can reach every man, woman, and child. It's fast—almost instantaneous. It's clean, easy, and it's lucrative, very lucrative," said Jacobsen, who had always wanted to move into that area.

"We can have people calling in their pledges," Pettersson chirped excitedly.

"Pledges?" scoffed Jacobsen. "Forget it. Stick to plastic money. With Visa or Master Card or American Express, we can convert numbers to immediate cash."

"Not everybody has credit cards," said Fitzgibbons levelly.

"But anybody can wire in money," said Jacobsen. "And in urban areas we can set up collection centers. Why, think of it, within twenty-four hours we could have three million—or close to that—sitting in piles right in this very room."

"But they want the money *tomorrow*. Christmas Eve."

"Screw them!" roared Jacobsen, feeling his oats and taking control. "If they want that kind of money they're going to have to give us a couple of days," he said, extracting a little black book of phone numbers. Wetting his finger, he hastily thumbed through the leaf-thin pages. "Rolf," he ordered, pointing to the phone, "Get me Silverman. If you can't raise him at the station, try him at home"

Pettersson was scribbling madly on a pad by the phone.

"Hurry man," said Jacobsen feverishly. "We don't have all day."

"Yes, sir," said Pettersson, grabbing the wrong phone and flashing an alert in the FBI office.

"Some winter we're having," said the man sitting across the aisle from her on the night Greyhound.

Doris turned in the darkened bus and saw the elderly man with his cane resting between his legs, his pale, freckled face illuminated by the passing traffic. She nodded courteously and then turned back to stare out her window.

"Never seen it this cold," he added a little later as the bus droned on through the flatlands of New Jersey. "And I've been around seventy-five years. Seventy-five years!" he repeated.

Out of politeness Doris turned again toward him and tried to smile.

"Got all my own teeth still," he said, taking his upper teeth between his two fingers and yanking them theatrically. "And my own hair!" he said, taking off his hat and bending his neck so Doris could see the top of his head.

"That's very nice," said Doris dully, and was staring back out the window. Over the eastern, icy marshlands the sky was slowly reddening, and as the bus shook and swayed over the potholed road, Doris was trying to think ahead. She was hoping that it would be light by the time they pulled into New York City. It was more than fifteen years since she had visited the city, and her imagination took her no farther than her arrival. Beyond that stretched a blank.

"Some folks say that it's all these nuclear accidents," said the man across the aisle a few minutes later.

"Huh?" Doris awoke from her thoughts.

"The weather. The ice age. Why it's coming back," said the man desperate for conversation. "But I know that's not the reason. It's because of our wickedness. We're being punished."

Doris looked at him blankly. Her head ached as ever, and she felt herself removed from the world.

"You ask me, the whole planet's going plumb crazy," he offered without being asked.

Doris looked away. She was in no mood for small talk. She was, in fact, interested in only one thing: finding Baby. Since the Schooleys had driven her out to route 79, where they had managed to flag down the night bus from Rochester, Doris had been able to think of little else. Even when the bus, just out of Binghamton, had skidded off the slick road into an abutment, lurching and coming to a crashing halt, Doris still had had her mind on Baby. New York. She had to get to New York, she had repeated to herself while the passengers sat stranded at the side of the road, waiting those interminable hours for a replacement bus to come and rescue them. New York. That's where Baby was.

"Now you take the kidnapping for instance," said the old gent reaching into a paper bag. Tearing apart a sandwich, he extended half to Doris. Without thought she accepted it and as she bit into the dry bread, her tongue made contact with something that tasted like warm salami. "Now if that isn't wickedness, pure and simple, I don't know what is," snorted the man.

Doris stopped chewing in midbite and turned to look at him. There were large, luminous tears in her eyes, and through them the man's face appeared misty and distorted.

"Now how can somebody do a thing like that? Take an innocent baby, a gift from God Almighty himself, and steal her?"

Doris shook her head as the tears coursed down her cheeks.

"What a pity!" said the man, wiping his own eyes. "What a crime of crimes." He blew his nose loudly into a stained handkerchief and, rolling it into a ball, stuffed it back into his pocket. "I know just how you feel, lady—" He shook his head in commiseration. "I'm a Babyist myself," he said. "See?" He opened his shirt and held up the golden lips that hung around his sinewy neck.

Doris leaned across the aisle and stared at the lips that dangled between his fingers.

"Baby," she muttered into her fist, seeing the lips that were a perfect replica of Baby's little birdlike mouth. "My sweet Baby." She broke down at the sight, weeping openly, the remains of the half sandwich flopping to her lap.

"Gee whiz, lady," said the man, taken aback by her copious tears. "There, there, now," he said, sliding into the empty seat next to her and patting her hand. "Everything's going to turn out all right. That's why I'm going to New York. Because of Baby. Sure," he said, when Doris quizzically turned her tear-splotched face up to him. "To see that telethon tomorrow. My nephew's a big shot, a cameraman for the network"—he grinned proudly—"does all the top shows. Said he could get me into the telethon. Knows how I feel about her music and all," said the man, still holding Doris's hand. "Why maybe he could get you in too," he said, noticing the way Doris's eyes were still fixed on the lips that now hung out of his shirt. "Here," he said, carefully removing the chain over his head. "You need this more than I do." He handed the lips to her. "Genuine fourteen carat gold-plated," he said wistfully. "But that's the message," he explained in his disconnected fashion. "Of her music. To share. To give a part of yourself to others who need it. I've heard her sing with my own ears. Yep. Really," he insisted when Doris looked at him through her continuing stream of tears. "Heard her in Cleveland. In Chicago once. Even heard her in Atlanta. I'm quite a bus rider"—he laughed at himself—"got myself one of them passes. They call them Discover America. I call them Discover Baby." He chuckled, trying to cheer up his silent companion.

"My heavens," he remarked later, still holding Doris's hand as they entered the Lincoln Tunnel. "You're cold as ice," he said, trying to warm her with his own bony hands.

Doris gave him a weak smile. She had been sitting for the last half hour with those golden lips pressed to her own lips. Watching her, the man knew now that he had done the right thing in giving them to her, that the act of parting with what he held most dear was the reward in itself, just as he had heard Father Tom once say.

"Well," he said, gathering up his meager belongings as they pulled into the Port Authority Terminal, "it's been nice riding with you. You don't talk an awful lot," he said candidly, struggling to his feet with his cane, "but you're sure a good listener."

From the very moment of its conception, the Christmas Day Telethon began to take shape as if possessed of a will and energy all its own. Everywhere doors magically opened. The network and its affiliates coast to coast agreed to push aside their scheduled Christmas programming to make way for the telethon. Some of the biggest names in show business—actors, singers, dancers, and comedians—were falling all over themselves to offer their talent. Volunteers were coming out in droves to man the phones and the collection units to be stationed in major cities. By daybreak of Christmas Eve, the telethon was already a reality, and even Father Tom, a staunch believer in divine intervention, couldn't help but be astounded by the speed and ease with which everything fell into line.

With a star-studded cast, everyone was predicting an unprecedented 95 percent Nielsen share of the Christmas Day audience. The network had already sold the commercial time, sandwiching the telethon for a phenomenal three times the going prime-time rate—the revenues, the network president explained, earmarked to cover the costs for the show. "Otherwise," he told Jacobsen, "consider the air-time and facilities *our* gift to Baby."

As Father Tom and Pettersson and Osgood worked with Jacobsen at his Madison Avenue office, feverishly putting together the program, Shockley found himself once again alone at the Plaza, waiting for the next contact from the kidnappers. He tried to fill the intervening time by listening to the news or reading the papers, but mostly he ended up sitting in the bedroom on the edge of his bed, staring at Baby's empty crib.

As the hours wore on, Shockley found himself alternating between the depths of despair and glimmering hope, his moods swinging wildly from minute to minute, giving him no respite. Yes, he would think in a flash of hope, he would get Baby back. Happy and healthy. No, he'd realize on second thought, as in the Lindbergh kidnapping, she was already dead. And all this activity was merely a futile death throe. Then he would re- member the drowning, Baby's miraculous survival. Surely someone was looking over Baby, someone who would protect her now, he thought in a moment of near prayer. No! If she were protected, this would never, never have occurred.

When his patience was near the breaking point, Shockley picked up the auxiliary phone and made contact with the same gravel-voiced Fed who had been on the case almost from the beginning.

"How're you holding up?" asked the man, sounding weary himself.

"Badly."

"Try to be patient. These things can take time. Time is in our favor." The cop tried to soothe Shockley.

"Have you ever been involved in a kidnapping before?" asked Shockley pointedly.

"Well, no," the man answered honestly.

Shockley laughed.

The man laughed.

"But seriously"—the cop tried to allay Shockley's fears— "we're trained to handle things like this. We've got over ninety men out in the field on this case."

"By the way," asked Shockley, hungry for conversation. "What's your name? We've been talking to each other all this time and I still don't know it."

"Nisbet. Jeff Nisbet."

"Nisbet," repeated Shockley, trying to imagine the face. "Look, Nisbet, do me a favor. Level with me. Do you *really* have any leads?"

"We do," he answered succinctly.

"Well?"

The man became silent.

"Come on, tell me," Shockley coaxed.

The line remained silent.

"I'm not going to talk about it. Do you think I would screw myself? Who the hell am I going to talk to, anyway?"

"OK," said Nisbet, knowing that Shockley needed something tangible to keep him going. "We know that the woman who slept in your bed did not have dark hair."

"So?"

"She was a redhead. She had dyed her hair black."

"And?" Shockley waited for the rest.

"Well, that's a clue."

"You're joking!" said Shockley. "Tell me, how many red-headed women are there on the loose in the city at this moment, huh?"

"There's more."

"Go on," Shockley prompted.

"We think that the kidnappers are part of a Puerto Rican nationalist group. That they're the same people who set off bombs in the Bank of America offices in Chicago and New York last week."

"Based on what?"

"They're trying to raise money to finance a revolution to break Puerto Rico free from the United States. They operate out of the South Bronx. The call you got from the kidnappers came from that part of the city."

"How does that connect with the red hair?"

"One of our informers identified the composite you made with our artist as looking like Mama Libre, one of the heavies in the organization."

"This woman was no Puerto Rican," said Shockley, thinking back again to Irina. When he visualized her in bed with him, chills ran up and down his spine.

"We've only got a description of her, no pictures, but from what we understand she's an American girl, one of these little college-type bleeding hearts—" The cop stopped himself.

Shockley sat silently holding the phone.

"You still there, Shockley?" asked the husky-voiced Fed.

"Still here, Nisbet." Shockley heaved a long sigh. "Not going anywhere."

"Listen, this was strictly between us."

"Don't worry. My lips are sealed. Your job is safe."

"Good," mumbled Nisbet, only vaguely relieved.

Shockly put down the phone. He sat trying to imagine Irina dressed in army fatigues, moving through the jungled hills of Puerto Rico carrying a machine gun. By no stretch of the imagination could he fit her into that image. There was something about her, however, that continued to nag at him. There was something indefinable he had spotted in her from the beginning, something that went deeper than her beauty, a certain sense of genuine kindness, of compassion, of warmth. Yet, yet that miserable bitch had stolen Baby. The contradiction made him dizzy.

Leaving the bus and emerging into the Port Authority Terminal, a shopping bag in hand, Doris was immediately overwhelmed. On this morning before Christmas the bus station was sheer bedlam. The crowded hall was swirling with holiday travelers, people scampering back and forth with their bundles and bags, bawling children dragged along behind their arm-yanking parents, all kinds of people frantically rushing around. And there were lines everywhere. Lines snaking through the hall to the ticket counters. Lines to the information booths. Lines for doughnuts and coffee. Lines for escalators. As Doris stood on tiptoe searching for an exit to the street, a huge woman lugging a suitcase charged smack into her from the rear, nearly bowling Doris off her feet—the woman pushing on without so much as a second look. An instant later a teenager with festering pustules covering his face tried to interest her in a digital watch hot off the trucks. Overhead speakers blared out garbled messages. A vendor vaulted over the counter of his stand and dashed past her, chasing a woman who had stolen a pack of M&Ms. Swept up in the eddies and swells of the crowds, Doris finally found what appeared to be an exit and, before she knew it, was propelled out the door by the surge of bodies.

Out on the street, Doris stood for a moment on the corner near the terminal trying to get her bearings amidst the morning rush of trucks and cars bouncing through the slushy potholes, the noise of jackhammers and horns and sirens blaring in her ears. Finally she picked a direction and began to walk.

Blowing on her frozen hands and pushing them deep into the pockets of her old wool coat, her shopping bag dangling from above her wrist, Doris pushed on through the thickening crowds streaming past her in all directions. She was looking for Baby, she told herself, beginning to realize the enormousness of the task that lay before her. Somehow time and memory had shrunk New York to the manageable proportions of Ithaca. But this was no Ithaca. This was madness, sheer chaos. Yet, she thought, crossing the street in the sea of people, somewhere amidst all this pandemonium, somewhere in this city, was that woman who had stolen her Baby.

"I've just got to find her," she said to herself, reaching a wide avenue. Turning onto it and instinctively heading northward, Doris continued to trudge on, the icy headwind freezing her cheeks and causing her nose to run.

"Oh, dear God," she prayed ten blocks later, when her feet began to ache, her hands had gone beyond numbness, and her resolve had begun to falter. "Please give me the strength to find my Baby," she uttered, looking up into the gray sky lodged between the buildings. A lone snowflake fluttered down and hit her in the eye.

Shuddering in the icy, raw air, Doris pushed on. She managed another few slushy blocks and then, looking for a place to rest, noticed a small luncheonette. She went in, thawed out her hands while waiting for an empty stool, then sat down at the counter and ordered tea. While people stood behind her waiting for an opening, she sat nursing her cup of tea and trying to puzzle out a plan. She sat and sat and sat over that half-finished cup, stalling, waiting, hoping, praying as the waitress came past repeatedly, busily cleaning the counter in front of her and trying to shame her into leaving.

When the morning rush had finally thinned, Doris picked up her bag and continued her northward trek. When she reached the edge of Central Park, Doris sensed she knew where she was—she had been here once during a school-librarians' convention in 1958. Recalling the horses and carriages she had seen that year, that very happy year, she turned east on the cross street and soon found herself standing in the small plaza near a rather ornate hotel. Reading the sign on the awning, she made the connection with the news report. Finding a telephone booth down the street, she slid in, closed the door, and hunted in her purse for a dime.

When the hot line sounded, Shockley could barely restrain

269

himself from picking it up. With clenched fists he stood poised over it and finally, on the fourth ring, grabbed the receiver.

"Dees da professor?" asked the now-familiar voice.

"Speaking."

"You got dee money, meester?"

"How's Baby?"

"She happy as a bird. Now, dee money."

"We're getting it."

"What you mean? We tol' you, mahn, today ees dee day!"

"I know you did. But you're asking for an extraordinary amount of cash. If you'd consider a smaller—"

"Hey, you playin' games weet me?"

"If you want three million dollars you'll have to—"

"You know what we wan', meester. You don' fuck weet me or dat baby—"

"Look. Try to be sensible. There's no way in the world we could have scraped together that kind of money in a few hours. You must know that," said Shockley.

"Meester, I don' wanna hear 'bout your problems."

"It's your problem too," said Shockley bluntly.

"I wan' dee money an' no bullsheet, meester, get it?"

"If you're willing to take less, you can have it now. I could give you a hundred thousand in a matter of an hour."

"Three million, mahn. No less!" The man sounded enraged and Shockley backed off.

"OK, OK, but we need time."

"Today, meester, or your baby she is dead."

"Three days," said Shockley.

"Today!"

"We've got a telethon benefit coming on tomorrow to raise the money. Surely you must have heard—"

"Hey, mahn, you stallin'?" The man sounded worried.

"No, no. But we need time. Give us at least two days then."

"Mahn, what you talkin' about?"

"Two days. And that's the best we can do," Shockley pushed on stubbornly. "We'll give you three million dollars, any denominations, any way you want it."

"You agreed today."

"Impossible. It's *absolutely* impossible. What's an extra couple of days going to matter to you?"

"Stop hustlin' me, mahn!"

"Three million dollars. It's yours. All of it. But you've got to give us a chance."

"I gotta think, mahn—"

"Just two lousy—"

"You rushin' me, meester!" said the man, now sounding frantic.

"But—"

"I gotta think!" he screamed and then hung up.

Immediately the auxiliary phone was ringing.

"Good going, Shockley," said Nisbet. "You're taking control of the situation. And you had him on for a good couple of minutes. Hang on."

Shockley waited tensely.

"OK," Nisbet returned. "We got a make on that call. Call you back as soon as—"

The hot line began to ring again.

"It's him!" Shockley gasped.

"Let it ring," the cop warned.

"What do I do if he won't wait?" said Shockley, panic surging in him.

"He'll wait," said Nisbet. "Take control. Don't clutch!"

The phone kept ringing.

"OK. You relaxed?"

Shockley took in a deep breath and let it out slowly.

"Yes?" he said, trying to slow his racing heart. If he screwed up, she was finished. He'd never see her again. She'd never sing again. He had to be cautious. Calm. Not let this guy stampede him.

"OK," said Nisbet. "Pick up the line now."

Shockley put down the one phone and picked up the other.

"Yes?" he said, trying to sound determined.

"Professor Shockley?" asked a creaky old lady's voice, taking him by surprise. "This is Doris. Doris Rumsey."

"Doris? How'd you get through on this line?"

"I told them who I was. I'm calling about Baby," said Doris, beginning to weep despite her resolve.

"Listen, Doris, you're calling on the wrong line. And at a terrible time. The kidnappers are supposed to call back in a minute and you're tying up the phone. Please," said Shockley, rushing his words, "just hang up. I'll call you right back. I promise."

"But—"

"Please. Now!"

Doris hung up.

The auxiliary phone rang again.

Then the hot line rang.

Shockley feared he would go insane. He didn't know which to grab first.

The auxiliary phone fell silent and he picked up the hot line.

"Eight in dee mornin'. Day after Christmaas, got it?"

"Too early. We need the full day."

"Tha's all you got. Not a meenit more!"

"Where do I drop it?"

"You' find out."

"How do I know if Baby's alive and well?"

"She OK."

"I want assurances."

"You've got it, meester."

"Huh?"

"My assurances," said the man with a chilling laugh, and hung up.

The auxiliary phone rang.

"Hang on, Shockley," said Nisbet.

Shockley sat holding the receiver in his trembling hand. In the background he could hear garbled radio chatter. Tensely he waited, feeling sweat soaking through his shirt. A minute later Nisbet was back.

"Hell," he muttered disgustedly. "We almost had the son of a bitch. It was another coin box eight blocks away. Damn, that was close! Next time," he added, trying to sound optimistic. "Next time we'll nail him."

Shockley put the phone back into its cradle and stood up. He poured himself three fingers of whiskey and downed it in a single gulp. Slowly the warmth spread outward from his stomach, untying the knots in his nerves. Then, suddenly, he remembered Doris.

"Nisbet," he said, picking up the auxiliary phone.

"Yeah?"

"I'm going down to the lobby to make a call. I'll be back in a couple of minutes."

"Why don't you use the hot line? I doubt if he's going to call back. It's better you stick around here."

"OK," said Shockley and, picking up the outside line, suddenly realized that he didn't know Doris's new number. He called information in Ithaca.

Standing in the phone booth on the street, Doris put in her dime, called the Plaza and, identifying herself, asked for Shockley's room. The line, so she was informed by the switchboard, was busy. She hung up and waited.

Shockley put down his phone. Doris had no listing for her new home, which meant probably no phone. He debated calling Ruth and asking her to drive out to the trailer park, but knew that Ruth had had her fill of playing messenger and courier. He picked up the phone and, calling Ithaca information, tried to get Olive Eldridge's number. There were three Eldridges listed, none with Olive's first name. Shockley scribbled down all three.

Doris put another dime in the phone.

Shockley dialed the first listing.

Doris dialed the hotel again.

"Olive Eldridge?" said a man. "Why, that's my sister-in-law. You got the wrong Eldridge. She lives down on Third Street."

"I'm sorry, that line is still busy," said the woman on the hotel switchboard. "Do you want to hold the line?"

"I'll wait," said Doris.

Shockley depressed the button on his phone for an instant, then dialed the eleven digits that were Olive's number.

"Still busy," said the switchboard lady. "Please hold."

Olive's number in Ithaca rang. It rang three times, but no one answered. Shockley let it continue to ring.

Disgusted with waiting, Doris finally hung up.

The auxiliary phone rang.

"I just learned from our lady on the switchboard that she's been trying to get you," said Nisbet.

"Who?"

"Doris Rumsey."

"Oh, damn!" muttered Shockley. "Do you have her number?"

"Yeah. They put a trace on it. Just to be sure."

Doris swung open the door to the booth. She had used up her last dime and wasn't about to waste any more time or money trying to contact Shockley. She didn't need him, and she had been stupid to even try to call him. Picking up her bag, she moved to the corner and waited for the light to change. Enough was enough, she thought crossing the street and heading up the avenue as the phone in the booth started to ring.

"Oh, honey," sighed Fay when Baby suddenly stopped singing, her little chest racked by a deep, painful cough. "Save your strength."

Baby coughed up a small glob of rusty sputum and tried to sing again. She forced out a few feeble notes, took a quick, wheezing gasp, and gave out a few more.

"You don't have to sing for me," said Fay tenderly to the child, who lay drooping in her arms. "I know what a good little girl you are."

"She's suffering." She cornered Sloan when he came back from his latest foray. "Just listen to her," she said, distressed as Baby was gripped by a loud, hacking spasm. Fay picked her up and patted her back until the coughing subsided—Baby lying spent in her arms, flushed and soaked with sweat.

"Sure. I hear her. And so does probably half the neighborhood. In fact, I heard her all the way down the stairs," said Sloan, preoccupied. He was thinking about the two days that that professor had wheedled out of him. Was it a trick? Were they trying to hold him off as they zeroed in? Maybe he should have taken less and split? Two days. Two long days. How would he last with this broad driving him up a tree? He must have been out of his skull to ever think he could spend the rest of his life with her.

"We've got to do something for her."

"OK," he agreed a moment later when Baby started to hack again, "we'd better get her some cough medicine." He didn't want anything happening to the baby before the payoff.

"She needs a doctor, a pediatrician, dummy, not cough medicine!"

"Hey, who are you calling a dummy, huh?"

"Myself. That's who. I must be to have ever gotten into a mess like this with you."

"Christ Almighty, will you stop harping on the same thing!"

"Harping?" she mimicked. "Listen, I'm the one they can finger. Not you. *Me!*"

"Well, you're in it. And while I'm trying to pull off a three-million-dollar deal for us, all you do is get bent out of shape on

274

piddling little shit. It's too cold in here. It's too drafty. The kid needs baby food. The kid has a cold. The kid needs a doctor. I'm not running a fucking nursery here," he fumed.

"I think," he continued, calming himself, "that you've been listening too much to that baby's singing. It's going to your head."

"What do you know, anyhow?"

"That if this keeps up I'm going to have to go out and buy you a set of those lips to hang around your neck or stick in your twat or whatever."

"You really are disgusting!"

"Let me put this very straight to you, Fay dearest"—he spoke through gritted teeth—"I don't want you holding the kid anymore. I don't want you listening to her or talking to her or touching her."

"I'll do whatever the hell I feel like!"

"You do and you'll end up *really* wishing you had never gotten into this. Do I make myself perfectly clear?"

26

Shuffling northward along Fifth Avenue as it skirted the eastern rim of Central Park, Doris was struck by how much more peaceful and habitable this part of the city seemed. The tall, ornate buildings across the street were clean and orderly with their sidewalks neatly shoveled and a doorman in every entrance. On her side was the stone wall bordering the park and beyond it the small, undulating hills and sturdy, ice-encrusted trees that brought to mind the serenity of Ithaca. Though it was still noisy, the sleaziness and detritus of the terminal area had yielded to civilization as she thought of it, and slowly, as though a veil were being lifted, her mind began to clear.

Spotting in the distance a line of deserted benches, Doris

pushed ahead, and when she reached the first bench, she brushed a spot free of snow and sat down on the hard wooden slats. Reaching into her bag, she extracted the remains of the sandwich the man on the bus had given her, and biting into the bread, she chewed slowly, trying to formulate a plan. Faced with the enormousness of this city, she understood that there was no earthly way she could attack the problem of finding Baby. It was hopeless, she told herself. She didn't even know where to start. Yet, since arriving in the city, she realized that she had been steadily moving in the same direction, driven by some strange whim. Logic—that old common sense of the librarian that craved ordered thoughts like neatly arranged books—warned Doris that she was just wasting her breath. Her instincts, however, kept gnawing restlessly, prodding her to get back on her feet and stop wasting precious time. But what instincts? She wondered. It was absurd wandering aimlessly through the endless canyons of this city looking for Baby. Downright ridiculous. As ridiculous as it had been for her to have gotten pregnant, carried a child, been given an infant who could sing. If she were to worry about a logical explanation for what she was doing now, she thought swallowing her last bite of sandwich, why then she'd have to go back and explain—

Doris suddenly stopped and looked up.

Above the noise of the city she thought she heard something calling to her. She strained to hear it again, tilting her head from side to side, but it was gone.

With a grunt she rose from her bench and looked around. Then suddenly she heard it again. It was Baby's voice. Faint, faint, faint. A few feeble notes. Then it stopped.

Doris cocked her head to one side and waited. Yes, she thought excitedly when it came back again, a short string, barely audible. It was Baby singing, calling out to her, the child's voice raspy and weak. And it was coming from the distance ahead, she thought, hurrying forward as the faint sound disappeared, lost in the jumble of city noises.

"Am I losing my mind?" she asked herself later, continuing to plod up the endless avenue. "Was it real or just in my head?" she fretted, inching wearily ahead as the day slowly began to wane.

"Baby, where are you?" she mumbled to herself exhaustedly,

leaving the park behind her and moving through the darkening streets of Harlem, loitering men on the streets watching her through the corners of sleepy-lidded eyes, giving no more than a desultory glance to the old, broken-down shell of a white lady, a nonperson moving through their territory, a shopping-bag lady muttering to herself, drifting up along Lenox Avenue toward the Harlem River.

When Sloan saw the headlines splashed on the front page of the evening *New York Post*, he was delighted.

"Look at this!" he piped, holding up the paper for Fay, trying to shake her out of the doldrums, hoping against hope that he could still win her over and unknot their entangled situation.

"Look at this." He waved the paper in front of her eyes as she sat by the heater holding Baby pressed against her body, her coat enclosing the two of them like a cocoon. Baby's parted lips were dry and cracked, her nose running, and that telltale gurgling in her chest had gotten worse. "Look!" he said, and Fay shifted her glance just enough to catch the headline.

PUERTO RICAN TERRORISTS BEHIND $3M BABY SNATCH

When she failed to react, he approached her cautiously.

"Don't you see? I really pulled it off."

"You're going to get an Academy Award," she said woodenly.

"Fay. Please," he began, nuzzling her ear, "let's be friends, huh?"

Her head hanging limply out of the front of Fay's coat, Baby opened her feverish eyes and rolled them languidly up toward Sloan.

"Whew!" he gasped, pulling away abruptly as a putrid odor hit his nose. "What is it that stinks like that?"

"She's got diarrhea. What do you think it is? She's dying, don't you understand? Dying! This little tiny kid is dying, and you're coming up here kissing me and trying to make nice as if nothing's wrong."

"I was just—" he began, and then stopped.

"Just what? Don't you have *any* human decency at all?"

"Aw, shit," he mumbled disgustedly and, flopping down on his mattress, opened the paper and began to read.

By the time Doris crossed the bridge into the Bronx, she had heard Baby's voice twice more. Each time the faint, short burst of notes seemed slightly closer, more urgent—reaching her at a point just as her strength began to flag. It was dark now as she reached the end of the bridge and, ahead, the traffic was light, the snow faintly cleaner, the sounds of the city falling upon her ears muted and subdued. By now, Doris reckoned to herself, people were already in their homes eagerly preparing for tomorrow's holiday. She thought about friends and families together. Mothers with their children. And she envied them.

A sharp wind gusted down the river, lifting the flaps of her coat. Shivering, she tightened her scarf and looked out. From her vantage at the end of the bridge, she could see the vast desolate miles of tenements stretching awesomely before her, and once again her determination began to wilt.

Which way now, she sighed, wondering how much more she could press on. She felt herself inexplicably drawn ahead to the left but resisted the insistent pull. She strained her ears to hear above the wind that howled through the frame structure of the bridge, but try as she might she could not discern Baby's voice.

"Baby," she called out hoarsely into the night. "Baby, Baby." She strained her ears, moving her head from side to side, but could hear only the rumble of a train, the dull throb of a distant jet.

"Baby, darling. Where are you?" she called out again. Still nothing, just that ineffable tug to the left.

"Oh, Lord." She turned her face up to the sky, afraid to trust her own feelings. "Please guide me," she prayed, continuing to gaze into the low sky, milky from the reflected lights of the city. "Give me some sign," she begged, and suddenly, as she uttered those words, Doris saw a break in the low clouds, saw the deep chasm that magically appeared leading out into space, saw the distant but bright, starlike light that moved slowly but unwaveringly across that gap, traveling across the heavens and following the identical path that her instincts had all along been urging. And then she knew, recognized that the song she had heard, the message that was in her soul had been real all along. Gaining heart, the hint of a smile forming on her frozen face, she picked up her bag and hurried off to the left, following the guiding light that was the night flight to Montreal.

The South Bronx was crawling with cops—city police drawn from precincts in all five boroughs, detectives from the state Bureau of Criminal Investigation pulled off other less-prominent cases, Feds flown in from offices all across the East. From Bruckner Boulevard in the east to the Major Deegan Expressway in the west, from the Triborough Bridge at the southern tip of the Bronx to a line running east-west through Fordham Road, the place was thick with police of every description. There were cops in cruisers, cops in unmarked units, cops in disguises, cops in uniform, cops hanging around the South Bronx precinct house just waiting to be dispatched at a moment's notice.

"Not a living thing is going to move on those streets without our knowing about it," said Inspector Albert Heath to Special Agent Nisbet. Heath, a ranking fifteen-year veteran who headed the Philadelphia field office and was considered a specialist in kidnappings, had been brought in to coordinate the search for Baby. With public attention focused on what was being called the case of the decade, law enforcement agencies knew they had their reputations on the line and they weren't taking any chances. There were now close to one hundred and forty cops either directly or indirectly working to crack the case.

When Shockley saw the *Post* story, he immediately called Nisbet.

"Have you seen the paper?"

"I heard."

"What the hell kind of shoddy operation are you people running there, anyway?"

"Who says the leak came from this end?"

"No. It came from me!"

"That's a distinct possibility."

"Nisbet, are you accusing me?"

"No. I just said it's a possibility."

"Stop playing games with me. You know I didn't talk to anyone. The leak came from your end. And if that's the slipshod way you people are going to run this investigation, then we're never going to get her back!" he fumed, slamming down the phone with a crash.

Later, when his anger had dissipated, Shockley went back to the paper and carefully read through the articles, combing the long piece on the coordinated police search, the background on the terrorist group, even the article on the upcoming Christmas telethon. Nowhere, absolutely nowhere was there mention of the South Bronx. Then he understood: The business about the terrorists had all been pure, unadulterated bullshit. They were trying to flush out the kidnappers by lulling them into a false sense of security. Which meant they had been stringing him along as well. They had nothing, not one lousy lead to Baby except that she was somewhere in the Bronx. Maybe.

Led by her impulses, Doris had now been walking in the South Bronx for almost two hours. Cutting through back lots and over mountains of rubble, she made her way through the maze of burned-out brick shells, pressing forward in an inward-spiraling loop. Dizzy with hunger, numb with cold, her head thrust resolutely forward, Doris drove herself on. She was closing in and Baby was near, she sensed, tightening again the helix that now enclosed little more than three blocks at its widest point. At that moment Doris was so near, in fact, that had Baby's kidnappers looked out their side window they might have caught a glimpse of her as she shambled along a cross street at the far end of the block. The pair, however, had momentarily let their vigil lapse, for as Doris was steadily homing in on their hideout, Sloan was lying sprawled on his back on his mattress, snoring deeply, while Fay, holding Baby, sat dozing in her chair by the kerosene heater.

Doris's progress through this torched-out section of the city, however, was not going entirely unnoticed. Two patrolmen in an unmarked cruiser had spotted her early on, wedging her way through a hole in the mesh of a high cyclone fence. For a minute they had sat in their darkened car observing her as she picked her way through the garbage-strewn lot. Their radio had squawked, they had exchanged knowing glances, and then moved on.

Doris had been spotted twice after that. Once by another patrol car. And once by a city cop by the name of Len Alicki. Alicki, who was disguised as an aging and disheveled hippie, had been sitting on the front stoop of an abandoned building apparently catching a few, drug-induced winks when Doris had come plodding by. Out of the corner of his eye he had watched as the old lady had stumbled past, weeping and jabbering to herself. Alicki, a hardened, street-wise cop, who had worked some of the toughest precincts in the city, had seen people like Doris and worse, much worse. Yet, watching her, he had been inexplicably pricked by a sense of pity. Here was this poor, old, shopping-bag lady on a dismal Christmas Eve with no place to go but the war-torn streets of the Bronx. It was a downright shame, he had thought, stung by reminiscences of his own mother, who had died almost five years ago after a long and debilitating senility. Doris had then disappeared around a corner, and Alicki had conveniently forgotten her, returning to his surveillance of the near-empty, snowy streets.

A scant minute before ten, plainclothesman Alicki pulled up his sleeve and, checking his watch, saw that it was finally time to end his shift. Rising off the cold concrete steps, he stretched himself, yawned, and began walking the six blocks to the rendezvous point where he was to be picked up for the night. He had hardly gone a few blocks when he spotted Doris for the second time. She was on the opposite side of the street, shuffling ahead as she wound in on her final loop, now but a few doors away from the entrance to the building where Baby was being held. Striding on toward the point where he was to meet with his pickup, Alicki continued on down the street, passing an unmarked unit that stood parked in the shadows. Exchanging a brief nod with the men who sat in the car taking a smoke, he went on a few more steps, came to a full stop and, suddenly turning around on his heels, marched back down the street. He knew that what he was doing was utterly meaningless, but something in his head warned Alicki that if he didn't go back to the old lady tonight, tomorrow would be a miserable Christmas—that thoughts of the old woman would plague him all through the night and the next day. A soft touch, he told himself as he saw Doris come to a stop at the doorway of the abandoned tenement in front of him, that's what he was, just an old, soft touch.

Checking his watch, Alicki picked up his pace. He was already late for his rendezvous, and he knew the men in his team would be getting itchy.

"Excuse me, lady," he called out, approaching Doris from the rear.

Doris slowly turned her hunched back and looked up at him.

"Where're you going?" asked this strange man dressed in fringes and beads, his face covered with hair.

Doris looked at him in confusion.

"Can I help you?" he asked, as Doris stared at him in continued bewilderment. "Are you lost? Are you looking for someone?"

"Baby," she finally mumbled through her cracked lips. "I'm looking for Baby," she said, exhausted, glad for any offer of help.

"Which baby?"

"My Baby," explained Doris, wiping her runny nose with the back of her hand. "My Baby," she repeated. "The one who sings," she added for clarity.

"Oh," said Alicki, taking a second look at Doris. Though she certainly didn't seem prosperous—wisps of ice-encrusted hair stood out from under her frayed scarf, her coat looked old and worn, her body broken and decrepit—Alicki couldn't help but note the glimmer of intelligence in her face. And her speech, though halting and weak, seemed clear and educated. She was not a shopping-bag lady, he now realized, and that was what had bothered him from the first. She was just a poor, old woman, one of those nutso Babyists. Probably someone's gaga mother. But what the hell was she doing out here?

"Please, help me," she said imploringly, feeling her last vestiges of strength dwindling. "I'm close, so close."

Alicki stared at her, debating what to do. He certainly couldn't leave her around here, prey to every lousy mugger and thug. He scratched his head and tugged at his frozen beard as Doris looked up at him with her rheumy eyes. Then, reaching into his back pocket, he extracted a walkie-talkie.

In less than a minute a dark car screeched up to the curb. Seated in it were three men dressed as hoboes and derelicts.

"Come on, get in, lady," he gently urged her, taking Doris by the arm.

"No," said Doris, resisting. "I have to—" she tried to shake free his hand.

"It's OK. We're police officers," he said, flashing his badge. "We're going to help you," he tried to soothe her.

"What's this, Alicki?" complained the man in the front seat, wearing a torn stocking cap. "We're supposed to go off duty now."

"Come on, Len. It's Christmas Eve. Give us a break," whined the other.

"We're going to find you a warm place," said Alicki to the old woman, ignoring the complaints.

"No. I can't leave. Not now! Please. Baby. She's here. I know she's here!" Doris struggled, feeling Officer Alicki's powerful hand tightening on her arm as she tried to wrestle free.

"We'll get you a good, warm Christmas meal and you can have a nice, clean—"

"Please. No. Don't! I have to—" Doris struggled with her last bit of strength.

"Come on now, lady. No one's going to hurt you."

"Oh, please." She struggled, feeling herself weaken. "Please don't take me away," she pleaded, crumbling into an exhausted heap into the man's arms.

"Chrisake, leave her!" said the cop at the wheel disgustedly, as Alicki lifted Doris into the car.

"I'll lose her! I'll lose her!" Doris objected as she felt herself being hoisted into the rear seat. "My Baby, my Baby," she sobbed, turning and looking out the back window as the car drove off with her. "She's here. I know it!"

27

Those lights," said Jacobsen, dispatching one of his assistants as he stared through a monitor into the darkness of the theater. "They flare in camera two. Tell those guys they should either turn or kill them. Rolf"—he motioned for Pettersson who stood watching a line of shapely dancers going through a dry run of their routine, their choreographer snapping his fingers and counting out the beat— "who told them to put those phones there? They should be more toward center stage. Where they've got them now they're almost off into the wings," he said, referring to the technicians who had started wiring in the lines in the late evening and would probably have to work through most of the night to meet the 9:00 A.M. start of the telethon.

"I told them to put them there," injected Father Tom, coming up the aisle from the stage. "If you place the phone bank more toward the middle it'll block half the stage for the audience on that side."

"Yes that's true," said Jacobsen as if it hadn't occurred to him. "But don't you think it would be better if the phones were always on camera?" He smiled patronizingly. He was feeling too good to argue. The show was coming together beautifully like a flower ready to bloom at the optimum moment, the telethon airing on Christmas morning just as gifts were being unwrapped and people's hearts were most open to giving. Why mar it with petty bickering?

"Well," Fitzgibbons deferred, "I'm hardly an expert when it comes to putting on shows."

"True"—Jacobsen smiled, putting his arm around Fitzgibbons—"leave it to me. I know what the priorities are. Just keep everybody happy as you've been doing and you'll be doing more than your share. Your contribution so far has been nothing short of spectacular."

Fitzgibbons smiled uneasily and slipped away from Jacobsen's arm.

"Rolf, my boy" said Jacobsen later, still in an effusive mood. "You're watching television history being made."

"Yes, sir," Pettersson grinned.

"They're going to be talking about this program for years to come. That you can count on."

Shortly thereafter, just when Jacobsen was sure the program was in the bag, the telethon was hit by a seemingly endless barrage of calamities.

Just after eleven there was a mysterious power failure that confounded the theater crew. After forty minutes of struggling around in the darkness and trying to unsnarl the confusion of circuitry, a young man, proudly claiming to be a CURBist, was discovered hiding in the theater. He had been flipping power switches in an effort to disrupt the program. The man was arrested, security immediately tightened, and no one was allowed to enter or leave the premises without passing through a phalanx of armed guards.

Soon thereafter, a man claiming to be an official from the union representing the telephone technicians installing the phone bank appeared on stage and announced that, according to a contract negotiated with the phone company last fall, his men were strictly prohibited from working after midnight. Anxiously, Jacobsen pulled the man aside and tried to reason with him. Weren't there exceptions to the rule? Yes, said the man. In cases of national emergency. Well, this was a national emergency! The man laughed away the notion. Jacobsen offered a cash bonus to the men on top of their double time if they continued to work. The man said he would take the suggestion under consideration and turned to leave. Jacobsen slipped something into the man's pocket. Yes, said the man stopping for an instant, maybe this telethon did, in fact, come under that emergency provision. He would ask his men to stay on the job.

"I'm sorry to call you at this hour," said Harry Terkel, sounding half asleep himself.

"What's the matter?" asked Olive groggily. She yawned, flipped on the light, and, squinting at the clock, saw that it was just about three.

"I just got a call about Mrs. Rumsey," he explained.

"Doris?" exclaimed Olive, trying to clear her head. "Where is that woman? I've been trying to get ahold of her. I went out to the trailer today, but the place was locked and her cat's gone." Olive suddenly stopped short. "Is she all right?"

"She's in New York City," said Terkel tersely. "Bellevue."

"Oh, Lord." Olive sat up in her bed alert. "You don't mean that poor soul went to the city to—"

"She was picked up somewhere wandering the streets in a state of confusion. They asked her for the name of a family member," Terkel explained, a little embarrassed, "and she apparently gave them my name and number." He paused and waited.

"What're we going to do?" asked Olive.

"We ought to get her out of there. As fast as possible."

"You want me to go down and get her?"

"I was hoping you'd say that," said Terkel, noticeably relieved. "They'd be willing to release her in your custody. All you have to do is sign for her."

"Why, of course," said Olive, preparing herself mentally for the trip.

"And Mrs. Eldridge?"

"Yes?"

"This thing. It could really hurt her custody fight."

"But—"

"I'm looking ahead, Mrs. Eldridge. So, for her sake, please don't mention this incident to anybody."

"Don't you worry none about that," said Olive, reaching for her robe. "My lips are sealed."

Fay awoke with a sudden start in the midst of a nightmare. Seated by the kerosene heater, she had been sleeping with Baby tucked under her coat. Dazed, she looked around the room trying to place herself. Though it was after daybreak, the apartment was still dark, only faint swatches of gray outside light seeping in through the plastic-covered windows. Immediately she realized something was terribly wrong. She looked down. In her lap lay Baby writhing convulsively, the child gasping for breath.

"Oh, God!" She sprang to her feet, holding the jerking child in her arms. "She's choking!" she wailed, seeing Baby's face turn blue, the child struggling for air, her arms and legs thrashing out wildly. Gripped by panic, Fay dashed with Baby to the front door of the apartment.

Sloan was already scrambling to his feet as Fay stood fumbling with the door lock.

"Stop!" he barked, shoving her roughly aside and blocking her exit.

"Sloan,"—she wept hysterically—"she's dying! Let me out! Let me OUT!" she cried as his fist came flying across her face, knocking her to the ground with Baby. "Sloan. Oh, Sloan!" she pleaded, getting up on her knees and grabbing onto his leg. "Please let us out. You can still get away. I'd never tell. I swear. Please. Please!" she begged, the shadow looming above her.

Sloan kicked his leg free.

"Look," she said, holding Baby out to him, the child's pitiful body torn by convulsions as she frantically fought for each gulpful of air. "Don't you have an ounce of humanity in you?" she beseeched as he remained planted squarely in front of the door, staring tight-lipped out into the darkness, refusing to look down at the dying infant.

Seeing him standing hard and silent, immovable as stone, Fay leaped to her feet and charged to the kitchen. Laying the gasping child on the icy floor, she tried to pry open the window, and when it wouldn't budge, she picked up a chair and swung it with all her might. The glass and frame exploded into the alley in a shower of fragments that tinkled down the metal steps of the fire escape. As she bent down to take Baby, Sloan was already behind her, grabbing a fistful of hair and yanking her violently away from the shattered window.

"You bastard," she hissed, reaching out and swinging wildly at him as he held his grip. "You miserable bastard!" she snarled, lashing out in a last frenzy, catching his face with her nails and ruthlessly ripping his flesh.

"Augh!" he cried out and flung her by her hair against the wall.

Moaning, the wind knocked out of her, Fay raised herself weakly on one arm. She looked at Baby, who lay sprawled next to her. The child now lay flaccid and barely conscious, her breath little more than a feeble, gurgling rattle. Fay stared back up at Sloan, who stood glaring down at her, clutching his torn face as he waited for her next move. She could feel the warm blood that coursed from her nose and into her mouth and seeing Sloan standing there, personifying all that was cruel and mean in life, she became an animal herself, cornered and enraged, ready to fight to the death. Slowly she raised her bruised body, sliding upward against the wall, her head throbbing, her eyes widened in rage, her bloodied mouth open and panting. With her eyes locked on Sloan as he stood ready for her, his feet spread, his fists clenched, she searched for an opening, a point of weakness, a momentary lapse. Seeing the murder in her eyes, Sloan backed up a foot and stood poised for her next assault as she circled to one side, her hands up, nails extended. Her eyes darted about the room. The vague form of an iron skillet that stood on the counter suddenly caught her attention. Still fixing Sloan with her eyes, Fay continued to circle to her right, moving steadily inch by inch toward the counter, frantically hoping she could reach the pan before he lunged for her. When she was but an arm's length away, Baby suddenly let out a loud, gasping, barklike sound. Sloan looked for an instant at the child, and in that fleeting second, Fay, in a single, coiled movement, leaped for the pan, grabbed its handle, and let it fly with all her strength.

Coming out of the dimness, the skillet caught Sloan unawares, the heavy iron slamming into the bone between his eyes in a searing white flash of pain. Crying out, he stumbled drunkenly backward, his hands going up to his eyes. In that split second Fay had Baby in her arms and, in one jump, had broken through the shattered remains of the window.

By the time Sloan realized what had happened, Fay was already out on the fire escape, clattering furiously down the stairs. Sloan flung himself through the opening, feeling the jagged edges of glass slicing into him, warm blood spurting out against his skin. Grasping the rusty railings of the fire escape, he clambered down the steps.

"Help! Help!" Fay screamed desperately, her voice shrill and breaking. "Help! Someone! The baby's dying! Help!" she cried, holding the infant under one arm as she bolted down the metal stairs, tripping and recovering her hold and seeing Sloan narrowing the gap between them. "Oh, dear Lord. Someone! Help us!" she wailed in the raw deserted dawn, her voice echoing hollowly in the narrow alley between the buildings.

Scampering down past the landing, Fay suddenly found herself dangling in the air, futilely searching for the missing rungs, the final extension that should have bridged the last twenty feet to the littered alley below. She saw Sloan closing in, his face twisted in hatred, rivulets of blood streaming down his eyes and cheeks. Fay looked back down into the darkness of the narrow alley, trying to estimate the long drop. In another second he would be within arm's length. She stared down into the dimness, pressed Baby tight against her body and, bending her legs, leaped out blindly.

Fay felt herself flying through the cold air, saw that elusive ground suddenly appear and move up at her, then felt the shock of impact reverberate through her bones as she hit the concrete, her feet crumbling under her in a bone-crunching jolt. Moaning in stunned pain, she looked up and saw Sloan dangling by his hands from the last rungs, ready to leap after her, the bones of her legs jutting out through her torn flesh. Desperately, still holding Baby, she began to crawl, pulling with her free arm and dragging her shattered legs behind her. Reaching the end of the alley and nearly the front sidewalk, she heard Sloan land behind her with a loud grunt.

"Please! Dear God, help me!" she called out, hoping to reach the empty street. "Help!" she cried as Sloan stumbled to his feet and began to hobble toward her. "Someone! Baby's dying!" she called out with her last breath, fainting as the pain became unbearable.

The harsh bell jarred Shockley out of sleep. Stumbling to the phone, he picked up the receiver to the hot line. A dial tone hummed in his ear while the other phone continued to ring. He put down the first receiver and picked up the second.

"We found her," said Agent Nisbet without preliminaries.

"Baby?" he asked in disbelief.

"Yes," answered Nisbet in a subdued voice.

"Thank God!" he said and then stopped short. "What's the matter?" he asked, picking up the agent's tone.

"She's not—not in good shape."

"She's dead!" Shockley exclaimed.

"No. No," Nisbet answered quickly. "Look, let's not waste time. Can you be ready in a couple of minutes?"

"I've just got to throw on some clothes," said Shockley, rushing his words.

"Good. We'll pick you up at your hotel. The car'll be waiting in front."

Shockley hung up, pulled a pair of pants over his pajamas, and put on a shirt that was lying on a nearby chair. He yanked on a pair of socks and shoes and, grabbing his coat, bolted for the elevator.

"Come on. Come on. Come on," he fretted, repeatedly pressing the down button and watching the indicator, which seemed to move with deliberate slowness. Finally the elevator arrived and Shockley rode down in shaky silence, his hands nervously clenched at his side.

Idling in front of the main entrance to the hotel was a late-model dark sedan with a short, telltale antenna sticking up in front of the trunk. As he raced down the stairs, the front door to the car swung open. Shockley jumped in.

"You Nisbet?" he asked the youngish, dark-haired agent as the car peeled away, its siren going.

"I'm Special Agent Howard," said the man with the long nose and square-cut jaw.

"How's Baby?" he asked anxiously as they whizzed eastward, flying through chains of red lights.

"I don't know. I really don't. I'd tell you if I did. I just got a call to pick you up."

"Where are we headed?" he asked as they reached the Eastside Highway and Howard took the northbound entrance.

"The Bronx. Bronx Hospital."

"Oh, God," uttered Shockley, his hands locked together, blocking out the gruesome images served up by his fantasy. Sitting stonily in the car, he looked out at the river as they raced up the near-empty highway. A lonely tug was making its way down the ice-choked river and he concentrated on it until it fell out of view. Baby was alive, he told himself, hanging on to that tenuous thread, and that was the important thing. Overhead, the sky, which had been gray since daybreak, turned ominously black.

"We're in for another one," said Howard, trying to ease Shockley's wait.

"Huh?"

"Snowstorm. Some pisser of a winter we're having, isn't it?"

Shockley nodded.

"What time is it?" he asked, breaking the silence a little later.

"Eight"—Howard glanced at his watch as he zigzagged through a jumble of cars blocking both lanes—"Eight fifty-seven. Hang on. We'll be there in no time."

"I appreciate your calling me," said Jacobsen.

"I only wish it had been better news," said Nisbet.

"Have your people made an announcement?" he asked, staring nervously up at the clock in the busy control room. There were scant minutes before the telethon was scheduled to start in the eastern- and central-time zones, and they were already on a countdown, the network affiliates waiting to be fed. The audience was seated and the orchestra was playing, warming them up.

"Not yet," answered Nisbet. "We want to make sure we've nabbed everyone involved. We want to hold a little longer."

"Of course. I understand," said Jacobsen, striving to sound cooperative. "Will you let me know *before* you announce it?"

"I'm not announcing anything. I'm going home to sleep. That isn't my department, anyhow."

"Then whose is it?"

"Press-liaison people."

"Can you give me a name?"

28

This way," said the uniformed city cop, taking a sharp turn in the corridor as they raced through the hospital halls, the pungent odor of disinfectant and drugs and sickness assaulting Shockley's nostrils.

At the far end of the hall another cop standing guard in front of a door looked up as the pair hurried toward him. A nod from the officer accompanying Shockley and he quickly opened the door and moved aside.

Shockley stepped into the room and heard the door close behind him. In the room he saw two men in white and a nurse standing around the large crib at the far side of the room. His heart thudding, Shockley looked past them, past the tangle of drip bottles and wires and monitors.

"Baby!" he whispered in anguish, spotting the little figure that lay inertly encased in a plastic tent. "Oh my God, my God, what did they do to you!" he gasped, biting his lip as tears rushed in to cloud his vision. Approaching Baby's crib he saw Baby's bluish-white body pressed cold and lifeless against the crisp sheets, her eyes sealed, her face slack. Sinking down to his knees, bitter tears searing his cheeks, he slid his hand under the tent, reaching in until he finally made contact with Baby's tiny hand. Taking her fine fingers in his, he was almost shocked to find that they were not icy, but hot, burning hot.

"I'm Dr. Martinez," said the first man, gently trying for Shockley's attention. He was brown-skinned and short and had an accent faintly reminiscent of the kidnapper's. "I'm the chief pediatric resident," he added.

Shockley stared up at him in a daze.

"We're doing all we can," the doctor said in a subdued voice. "But she's very sick."

"She's got a severe pneumonia. She has had a very high fever—we don't know for how long. She's dehydrated," added the second man.

"She's been in a coma ever since she was admitted," continued Martinez, Shockley's eyes moving from one doctor to the other.

"We've got her on ampicillin, and we're trying to replace her lost fluids," said Martinez, and Shockley's eyes drifted up to the bottles and then traced the lines that ended in large needles that were taped into Baby's frail arms. He brought his head close to Baby, pressing it against the cold plastic, and stared in at her. There were beads of perspiration on her face, her angel locks damp and plastered against her head. Her chest was rapidly rising and falling as though she were a wounded animal panting its last breaths. Then he heard a strange gurgling that sounded as though air were being bubbled through water. At first he thought it was a respirator or one of the machines. Then, in horror, he realized it was Baby herself, fighting for air, her lungs filling with liquid.

"We did one aspiration already, when she first came in," said the doctor as though reading his mind. "But her chest has filled up again," continued the man, who also had an accent.

Shockley looked from one man to the other, looked searchingly at the nurse. The woman tried to give him an encouraging smile. Shockley swallowed. Wiping his eyes he tried to clear his head. He began to formulate the question that was on the tip of his tongue, but he was afraid to ask, fearing that posing it would be giving substance to his deepest dread. He stared fixedly at Baby's face, trying to match it to the little girl who had, only days earlier, cooed and sung for him, but those images refused to converge. She had moved away, he feared, her fragile body dangling over the edge of that eternal abyss.

"Will she make it?" he finally asked, the words needing to be forced out of him.

"I honestly don't know," answered Martinez. "We're doing all we can," he explained softly. "It's in God's hands," he commiserated, nodding his head sadly.

Within the next hour Baby's condition became even more acute.

"I don't like the sound of her heart," said Martinez.

"What do you mean?" asked Shockley, trying to tie him down.

"There's a frictional rub synchronous with her heartbeat," he said, as his colleague, after listening to Baby with a stethoscope, looked up and nodded.

"I don't understand," said Shockley.

What Martinez meant was that Baby's pneumonia looked as if it were becoming complicated by an acute bacterial endocarditis. There was an ominous sound in Baby's heart, and the doctors suspected that the infection had turned metastatic and was now attacking the child's aortic valve.

"If this endocarditis goes any farther," explained Martinez yet later, looking plainly worried, "there's a real danger that a rupture or perforation of the cusps might occur, or even a rupture of the aorta itself. We're going to have to monitor this *very* carefully."

Shockley looked at him blankly.

"What I'm saying is that we may have to consider surgical repair."

"Oh," said Shockley, his stomach twisting.

"Would you mind," he asked Martinez a few minutes later as Baby was wheeled in her tent together with her i.v. bottles down to the x-ray room, her police guards following on either side, "if we brought in some other specialists?" Shockley was only going through the formality. He had just made up his mind to get a second opinion.

"No. Not at all. In fact"—Martinez smiled, almost relieved—"I was going to suggest that myself."

Shockley wasn't quite sure how to go about getting a specialist in the city, but he knew that Baby required the best that money could buy. The logical person to call was Jacobsen, who seemed to know everybody.

"Yes. I just heard about Baby," said Jacobsen, shielding the receiver to blot out the music in the background. "How is she?" he inquired hastily.

"It looks bad," answered Shockley dully.

"Is there anything I can do?"

"Yes. That's why I called."

Shockley then quickly told him about Baby's condition, about the complications, about the need for specialists. For a good pediatrician. A good cardiologist.

"Consider it done," said Jacobsen.

"I've got to run," said Shockley, seeing Baby's bed being wheeled back toward the elevator.

"Keep me posted, Shockley. I'll try to get over to the hospital later."

"Is Father Tom there?" Shockley asked.

"Let me see," said Jacobsen, looking straight at Fitzgibbons, who stood no more than a few yards away from him in front of the control room. "No. No, I don't see him. He was around earlier but—"

"As soon as you can find him, please tell him what's happened," said Shockley, his voice breaking.

"Certainly."

"Thanks," said Shockley weakly and started to hang up.

"Shockley," Jacobsen caught him in the last second.

"Huh?"

"The police don't want any announcements made about Baby's return until they're sure they've rounded up everyone involved. Please, don't break the news to the press. There'll be a joint release at the appropriate time."

"Sure," agreed Shockley. The last thing in the world he wanted to do at this point was talk to reporters.

Around eleven o'clock Shockley got a call, which he took at the nurses' station down the hall from Baby's room.

"How's it going?" asked Nisbet. The agent was calling from his home in Queens. He was getting ready to hit the sack and just couldn't go to sleep without first checking with Shockley.

"Not so good. They had her on penicillin, but she's not responding. They suspect the infection might be penicillin resistant. They're trying another antibiotic now. She's got heart trouble too."

"It's a bitch," commiserated Agent Nisbet, who had children of his own. "If it's any consolation—" he began.

"The kidnappers?"

"Yeah. I thought you'd want to know."

"Yes."

"It looks like it was a couple. A boyfriend and girlfriend team. Just two. No one else. The woman's confessed. They weren't Babyists or CURBists or anything. Just your average greedy

294

people. The woman's in surgery right now. She fractured both her legs trying to escape with Baby from her boyfriend. She's in pretty tough shape."

"And the man?" he asked, picking up the cue.

"One of the city stakeouts pulled up just as she was crawling to the street after jumping from the second story. Her boyfriend was right behind her. When they told him to freeze, he reached into his pocket. That's what they say, anyway. They shot him. One shot. Through the head."

Silence.

"They didn't find a gun," Nisbet added uneasily, filling the void. "Look, if there's some way I can help, just give me a call," he said and gave Shockley his home number.

"I appreciate that. I really do," said Shockley, scribbling down Nisbet's number and stuffing the slip of paper into his pocket.

Replacing the receiver, Shockley remained standing in the glass-enclosed cubicle that was the nurses' station. A nurse stepped in, reached past him to take a clipboard off a hook, and left. He watched her move down the corridor, then looked up at the clock and followed the second hand as it swept across the large face. Somewhere in the back of his mind a thought was stirring. He was thinking about Baby. About Doris. About the connection between the two of them. He knew he was probably grasping at straws, but—but—He recalled the time Baby had fallen despondent and stopped singing. Now that he thought about it, it had coincided with Doris's confinement to Willard. He wasn't positive, but it seemed that Baby had started to sing again just about the time Doris had been released.

Shockley's pulse began to quicken as he dug further back into the recesses of his memory. He then remembered the onset of Baby's elegiac song, that longing, mournful melody that began just about the time Doris had become deathly ill. And then, of course—Then there was that gruesome day that Baby had almost drowned. Looking out during the television interview, he had seen a hunched-over, snow-clad figure moving fleetingly past his window. It could only have been one person, he now realized, and the odds in his mind were now stacked against sheer coincidence. Doris had come because she knew Baby was in trouble. She had known about Baby, just as Baby had always known about her. Suddenly a multitude of small, seemingly meaningless and disconnected occurrences all jelled. As utterly absurd as it was, as much as it defied all experience, now in this moment of desperation it made perfect sense.

Shockley fumbled through his pockets for Nisbet's number. He grabbed the phone and punched out the numerals, waiting impatiently as the call wended its way sluggishly through the system. The phone on the other end began to ring. Someone picked up the line and without waiting Shockley hurriedly asked, "Nisbet?"

"Yeah," said the agent, sounding a bit startled.

"Can I take you up on that offer? Of a favor?"

"Sure."

"Baby's real mother. Doris Rumsey."

"Yeah. The lady who tried to call."

"Right."

"You want me to try and locate her?" he asked, anticipating Shockley's request.

"More than that. I want you to find her and get her here to the hospital. Quick."

"It may not be that easy. This is a big city."

"Nisbet. It's important. Urgent."

"I understand," said Nisbet.

"No, you don't. Not really," said Shockley, guessing what the cop was thinking. "I know this is going to sound nuts, but, Nisbet, I've got this feeling in my bones that she's the only one now who can really save the child."

"Shockley," said Nisbet, trying to pull him back to earth.

"Look, there isn't time for me to go into the details. You offered me a favor. I'm asking for it. Just tell me, will you do it or won't you?"

"OK," came Nisbet's slow reply. "OK."

"I know you're exhausted."

"I'm on my eighth wind," Nisbet tried to sound up.

"Thanks."

"Don't thank me yet. I haven't found her."

"Just thanks. And listen. I'm sorry about snapping at you earlier."

"You don't owe me an apology. I would have been pissed, too."

At 11:10 a team of three high-powered physicians converged on the Bronx Hospital. There was a specialist in pediatric medicine from Columbia-Presbyterian, a world-famous cardiologist who had pioneered new techniques in heart repair, and a specialist in internal medicine from the Cornell School of Medicine. Dr. Martinez and his aide stepped aside deferentially to let them take over. They reran all the tests that Martinez had performed, from sputum and spinal-fluid cultures to a complete blood and urine work-up to a fresh series of lung X rays. They listened to Baby's heart and ran an EKG. They ordered frequent alcohol rubdowns in the hope of dampening her stubborn fever. They slid long needles into her side, aspirated the thick, viscous fluid filling her chest, and instilled erythromycin—all just as their predecessor, Dr. Martinez, had done through the early morning. After they had finished, they gathered for a second huddle and then finally spoke with Shockley.

"She's got a severe pneumococcal infection that appears metastatic. There appears to be endocarditis," said the pediatric specialist from Columbia. He was an elderly man with deep furrows in his brow and a cold, professorial manner that reminded Shockley of Krieger. When he spoke, he fixed Shockley with his unrelenting greenish blue eyes. "The bacteria seem to to be penicillin resistant, and from the beginnings of Dr. Martinez's sensitivity study, it looks as if it might respond to erythromycin. We're going to run a second study to be sure. But we need time. Right now we're running blind."

"Will she live?" asked Shockley bluntly.

"I don't know," said the man without flinching. "Babies are not little adults. The outlook for children under a year in her condition, at least in my experience, is not good. I'd like to be more positive," he said, finally looking away, "but I don't want to raise false hopes."

"I see," murmured Shockley.

"If the new antibiotic works, you may see a remarkable turnaround," he said, trying to hold out a glimmer of hope.

"I see," repeated Shockley, lacking words. But what he saw was that money and high-powered physicians were not going to save Baby. The prognosis of these illustrious doctors was no more heartening than that of Dr. Martinez, and their treatment was merely a continuation of what that doctor had done already. Despite his lack of fancy credentials, Martinez was just as competent as they were and, Shockley was coming to understand, much more of a human being.

"What are we?" said Martinez, bringing Shockley a much-needed cup of hot coffee. Even though the other three doctors had taken charge, Martinez had stayed as if to console Shockley. "We're a bunch of technicians. That's all." He spoke with his hands, his eyes dark and alive. "We give bacteriostatic chemicals, antibiotics, but these drugs don't lick the infections. They merely hold them in check. It's the body itself that must ultimately eliminate the infection," he said, making a fist. "At times like this we become almost helpless, superfluous," he added with a sad nod.

"Do you think maybe she doesn't have the will to live?"

"Well, I—" began Martinez, taken aback by the question. "Why do you ask?"

"I was just wondering, that's all," Shockley answered vaguely, his eyes drifting back to the bed.

"She's just a baby. All babies want to live. It's built into them by creation."

"Are you religious?" Shockley asked Martinez, trying to pin down the doctor.

"I never heard her sing, if that's what you mean," he said with a smile, referring to Babyism.

"No. I meant in general." Shockley brought him back on track.

"Well"—Martinez laughed uneasily—"we're not supposed to be. Oh, nobody in med school ever said it right out. But it's something that's infused into your system by osmosis. Am I religious?" He raised his dark eyebrows and looked up at the tile ceiling. "No. Not in the conventional sense. But in my own way, I suppose—Yes. Yes, I am," said Martinez, gaining resolution as though he had not pondered the question in years. "I believe there is a God. Someone looking over us now, watching over this sick child." Martinez stopped and looked straight at Shockley. "Prayer certainly never hurt," he added as if reading Shockley's thoughts.

Nisbet called Shockley back at eleven-thirty.

"How's Baby looking?" he asked.

"No change. Did you locate Doris?"

"Yeah. She was picked up—now listen to this—of all places right in front of the building where that pair was holding Baby."

"When?" he asked tensely.

"Before. Almost *twelve hours* before we caught them."

"Then she knew!" he uttered.

"It's weird," said Nisbet, sounding baffled.

"But where's she now?"

"She was acting very disoriented and confused, so they took her to Bellevue for observation."

"She's there?"

"No. She was released a couple of hours ago. Some friend came to pick her up."

"Damn!" muttered Shockley.

"Well, that's how things stand. I thought you'd want to know."

"Please. Please, don't give up," he urged. "Keep looking for her."

"Have I given up so far? I can't give you any guarantees that I'll find her, but I'll stay on the phone and keep trying. That I promise."

"You're an angel," he said, and Nisbet laughed. "I mean it. An honest-to-goodness angel."

The hospital chaplain came by a few minutes later and offered to pray with Shockley for the health of the child. Shockley thanked him but declined.

Dr. Martinez dropped by after seeing to another case and suggested that Shockley take a few minutes off and come down to the cafeteria with him to have some breakfast. Shockley declined that offer too. He was waiting for Nisbet's call.

Finally, a couple of minutes later, it came.

"Shockley?"

"Shoot," said Shockley.

"She was released in the custody of a Mrs. Eldridge. Olive Eldridge. That ring a bell?"

"Yes. Yes, that's her friend from Ithaca."

"Well, they left in her car about two and a half hours ago—but that's only an approximation. They're in an old Volkswagen."

"Do you have the license number?"

"I'm ahead of you."

"Well?"

"This is not very kosher," said Nisbet, knowing what was coming next.

"I know. But for the child's sake. For the sake of her music. For the sake of us all, please," he pleaded.

"How in the world am I going to explain this?"

"Don't!"

"I've got superiors to deal with, Shockley. I've got a job I want to keep. Kids to support. I don't want them thinking I've gone off the deep end."

"Please, Jeff," said Shockley.

Silence.

"OK, OK. I'll alert the state police."

"If they're headed back to Ithaca they're probably somewhere on Route 17"—Shockley did a quick calculation in his head—"somewhere between, say—say—"

"Between Liberty and Binghamton," chimed in Nisbet, who had already consulted a map before calling Shockley.

29

As the minutes ticked by and the hunt for Doris went on, Shockley kept his vigil by Baby's crib, searching her comatose face for some small hint of consciousness. Once, for an instant, he thought he saw her eyebrows knit and nearly flew out of his skin. The brief twitch passed, however, and her features remained as dead still as ever, only her gurgling breath giving any hint of life. Hoping to penetrate the shroud of unconsciousness enveloping her, Shockley tried to rouse Baby by talking to her. When that failed he sang to her, singing in his unsteady voice a lullaby his mother had crooned to him as a child. Nothing seemed to work. Baby just lay there inert, her lifeless face cast in an eerie bluish hue. Finally, in desperation, Shockley broke down and took Martinez's advice.

"Dear God in heaven," he whispered under his breath, hoping that the nurse in the room wouldn't hear him. "Please save her. Because of my greed and selfishness, I brought this upon her. She doesn't deserve to die for my stupidity. Please, dear Lord, if you're there, save this innocent baby."

Later, as Baby's breathing became shallower, her heart

showed signs of faltering, and Shockley was dispatched to the corridor as the doctors rushed into the room, he tried praying again. He prayed louder and more fervently than before, no longer afraid that someone might overhear him. It didn't matter. All that counted was Baby.

"Dear God, if you let her live, I promise that I'll change all my ways. I promise that I'll never again exploit her as I've done. I'll serve *her* instead of letting her serve my ends. I know now that she's more than just a genetic quirk. She *is* a gift from you. If she lives I'll dedicate my life to her and you. Please. This one favor. Spare her."

Shockley paced the corridors waiting for the doctors to emerge. He circled up and down the halls, repeatedly checking the door to Baby's room. As he wandered along one of the corridors, it suddenly dawned on him that most of the televisions were on in the patients' rooms. Not only that, but they all seemed to be tuned to the same channel.

Entering one of the open rooms, he approached the bed of an emaciated old man and looked at his set. On the screen at that instant were Donny and Marie Osmond, and what Shockley saw and heard he could hardly believe.

"The money that you call in this morning," said Donny woodenly, obviously reading from a cue card.

"Your dollars, even quarters and dimes, however much," chirped Marie.

"All will help gain release of Baby."

"Our operators are standing by," said Marie as the camera panned the men and women sitting at the bank of ringing phones.

"Minutes count," urged Donny as a toll-free number traveled across the bottom of the screen.

"On this Christmas morning with your loved ones—"

"Think of Baby, who loves us all."

"And now while you're calling in your donation," announced Donny on an upbeat note, "here is—"

"Mr. Ray Charles!"

Applause.

Up the corridor at the nurses' station, the phone rang. It was for Shockley.

"We found her," piped Nisbet. "Got her right before Binghamton. It was close. She's already on her way back to the city."

"Get her back *fast*," said Shockley, looking at Baby's closed door.

"We're moving mountains. The state police are using a chopper."

"Hurry. Please. She doesn't have much time."

"Hang in there."

"Jeff?"

"Yeah."

"The telethon," said Shockley succinctly. "It's still running."

"Yeah. I just noticed. My kids turned on the tube."

"What's going on?"

"That's what I'd like to know. From what I understood the Mayor's office was supposed to make a joint announcement with your people hours ago. I can't figure it."

"I can," said Shockley. Then the door to Baby's room opened slowly and he hung up.

"For those of you who've just joined us," said Osgood, looking earnestly into the camera, his back to the tiers of operators feverishly answering the phones, "we're steadily moving toward Baby's freedom and our goal of three million dollars. And—"

The screen cut to the large electronic billboard on center stage that was continually tallying up the donations.

"And, as you can now see, we're at"—Osgood sneaked on his glasses and took a squint—"at one million, two hundred and fifty-six thousand—Whoops!—fifty-eight thousand, one hundred and sixty-two dollars and seven cents!" he crowed, grabbing at the latest digits in the ever-changing display.

"And this is *your* money, *your* gift, every single penny of which is going to Baby. Somewhere in this city our precious child's life hangs in the balance. With your help we can tilt that balance in her favor. Please, don't hesitate. There is no one to save her but *you*!" He leveled a finger at the camera. "It is for you that Baby has sung and for you she will continue to sing if we can rescue her. Spare the life of this God-sent child," he said, the screen dissolving into a picture of Baby in concert, her mouth open in joyous song. At the bottom of the screen the toll-free number was urgently flashing in a hot shade of red.

As he stood in the rear of the control room, Jacobsen's eyes shifted from Osgood on the outgoing monitor back up to the series of clocks lining the wall. It was now almost twelve in New -

York. In a couple of minutes it would be nine o'clock for the network affiliates in the Pacific time zone, the moment at which the central control in Rockefeller Center was scheduled to start feeding the first hour of the New York tape just as they had fed the mountain-time stations the first tape an hour earlier. If they could just squeak through the next hour without word leaking out that Baby had been found, thought Jacobsen nervously, they could wrap the last hour of the show in New York and keep the tapes running and the money rolling in. If only those who had agreed to keep the lid on this thing could hold out for a few more hours, they would break the three-million mark with ease.

Jacobsen stared tensely out the window of the control booth and saw Fitzgibbons standing partially hidden in the wings of the stage. Father Tom looked back up at Jacobsen, then at the electronic board and, making a sign of victory with his fingers, gave a broad smile.

"One million, two hundred and eighty-three thousand," crowed Osgood when he was cued, "six hundred and forty-two dollars and sixty-three cents!" he laughed, pretending to catch his breath. "We're getting there. We're getting there!"

"Roll the number," cued the director into his mike, and slicing across Osgood's waist there appeared in red that now familiar train of numbers: 800-555-2000.

"Our operators have been working tirelessly," said Osgood, extending his hand toward the line of people answering the phones, which continued to ring almost as fast as they could put them down. The audience burst into spontaneous applause. "And I want you people around the country, all around this great, generous nation of ours to just keep these phones ringing right off the hooks. Let's show the world on this Christmas Day that we care, care about Baby! And now to start our fourth hour—"

"OK. Camera three. Get ready. Move to the left. Little lower. That's it. Hold it!"

"It's coming up on noon," said a woman at the far side of the console into her headset. "Let's get ready to roll for Pacific. Five, four, three—"

"Our last big hour. Here's the maestro of comedy, the man who taught America how to laugh, America's own—"

"Roll tape one on Pacific."

"Mister—" said Osgood, building suspense for the next act.

"And now," issued a slick, deep voice from the monitor marked Pacific. "From New York City's Town Hall—" fanfare of trumpets—"the Christmas Benefit for Baby!" Applause. "With a star-studded cast including—"

"Welcome back to the second hour," chirped Osgood on the mountain monitor, sweat glistening on his brow as it had two hours earlier.

"Mister Jerry Lewis!" crowed Osgood live as the orchestra came on with a blast of an intro, Lewis striding across the stage to a thunderous ovation, his toothy smile flashing in the lights, his arms outstretched as though he could enfold the country in his arms.

"Rock-a-bye your baby with a Dixie melody," he crooned, coming in on beat. The music built on the insistent beat.

"A million baby kisses I'll deliver / If you would only sing—"

As Jacobsen stood in the rear of the half-darkened control room, his eyes traveled across the line of monitors. He flicked a tail of ash off the end of his cigarette, brought the cigarette to his lips, and took a long, slow drag. The end glowed brightly, then slowly faded and disappeared in a cloud of swirling smoke.

"What the hell is going on there?" asked Shockley when Pettersson picked up the phone backstage.

"A million baby kisses I'll deliver—"

"What do you mean?" asked Pettersson above the roar of the music.

"Why is that show still on the air?" asked Shockley, one eye peeled on the hospital corridor.

"Still on?"

"Baby's been found."

"Why that's just great—!"

"She was picked up hours ago!"

"Hours ago?" he repeated amidst the bustle. A team of acrobats was setting up for their high-wire act, which came right after the Lewis act and, with minutes left, they were frantically trying to reinstall a set of lines that had just come loose. "I think you'd better speak to Mr. Jacobsen," said Pettersson cautiously as a pair of twins in lavender tights edged past him. "He's in the control room. I can have you transferred," he said, looking up and seeing his boss's glasses glinting in the light of the control's and color monitors.

"No!"

"But—"

"Absolutely not! I don't want to talk to him, I want to talk to Fitzgibbons. Is he there?"

"Why, yes. He's right—"

"Let me speak to him. Now!"

Pettersson waved across to Father Tom, who stood on the other side of the stage talking to a man.

"Irwin?" asked Fitzgibbons, covering an ear as he watched Pettersson scurry off to the control booth.

"Why is that show still on the air?"

"I don't follow you."

"You didn't know about Baby either?"

"Talk sense, man!"

Shockley told him the whole story about Baby.

"Hours ago?" he said, dumbfounded.

"I spoke with Jacobsen myself. He's known all along."

"He hasn't said a word to me or anybody."

Shockley suddenly spotted Doris and Olive rushing down the hall escorted by a state trooper, the trio dashing up the corridor toward Baby's room.

"I've got to run," he said hurriedly. "Doris has just come."

"Go ahead. I'll take care of everything on this end. I'll see you at the hospital as soon as I can break away."

"Let her," Dr. Martinez urged the pediatrician from Columbia when Doris reached in below the tent to take hold of Baby. Shockley had just stepped into the room and stood with Olive by the door watching as Doris knelt down and lovingly lifted Baby's slack body into her arms.

"Be careful of the i.v.s," warned the specialist with the silver-rimmed spectacles, but Martinez put a quieting hand on his arm.

All eyes in the room were fixed on Doris, who had moved in under the tent and stood hunched over the bed, rocking Baby in her arms. "Baby, Baby, Baby," she intoned in her creaky voice, fighting her tears as she pulled her child's feverish face against her own cold cheek.

Shockley watched as the old woman cradled her unconscious

child and continued to rhythmically chant, her rounded shoulders swaying with each deep call to life. "Baby, Baby, Baby," Doris continued to sing, oblivious to all in the room.

The pediatrician heaved a sigh and left the room. Soon Martinez excused himself, and Olive slipped out into the corridor. Shockley remained frozen as the minutes passed, waiting expectantly, hoping for some change in Baby. But the child continued to hang limply in her mother's arms, rolling with each sway of the old lady's body.

Father Tom Fitzgibbons wasted no time. As soon as Jerry Lewis had completed his song and was taking his bows, he darted onto the stage and, grabbing the microphone from a bewildered Mr. Lewis, boldly stepped in front of the camera with the red light.

"Ladies and Gentlemen," he began, but suddenly the light went out.

The camera that stood facing Osgood in front of the phone banks unexpectedly flashed on.

Dropping his mike, Fitzgibbons made a dash for it. The stage crew looked on stunned as he raced headlong across the length of the stage.

"He's running over to camera one!" shouted Jacobsen in the control booth to the director. "Go to camera three!"

"What's he doing?" asked the director.

"He's gone nuts. Get him off! Call security!"

"That's Father Fitzgibbons," said the woman who was assistant director. "I think he wants to say something."

"Cut to camera three," ordered Jacobsen, and the director looked up at him, his face flushing.

"Ladies and Gentlemen," began Father Tom, out of breath. "I—"

"I said three!" fumed Jacobsen and, reaching across the director, pushed a button on the console. Immediately the broadcast monitor cut to the acrobats, catching them unawares as they stood in a group waiting for their cue. One of the twins in the troupe, seeing the camera light, poked her mother who, in turn, alerted the others, the whole family staring blankly into the camera.

"Get your fucking hands off my controls!" snapped the program director. "Get this man out of here!"

Father Tom was already sprinting toward the acrobats when the red light on camera three went off and the ongoing monitor displayed a startled Judson Osgood.

Quickly Osgood gathered himself.

"Well"—he forced a nervous smile, trying not to appear rattled—"we're approaching our goal of—"

Father Tom was racing back to the phone bank.

"Excuse me, Judson," he said, delicately twisting the microphone out of Osgood's hand. "Ladies and Gentlemen! I have a vital announcement," he began, blocking Osgood who kept trying to snatch back his mike. "Baby"—he took a breath—"Baby has been *found* by the police."

For an instant, dead silence.

Osgood froze.

Then the audience broke into loud cheers and applause. Fitzgibbons, raising his hands to quiet them, shook his head. The theater fell quiet.

Jacobsen, who had been wrestling with two technicians, gave up struggling and stood passively in their grip, facing the monitor, his eyes narrowed into a pair of angry slits.

"At this moment Baby is in the hospital in grave condition. She's suffering from acute pneumonia with very serious complications." He paused. "Her life, I'm sorry to say, is in critical danger." Father Tom wet his lips and took a long breath.

In the control room, the director had just halted the tapes and was feeding Father Tom's address live to all stations across the country. His assistant was on the phone to the news department. The performers who had been in the wings began drifting onto the stage of the hushed theater and stood watching Father Tom—the women dabbing at their mascara-smeared eyes.

"This morning, by your generosity, you have shown the world how much you truly care for her. But, unfortunately, the problem facing us right now cannot be surmounted with the power of money. Nor apparently, science. The doctors caring for Baby have done all they can. Their medicine has gone as far as it can go. There is now only one power that can rescue this miraculous child. And it is the power of prayer. Ladies and Gentlemen, in your homes all around the country on this Christmas Day, I ask you to please raise up your voices as one for this child," implored Father Tom, lowering himself to his knees and bending his head as the camera tilted down to follow him. "Let us all pray together," he entreated as millions of Americans saw how the people assembled on the sides of the stage, comedians and soundmen, wardrobe workers and celebrities, grips and security men, sank to their knees.

"Our Father in heaven, save this precious child," he said, and the voices of the crew and the theater audience echoed his plea in unison, their prayer going out over the airwaves to be joined by millions of other voices, all calling Baby back to the living. "We beseech thee to forgive our sins and continue to grant us the comfort of her presence—"

When Father Tom finished, he remained kneeling, his head silently bowed as instinctively the director slowly faded to black, bringing the program to an end.

Shockley couldn't quite believe what was going on. It started in the ward rooms with televisions, the ill and their visitors responding to Father Tom's plea, clasping their hands, lowering their heads, and mumbling a few halting words. Almost immediately it began to spread, moving up and down the corridors, touching the nurses and orderlies, until even the cops who stood guard in front of Baby's door were bowing their heads uncertainly. Everyone in the hospital, it seemed to Shockley, even the doctors, had stopped what they were doing and were praying for Baby. It was uncanny, he thought, before lowering his own head to pray for the dying child, who lay in her mother's arms.

As quickly as the prayer had begun, it was over, nurses, looking a little sheepish, returning to their rounds, visitors picking up their conversations with their bedridden friends and relatives, orderlies moving hurriedly as before, pushing baskets of dirty linen or serving lunch up and down the halls. When Shockley raised his eyes, the first thing he saw was that Baby's eyelids were twitching, fluttering weakly as she tried to open her eyes.

"I don't believe it!" he gasped, turning to Olive Eldridge to confirm what he was seeing. Olive just looked at him, shaking her head in disbelief as tears of relief glistened down her cheeks.

"Doctor! Doctor!" said the nurse, racing out of the room, looking for the specialist from Columbia.

Word spread like wildfire through the hospital, and in less than a minute Baby's room was packed. They were all there: the pediatrician from Columbia, the world-renowned cardiologist, the internist from the Cornell School of Medicine, Dr. Martinez and his colleague of the earlier morning, the chief of nursing and as many of her staff who could acceptably squeeze into the room—all staring down in amazement at the child who was making her first tentative movements.

"My God!" uttered Shockley beside himself with emotion, watching as Baby wriggled in her mother's arms, her big, feverish eyes sweeping across the panoply of faces staring in at her.

"Thank you, Jesus," said Olive emphatically, clasping her hands.

"It's a miracle," said Dr. Martinez, his face aglow. "A real honest-to-goodness miracle."

"I wouldn't have believed it if I hadn't seen it with my own eyes," said the nurse who had been on duty since Baby's arrival.

"The hand of the Lord," said one of the older, more hardened nurses.

"It was the erythromycin," said the pediatric expert after conferring with his colleagues, who nodded in agreement. "Once it starts to work, you get these dramatic turnarounds," he explained to Shockley, who listened politely, but was no longer certain just what to believe.

FOUR

30

Over the next days, Doris and Shockley took turns watching over Baby, the two never exchanging more than a word, their pattern of shifts developing out of a tacit understanding—Doris leaving when Shockley arrived and vice versa. While Shockley continued to stay on at the Plaza in midtown, Olive had taken a nearby motel room and made it a point of ferrying Doris in her Volkswagen to and from the hospital.

Each shift brought new and startling improvements in Baby's condition. Her fever plummeted, and within two days it was only slightly above normal. Baby's periods of wakefulness began to stretch as she became progressively more alert and the phlegm that she coughed up started to clear. Though Baby at first refused to eat, Doris was able to coax her into accepting a few mouthfuls of juice. Soon that gave way to part of a bottle and that to some spoonfuls of baby food. As Shockley also continued to ply Baby with nourishment and liquids, the doctors finally ordered removal of the i.v.s, and within another three days a very debilitated but recovering Baby was eating near normally and gradually beginning to recoup some of her lost weight.

Around the clock, Doris's and Shockley's vigil continued unabated, night and day merging for the pair. And through it all Father Tom was there, spending long hours watching over Baby, praying and waiting.

"You're worried that she won't sing again, aren't you?" asked Shockley late one evening when they were alone in Baby's room and she was sitting up for the first time, holding her own bottle and drinking busily. Though she was now breathing easily and cooed and made her usual baby sounds, nothing even faintly resembling song had yet emerged from her lips.

"My first concern was for her life," said Father Tom, brushing back a lock of white hair that had fallen over his forehead. "Now that we're over that crisis, thank God, well—Yes, I am frankly worried. I spoke with one of the doctors in our congregation, and he told me there might have been brain damage either from the high fever or oxygen deprivation."

Shockley nodded. The same fear had been running through his mind.

"But she does seem normal." Father Tom tried to look on the bright side of things. He felt Shockley had gone through enough trauma and didn't need his anxieties stoked.

"Whatever is, is," said Shockley with a fatalistic shrug. "At this point there's nothing we can do about it, is there?"

Father Tom's whole face broke into a smile. Even his eyes were smiling.

"If I believed that, Irwin, I wouldn't be here," he said.

"The power of prayer."

"Don't knock it."

"Oh, I'm certainly not knocking it." Shockley fell serious. "It's just not easy for a dyed-in-the-wool atheist to change colors this late in the game."

"Anything is possible. Even that," said Father Tom with a laugh, and then Doris appeared. Seeing her, Shockley automatically rose from his seat and took his coat. Baby dropped her bottle, smiled, and stretched out her hands in greeting.

"Doris," he said, putting on his hat and stalling by the door as she greeted Baby with a hug. "Can't we at least talk?"

Doris shed her heavy wool coat with an audible sigh and sank down in the chair still warm from Shockley's body.

"No," she answered woodenly. "I have nothing to say to you. There's been too much talk already."

Shockley gave a hopeless shrug and, seeing his glum look, Father Tom gave him a reassuring nod.

Later that evening, as Baby lay sleeping soundly, Father Tom tried to approach Doris.

"Don't you think, perhaps," he ventured, "that the time has come for some sort of reconciliation between you and Irwin."

Doris slowly turned her head and looked at Fitzgibbons.

"If for nothing else," he continued cautiously, "then for the sake of Baby."

Doris continued to stare at him.

"Don't you think it would be a good idea?"

"No," she answered flatly, putting an end to that. "Absolutely not!"

Yet another couple of days passed, and Baby became her old self. The color returned to her cheeks; she seemed happy at all the attention lavished on her and took an active interest in the endless parcels of toys and gifts sent by well-wishers from around the world.

"If only you'd sing," Shockley said to Baby as he held her in his lap on New Year's Day, trying to give her a spoonful of her apparently awful-tasting antibiotic as she twisted her head back and forth. "Come on, you little troublemaker," he struggled to get her to take the shimmering, red medicine balanced on the spoon. Finally, as she swung her head past, Shockley managed to target the spoon, sluicing the cherry-flavored liquid into her mouth.

Baby pulled a disgusted face.

"Ah, there," he exclaimed victoriously, only to have her spit it all out, the syrup running down her chin onto the front of her bib.

"I'll tell you what," he joked indulgently. "I'll make you a deal. If you sing," he carefully poured a fresh spoonful, "you don't have to take your medicine."

Baby looked at him in puzzlement.

"You know," he smiled. "La la la la," he gave her a quick sequence of notes reminiscent of her earliest song.

Baby cocked her head quizzically, but Shockley, intent on not spilling the full spoon, failed to notice the expression. Baby's eyebrows began knitting furiously as she held her head still. Seeing his chance, Shockley eagerly raised the spoon to her lips and just as he was about to slide it into her mouth, out came a high, tentative sound. A single, clean note.

Shockley dropped the spoon into his lap, the sticky syrup soaking his pants. Excited, he sat motionlessly waiting for the next note, but as quickly as it had appeared the tone vanished, and in its place there was nothing but the ordinary hum of the hospital. Shockley looked beseechingly at Baby, who stared back at him. He waited, but there was nothing more.

Baby began to fidget in his lap.

"Sing, darling," he whispered to her. "Come on, sing," he coaxed and gave out a few notes himself.

Baby looked at him and cocked her head again.

"Sing. Please sing."

Baby took a small breath.

"Yes," he urged. "Yes."

Then she let out three more tones, her notes this time more certain, crisper, clearer than the first. Baby stopped and looked questioningly at Shockley. He smiled at her reassuringly, afraid to speak.

Baby grinned, showing her two little milk teeth on the bottom row. Then she took a long, deep breath and began to sing in earnest, her voice low but steady, note after perfect note emerging from her lips. Shockley nearly went out of his mind with joy. She was singing. Baby was singing! he exulted. It was almost too good to be true. At that instant he wanted to race up and down the corridors of the hospital shouting with joy, get on the phone and call half the world, tell the reporters who had been hounding him for days, call Father Tom, alert Doris and Olive, even call Ruth. But instead he sat glued to his seat, spellbound, listening to that near-forgotten song, that heavenly melody emerging from a previous life and moving through the eons of time to reach his ears, that velvety clear song of chirping birds and water lapping a forgotten shore, of wind whistling through the trees.

"Oh, darling," he sighed when she had finished and sat in his lap looking proud and happy. "That was gorgeous. Thank you, sweetie," he said and kissed her cheek that tasted of cherry syrup. Then he remembered the spoon that lay in his lap. He looked down at the clinging mess and laughed. Picking up the spoon Shockley debated with himself.

"I'm afraid," he said to her, filling up the spoon for the third time, "that I'm a liar. But, please," he said, trying to slip her the medicine, "understand. It's for your own good." And with that he plunged the spoon into her mouth and, holding her jaw shut, waited until she finally swallowed. "Will you ever forgive me?" he asked.

On Thursday, Jacobsen finally appeared at the hospital to see how his client was faring, an entourage of new assistants in tow. He was already talking about the future, a new tour, a European swing—all as if nothing had happened.

"We could start with a big bang opening at La Scala. From Milano we could shoot up for, maybe, two nights at the Vienna Opera House. From there—"

Shockley listened speechlessly as Jacobsen rattled on, dropping names from the Gewandhaus in Leipzig to Tel Aviv's Mann Auditorium. When Jacobsen finally finished his spiel, Shockley looked him straight in the eye and answered him with one word.

"No."

"No?"

"No!" repeated Shockley emphatically—his single-worded obstinancy reminding him oddly of Doris.

"What are you talking about?" asked Jacobsen, looking genuinely surprised. He turned to his three assistants, who all shrugged their shoulders.

"I'm talking about your relationship with Baby. Consider it at an end."

Jacobsen looked at him blankly.

"You know, finished. Fini. The end. This is the last time you're going to see Baby. Say good-bye to the man," he said to Baby for effect as she looked at him with her blue eyes and grinned.

"You mean, because of the benefit?" he asked, supinating his hands in a gesture of apology. "Shockley, look. I'll be the first to admit that I got a little carried away. But after all that work and preparation, I just couldn't see—"

"It's not just that. And it's not just that you're thick-skinned and don't really give a damn about Baby. It's basically because I've decided that I'm not going to exploit her gift anymore."

Jacobsen glared at him menacingly.

"I made a promise to myself and I intend to keep it," he said, ignoring the look.

"It's those Babyists." Jacobsen's face boiled a deep red, his nostrils flaring as his temper broke loose. "Fitzgibbons and those fucking Babyists. They've gotten to you!"

"Absolutely not," he answered sharply, which made Jacobsen all the more convinced. "It's a decision I reached solely on my own. From now on anybody who wants to hear Baby can hear her for free. She doesn't belong to you or me or the Babyists or *anyone*."

"That's very noble." Jacobsen snorted. "Very lofty."

"It's not meant to be."

"But, before you go off on your little religious kick, I suggest you take a good, hard look at your contract."

"I don't have to read a contract to know what I have to do."

"For the next five years Baby belongs to me." Jacobsen leveled a threatening finger at Shockley.

"She doesn't belong to anyone!" Shockley shouted back.

"Unless she sings for me, she sings for no one!"

"That's ridiculous!"

"Oh? Is it now?" asked Jacobsen, a nasty smile dancing across his lips. "Well, we'll just have to wait and see how 'ridiculous' it is, won't we?" Then he turned with a contemptuous smile and marched off, his people trailing single file down the hall.

"Yes," said Kiely, responding to Shockley's phone inquiry. "You're most definitely bound by the terms of the duly executed contract you signed with the Jacobsen organization."

"But—But—"

"You were appointed guardian *ad litem* by the court. The court gave you authorization to make that contract. In it, you specifically agreed to make the child available for performances, granting the Jacobsen association sole agency. As far as I can see, once she is sufficiently well to perform again, that contract becomes binding upon you and the child. For the next five years she can never sing in public—that being clearly defined as more than five people—unless it's under their aegis."

"That's crazy."

"Perhaps. But that's what you get for signing an agreement without first consulting an attorney."

"Can I fight this thing?"

"Of course. I was going to bring that up. If we can prove in some way that the child, in the process of going on these concerts, was abused or subjected to—"

"What? Do you think I want to undermine my own credibility as guardian and end up losing custody of Baby?"

"Or," Kiely went on, "that the contract was misrepresented or signed under duress."

"What does it all mean?"

"It means that there are plenty of grounds for challenging that agreement. But it also means a tough battle. A knock-down drag-out court fight."

"More publicity?"

"More publicity. More accusations and counteraccusations. More expense. A lot of expense," he warned with characteristic bluntness. "Jacobsen's no small fry. He'll have the best legal minds at his disposal."

"What do I do?"

"Nothing. Nothing yet. Sit tight. Wait for him to make the first move. It might all be bluff."

"Not likely."

"No. It's not likely."

"You know what he's trying to do."

"Sure. He's trying to grab Baby from you. He might even succeed. But just remember one thing."

"What's that?"

"You set yourself up for it."

"I was thinking about all that money raised by the telethon," said Shockley to Father Tom the next day as they walked together to the subway station near the hospital. It was a bright, windless January afternoon and, as they strolled in the sun, there was a vague, springlike thaw in the air. "There must be quite a fortune there."

"I got a peek at the accounting the Jacobsen people had made, and it looks like there's just a shade under two million dollars," said Father Tom, squinting in the light.

The two walked on, passing a line of elderly people sitting in chairs against the sheltered front of a building, their faces turned up to the sun.

"What's going to happen to it?"

"I think that's partly up to you. It was intended to be used for Baby—or at least in her name. I keep getting calls and letters from people urging us to build some sort of shrine for her. Perhaps a place where people could go into retreat."

"That's a good idea," said Shockley. "But I've got an even better one," he said, brightening noticeably.

"Oh?"

A garbage truck roared by, drowning them out, and Shockley waited for it to pass.

"Let's use some of it to buy out Jacobsen's contract," he suggested excitedly. "Get rid of him once and for all."

"I'm afraid it's not going to be that easy. Yesterday, after you told me about Jacobsen's threat, I took the initiative and went and spoke with him. I brought up the notion of buying back his contract."

"And?"

"He just laughed at me. Laughed right in my face," said Fitzgibbons as they descended into the subway station, a rush of stale air rising up to greet them. "He doesn't want money, Irwin."

"Yeah, I know," said Shockley worriedly. "The bastard wants blood."

"No. Not blood." Father Tom put two tokens into the turnstile. "Just Baby."

Regrets, Shockley had long ago concluded, were like lifelong hangnails. They were always there at the corner of your life, nagging, gnawing, irritating. The more you clawed away at them, the more inflamed they became. And Shockley felt he already had more than any man's share.

He had old regrets: that he hadn't stood up to his father and protected his sister when he saw how the old man was destroying her; that he had let his mother die without ever visiting her bedside; that, at the end of the old man's life, he hadn't been big enough to forgive and forget. And now he had new regrets: that he had destroyed his marriage, broken up his home, hurt his children, misused Baby for his own ego gratification.

Between the old and the new, there lay that wasteland of mistakes, small regrets at having unnecessarily offended someone, taken unfair advantage of a friend, lied, bragged, and all the other human foibles.

The last thing that Shockley wanted was another inflamed hangnail to carry through life. So when he heard from Olive that

Doris was planning on returning to Ithaca now that Baby was almost well, Shockley decided the time was ripe to attempt reconciliation once more. It was a delicate situation. He realized it was wrong for Baby to be separated from her mother. Yet, he couldn't in good conscience return Baby to Doris's sole care. To his mind came visions of Leeming's Trailer Park, the surrounding shanties and shacks and junk-piles. The thought of sending Baby out to that made him shudder. He loved Baby, cared about her deeply, and could never live with himself if he just dumped her out there. Baby was an extraordinary child who deserved something at least a little better than that. Shockley thought back to the first time he had entered Doris's house on Willow Avenue, the disorder and sloppiness of that dingy place, Baby's obvious undernourishment. He recalled Baby's state of neglect when Doris had grabbed her back after breaking out of the hospital—the bleeding diaper rash that took weeks to cure, Doris's barren refrigerator, the turd-deep boxes of unemptied kitty litter. Baby was a princess. She didn't deserve to live stifled in bleakness because of her aged mother's obsession with total control. Love was necessary, but it wasn't enough to warrant what Doris would ultimately subject Baby to. If only some reasonable settlement could be hammered out—

"Doris, please," began Shockley, arriving early for his shift at the hospital that Saturday morning. "Let's try to talk this thing over."

With Shockley was Father Tom, who had offered to come along to mediate. Olive Eldridge was also in the room.

"I know you're going back to Ithaca this afternoon and before you leave I—"

"Who told you I'm leaving?" asked Doris, looking accusingly at Olive. Olive turned and pretended to play with Baby.

"It's not important," he said, holding up a pacifying hand. "What is—is—well, there must be a way for us to work out some sort of compromise."

Doris looked at him with her rheumy eyes and then, turning and hunching over the chair holding her coat, said to Olive, "Come on, Olive. It's time to go."

Olive stalled.

"I don't want you to be separated from Baby any longer."

Doris looked over her shoulder at him through the corner of her eye, her body stooped over farther than ever, it seemed to Shockley.

"Don't you try and sweet-talk me again in this lifetime," she said, trying to control her seething resentment.

Shockley threw up his hands.

"Christ, Doris, I'm trying to undo some of the damage. Don't you understand that?"

"I understand perfectly. You want to keep Baby for you and your friends and salve your conscience at the same time. Oh, I understand perfectly."

"No, I want to return Baby to you!"

"Oh, really? Then give her to me and let me take her home this instant." She abruptly picked up Baby from the bed to call his bluff.

Shockley shook his head and turned to Fitzgibbons in frustration.

"Let me make a suggestion, Mrs. Rumsey," began Father Tom. "Please, just hear me out."

Doris gave an impatient snort.

"We've got lots of money from the telethon. We want to build a house for you and Baby. You wouldn't have to live in a trailer park any longer. You wouldn't have to worry about—"

"I don't want any handouts!"

"It's not a handout. Look, Doris," Father Tom said gently. "All Irwin wants, all anybody wants, is to ensure that Baby is well cared for, that she's not hidden from the rest of the world. She's growing, she's getting older. She's going to blossom into a wonderful human being. She—"

"You may be a priest," said Doris, interrupting him, her jaw set firmly, "but you're awfully thick."

"Doris!" scolded Olive.

"Don't Doris me! I've had enough of all this sanctimonious—" she said, searching for a shocking word, "sanctimonious crap! And that's what it is. Crap!" she repeated angrily. "You steal my very own baby from me, the child that came from my body, that I carried for—"

"You weren't able to care for her!" Shockley finally burst out. "And you're not able to properly care for her now. You don't even have the vaguest idea of what a child needs. Admit it!"

"Have you been any better?" Doris shouted back. "Look at the state she got into, thanks to you!"

"Please. Please," said Father Tom, stepping between the two adversaries. "I think we're getting somewhere," he said, trying to be positive.

"Don't fool yourself," said Doris, picking up her wool coat and pulling it over her shoulder.

"You're still blaming me for the time you were in the hospital and I deceived you," Shockley tried again. "And rightly so. But that's ancient history."

"For you, maybe," answered Doris, a blue vein bulging at the side of her forehead.

"There are lots of alternatives," said Fitzgibbons.

"There's only one," said Doris, and there were tears in her eyes as she said good-bye to Baby who clung to her neck.

"Why don't you at least listen to these folks?" said Olive, reluctantly picking up her own coat. "Try to be just a little reasonable."

"Be reasonable! Be reasonable!" Doris pressed her fist against her mouth to stifle a sob. "How many times have I heard that? I'm sick of it. Whose side are you on, anyway?"

"I'm on your side, dear. Always have been," said Olive coming up and putting an arm around Doris's shoulders. "You know that."

Doris nodded through her tears.

"I'm sorry," she muttered feebly.

Shockley looked forlornly at Father Tom, Shockley himself verging on tears.

"I'm going," said Doris, giving Baby a long, hard hug. She kissed both her cheeks with big, wet, sloppy kisses. Baby opened her mouth and started to sing, but Doris took a finger and resting it against the child's lips silenced her.

"There isn't that much time in life," said Olive astutely. "And every day you go without Baby is a day lost. Talk to these gentlemen. Please. For your own sake."

Doris turned away from Baby.

"Come on," she said to Olive. "I've waited this long. I can wait just a little longer."

31

When by chance Shockley turned on the television in his hotel room that Sunday evening, he was taken completely by surprise. There, suddenly, on "On Line" was the story about Baby that had been scheduled for airing at the end of the month.

"Tonight," began Joel Webster opening the segment, sitting as he had in the Shockley living room, Baby in his arms, "we have a rather unusual story for you. Some say this little girl sings and could do so from birth. Many, including the sixty-year-old mother of this child, insist that she was the result of a virgin birth. To others, this has been one big hoax."

Shockley grabbed a chair and pulled it up close to the set as the scene cut to Webster sitting in the studio in front of a blown-up picture of Baby with production credits.

"But the story we're about to tell is not about the alleged mystical or curative powers of her singing, nor her conception. But rather, it is the tale of a power struggle, a veritable tug-of-war involving big money, fame, greed, mendacity, and a host of other human foibles. And, at the center of this maelstrom is one innocent child. A little girl. A little girl called Baby."

His heart beginning to pound in his ears, Shockley leaned forward and anxiously turned up the sound.

"Enter one Dr. Irwin Shockley, a university professor of music, Pulitzer Prize-winning composer."

Shockley watched as his own owl-eyed face stared back out at him from the screen. It looked haggard and harassed, his skin washed in hues of green on the out-of-sync color set.

WEBSTER: How did you get the child?

SHOCKLEY: She was put in our foster care by the Department of Social Services.

WEBSTER: Why?

SHOCKLEY [*Swallows uneasily.*]: Why? [*Shrugs and tries to appear nonchalant.*] Apparently she was being neglected in her previous home.

The screen suddenly cut to Olive Eldridge.

OLIVE: Neglected? That woman loved that baby more than anything in the world. She was her whole life. Now, I'm a retired elementary-school principal. Children have been my business for almost forty years. [*Getting feisty.*] So I know what I'm talking about. Now Doris may not have been as wealthy as those other folks or as well educated or as important, but she loved that child and in *my* book that's more important than all the fancy clothes and toys. It's love that counts, not money! Neglected? My foot!

WEBSTER [*Voice-over as Shockley sits uneasily on the sofa beside his wife.*]: Was Baby in fact neglected?

SHOCKLEY: Well, according to the people at social services and according to the courts and whoever else was involved, it was determined that she was not getting proper care. I really don't know much more about it.

WEBSTER: Come now, Dr. Shockley. You don't mean to say that you didn't know the mother well *before* the child was placed in your custody?

SHOCKLEY: If you're implying in any way that I was instrumental in her removal from her mother's custody, the answer is emphatically no! When I learned of the court decision my wife and I offered our services. Period.

WEBSTER: And not before?

SHOCKLEY [*Irritably.*]: I said *no*. If you want to know more, why don't you talk to the authorities?

WEBSTER [*Voice-over.*]: And that's exactly what we did.

As Shockley looked on in helpless dismay, cursing himself for his blunder, Andrea Cassaniti appeared on camera. She was standing on the corner of Cayuga and Green streets in front of the old brick building housing the Department of Social Services.

WEBSTER: Miss Cassaniti, what precisely made you choose the Shockleys as foster parents?

CASSANITI: The Shockleys seemed well suited to be foster parents. The home environment seemed a very positive one. And, since Dr. Shockley was very interested in her musical ability, we thought that would be of special advantage to the child.

WEBSTER: When did the Shockleys offer their services as foster parents?

CASSANITI: Let me see—[*Stalls.*]

WEBSTER: Was it *before* the family court hearing?

CASSANITI: I'm just not exactly—

WEBSTER: Surely you must know. You do have records, don't you?

CASSANITI: Well—

WEBSTER: These copies I have here—[*Produces a sheaf of papers.*] Aren't they copies of the file your department has on Baby?

CASSANITI [*Looks surprised.*]: Yes. But those are confidential and are not supposed to—

WEBSTER: And doesn't it very explicitly state here, right here, that Dr. Shockley in fact spoke with your agency well *before* Mrs. Rumsey was ever subpoenaed to appear in family court? [*Puts on glasses and reads.*] Two full weeks before?

CASSANITI: Why, I suppose it's possible. My memory is not that great and—

WEBSTER: [*Zeroing in.*] And that here, a day before the issuance of that show-cause order for the removal of the child, you've logged—and this is your handwriting, isn't it?—an interview with Dr. Shockley during which he provided you with detailed information supporting allegations of neglect?

CASSANITI [*Looking around nervously.*]: I think that's all I can say at this point.

Shockley again found himself on camera.

WEBSTER: Dr. Shockley, you launched Baby's career by first visiting a number of music schools around the country.

SHOCKLEY: Yes. That's correct.

WEBSTER: Did you have permission from the mother to take her child on that tour?

SHOCKLEY [*Taken aback and unprepared.*]: Tacitly. There were many factors involved, including the mother's health. [*Clears his throat.*] The woman was very sick and apparently dying. Yes. I would say that there was a tacit understanding.

The screen suddenly cut to Doris sitting in her trailer, stroking a cat in her lap.

DORIS: Never! I never gave any permission. When I asked to see Baby at the hospital, Mrs. Shockley tricked me by parading a bundle or something wrapped in a blanket in front of my window, trying to make me think that Baby was still in Ithaca when all along she was on that tour.

Olive returned to the screen.

OLIVE: I didn't always agree with Doris, but she had always made it clear that she would not approve of Baby going on any

326

tours or shows. She just didn't want that child leaving town. She was firm as a rock on that!

The screen cut back to Doris.

DORIS: I was railroaded. By the Shockleys. By the social services people. By the court. By my very own lawyer.

Shockley then watched as Kiely appeared on the screen, was introduced, and promptly raked over the coals.

WEBSTER: You represented Doris Rumsey in her custody fight?

KIELY [*Looking suspiciously at the camera.*]: That's correct.

WEBSTER: And took a very handsome retainer.

KIELY: My legal fees are purely a matter between myself and my clients.

WEBSTER: And didn't even appear at the hearing!

Shockley watched as Kiely tried to weasel his way out of Webster's tightening grip. Though Kiely was more adept than Andrea Cassaniti, it soon became apparent where the truth lay.

WEBSTER: Sending instead a neophyte assistant, fresh out of law school, with no prior trial experience, who was totally unfamiliar with the case.

KIELY [*Indignant.*]: Mr. Bennett is a perfectly competent attorney, licensed by the state bar association. I was ill that day and asked him to take my place. He was thoroughly familiar with the case from the beginning.

Doris popped on the screen.

DORIS: Ill? I was told by Mr. Bennett that he was on another case. But that doesn't really matter, does it? I hired him and he never appeared. I paid him one thousand dollars!

Kiely came back on camera.

WEBSTER: Mr. Kiely. You represented Mrs. Rumsey.

KIELY: Yes.

WEBSTER: Not long after the hearing you became the attorney responsible for managing Baby's business affairs, essentially in the employ of Dr. Shockley. Isn't that [*Looks dramatically puzzled.*], well, isn't that a conflict of interests?

KIELY [*Rising up from his chair.*]: Mr. Webster, I'm tired of sitting here and listening to your insinuations. I was kind enough to grant you this interview, and you're using my hospitality to impugn my good name. I don't believe in trial by television, and as far as I'm concerned this meeting is over. Now turn off those damn cameras!

The screen returned to Olive.

OLIVE: Doris didn't have a chance. There was big money involved. Everybody wanted a slice of Baby. There were movie contract offers. Offers to appear on television shows. Offers for interviews. She refused to cooperate, so they went after her.

Doris came on screen again. She was now walking with Webster through the snow outside her trailer, telling him about how she sold her house to pay for her court appeal, about her further determination to fight Shockley for the return of Baby.

DORIS: That man forced his way into our lives. Right from the beginning he wanted Baby for himself. He wasn't the only one, but he was the most persistent. I suppose it was my fault. I wasn't strong enough. I was tired, I was weak after the birth.

Shockley got up and poured himself a stiff drink, the glass trembling in his hand. The program rolled on.

DORIS: The facts have been twisted, have been distorted [Chokes up, speaking haltingly but effectively.]. They even tried to have me adjudged insane. Everybody wants a share of Baby, and they're tearing her to pieces for their own greed.

Shockley downed his drink in a single gulp and looked at the set where Father Tom was being interviewed, obviously well before the kidnapping.

FITZGIBBONS: Our main concern all along has been accessibility to this miraculous child. She is a gift from God and was not meant to be used as a trained seal. Our congregation feels that certain people are exploiting her and using this poor child in a rather immoral way.

Shockley poured himself another drink. After Fitzgibbons, on came Jacobsen, acting predictably arrogant.

JACOBSEN: Look, I'm a busy man, Mr. Webster. Let me put it to you simply. Dr. Shockley and I have an arrangement. He wants to give Baby exposure by putting her in concert. I am meeting that need. Our arrangement is sanctioned by the courts and, as far as Baby is concerned, it's an exceedingly generous one. I might add that all the child's earnings are being held in a trust for her.

WEBSTER: Do you make money under that "arrangement"?

JACOBSEN: Well, of course I do! I'm not running a church here. [Scoffs.]

As Shockley began to pace the floor in front of his television, Webster brought the program up-to-date, explaining over a shot of the Plaza Hotel about the woman who had wormed her way past Shockley's defenses, of the seduction and ultimate abduction.

On and on the program went, the point being hammered home: Shockley with his music, the Babyists with their religion, Jacobsen with his business, the kidnappers with their extortion, the social services with collusive interests of their own, all were trying to get their grips on Baby. It was true, thought Shockley, and yet it wasn't quite true.

Shockley felt disgusted. To all the regrets he had in life, he added a couple more. One was lying. The other was ever having let a TV camera into his house.

Shockley stared back at the set. Webster was finally winding up the segment.

"All this raises more questions than it really answers. But at the heart of it all lie some very central questions that go beyond even this fascinating tale. What constitutes neglect? Do, in fact, unusually gifted children have requirements and needs that lawfully go beyond those of normal children? To just what extent do the courts have a right to intercede within a parent-child relationship? When the appellate court finally hears Doris Rumsey's case, some of these questions may well be resolved."

Shockley reached over and snapped off the television.

32

On Tuesday morning, three days after Doris had departed for Ithaca, Shockley checked Baby out of the hospital. Lining the hallway were well-wishers from the hospital staff who turned out to say good-bye. There were the nurses who had seen Baby through her crisis, Dr. Martinez and his colleague from that first, frightening morning, countless orderlies and candy-stripers. Even the pediatric specialist from Columbia journeyed all the way uptown that early morning just to see Baby off.

"Godspeed," said Martinez, taking Shockley's hand in both of his and holding it tightly. "Take good care of our little girl."

Shockley tried to thank Martinez for all he had done, but somehow the words didn't quite come and all he could do was nod and smile gratefully.

Baby went from hand to hand, moving down the length of the ward corridor, getting hugged and kissed and tickled. When she finally reached Shockley's arms she opened her mouth and spontaneously burst into song. It was a short melody but clearly a new one. To the hospital staff, who listened in awed silence, it sounded like a song of expectation, a song of promise and relief. Caught in the swirling undertones of her voice they could detect the sounds of the coming spring, the sounds of icicles dripping, flowers opening into delicate blossoms, a newborn chick emerging from its shell.

When Baby finished, the staff broke into delighted applause.

"Thank you," said Shockley, addressing the throng. "Thank you one and all for everything you've done for Baby."

Then, following the two city cops who had been on the morning shift with Baby from the beginning, Shockley took the elevator down to the ground level and hurried past the throng of reporters anxiously waiting in the lobby.

"Is it true, Dr. Shockley, that Baby will no longer be performing?" asked a reporter, sticking out a mike. Deftly avoiding it, Shockley hurried toward the car that stood waiting, Father Tom holding open the rear door.

"What about the upcoming appeals hearing that could—?"

A phalanx of waiting motorcycle cops moved in and helped clear the path.

"Whew!" said Shockley when he and Baby were safely ensconced in the limousine and the motorcade was ready to roll.

But the car remained motionless.

"What are we waiting for?" asked Father Tom, leaning forward to the driver. The driver shrugged, then motioned toward a man in a brown suit that the police had let through their lines. The man approached the car and knocked on Shockley's window. Puzzled, Shockley rolled it down.

"Are you Irwin R. Shockley of Ithaca, New York?" asked the man, identifying himself as a federal marshal.

"Yes, I am," admitted Shockley warily.

The marshal then served Shockley with a document, signaled the police, and the convoy took off.

As the car sped out to the airport under escort, Shockley opened the paper and read it. It was, from what he could make out, a show-cause order from the district federal court. Shockley was to show cause within ten days why an injunction should not be granted to Jacobsen Associates, preventing Baby from singing in public.

Shockley handed it over to Father Tom.

"That's not an injunction," said Father Tom, showing anger for the first time. "It's a gag order!"

Shockley said nothing, just stared glumly out the window.

Emerging from the plane after landing in Ithaca, Shockley was immediately jolted by the arctic air engulfing them at the top of the open ramp. Bundling Baby up, Shockley rushed with her over the snow-encrusted tarmac toward the one-room terminal as around him the wind swirled, picking up funnels of snow that traveled furiously across the high, barren airstrip. Moving through a howling headwind that made Baby bury her face against his shoulder, he was suddenly struck by a sense of having been cut loose from the world. Today there would be no Ruth waiting to meet him. Nor the expectant face of one of the children who had come along for the ride. It was over. He was alone. A single man. Nevertheless, Shockley searched the waiting faces pressed up against the glass in the warm terminal, searched them only to be keenly stung by disappointment.

In the lobby was a small contingent of reporters and cameras waiting for him. There were familiar faces from the *Ithaca Journal* and local radio stations as well as a couple of television people who had come from nearby Binghamton and Syracuse. Compared to the hubbub in New York, the reporters were quiet and low keyed. In a way it was a pleasant welcome that eased the pain of his loneliness, and he took a few minutes to answer their questions as patiently and honestly as possible.

No, he admitted to one reporter, he didn't know what the future held. There were legal entanglements that would have to be unsnarled. No, he was not afraid of losing Baby.

"Ivar Jacobsen obviously has no further claim to Baby's services, especially in light of—"

"Dr. Shockley," interrupted the young woman from the *Journal* who had posed the question. "I was referring to the appellate court."

"Huh?" said Shockley, a little confused. "Oh. Yes," he nodded, remembering Doris's petition. "I'm not too worried about that. That's still far off and when it does come around I think that the higher court'll sustain the family-court decision considering the child's history. In the meantime I'm trying and hoping to circumvent the whole appeal process by reaching some sort of compromise with the mother that would permit her to live with Baby while—"

"Excuse me," interjected the woman, looking surprised. "Aren't you aware of the announcement made this morning by the appellate court?"

"No. What announcement?"

"They're scheduled to hear Mrs. Rumsey's appeal tomorrow."

Shockley looked flabbergasted.

"The program," he uttered under his breath.

"Yes," she said, picking it up. "Justice may be blind," she closed her notebook, "but apparently it does watch television."

As soon as he had taken a room in the downtown Ramada Inn, Shockley called his lawyer. Kiely was out of the office, so he left urgent word for the attorney to get back to him.

After waiting a full hour he called back and once again the secretary assured him that Mr. Kiely would promptly return his call.

For most of the afternoon Shockley sat glued by the phone in his motel room, awaiting Kiely's call. As he waited tensely, valuable time ticking away, Baby seemed oblivious to his anxiety. She spent much of the time playing on the floor with her toys, often singing happily to herself, her songs more exuberant and joyous than at any time in the seven months of her life.

Shockley, however, failed to give her singing much attention. His ear was tuned to a different sound, the sound of a ringing phone, which never materialized.

When Shockley realized that the secretary's promises were just putoffs, he took the initiative and began calling around town trying to locate the lawyer. He tried Kiely's home, the courthouse, the county clerk's office, and even some of Kiely's colleagues' offices. Finally, in the early evening, Shockley located him in Collegetown at one of his properties. It was his Eddy Street apartment house that had just been closed down by an order of the Ithaca Housing Authority during one of its sporadic crackdowns on student slum housing.

"Where have you been?" Shockley asked, his voice nearly frantic. "I've been trying to get you since the morning."

"What's the problem?" asked Kiely. In the background Shockley could hear the sound of power saws and pounding hammers. On his end Baby was belting out a happy song, and he had to cover his ear to hear.

"The problem is that the appellate division is hearing Mrs. Rumsey's appeal tomorrow. That's the problem."

"Relax. I'm fully apprised of the situation. We're on top of it."

"How?" asked Shockley, dispensing with any politeness.

Kiely gave a thin laugh trying to embarrass him.

"We're filing an amicus brief—that's a friend of the court's brief—and we're also going to be giving input when oral arguments are heard."

"Who's *we*?"

"I sent my associate Mr. Bennett to Albany. He's already there. So just relax and take it easy."

"Your associate?" asked Shockley incredulously, suddenly realizing that Kiely was going to screw him just as he had screwed Doris. "I retained *you*, not your associate."

"Mr. Shockley," said Kiely above the whine of a saw, "I don't work for you. You're not my client. I represent Baby. I am the executor of her trust. I do what I deem to be in her interests. And, I felt that it was in her best interest to send Mr. Bennett. Discussion completed," he said and abruptly hung up.

Shockley sat stunned on the edge of the bed holding the phone as Baby continued to sing.

"Sh-sh, honey." He tried to hush her, but she just smiled cheerfully and continued to croon. Shockley pulled his hair and tried to concentrate. It was too late to get another lawyer by tomorrow morning. Damn, damn, damn! He pounded his fist into the palm of his hand until it burned. He knew what was happening. It was the rats-deserting-the-sinking-ship syndrome. And he was the ship.

Terkel drove directly out to Leeming's Trailer Park as soon as he got back from Albany.

"Our case looks very promising," he said, taking Doris's hand excitedly. Doris was dressed in new clothes that she had bought with Olive on the way back from the City, and the trailer looked neat as a pin. In the tiny kitchen and living area there were bouquets of fresh flowers wired by well-wishers who had seen the program about her plight, and the air in the trailer smelled fragrantly sweet. Doris herself looked radiant. There was lipstick on her lips, and there was the hint of rouge on her cheeks. Her hair had been done up in small waves by a lady in a neighboring trailer who ran a hairdressing business. Even the cats looked as if they had been spiffed up, their coats gleaming and silky.

"I submitted our brief and the court agreed to hear oral arguments." Terkel was now pacing back and forth in the tiny enclosure and spoke as though he were in court presenting his case. Doris watched the performance with obvious pleasure. "It went beautifully, if I may say so myself. And not just because of my splendid arguments," he said with a quick, happy laugh. "There was a lawyer there from social services as well as your acquaintance Mr. Bennett. They were in such a state of disarray that they really botched it up. They couldn't have helped us more if they had tried."

Doris smiled from ear to ear. She was so excited she could barely catch her breath.

"Now, all we have to do," he said, stopping and facing her, "is sit tight and wait for the decision. I'm usually very cautious about saying anything before an opinion, but—well, I could just sense where the judges' sympathies lay. Heck, I'd almost be willing to bet my last dollar," Terkel threw off all restraint. "I really think we won. I think you're going to get Baby back."

"Oh, Mr. Terkel," exclaimed Doris, unsure whether to laugh or cry. "You don't know how happy this makes me!" she held her hand to her chest. "I'm actually going to get Baby back."

"I think so."

"I can't quite believe it."

"You deserve it. And much more. If this thing goes the way it should, I'm also going to see to it that you get your house back, as well as some sort of settlement for damages."

"I don't want anything but Baby," she said dreamily. "Nothing at all."

"Let's make this brief and to the point," said Ruth when they sat down in the Gazebo Room of the motel and Shockley suggested lunch. People kept stopping by their table to touch Baby and listen to her as she sang on to herself, and for once Shockley wished she would just be quiet. Her song actually seemed to be aggravating an already-tense situation.

"After eighteen years, a bite of lunch with me is not going to kill you," he said, ordering.

"We can either settle everything amicably or—" Ruth broke off her sentence and waited until the waitress had served them. Then she continued, "Or we can let the courts decide an equitable settlement."

"What are you talking about?"

"Property."

"Yeah. I know. But that sounds like a prepared speech."

"I've already seen a lawyer," she said ominously over Baby's song.

"Look, what do you—?" He stopped in midsentence as a fat woman stood by Baby's high chair clasping her hands in rapture as Baby sang with a mouth full of crumbs. "Please," he muttered. The woman excused herself and reluctantly moved on. He turned back to Ruth. "What do you want?"

"Whatever's fair. We've been together for many years. During a good portion of that time I worked. When I wasn't working, I was making a home for you, serving your needs, taking care of your children."

"Is that what your lawyer told you to say?" asked Shockley, his hamburger tasting of bile.

"As a matter of fact."

"Look, let's make it simple. Why don't you take it all?"

"Huh?"

"Everything. The house. The cars. The savings accounts."

"Are you kidding?" she asked, taken aback.

"No, I'm not 'kidding.' I don't want any of it. It's all yours."

Two days later the appellate division of the New York State Supreme Court handed down its opinion.

Citing what they termed manifest injustice, the judges in a unanimous decision reversed the family court's action. In its written opinion, now a matter of public record, the court held that in the case of the *Tompkins County Department of Social Services* v. *Rumsey*:

1. The presiding justice had been in error when he admitted into evidence the child's entire case file from the county Department of Social Services since many of the entries in the file consisted of statements, reports, and even hearsay made by persons under no business duty to report to the department.

2. The defendant had no opportunity to examine said documents prior to the hearing.

3. There appeared to be some element of collusion between individuals within the Department of Social Services and the foster parents.

What it all meant, Shockley learned from Ed Lutz, the new lawyer he had retained to examine the opinion, was that the appellate division had definitely wiped the slate clean, putting the onus on the Department of Social Services to begin an action in the higher court of appeals if they so desired.

"Considering the fact that Andrea Cassaniti was swiftly discharged today," said the lawyer, looking curiously at the child, who sat on the floor of the motel room singing to herself, "I'd say that the possibility of their initiating a new action is very small."

"And the bottom line?" Shockley asked as Lutz got up to leave.

"You're going to have to return the child to her mother," he said, snapping closed his briefcase. "Immediately."

After Lutz left, Shockley stood by the door looking sadly at Baby, who now lay on her back with her feet in the air as she dreamily serenaded herself, her voice soft and lilting. Biting his lip, Shockley closed his eyes and listened to her song, listened as though for the last time, soaking in her mellifluous voice as it unraveled the knots twisting his soul.

Suddenly Baby stopped singing in midnote.

Shockley immediately opened his eyes.

The child lay on the floor, her eyes wide, her body rigid as a board. She had stopped breathing.

Shockley charged over to her. But by the time he reached her and knelt down, whatever it was that had occurred had passed and she now seemed normal again.

For a long time Shockley carefully observed her. He watched as Baby rolled over, hit a ball with her hand, and scampered repeatedly after it as it tumbled across the floor. Letting out a loud sigh of relief, he realized that it had been nothing serious, just a momentary stomach cramp. Kids got them all the time.

Shockley procrastinated. Though he expected the phone to ring at any moment or the police to come marching into the motel in search of Baby, Shockley couldn't pull himself to take

Baby back to Doris quite yet. For a while he thought about running away with her, to another state or another country, but in his heart he knew he could never do it. He also considered trying to gum up the transfer, dragging his heels until—as Lutz had warned—the courts would cite him for contempt. He knew, however, nothing would be gained by it and in the end he would have to return Baby.

What Shockley did instead was stall a little, buying himself a few hours in which to come to grips with losing Baby. And it wasn't going to be easy, that. Not after all these months of being so close to her, he thought staring out the motel window with Baby in his lap, watching as the day began to dwindle, darkness creeping up in the late afternoon as a fresh snow started to fall.

"Well, this is the end of the road," he said as Baby remained nestled quietly against him, her head tucked under his chin, her eyes following the passing traffic. In his mind Shockley ran through the closing loop of his life with Baby, starting at the very beginning that spring evening when he had almost run into Doris with his bike, unaware that buried within her swollen body lay the fetus destined to leave its mark on him and history. He recalled his children telling him of the miraculous infant who lived down in the flats and how he had laughed at the absurd notion of a newborn child who could sing—remembered then how his skepticism had crumbled before her unearthly song, how incredulity had given way to elation and ultimately that single-minded obsession with her music. Through his mind passed those notes of her first song, and he thought back to how that music had stirred his soul, evoking feelings that he had been sure were dead, her flutelike voice catapulting him to dizzy heights of joy and ecstasy, unlocking a flood of forgotten creativity. How—Shockley shook himself out of his reverie and looked at Baby. This was ridiculous, he told himself. Here he was in essence eulogizing her. But she was not dead; it was only their life together that was finished. Once returned to Doris, Baby would go on playing, singing and living, probably even happily. She didn't need him in order to exist. It was the other way around.

It was then that he was struck by the continued absence of Baby's song—her silence as hard to ignore as her recent burst of constant singing. Except for the sounds of passing traffic drifting in through the plate glass, the hush in the motel room was unsettling.

"Sing, Baby. Sing for me again," he urged her. "One last time."

Baby looked up at him, tilted her head to one side as she usually did before singing, even opened her mouth, but failed to sing.

She was hungry, he thought, checking his watch and realizing that it was well past her dinnertime. Putting on her sweater, he took Baby to the restaurant and fed her. When they came back, he let her play on the floor while he continued to watch her. She played for a while, scattering her brightly colored cars and stuffed animals across the floor, and then let out a long yawn. Shockley watched and waited. Waited, but still no song.

As evening yielded to night, he picked Baby off the floor, bathed her, dressed her in her pajamas, and lay her down in the crib and waited. Leaning over the bars of her crib, he looked down at her and watched as she stared back up at him, her eyebrows knitting. She yawned again, closed her eyes, and went to sleep. The silence was deafening.

Baby's soundlessness continued to bother Shockley that night. He debated with himself, put his fears to rest, only to have them pop up again. It was silly, he told himself, to get all upset simply because she hadn't sung that afternoon and evening. There were other times besides illness that Baby had not sung for hours. Yet—yet—Still dressed in his clothes, Shockley fell asleep on top of his bed.

When he awoke in the morning, Baby was already up, standing in her crib and waiting for him. When he looked at her, she smiled. Drawing apart the curtains he stared glumly out at the morning. The snow that had started to fall last night was still coming down and was getting deep. Remembering the court order as if recounting a bad dream, he wondered if the roads out to Doris's trailer would be passable. With the clarity of morning he knew that he was just looking for an excuse. Today, he realized without equivocation, today he would return Baby. Shockley pulled some fresh clothes out of his suitcase, showered, shaved, and dressed slowly. All the time he kept listening, hoping that Baby would at least leave him with one last song to erase that nagging worry that kept chafing at the back of his mind. He lifted Baby out of her crib, changed her diapers, dressed her, took her to breakfast and, finally, when he could stall no longer, bundled her up in her snowsuit and carried her out to the car.

Driving out along the highway that rose above the lake, Shockley skirted the edge of Cayuga Heights and then passed the shopping malls, Baby sitting in her little seat and contentedly watching the passing scenery. As he drove past the airport, the land turning into high plateau, Shockley debated making a last plea to Doris but knew it was hopeless. Baby was hers, he thought, glancing at the child who sat ever silent, and that was the end of that. From now on he would have to concentrate on picking up the pieces of his own life.

Shockley turned off the highway and onto the road that led him past all the shacks and shanties of West Dryden. Under the soft blanket of fresh snow they looked benign and peaceful, the junk piles pristine mounds of white. Even Leeming's Trailer Park seemed pretty this early morning, he thought, turning into the entrance, the road winding through the park deep and clean with fresh lines of tire tracks cut through the perfect snow, sharp and incisive. A graceful roof of snow arched over each trailer, making them look like oblong mushrooms. The trees were plastered with white, like frosting on pastry.

Shockley pulled off the road. He unfastened Baby from her seat, took her in his arms, and tramped through the hushed maze toward Doris's trailer. As he approached the door, his eye was immediately caught by Doris's two cats, who stood huddled in front, the snow deep and undisturbed except for their prints. When they saw him, they began to meow loudly, and Baby reached out toward them. Mounting the steps, Shockley knocked on the aluminum door. No response.

He knocked again and, tilting his head toward the trailer, listened for some noise. Seeming to imitate him, Baby also tilted her head. Shockley strained to detect a sound from inside, but all he could make out were the cats crying and the noise of a snowplow grinding down a distant road.

He rapped again, louder, and waited, stamping his feet to keep warm.

"She's in there. Just keep knockin'," said a voice from behind, startling him. He turned around. Mrs. Schooley was standing behind him, wearing only a thin blouse and flowery summer skirt, her bare, white legs plunged into a pair of men's high rubbers.

Shockley turned back to the door and pounded loudly.

"Are you sure she's in there?" he asked, his suspicions gaining momentum.

"She hasn't gone out. I'd know. Why, I jus' live right—" the woman continued to rattle on.

Shockley moved away from the door and, leaning over the front steps, looked into a window.

"She's been just sitting there an' waiting for— Now, I'll just bet that little girl there is Baby. Now aren't you?" she chuckled, coming closer to the child.

Blocking out the morning glare with his free hand, Shockley peered in the front window. There was not a single light on in the trailer and from what he could see, the living room was empty. The kitchen area was deserted, too. Craning his neck to see through a partially opened door, Shockley then spotted something on the floor in the tiny, dim bedroom. Pushing his face hard against the icy glass, he looked closer. Suddenly his jaw fell open and he let out a gasp. It was a leg.

"You gonna sing for us, honey?" asked Mrs. Schooley, taking Baby's mittened hand in hers. "You gonna—"

"Quick!" Shockley shouted to the woman. "Get someone to open this door!" Jumping off the steps into the deep snow, Baby tucked under one arm, he plunged through the layers of snow drifted up against the side of the trailer, fighting his way to the rear bedroom window, his heart echoing loudly in his chest. "Hurry!" he cried out to the startled woman, who stood frozen in her tracks. "Get someone with some tools!"

The fat woman turned and scurried back to her home.

Around the rear of Doris's trailer the snow was crotch-deep, and by the time Shockley had broken a trail to the window, he was dizzy and spent, his lungs on fire. Forcing himself up on tiptoes, he stared into the window.

"Oh, God!" he cried, looking in and seeing Doris's inert form lying on the floor, her curved body forming an almost perfect **U**.

Quickly he circled back around the trailer, following his broken path. By the time he had waded back to the front, the woman's husband was standing by the door with a crowbar. Shockley nodded, and with a single fast jerk, the skinny man sprung the lock and they all bolted in.

"Sweet Jesus!" uttered the man, looking down at Doris, who was lying there as she had since the previous afternoon, her face ghostly white and contorted, her body rigid as though frozen in an agonizing cramp.

"She's dead!" cried Mrs. Schooley horrified. "Dead!"

From the vantage of Shockley's arms Baby looked down at her mother's body, then looked at the frightened couple who stood in the trailer—the man dangling a crowbar from a limp arm, the woman weeping tears that spilled over her round cheeks. Then, slowly, she turned her head and looked at Shockley. Shockley shifted his eyes away from Doris's body and looked back at Baby. Baby tilted her head, took a breath, opened her mouth and emitted a sound, a sound that echoed like a roar through Shockley's brain.

"Mama," she said, speaking her first word. "Mama, Mama."

EPILOGUE

Baby never sang again. Though she learned to walk and talk like other children, grew and developed normally, never once did she emit so much as a single, unearthly note.

Shortly after Doris Rumsey's death, the Department of Social Services, while repeatedly denying Irwin Shockley's petitions for custody, initiated an extensive search for relatives of the deceased mother. The agency managed to uncover a second cousin in Alabama, an aging aunt in Maine, and an even-more-distant cousin in Minneapolis, all of whom expressed an interest in adopting the child. When the relatives learned, however, that Baby was no longer singing, they indicated no further interest in the orphaned child. As the search dragged on and no one was forthcoming with an offer to adopt the little girl, the agency decided it both prudent and in the best interests of the child that she remain in familiar surroundings and, upon petition, she was returned to the foster care of Ruth Shockley.

With Baby's singing at a clear and definite end, Ivar Jacobsen's request for an injunction became a moot question and was subsequently dropped. The controversy surrounding the nearly two million dollars raised for Baby's ransom, however, continued to rage. Many Babyists were urging that the money be used to build a shrine to the mother and child. A consumer group in Washington was demanding that the money, acquired on a fraudulent basis, immediately be returned to its original donors, and there was a strong movement in Congress calling for a joint House-Senate investigation of the matter. A number of prominent clergy originally associated with the CURB movement were insisting that the money be confiscated and distributed among relief organizations and established churches around the country.

The controversy surrounding the money, however, was brought to an abrupt close when it was discovered that Mr. Ivar Jacobsen had absconded with the entire fund. Jacobsen was first spotted in his native Denmark approximately one month after his sudden departure, but when proceedings were initiated to extradite him, he conveniently dropped out of view, reported sightings having since been made in such far-flung places as Tegucigalpa, Singapore, and Johannesburg.

Two months after Doris's death, Father Tom Fitzgibbons moved to Ithaca, accepting a part-time position as chaplain at the university. He divided his time between counseling students and continuing his avid pursuit of Babyism.

As Baby's singing faded to little more than a memory, many of the people who had firmly believed in Baby's descendancy from God began to falter in their conviction. What had once been a vast congregation steadily dwindled, and soon even those who had actually heard Baby sing began to doubt. Through it all, however, Father Tom Fitzgibbons never once wavered in his faith.

The Baby who had sung, he would explain to anyone who would listen, had died when the mother died, its spirit departing from the earth. It was the soul invested in this child that he had worshiped and continued to worship, not the little girl herself. Through the child's singing, God had sent a message to the people of this earth and it was there, and continued to be there, for those who would only open their hearts and listen.

Father Tom continued to correspond with the faithful, writing and printing a monthly newsletter linking the remaining Babyists around the globe. Through friends he managed to raise enough money to purchase the Lansing field in which Doris had given birth, and after a protracted fund drive, a modest five-room building was constructed the following year at the edge of that field, the structure's large front wall of glass looking out on the jutting shale rock marking the point where Doris had lain that morning. Ultimately the A-frame-type building came to serve as the International Center and Archives for Babyism as well as a home for Father Fitzgibbons and Irwin Shockley.

That fall, following Doris Rumsey's death, Harry Terkel ran on the independent ticket for Tompkins County District Attorney. Running against his better-financed, better-organized Republican opponent, Frank Kiely, he nonetheless won by an impressive landslide, his victory due in part, it was felt, to his success in the Rumsey appeal. Upon being sworn into office he immediately launched an investigation into the activities of the department of social services, his probe resulting in a number of important reforms.

A few months after Terkel's election, Ruth Shockley was quietly married to a colleague of hers in the physics department and became Ruth Goldman. She, together with her new husband, began adoption procedures, and within a short time Baby became their legal daughter. Along with the child, who had grown into a rather happy-go-lucky tomboy, went a sizable trust fund, totaling nearly three hundred thousand dollars.

Walking down Willow Avenue one morning in June just after a freak snowstorm, Olive Eldridge slipped and fell on an unshoveled walk, breaking her hip in two places. As coincidence would have it, it was the sidewalk in front of what had once been Doris's house. Olive initiated suit against the new owner for contributory negligence, and upon receiving a substantial out-of-court settlement, moved to Florida, where she now lives happily in her own condominium.

Fay Dworkin, the convicted kidnapper of Baby, is serving a life sentence in a federal women's prison in the state of New Mexico. A few months after her conviction, she wrote a long and rather touching letter to Irwin Shockley, explaining that not a day goes by without her thinking about him and Baby and how she regrets having brought about the end of Baby's singing. Could he, she concluded in her letter, ever find a way to forgive her for what she had done? Shockley promptly replied that she was not to blame herself for precipitating Baby's change. And, as far as he was concerned, she was forgiven for her part in the kidnapping, thought it wasn't really for him to forgive. Thus began a continuing correspondence in which Miss Dworkin expressed her sincere desire to continue spreading the message of Baby's song while in prison. If and when she ever got paroled, she hoped to come to Ithaca in order to serve, in whatever way she could, the cause of Babyism.

To this very day, five years later, Irwin Shockley continues to reside in Ithaca. He lives an exceedingly simple, essentially ascetic existence. He earns a small amount of money giving violin lessons. He wears the same set of worn-out clothes, eats sparingly, remains strictly celibate, and has no possessions of his own other than his violin. Shunning all modern contrivances, he gets to his lessons by walking long miles. His hair has turned snow white, and he can often be seen moving across the countryside in the scorching heat of summer or the midst of icy winter, shuffling along in his broken-down shoes, his shoulders hunched over, a small pair of golden lips dangling from a chain around his neck. Some say he has gone off the deep end. Others claim that he is doing penance, begging God for forgiveness for all his sins, both real and imagined.